THE
EMPTY
SHRINE

# WILLIAM E. BARRETT

# THE
# EMPTY
# SHRINE

### WILLIAM E. BARRETT

DOUBLEDAY & COMPANY, INC.
GARDEN CITY, NEW YORK

*All of the characters in this book are fictitious, and any resemblance to actual persons, living or dead, is purely coincidental.*

To B. V. M.

# CONTENTS

# CONTENTS

# I
## THE MIRACLE?

# I

The island is old in recorded history, older in time. It is a place where a miracle might reasonably happen if it is reasonable for a miracle to happen anywhere. There is blood in its soil and there are people who maintain that it is the blood of martyrs. The martyrdom is open to question. Certainly, the Iroquois, long ago, slaughtered Hurons on the island, and rather horribly, making them last a long while *pour le sport*. The island Hurons were Christians, but that may have been an irrelevancy. The Iroquois habitually massacred Hurons, who were a tribe of particularly ineffectual Indians; the creed and color of the victims did not seem to be the main point.

The French, who still live on the island and who are as French in spirit as they ever were, let the Hurons pass into history without settling the martyrdom question, contenting themselves with settling the more urgent matter of the Iroquois. They had legends of their own to write and they wrote them with muskets, with wooden crosses, and with primitive farm implements. They are still writing them.

You have to know all of this in order to understand the story of Valérie Rivard, who may, or may not, have seen the Blessed Virgin on a summer afternoon in 1945, and of Keller Barkley, who came to the island as her enemy in 1957; of all the people whose lives were changed, in one way or another, by what she did, or did not, see. Events belong to the places where they occur, and if they are strange events they cannot be understood in another setting; the setting must accompany the story.

Physically, the island is not impressive. It is slightly less than ten miles long and it is five miles wide where it is widest, when the tide is low. The tide rises sixteen feet there, and it is possible to draw both fresh water and salt from the Saint Lawrence, which surrounds it, although the sea is more than five hundred miles to the east. The Laurentians, the oldest mountains of North America, dominate the horizon beyond the north shore of the river, which is five miles from the island. The south shore is twelve miles away. If one of the huge geese which rendezvous in the island coves feels an impulse to visit the United States, he flies southward for fifty miles and he is in the State of Maine.

That is the geography of it.

Jacques Cartier, who discovered the Saint Lawrence, and who made as many memorialized landings as George Washington made overnight stops, landed on the island in September 1535. Francis I was King of France. Henry VIII was King of England and Anne Boleyn still retained her head. On the day that Jacques Cartier's chaplain said the first Mass on the island, Anne's daughter, the famous Elizabeth, celebrated her second birthday. Martin Luther was preaching in Germany and the Protestant Reformation was very young, not much older than Anne Boleyn's baby. Jacques Cartier knew nothing about the Reformation and had never heard the word "Protestant"; which would be irrelevant and unimportant if it were not for the fact that the people who live on the island today, 675 of them, know very little more on that subject than he did. They entered history as French and Catholic within fifty odd miles, as a goose flies, from what is now the United States. They remain what they were.

Jacques Cartier christened the island "Ile-aux-Erables," which means "island of the maples." He sailed on, then, to spend a miserable winter huddled under the bluff where Quebec was born. Like most of the island legends, the naming of it has raised questions. Historians have wondered why Cartier was impressed with the island maples when he must have seen such trees everywhere that he landed. Romantic people have advanced the explanation that the island is shaped like a maple leaf when the tide is low, a fact apparent only from an airplane and not too apparent then, not at all evident in any of the maps, early or modern. At any rate, Cartier named it, for one reason or another, and it has retained the name that he gave it.

The first habitant families of Ile-aux-Erables cleared the land and started farming on it in 1725. The direct descendants of three of those families are still farming the land of their forefathers today, and the other families on the island have unbroken lines that are nearly as long. Their names are the same names that one encounters along the Beaupré coast of the river, in the towns of the south shore, and in solid pages of the Quebec telephone book. The family trees are ancient and their growth is strong.

In 1759, when the British fleet sailed up the river, accompanying Wolfe on the expedition which climaxed upon the Plains of Abraham, the island was raided by British sailors, the habitants driven from their homes, and their church burned. The people were back on their island before Quebec fell and they have remained on it, speaking their own language as they did before the British flag was unfurled above Quebec.

The British conquerors were in an odd position. They were soldiers and sailors who lived in barracks and aboard the ships of the fleet, superior in the machinery and the equipment of destruction, but inferior to the conquered in all of the arts that sustain life. The French were more numerous and they lived on the land which they understood and which worked for them. The people of the land succeeded, then, in forcing their conquerors to accept the language of the conquered as equal with their own in the writing of laws, highway signs, and public announcements of all kinds, an agreement between opposing forces which is still in effect. In fairness, since they were treated justly, her French-speaking sons saved Canada for Britain twice, by repelling the American attempts at invasion in 1775 and 1812.

The people of Quebec Province, which includes the island, are now Canadiens, spelled with an "e" instead of the English "a," and pronounced accordingly as a French word. Their allegiance to France was canceled when Louis XV, ruled by his mistresses, abandoned New France to the English assault. Their last tie to the mother country was severed by the guillotines of the French Revolution from which they recoiled in horror. If they are French still, apart from language, appearance, and custom, they are French of the Louis XIV era. The term "Canadien" not only identifies them, it is their pride. They have played a vital role in the creation of Canada's government, the extension of its frontiers, the preservation of its traditions, the formulation of its political faith. They are not the wealthy of their

5

land, but they are many and they have an enduring strength. The earth that they have turned and tilled for centuries holds them close.

That is their history.

There are, of course, legends; of phantom bells that ring for deaths in certain families, of a sunken cannon, the ghost of an unhappy Huron who walks the beaches, of flickering spirit candles on the night of All Souls at the site of the first small mission chapel. No one quite believes them. They are merely tales to tell. The island itself is a place where ordinary people live their ordinary lives, untroubled by dreams of renown.

In the summer of 1945, the people of the island experienced a night of wonder; a night when the world of the supernatural, the world of their deepest believing, seemed very close to them. Confronted with the *possibility* of a miracle, they were afraid; and their fear was stronger than their faith. No miracle occurred and that, if one believes that the rightness of earlier action is confirmed by later events, proves that there was never any challenge to either faith or fear in the first place; that nothing happened, nothing at all.

And yet . . .

# II

Valérie Rivard was eight years old. No one on the Island of the Maples had ever considered her remarkable in any way, nor worthy of more than polite and casual comment. She was merely another of many eight-year-old girls, average in height, sturdy as most island children were sturdy, with large brown eyes and dark hair that would not curl without help. She was the daughter of the notary, but that was a distinction more readily understood in the adult community than in her own world of children, a reflection of her father and not a light of her own.

To herself, of course, she was unique.

Her main point of distinction was a negative point of difference, a peculiarity like the possession of two heads; that she was an only child, living with her father and her aunt in a community where large families were the rule. Every other girl of her age had sisters and brothers who were privileged in being permitted to do the many fascinating tasks of the farm and the farm home. Valérie envied them. In their company, she lacked prestige and she was without interesting conversation. She had one other distinction, peculiarly her own, and she made the most of it.

She had been born in Trois Rivières. No one else had been born anywhere. That, at least, was as she phrased it to herself. One could not say, "I was born here," because it did not mean anything to be born where you were. It was impressive to say, "I was born in Trois Rivières," because that was a place and it had an exciting name, and nobody, none of the girls on the farms, had ever seen it. Sometimes she made herself one with the other girls, while yet apart, by saying, "In Trois Rivières when I had a mother."

Valérie assumed that she had seen Trois Rivières herself and had experienced it. The assumption was enough for her. She had been brought to Ile-aux-Erables when she was two years old, before her memories began, but memory was not important. Her father had pictures of the city and the waterfront and the old churches and the houses with odd iron staircases on the outside. She had looked at the pictures and she had read some of the easy books.

"In Trois Rivières where I was born," she said often, "there is a river called the Saint Maurice. It runs into the Saint Lawrence in three different places but it is only one river."

This always interested her auditors, no matter how often she repeated the statement, because it was something beyond their knowledge and experience. It exasperated some of the girls, too, because the fact was simple and complete in itself and there was nothing that they could add to it. Once, in a burst of inspiration, Valérie had expanded the picture in her mind.

"It is like God," she said thoughtfully, "one river and three persons."

One did not compare anything to God in a religious community like Ile-aux-Erables without shocking sensibilities, not even in the world of the very young. One of the girls reported the remark to the nun in charge of the class. Sister Thérèse was not angry or stern but she talked solemnly to Valérie and told her that she must never say anything like that again. Valérie never did, but she thought of the Saint Maurice River in that way because the thought was in her mind when she pronounced the magic name of Trois Rivières. It was wrong if the sister said that it was wrong, but she did not know why.

Her father laughed when she asked him about it. He was a large man who laughed often, even when he did not believe that a remark was funny. When he laughed at something that was not funny, he made an odd snorting sound, and sometimes he pounded the table.

"Of a certainty, the Saint Maurice is like God," he said. "If there is a God, then everything that He ever made is like Him."

No other person on the island would say "if." That was part of what people said about Valérie's father, of what she had heard people say; that he was a "freethinker." The term had no meaning for her, and when she questioned her aunt, Laure Rivard told her that some

8

people will say anything and that she must not think about it. She thought about it.

Her father, she decided, was different from other people, as she was different from other people, but in another way. Her father was different because he did not go to church. "Freethinker" must mean that. The definition, like the fact itself, was something that she accepted among the many things that she did not understand. The quality of passing judgment, or of deploring, was not in her. She was sorry that her father did not go to Mass with her as she was sorry sometimes that he was not a farmer.

The girls whose fathers were farmers did many interesting and wonderful things with animals and with the seeds that were planted in the ground. The children of farmers knew all about what farmers did and knew with such certainty that they were impatient with anyone who did not know, too impatient to explain anything. They answered questions with mocking words that were not answers at all.

On the other hand, Valérie's father knew many things that no farmer on the island knew. He had many, many books and she felt that they were all hers because they were a part of the house in which she lived. Valérie owned books of her own and few of the other girls ever saw any books except those that they studied in school. They did not envy Valérie as she envied them; they did not want to own books. That, of course, was exasperating.

Valérie's father read stories to her, or told her stories. He had done that all of her life. The winter was the best time and she loved it, not for the deep snows and the cold, and the warm blankets on horse-drawn sleighs, the exciting feast days and the building of snow men; not these so much as the great fire and her father's voice as he held her on his lap. He took her into lands of enchantment and sometimes, when he did not feel like telling stories, he told her about real places that were far away: her own personally beloved Trois Rivières, Quebec, Montreal, and places of such marvelous names as Sainte-Anne-de-la-Pérade, and Sainte-Geneviève-de-Batiscan. All of these places he knew and had seen, but he told her, too, about the United States, where the cities were all big and strange, about France, where the names of places sounded familiar and friendly. Even if she never saw all of the cities and towns and countries, she felt that she knew them and loved them and would hold them forever inside of her because her father had put them there.

Her aunt, Laure, listened to the stories, too, while she knitted or sewed or did crochet work. Often she fell asleep listening to them and her work, whatever she was doing, fell on the floor. Laure slept with her mouth open and her glasses away down on her nose away from her eyes. To Valérie she was very old, a thought that she never had about her father, who had no age at all. Laure, however, loved her and was kind to her and was interested in many things that interested Valérie and that did not interest her father. She made Valérie's clothes but she did not teach Valérie to make clothes, nor to spin and weave and make hooked rugs in the way that mothers did. That, Valérie thought, was because she was an aunt, but Laure always gave another reason.

"I won't teach you to be a farmer's wife," she said. "That is not the life for you."

There was no understanding a statement like that because nearly everyone was a farmer's wife except Madame Drolet and the nuns and Madame Masson, the wife of *le bedeau*, and Laure, herself, who was an aunt. Valérie, who did not want to be Madame Drolet or Madame Masson or a nun or an aunt was certain that she would be a farmer's wife whether Laure wanted her to be one or not. She often said so, and, at such times, Laure's mouth would get very tight and she would bang things around as she did when she was angry with her brother, who was Valérie's father.

Valérie Rivard, who was born on July 10, 1937, was quite a normal little girl, then, on July 30, 1945, with no extraordinary gifts, no noticeably devout tendencies, inclined on the whole to conform rather than to differ from her contemporaries when she had a choice. She had more innocent curiosity than knowledge, and she was too frank and direct to be calculating or subtle. She either succeeded in reducing the complexities that she encountered to her own simple terms or she dismissed them. She was not a moody child. She was loved and protected and she had no personal knowledge of unhappiness.

July 30, 1945 was a bright, clear afternoon with a white cumulous pack riding high in the sky, a day of calm, with a light breeze blowing down-river in the afternoon when the tide went out.

Valérie was helping her aunt to weed the flower garden. It was a task that Laure performed capriciously, usually having an urge to weed when there was some task to be done indoors that she particularly disliked and wanted to avoid. Laure had no great love for gardening, and she welcomed interruptions when she worked in her flower patch, which was the smallest in the village. She welcomed Céleste Drolet this afternoon. Madame Drolet seemed worried and upset, which was not unusual.

"I must talk to you, Laure," she said.

"Certainly. Certainly." Laure rose, rubbing her hands together. She was a short, heavy woman, and she always sounded breathless when she was called upon to change position suddenly or to speak before she thought about speaking. "You must come into the house, Céleste," she said.

Laure's eyes found Valérie, as Valérie had anticipated, blinked at her, then fixed upon young Robert Drolet, who was moving a pebble back and forth on the path with his toe, frowning at it.

"Valérie," Laure said, "the tide is out. Take Robert with you and find for me some shells. Real pretty ones! My box is nearly empty."

"Yes, Aunt Laure."

Valérie rose, rubbing her hands together as her aunt had done. She looked at Robert without enthusiasm, a tall, strong, light-haired boy, who wore a T shirt with the name of a soft drink across his chest. Robert was nine, one year older than she was, and he was either loud and noisy or, as he was today, sulky and brooding. He either yelled at people and called them names and whistled shrilly, or he did not notice them at all, or speak to them. Either way, there was no fun in him and nothing interesting.

"Wait here for me," she told him, "I must get my basket."

Robert did not answer her. He was still rolling the pebble around with his toe when she came out of the house with the basket on her arm. He walked behind her and she paid no attention to him. The road through the village was an aisle between stately poplars and friendly, sprawling willows. The houses were set back from the road, not close together as in the pictures of villages on the mainland. The houses all had steep roofs so that the snow would slide off in winter. The roofs were of different colors and the shutters on the windows were brightly colored, too, and the doors, none of them ever matching the colors of the roofs. If anyone named three colors, starting with the roof color, any child on the island could name the house that those colors identified. The houses had big chimneys and porches on which the families sat on Sunday afternoons. The larger houses had dormer windows.

In front of the church there was a cleared space which had gravel on it. Robert spoke to her suddenly, so suddenly that Valérie turned, startled, to look at him.

"My mother does not like it because my father is home," he said.

"How do you know?"

"She tells people. That is what she is telling your aunt."

Valérie pondered that, stopping on the edge of the gravel to permit Robert to draw even with her. She did not understand why Madame Drolet should come to her house to tell her aunt something that everyone knew. She had known for a long time, without knowing how or where she learned, that Robert's father and mother did not like each other. It was not the same thing as her own father and Laure being angry with each other often; it was something else.

Robert raised his eyes, saw that he had her attention, then looked at the ground again. "She says that—'he comes home only long enough to make me pregnant.' She says that to Madame Lepage. What does it mean, that word?"

Valérie repeated the sentence to herself. The way that Robert said it was: "*Il ne vient à la maison que juste le temps de me rendre enceinte.*" She knew many words because she read books, even books that she did not understand. It was a habit that her father encouraged. Instinctively, as she repeated Robert's sentence, she made a rotating motion with her right forefinger. She had seen that word, "enceinte," and she had a half-formed picture in her mind. It was a circle, a circle of walls. She nodded, pleased with herself. When she knew anything, she knew it positively.

"It means that he make walls for her in the house," she said. "In a circle."

Robert looked startled. "He never does."

"He must do it. That's what the word means."

"He doesn't. He doesn't make anything."

Valérie blinked in the bright sunlight. "Maybe he makes a fence for her. A fence in a circle."

Her voice was less certain because she could not imagine that fence.

Robert shook his head vehemently. "He doesn't. He doesn't make anything for her."

It was very baffling. Valérie walked again, letting Robert lag behind as he did before. They passed the church with its tall spire gleaming like silver in the sun. It was the church of Saint-Thomas-Apôtre, and there was an image of Saint Thomas in a niche over the wide main door. Valérie made the sign of the cross passing it and she heard Robert's voice, a deep sullen voice now.

"I don't like my father," he said.

Valérie turned and Robert was just finishing his sign of the cross. That made his statement doubly shocking to her. He was breaking the fourth commandment about honoring his father and his mother, and he was doing it in front of the church.

"You have to like him," she said.

"I don't."

The scent of honeysuckle was strong as they approached the presbytery to the south of the church. Antoine Masson was standing inside the gate of Monsieur le Curé's residence. Antoine was seven, a year younger than Valérie. He was taller than she was, nearly as tall as Robert, but not as strong. He was a thin boy with dark hair and blue eyes. He was very shy, which was strange in a boy, and when he spoke to anyone, he always looked as though he had just stepped on a frog.

"Where are you going?" he said.

"To Anse-Saint-Jean to find shells for my aunt."

Valérie told him reluctantly, knowing that he would come with her. He followed her often, not saying much, not doing anything, just following. She liked him better than she liked Robert, and she did not mind having him with her, but today she wanted to think about Robert and his parents and the word which would not fit into something that had happened.

"I'll come with you," Antoine said.

Valérie sighed. The two boys did not speak to each other and that was going to make matters difficult. Antoine walked beside her, a little ahead of Robert. They kicked up dust from the road as they walked, all three of them. Robert's feet were bare and she envied him that. Her aunt would not let her go out barefooted. She wore moccasins. Antoine, however, wore shoes. He wore a T shirt, but it was the wrong kind; it had brown and white stripes. A T shirt should be white and it should have some advertising on it, like Robert's. Antoine never looked like the other boys. Never.

The fragrance of clover was heavy in the air as they neared Rosaire Gagnon's farm. Rosaire was married to Marguerite Hamel but he did not have any children old enough to go to school. His sister, Léonie, did go to school. She was a year older than Valérie and lived with her parents on one of the mid-island farms. Valérie liked to visit her. The buttercups and daisies were bright beside the road.

Small thoughts and small impressions crowded into Valérie's mind, but they did not force out of her consciousness the big thought that Robert did not like his father and that Robert's mother did not like his father, and that there was something that Monsieur Drolet, the father of Robert, came home to do.

Antoine, beside her, made a swallowing sound. "Are you going to say the rosary?" he said.

She looked at him, startled. "No. Why?"

"So that you will know how far it is."

She stopped and turned. "That was a secret," she said angrily. "A very special secret."

Robert was looking at her over Antoine's shoulder. "What's secret about the rosary?" he said.

She did not answer him. She turned and resumed her walk toward the cove where she gathered shells for Laure. She had confided her secret to Antoine because she was sorry for him and because, although he was a boy, he was more like she was than anyone else. He did not have any brothers or sisters, and he had not been born on the island, either, although he would never talk about that. There was some mystery about him. Monsieur Masson, his father, was *le bedeau*, the sexton of the church, and his mother was the housekeeper for Monsieur le Curé. Antoine lived in the presbytery. To tell a secret to somebody who lived in the priest's house should be almost like telling it to the priest in confession She walked with her head down, brooding on that.

Her secret was that she had discovered a way of telling the distance from one place on the island to another so that she could always compare them and know how far she had to walk in order to reach where she was going. It took her fifteen minutes to say the rosary, the five decades and the other prayers, when she was saying it herself. It took

1

twelve minutes with Laure who said it fast. Valérie had measured the distances from her house to all the places that she visited regularly.

It was one decade and an extra Our Father to the Drolet house; two decades, an Our Father, a Gloria, and two Hail Marys to the church; a rosary and a decade and a half decade to the place in the road where she could look down on Anse-Saint-Jean.

The stand of birches, which marked the place where she always went down to the beach, was immediately ahead, and the salt, sea smell here was stronger than any of the varied scents and fragrances of the island. Robert was teasing Antoine, trying to make him tell the secret of the rosary, and Antoine was refusing to tell him although his voice sounded as though he was crying. Valérie did not look back. She was afraid, suddenly, of what would happen if Antoine did tell someone like Robert, who shouted at people and who was so noisy that everyone could hear him when he wanted to be heard.

It had never occurred to her before that it might be wrong to use prayers to measure distances. It might be a very great sin to do that, and if Robert knew about it, everyone would know. She hoped that it wasn't a sin, and very slowly, very solemnly, she recited to herself the Act of Contrition. The saying of that prayer brought her to the exact spot where the little path went down to the beach. At high tide the river came up almost to the road and covered a quarter of a mile of beach, which lay exposed now as she came to a stop above the steep path.

It was amazingly clear and she could see the spire of a church on the south shore, which was a great distance across the water, greater than the distance from one end of the island to the other. Valérie had never been on the south shore and she knew nothing about that distant church except that she had decided long ago that it was very beautiful inside; more beautiful, perhaps, than Saint-Thomas-Apôtre, which was the loveliest place she had ever seen.

Robert was no longer teasing Antoine. He wasn't saying anything at all. With the saying of her prayer, Valérie had dismissed her own problem, and now she thought about Robert once more, about his mother and his father and about that strange word "enceinte." Robert had said that he did not like his father. He said it in front of the church while he was making the sign of the cross. That was worse, probably, than using prayers to measure distances. She wanted to tell him to say an Act of Contrition but she was afraid that he would laugh at her. She decided to say it for him. Her eyes remained fixed on the distant church spire. She imagined herself inside the church, saying the prayer for Robert.

Robert's jeering voice cut across the prayer. "What are you doing? Saying the rosary?"

She did not turn around until she reached the "Amen." Both of the boys were staring at her. She felt dizzy, as though she had actually been in the church on the south shore and had come back too swiftly.

"I was listening to the silence," she said. "Can't you hear it?"

Antoine looked frightened but Robert laughed. He laughed loudly. He picked up a small stone and threw it far out on the beach. "Silence is silence," he said, "because there isn't any sound. How can you hear it?"

He laughed again and ran recklessly down the path. Antoine held back, letting Valérie go down ahead of him. "I *can* hear it," she said. "I can."

She was remembering other days when she had been alone on the beach, when there wasn't anyone like Robert to spoil the day for her. There was a sound to silence or a sound where silence was. She had listened and she had heard it. She had reached the base of the path and Antoine slid down after her. Robert had stopped twenty-five or thirty yards away to bend over some object on the beach. Valérie wanted desperately to be alone, to listen, to test her memory of what she had heard. She picked up a broken shell and held it out to Antoine.

"Run down and give this to Robert," she said. When he hesitated, she pushed the shell at him impatiently. "Right away!" she said.

Antoine took the shell and ran with it, awkward and stumbling. Valérie, astonished at being obeyed, almost forgot her reason for commanding him. Robert lifted his head, saw the other boy coming, and ran away from him. He was very fast, and nothing on the beach, rocks, pebbles, sand, or shells, hurt his feet. Antoine looked back at Valérie and she waved him on. He ran again, hopelessly outdistanced, his shoes sinking heavily into the sand, his arms waving wildly. Valérie paid no more attention to him. She tilted her head to one side, concentrating.

There was a sound, lower than a hum, softer than the song of insects,

16

hardly a sound at all. She walked toward the towering black rock which formed the eastern boundary of the cove. This rock was known as the Little Point. It was much closer inshore than Cap du Canon, which formed the western barrier, and at high tide it was not impressively tall. Little Point was rounded on top and seemed to bend forward toward the west like an old farmer stooped in the shoulders. There was a hollow place below the shoulders facing the beach, the entrance to a cave that did not exist.

Valérie had looked at that rock many times, thinking about the doorway that did not have a door, a doorway with no room behind it, no house for anyone to enter. The tide, deserting the long stretch of beach, never went out so far as the rock, so the water rippled beneath the doorway, brilliantly blue in the sunlight, making exploration impossible for small girls.

A gull swept down to the surface of the water, rode on it for a moment, bouncing up and down, then took off again. Valérie watched it fly far out on the river. Antoine was coming back.

"I couldn't catch him," he said breathlessly.

Robert ran in behind him. He was laughing again and his voice was loud. "How does the silence sound?" he shouted.

Valérie waved one hand at him. "Be quiet and listen!" she said.

The two boys stopped running, very close to her now. Antoine was breathing heavily. Valérie closed her mind to the sound that he was making.

"It is like a voice," she said imperatively. "Listen! Please listen."

Antoine sank down on the sand. Robert stood staring at her. He seemed momentarily impressed. "I don't hear anything," he said.

"Listen!"

She looked toward the rock, away from Robert's puzzled eyes, and her indrawn breath was stoppered by sudden shock. There was a brilliant light in the shallow doorway, a light that seemed to come from somewhere deep within the rock, as though all the rooms that never existed before were illumined now for some great event. Valérie experienced a moment of dizziness such as she had when she returned too quickly from the church on the south shore; then the mist cleared from her eyes and her breath was released, rushing forth and carrying words with it.

"Look! Look! Up there on the rock! There is a lady in white."

Robert was frowning. He had his back to the rock and he did not turn his head. He made an impatient gesture as though he were throwing something away. "You're crazy," he said. "You and him, you're both crazy."

He ran away as he had run down the beach, but this time he was headed in the direction of the path that led to the road. Valérie was only vaguely aware of him. She was still staring at the doorway in the rock. She brushed her hand over her eyes, then leaned forward, no longer thinking of anything, living an experience.

"Look, Antoine," she said, her voice trembling with excitement. "Look! She is going to step into the water."

Antoine was crouched in the sand with his hands covering his face. Valérie was aware of him and of his bent position without actually looking at him. She took two steps forward, her hand groping behind her for the boy.

"Can you see her, Antoine?" she pleaded. "Please. She is standing on the water. Just like it was ice. She is trying to tell me something but she is too far away. I can't hear her. She wants me to come closer. I want to know what she wants. I'll go out there if you will go with me. Please, Antoine."

Antoine stumbled to his feet and ran as Robert had run. Valérie heard his feet pounding in the sand but she continued to stare out across Anse-Saint-Jean.

She took another half dozen steps forward and she could no longer hear Antoine. There was only the silence that came into the cove when the water went out. She could hear that silence like a low, compelling voice and the vision was bright in her eyes. Fear came to her then as it had come to the two boys, or to her from them; the fear of a strange mood, of the silence itself, of the strange and the unknown, of a light where no light had ever been. She wanted the reassurance of another pair of eyes, looking with hers at the suddenly bright doorway, at the radiant figure that walked upon the water, beckoning to her.

She was aware then that she was alone, and fright mastered her. She turned, as the boys had turned, and raced panic-stricken toward the path, the road, the security of home.

## III

André Drolet was thirteen. He was a tall boy for his age, solidly built, with wide shoulders and strong hands. His features were rugged rather than regular, his head long and narrow with prominent nose and chin. There was endurance in him, and patience, because his life demanded those qualities of him.

André's two brothers had left home to seek work on the mainland as soon as they were old enough to venture alone. Neither of them had ever returned. The children who would have rounded out the family between himself and Robert, who was nine, had died in infancy. His father came and went, unpredictably. André learned early in his life to work at a variety of tasks and to rely upon himself for anything that he needed. His mother was, in a great measure, his responsibility, although his father sent home money regularly when he was away, money which his mother never seemed to manage well. André did household chores that would have fallen to a girl if Céleste Drolet had had a daughter, and he worked for anyone in the village or on the farms who would hire him after school or during the long summer months.

André worked through most of the day on July 30, 1945 for Rosaire Gagnon, who had the farm on the edge of the village. Rosaire, who was twenty-five, was in the most difficult period of a farmer's life. He had one small child and his wife was pregnant. It would be years before his own children would be able to help him and his wife was limited in what she could do. He could not afford a regular hired man and, although he received help from his father and the other Gagnons at harvest time and during other heavy periods, there were too many daily

19

tasks for one man alone. André worked for him and was happy with the arrangement because he did not have to go too far from his own home, where his mother, too, needed help.

André was tired when he left the Gagnon barn in midafternoon. He cut across the field to the road, and when he reached the fence he saw Antoine Masson running. He looked instinctively for a pursuer, but there was no one else. His eyes followed the small runner and he shook his head.

"Scared of himself, I guess. Poor little animal!"

There had been no mistaking the fright in the small boy's face, but fright in such a boy as Antoine was not to be taken seriously. Antoine did not lead the life of a normal boy. The Massons were always worrying over him and watching over him, trying to protect him when he did not need protection. It was beyond André's understanding. He climbed the fence and as he dropped down beside the road, he saw Valérie Rivard.

She was not running but she was walking fast at an odd, stumbling pace. Her face was streaked with tears. She did not see André until he called to her.

"What happened, Valérie?"

She stopped and turned to him. "I saw a lady in white and there was a light in the door and Robert ran away and Antoine and——"

André went down on one knee beside her, making his height more nearly equal to hers. "Look!" he said. "Don't be so frightened. You're all right. Take it slowly. What did you see?"

"An angel, I think. She was all bright."

He did not laugh at her. He was too close to his own childhood, and he had been hurt by people who laughed. Living with his mother, who was always carrying trouble, he knew how to listen.

"Tell me about it," he said.

Valérie drew a deep breath. "She was in the doorway of the rock," she said. "The Little Point."

He nodded. He knew the doorway. Valérie was a very solemn little girl. She lived in the house beyond his own and he had watched her grow. Her wide eyes held his.

"They wouldn't believe me," she said. "They wouldn't look. But she was there! In the doorway. There never was a room before, only a doorway. It looked like it was open behind her when she stood in the doorway, and there was a room with lights in it. It was all bright. I think she came out of the room but I didn't see her come out. She was just standing there when I saw her."

The words spurted, with odd little pauses in midsentences. Valérie no longer looked frightened. She gestured expressively, tracing a picture in the air.

"She was all in white, André, and the light was shining on her and she was trying to say something to me. She called me with her hand to come close to her."

André watched her intently. He didn't like this. "Wait, Valérie," he said. "This didn't happen, did it? You must not say it if it didn't happen."

"It did!" Her body straightened. "I saw her. I begged Antoine to look. I begged and begged him."

"What did Robert do?"

"He ran away. When I first saw her, he ran away. She was standing in the doorway. Then she stepped down. She stood on the water just like it was ice. On top of it, André, and she didn't sink or get wet."

André rose. The fright which had left Valérie entered into him. He looked back toward the birches, where the path went down to the beach of Anse-Saint-Jean. This problem did not belong to him. He did not want it.

"I'll take you home," he said. "You can tell your father about it."

"Yes," she said.

André walked down the road beside her. There were children of all ages on the island, and he had taken care of younger children when he worked at various places. He knew how they were; the games they played, and the way they liked to frighten themselves. This was different. This wasn't like anything else that he had ever encountered. He wanted to talk to his brother, to hear his account of what had happened. Something must have happened; not what Valérie said perhaps, but something. He concentrated hard, trying to puzzle it out.

"What did this lady look like?" he said. "Anyone on the island?"

"No. I don't know. Not like anybody."

Valérie, after the momentary hesitation, was emphatic. A daring thought struck him then. They had reached the gravel stretch in front of the church.

"Did she look like the Blessed Virgin?"

Valérie raised her hand to her mouth, the knuckles touching her teeth. She turned her head and her eyes widened. "Oh, yes!" she said. "Yes. Not like the statue in the church, but—— André! She called me and I didn't come. I didn't know who it was. I turned my back on her. I didn't even genuflect."

She whirled and started back along the road. The boy caught her in two strides. "You can't go back. You don't know who it was."

"I do. It was the Blessed Virgin. All in white and shining. I've got to go back, André. I wasn't polite to her. I turned my back when she wanted me to come."

She struggled with him but he held her right arm firmly. "You've got to tell your father first."

"She might be gone."

"She's probably gone now."

Valérie dug her heels into the ground, resisting him. "Come with me, André," she said. "Come back with me. I want to see if she's still there. I want to tell her I'm sorry that I ran away."

André did not know what to do with her. He did not want to go to Anse-Saint-Jean, and he did not want to become more involved in something that he did not understand. He saw Madame Charbonneau and Suzanne Lepage coming out of the church, and the sight of the two women increased his desperation. If Valérie told them what she had told him, there would be a lot of excitement and talking and questions. He did not want to be around women who were excited and asking questions.

"Valérie," he said, "if you'll go home first, I'll go back with you."

He felt her resistance lessen as she considered his offer, and he took advantage of the lessening to start her walking toward home; then he saw his mother. He knew when he saw her that she was in one of her disappointed moods. She saw him, and there was sudden anger in her face. Sometimes he thought that his mother was pretty, but when she was angry her face was sharp and her eyes very small.

"Where have you been all day when I needed you?" she said. "Out looking for shells with little girls?"

He did not take the question seriously. His mother knew where he had been. She knew that he was working for Rosaire Gagnon. Pretending not to know was a way of feeling sorry for herself. She did that often. He braced himself to resist her, and he said the first thing that he thought of saying, the first thing, that is, which was unrelated to her question.

"Valérie saw the Blessed Virgin," he said.

Céleste Drolet started the sign of the cross, then let her hand drop as she saw the expression on Valérie's face. She dropped to her knees beside the child, reaching for her.

"What is this?" she said shrilly. "What did you see? Tell me, Valérie."

Valérie told her. Listening to it the second time, André accepted every word of the story. It no longer shocked or startled him because it was no longer new. He watched the little girl's face and there was a strange light in it. This was not something, he decided, that Valérie would be able to tell if it had not happened. She told the part that he knew and told it exactly the way it was; about meeting him on the road and telling him and walking with him—and not knowing that the lady in white was the Blessed Virgin until he asked her if she was.

"I wanted to go back and tell her that I was sorry I ran away," she said, "but André wouldn't let me."

Céleste Drolet sprang to her feet. There was fury in her face as she turned on her son. "Why didn't you go with the child?" she said. "The Blessed Virgin! And you wouldn't go. My own son!"

She hit him suddenly, a slashing blow with the back of her hand across the mouth, then gripped Valérie's arm, hurrying the frightened girl back along the road that she had walked from the cove.

Beyond his mother and Valérie, André saw Madame Charbonneau and Suzanne Lepage. They had been walking home slowly and talking as they walked, no doubt, because he had seen them leaving the church and that seemed a long time ago. They were standing still now and he knew that they had seen his mother strike him. That completed his humiliation. She had struck him in the presence of Valérie, one of the younger children, and in the presence of two gossipy village women. He heard his mother's voice, high with excitement.

"A miracle! The Blessed Virgin has visited us."

André was no longer interested in miracles. He touched his lips with his fingers, and when he took them away there was blood on them. It was years since his mother had last struck him. The humiliation outweighed the blood on his fingers. He always had a bad time with her when his father was home, but no one else knew about that. She was always saying that he looked like his father and she made it sound like a sin or a crime. *"Vous se ressemblez comme deux gouttes d'eau!"* Well, he did resemble his father. He was not certain that he was proud of that, but it was not a fault of his. He touched his lips again.

The three women were grouped around Valérie and she was repeating her story once more. He heard the voices of the women when she reached the end of it, but he could not distinguish their words. The voices were a cackling, like the voices of his mother's miserable chickens; then they were all hurrying along the road to Anse-Saint-Jean with Valérie.

He turned away and walked slowly along the path that led to his own home, to the garden patch and to the chores that were his to do.

# IV

The incident of Anse-Saint-Jean was a mystery of childhood. A little girl of eight either witnessed a remarkable vision, or she did not; she either misinterpreted some phenomenon of light and shadow, imagined what she did not actually see, or deliberately fabricated an elaborate falsehood. The small boys who accompanied her, nine and seven, either believed her or did not, were afraid of what they did not understand or actually did not know what had happened or why they had run away.

Someone capable of entering a child's world might have penetrated to the heart of the mystery, but the children themselves could bring no comprehensible answer into the world of adults, a world which impinged upon their own but of which they were not actually a part. They lacked the poise and the vocabulary. They were at a disadvantage in the presence of people who awed them, who disconcerted them with irrelevant questions, and who anticipated their replies to those questions.

Valérie Rivard, who was the key figure, stepped from wonder into confusion when she met Céleste Drolet on the village road. She never found her way back.

Céleste Drolet was thirty-eight years old. She was an unhappy woman. Nothing in her life was as she wanted it to be. She was the last of Ovide Gagnon's children. She was born on January 1, 1907, the first girl in a family of boys, eight of whom were still living. Her father considered her birth date significant, regarded her as a special gift from God, and spoiled her as he spoiled no other one of his children. She was educated in convents on the mainland and she taught school on the Côte de Beaupré. She fell in love with Pierre Drolet and insisted upon marrying him against the wishes of her family, an unheard-of thing on Ile-aux-Erables. Married to him, she was soon convinced that she had married an inferior, and since she could not manage him as she had managed her father, she fought with him for dominance and ended up hating him.

Céleste Drolet had seven children; an astonishing and calamitous number to her, but not at all remarkable in the opinion of her neighbors. Since she could not avoid having children, she would have preferred to have only girls; all of them were boys. Three of the boys died in infancy, two of them left her to try their fortunes on the mainland as soon as they were old enough to do so, and she had two at home with her.

André was indispensable but he resembled his father and she felt an irrational antagonism toward him. Robert, who was lazy, unreliable, and selfish, who could not be depended upon to do anything that she told him to do, was her idol.

Two years away from forty, Céleste still lived in daydreams. Her favorite daydream was of a vague, but stupendous, miracle that would liberate her instantly from everything in her life that she hated and that would, in the same instant, reveal her to her neighbors as a person of great attainments, ability, and importance, the shining soul in their midst whom they had never understood or appreciated. Her imagination was never equal to the task of supplying detail to the dream of a miracle, but she prayed with a peculiar devoutness for what she could not imagine. When she was lost in the dank fogs of self-pity, as she often was, she clung to the thought that "some day everyone will *know*."

On July 30, 1945, in a depressed hour, she met her son on the road and heard him say: "Valérie saw the Blessed Virgin."

The longed-for, dreamed-of, stupendous event had happened. As she knelt in the dust beside the child and heard the exciting details, her heart beat so hard that it threatened to smother her. She was aware, immediately, that she was the first adult on the island to hear the story of the vision. Children did not matter. She, Céleste Drolet, had been *chosen* to hear it. It was her miracle as she had always dreamed that it would be. She rose to proclaim it and she was scarcely aware that she struck her son. Like his father, he always stood between her and life as she wanted life to be.

André had been close to the vision, close enough that he might have returned with the little girl to witness it, to see with his own eyes the Mother of God! The clod had not done so. He was too much like his father. Her mind raced. She might yet be in time to witness the vision herself. The Blessed Vigin might wait there for her. The thought propelled her along the road. She saw Jeanne Charbonneau and Suzanne Lepage. They were her audience. Her voice hailed them triumphantly; a voice that, like her thoughts, verged on hysteria.

"A miracle! The Blessed Virgin has visited us!"

Céleste Drolet named the event and made it forever hers. She was the first. She had discovered it.

Valérie, at her urging, stumbled through the story again. The child was obviously tired, disconcerted by the doubt and disapproval in the faces of the two women, the sudden flood of questions. Céleste waved her hand.

"Enough!" she said. "We must hurry."

She had a sense of urgency. There was no sense in submitting Valérie to the questions of these two stupid women. She regretted that she had wasted time on them, but they had been necessary to her. She felt the sturdy little body brace itself against the tug of her hand and she bent low.

"Don't you want to see *Her* again?" she whispered.

Valérie hesitated, then moved forward. Céleste Drolet hurried her along the road and the other women followed, as she had been certain that they would. They were conversing together in low tones. She could not hear what they said and she did not want to hear. They would be loud enough with their tongues if they discovered that they were in agreement! If only the vision remained! There would have to be something, some evidence remaining of the stupendous miracle that had occurred. The Virgin did not come and go, leaving no trace.

This was meant to be. She, Céleste Drolet, had waited all of her life for this moment. Her heart was suffocating her again with its rapid beating when they reached the little path. She stood, silent, staring across the wide stretch of emptiness that the river would hide again with the turning of the tide.

The sandy beach of Anse-Saint-Jean was deserted. The shadows of the birches were dark stains on the sparkling sand, the distant south shore was hazed over and the haze was tinted pink. The sun was low in the western sky and the light of it passed over the island obliquely. The Saint Lawrence flowed northeast and the island angled slightly across the line of flow. The lighting effects of late afternoon were strange effects. Streaks of gold and silver light lay on the river and the river flowed under, or through, them.

The east rock, the Little Point, was dark, and the doorway in the rock was filled with shadow. Céleste Drolet could hardly contain her disappointment. She could feel, as something tangible, the triumphant skepticism of the two women behind her who merely looked upon emptiness as she did. She bent low again to Valérie, who was standing very straight and still.

"Where was it, *petite?*" she said desperately. "Where did it happen?"

"It was down there. I dropped my basket. I was standing there when I saw the lady and I dropped my basket."

Céleste released the child's hand and watched her as she ran across the sand. She followed her and the other two women followed. The basket lay on the beach, a silent witness only to the fact that it had been dropped. The little girl picked it up and brushed sand from it. She raised her head and looked at the three women. Her eyes were wide, clear. She was no longer afraid of them, nor unsure. The finding of an object that she had lost seemed to restore to her the reality of all that had happened. Céleste, reading her expression, was confident again. She heard Jeanne Charbonneau breathing heavily, then Jeanne's voice.

"There was a lot of running around here, it seems to me, and little standing still. Look at those prints in the sand! Bare feet and a boy's shoes! Those boys were not running away. They were running *toward* the river."

Valérie's eyes followed the pointing finger, calmly. "That was before," she said.

"Before what?"

"Before I saw the lady in the doorway."

"The Blessed Virgin," Céleste said.

Valérie looked troubled. "I didn't know. I thought that she was an angel."

28

Jeanne Charbonneau made an impatient sound. "Put enough words in her mouth, Céleste, and she'll be the Blessed Bernadette of Lourdes."

"I'm not putting words in her mouth."

Céleste knelt in the sand. "Valérie, *petite*," she said. "Can you tell us any more about the lady? Was she wearing blue with the white?"

"No. She was wearing white. A long dress."

"Did she wear jewels?"

"No."

"Or stars in her halo?"

"She didn't have a halo. I know what a halo is. It's a circle around a person's head."

There was a startled expression in Valérie's eyes. Her right forefinger cut a circle in the air. She stared at Céleste and her lips parted. She was remembering something, something that she hesitated to put in words. The woman's hand leaped to the small shoulder.

"You have just remembered something. What is it, child? Tell us."

Valérie shook her head. Jeanne Charbonneau turned her back. "We had better all go home," she said. "There is nothing here. There was never anything here. We were fools to listen to the child."

Céleste regained her feet in an instant. "What do you mean by that, Jeanne? What do you mean? Are you accusing this innocent child of lying?"

Jeanne Charbonneau turned her head. "I mean that this is all nonsense," she said coldly. "I don't know how much you had to do with it in the first place, but it is all nonsense."

She walked angrily away, rolling slightly as her weight thrust her shoes deep into the yielding sand. Suzanne Lepage, still silent, followed her. Céleste was afraid then; afraid that they would reach the ears of the island with a denial of the miracle before she reached them with an affirmation. She hurried after them with tight lips, and the small pawn in a contest between women stood for a hesitant moment alone, gripping her basket tightly with both hands. Valérie Rivard looked at the dark doorway in the rock and, suddenly aware of the deepening shadows, trotted after the women.

As they gained the top of the path and the main road once more, Suzanne Lepage spoke for the first time. "It would be a wonderful thing for the village and for the island," she said. "Think of it! The

Blessed Virgin! People would come here from everywhere. Like Beaupré."

Céleste drew a deep breath, holding back with an effort her impulse to speak. She had not thought that far, not beyond the point where newspaper people would come and interview her, discovering that she who had proclaimed the miracle first, was the most intelligent woman on the island, the only one sufficiently educated to talk to people who wrote for newspapers. Jeanne, obviously, had not thought so far ahead, either.

The Charbonneaus owned the general store. They were struggling to maintain a hotel in a place where few strangers came. What would it mean to them if many strangers were attracted, suddenly, to the island? It wouldn't be like Jeanne Charbonneau to throw bread out of the window if she thought about what she was doing.

Suzanne had done the thinking. She and her sister had a small shop, too. They were the only beauty operators on the island. One of their brothers owned the *fromagerie* at the northeastern end of the island beyond the village limits, and another brother owned a farm in mid-island. It would be a good thing for the Lepages if the island became famous and Suzanne was shrewd enough to see that.

Jeanne Charbonneau made an impatient gesture with her right hand, as though brushing away a fly. She was a short woman, putting more weight lately on a frame that was never lightly padded.

"No good ever came of a lie," she said. "No good to anyone."

"Suppose it is the truth?" Suzanne said. "We do not know. It would be a wonderful thing."

Jeanne Charbonneau pushed ahead, moving more swiftly than either of them. She did not answer until they reached the edge of the village. She repeated the impatient brushing motion of her hand then.

"Take it to Monsieur le Curé," she said. "I want nothing to do with it."

Suzanne nodded. She was a tall, thin woman with large features and eyes set close together on either side of a long, straight nose. She slowed her own pace, dropping back level with Céleste. Her voice dropped and she held her head on one side, looking toward the edge of the road rather than toward the person she addressed.

"That is right, I think. That is the thing to do, Céleste. You must go to Monsieur le Curé and take the little girl. I would go with you."

She coughed apologetically. "But no! He might believe that I sought some advantage. It is different with you. You comprehend?"

Céleste Drolet comprehended, and despised the other woman in that comprehension. She did not want to face Father Bélanger, the village priest. She was not at ease with him because she knew that he disapproved of her. It was not a matter of morals. No one, she prided herself, could utter a world of reproach to her moral character. The disapproval of the priest was purely a matter of understanding or misunderstanding. He did not understand her. She was too subtle for him. He was accustomed to women like Jeanne Charbonneau or the farm women.

She looked toward the church and then at the presbytery, which stood between her and the church. There was something symbolic in the way they were placed. The priest stood between her and the possession of her miracle. If he proved to be unreasonable, as Jeanne Charbonneau was, it would all be very difficult. She straightened her thin shoulders and brushed the hair back from her eyes.

"Of course I will go, Suzanne," she said. "It is only right that I should."

From her own positive statement she drew strength. Jeanne and Suzanne would have the opportunity of spreading the story of the vision through the village, as she herself longed to do, while she was facing the difficult task of confronting a priest on his own ground of miracles and visions; but nothing could come of the matter until the priest was told, so hers was the most important role.

Céleste nodded her head, satisfied with her own reasoning. She took three steps toward the presbytery and then she remembered Valérie. In all of the excitement she had totally forgotten the child. She looked around in a panic.

The little girl had passed her by and was twenty or twenty-five yards down the road. She had to run to overtake her and Valérie eluded her hand. There were tears in the child's eyes.

"I want to go home," she said.

As she had done twice before, Céleste went down on one knee beside her. "Yes, *petite*," she said. "But, of course. I know that you do. But first we must tell Monsieur le Curé about the Blessed Virgin."

"I've told it and I've told it. The lady is gone."

"Maybe she will come back again if you pray to her and if you tell Monsieur le Curé all about it."

"I don't want her to come back."

"What? That is a terrible thing to say, child. The Blessed Virgin! You don't want her to come back."

"I want to go home."

Céleste felt her miracle slipping from her fingers there on the road, without even the opportunity of facing the priest with it. She reproached herself inwardly for neglecting the child on the return journey from the beach, for permitting her to become tired and frightened.

"Madame Charbonneau says that I tell lies."

The small voice trembled and Céleste drew the girl close to her. "Valérie, sweet," she said. "I know that you told the truth. When Monsieur le Curé says so, too, everyone will have to believe it. Of a necessity! You must tell him about the lady, every little thing about her."

She looked into the wide, dark eyes, regarding her with such innocent trust, and emotion rose in her, bubbling into words. Her own voice was shaking now.

"Valérie, *petite*," she said. "You are like my own daughter. Have I not given you piano lessons? I never had a little girl of my own. Always I have wanted one. I love you. I will not let anything happen to you. Never!"

She hugged the stocky little figure, kissed the tear-stained cheek, and rose swiftly. Valérie permitted herself to be led again, but as they neared the presbytery, she resisted the leading. Céleste spoke to her, reassuringly, needing reassurance herself. She, too, was afraid. The moment before the priest's house was a long hour.

Germaine Masson opened the door, as was to be expected. She was the housekeeper; a tall, heavy, slow-moving woman with faded blond hair, broad features, and round, expressionless eyes. She looked from Céleste to Valérie, missing nothing in her inspection.

"Monsieur le Curé is not home," she said slowly. "He departed on a sick call. Me, I would like to know what has happened with the little girl on the beach. My Antoine came home crying and he is sick with it."

Céleste tightened her lips. It was a great disappointment not to have the matter settled at once with the priest after reaching this point through so much effort of will; but she had no intention of delivering herself into the hands of Germaine Masson, who was a placid cow but deeper than she looked. There was no predicting what kind of a tale she would spin for Monsieur le Curé if she had the facts upon which to build. No one else would reach his ear once Germaine had affairs in her hands.

"I saw the Blessed Virgin," Valérie said, "but Antoine would not look."

Céleste heard her with horror. The story was spilled now, and with Antoine mixed up in it. It was the first time, Céleste noted as an aside, that Valérie had said, herself, that the vision was the Blessed Virgin. Germaine stood tall, heavy lids blinking over her round eyes.

"So?" she said. "Is this possible?"

She looked more motherly than the mothers of ten, or a dozen, children. Valérie, who had come in obvious fear of having to talk to the priest, to whom she was accustomed only to listening, was at ease with Germaine Masson.

"Antoine can tell you," she said. "I begged him to look. I begged and begged . . ."

"We will have to go," Céleste interrupted. "We will return to see Monsieur le Curé."

Germaine was looking at Valérie. She nodded her large head. "Yes," she said. "I will inform him of it."

She withdrew behind the door, which she closed, and Céleste did not know if the woman was astonished, impressed, or even greatly interested, whether she believed or disbelieved. One way or another, it was a pity that she had to know of the miracle before the priest heard of it. In some intangible way, the mischance seemed to dim the luster, to make the marvel secondhand, its newness worn before it had had time to shine.

The deep dusk had settled on the village and it was dark on the path between the poplars that led to the presbytery. The shadows wrapped the mood of Céleste. Everything had gone wrong. The Blessed Virgin, the Mother of God, had visited Ile-aux-Erables, and where there should be the bright light of glory, and people prostrated in wonder and gratitude, there was only the gathering darkness. She, Céleste, had raised her voice. She had sought to proclaim the wonder of it and her voice had found no sounding board. She no longer felt that first fine excitement. The event was beginning to seem unreal. Her feet dragged as she walked down the path and then she saw the women.

They were gathered in a group on the road, waiting for her. Suzanne Lepage had been busy. Céleste straightened and her weariness dropped from her. She felt jubilant again; confident and alive. Faith in the miracle returned to her and her eyes swept the tense, curious faces of her neighbors. This time she would not be shouting down a well. There were human ears to listen.

"What is this of the Blessed Virgin?" someone said.

"She has appeared to us," Céleste said solemnly. "I have seen the place where she stood. Tell them, Valérie, what you saw."

Valérie shrank against her and she trembled when the women pressed close, trying to see her face in the dim light, waiting to hear what she had to say. Not until three or four voices urged her did she begin again on her story, slowly, falteringly. She had not quite finished her narrative when a booming voice cut across it.

"What in the name of sanity is this? What are you doing with my daughter?"

The women, a tight group one moment, blew apart in the next, like massed leaves touched by the wind. They seemed literally to whirl as they made way for the short, stout, angry man who ignored them all to concentrate the fury of his stare on Céleste Drolet.

Céleste was afraid of Louis-Charles Rivard. There was no man on the island whom she liked and respected more, nor whose tongue she feared as much. She had to rally all of her forces to stand up to him, but that summoning of her inner strength gave her dignity and called forth from her the qualities that had made her a good teacher once.

"Valérie has seen the Blessed Virgin," she said stiffly. "It is a great and holy miracle and——"

"Great and holy nonsense! I have been searching everywhere for her. The child has not had her dinner, and I have learned just now that you have been leading her around like a photographer's dog. You silly fool! What are you trying to make of her?"

"A saint, perhaps. The Mother of God chose her. Not I."

Louis-Charles Rivard seemed about to explode, or to float upward in an ascension that needed no balloon. He stood on short legs and his big body swelled with his indrawn breath.

"I did see her, Papa," Valérie said unexpectedly. "I did."

The held breath went out of the man with a swift, sighing sound. The explosion directed toward his daughter was mild compared to that which, for a moment, had threatened.

"*Tais-toi!*" he said sharply.

He stepped forward and took the child's hand, looking with hard eyes at Céleste. "I want no more talk of this absurdity," he said. "I will not tolerate it."

He pushed his way through the group, leading his daughter home along the road. For several seconds no one spoke, then babble was released, everyone talking at once.

"*Fi donc!* That freethinker!"

"Imagine it. He wants no more of the Blessed Virgin."

"He refers to Our Lady as nonsense."

"He would not let his child tell of the vision."

"Monsieur le Curé must be told of this."

Céleste Drolet was still shaken by the encounter but she heard the comments of the women with joy in her heart. They had been as skeptical as Jeanne Charbonneau, listening to Valérie, but there were no skeptics now. They were solidly united in their opposition to Louis-Charles Rivard and that opposition made them believers in the vision. Madame Simard, the wife of the mayor and the oldest woman in the group, made the sign of the cross.

"We should all say the rosary in the place of the vision," she said. "We should pray to Her to forgive him and to return again to our island."

There was a swift murmur of assent. Céleste Drolet held the knuckle of her right forefinger against her mouth in a swift gesture of dismay. She had forgotten! She had not thought! As she had ceased to think of Valérie on the walk back from the beach, so had she overlooked the Blessed Virgin herself in her concentration upon the vision. Since that first moment in the road when she had encountered her son and Valérie Rivard, she had not said a single prayer, not so much as one Hail Mary.

35

# V

It was dark when Father Henri Bélanger returned to the presbytery. He had spent a harrowing afternoon on the north shore of the island, a narrow strip of poor farming land and a partially deserted fishing village that had once been prosperous. The people on this strip were his poor, if anyone could be actually poor where there was no lack of life's necessities. The man for whom he had been called was a stranger, a fisherman from Gaspé, who had waited until he was dying to turn his thoughts to God.

It had been difficult to reach the man's consciousness, much less his soul, and the priest could not be certain that the frail bridge of communication had sufficed to carry the burden of the man's need of him. He was depressed when the man died. A man who offered only the last few moments of his life was offering so very little.

Father Bélanger was not in a mood to welcome the women who waylaid him outside the presbytery, stirred to the verbal hysteria peculiar to their sex, all talking at once, raising a clamor about visions and miracles and the Blessed Virgin walking on the water. He stopped for a moment, facing them.

"Who claims all these marvels?" he said sharply. "Who witnessed them?"

The clamor rose again, woman competing with woman for the distinction of being the first to reach his ear. He caught the name of Valérie Rivard and that was enough for the moment. It was some affair of childish piety, then. He was well aware that children have vivid imaginations and he did not consider it remarkable that this should be so. He cut the voices off with a slashing, impatient gesture.

"I will look into the matter," he said. "In the meantime, deport yourselves reasonably. None of you can speak the truth of what you have not seen. To shout it is absurd. Remember that."

He entered the presbytery, annoyed and, at the same time, critical of himself because he was annoyed. He was, normally, a patient man, but there was something about women en masse, particularly when they were agitated, that tried a man's soul. These women would, he had no doubt, ignore what he counseled and go fluttering from house to house through all of the parish, enlarging the story—whatever it was originally—with every telling. It might take weeks to undo the mischief of their tongues.

With the closing of his door against the bedlam of tongues, he became suddenly aware of one phrase that reached his ear and which stayed now in his mind—"The Blessed Virgin *walking on the* water." He stood in his spare, bleak little reception parlor, frowning in concentration.

The visions of fanatics, hysterics, and precocious children were invariably imitative; pale echoes of Lourdes or Fátima, crude paraphrases from manuals of piety, reductions in words of paintings, statuary, or the illustrations in childish books. There was no precedent, as far as he could recall, for the concept of the Blessed Virgin walking on the water. Christ had walked upon the water, calling upon Peter to walk with him, but a child's mind was hardly capable of substituting one figure for another in such a scene, particularly when the substitution called for the changing of storm to calm and the whole context of the scene.

"It is odd, decidedly odd," he thought.

A soft, apologetic voice intruded upon his concentration. "M'sieu le Curé."

Benoit Masson, sexton of the church, commonly referred to as *"le bedeau"* had come quietly into the room. He was a thin, stooped-shouldered man, bony-featured, with pale, blue eyes, the husband of the priest's housekeeper and a man of great fidelity, devotion, and humility. Father Bélanger raised his eyes.

"Yes, Benoit?"

"There is a matter of which you should know. Monsieur le Curé. It is rumored that the Most Holy Virgin has appeared at Anse-Saint-

Jean. Madame Drolet asserts that it occurred. She was here with the little girl, Valérie Rivard, to see you."

"It was not sufficiently important, this vision, to justify her waiting to see me?"

"That I do not know." Benoit Masson coughed apologetically. "In some manner, my son, Antoine, seems to be concerned in the matter. He was, I understand, on the beach with the child who claims to have had a vision. My Antoine acts in a strange manner. He does not obey me to tell what he knows of the affair. This has never happened before. I have not punished him until I could talk to you."

"That was prudent, Benoit. Were there other children involved, do you know?"

"Robert, the son of Madame Drolet. The older son, André, too, I believe."

The priest was frowning again. There seemed to be a preponderance of Drolets in this affair. He was not impressed with the quality of Céleste Drolet as a witness to any event. A most erratic and irrational woman! He nodded his head.

"Try to have all of the children here when I have finished my supper, Benoit. I would like to talk to them."

"Yes, M'sieu le Curé."

Le bedeau bowed himself out and Father Bélanger went to his own rooms to wash off the dust of the north shore and to prepare for his evening meal. He was interested now in the events of the afternoon, not in a mood to entertain miracles but curious about the situation which would inspire the rumor of a vision.

Henri Bélanger was thirty-eight years old and he was in the fourteenth year of his priesthood. He had served the parish of Saint-Thomas-Apôtre for eleven of those years, one year as assistant to his infirm and aging predecessor, ten years as pastor. He was short, dark, compactly built. His eyes were dark and he had a wide mouth, thin-lipped but not severe. There was strength in him but little combativeness. In vital matters he moved slowly. He was not in the least impulsive.

He was aware as he relaxed at his table that there were many callers who came to the door, callers who were sent away by the imperturbable Germaine. This would not be, certainly, a quiet, ordinary evening.

He was having his coffee when the housekeeper ushered in the caller whom she did not presume to send away.

"Good evening, Monsieur le Curé."

"Good evening, Monsieur le Maire. You are in good time to have coffee with me."

Father Bélanger rose from his place at the table to extend his invitation. Nicolas Simard was mayor of the village, but his real importance lay in the fact that he had three sons settled on the land of Ile-aux-Erables and owners of the island's finest apple orchards, another son priest on the seminary faculty, a daughter married to one of the Gravel sons, a fifth son studying law in Quebec, another daughter in the convent of the Gray Nuns. He was a short, slight wiry man with an untidy gray beard, sharp features, and shrewd eyes.

"No coffee, thank you," he said. "It's bad for my stomach." He seated himself in the chair that was offered to him. "I came to talk to you, Monsieur le Curé, about the appearance of the Blessed Virgin on our island."

"It is a little early to speak of that as a fact, isn't it?"

Father Bélanger smiled but, at the same time, he was studying the man across the table. A patriarch like Nicolas Simard, whose opinion would sway a large family and the many people linked to it, was not to be taken lightly. He was not an old dotard. He was a vigorous man of sixty-two who had retired to the village of his free choice, holding still a few financial strings on his farmer sons.

"It is a fact as you will discover," he said calmly. "And the place where the Blessed Virgin appeared was once the land of the Simards, the land of my first ancestor on the island. I want that understood by everyone."

His mouth set grimly, stubbornly, on the last statement. Father Bélanger met his eyes. "I do not believe, if it ever comes to that," he said, "that there will be any question."

"No." Nicolas Simard rose. "No question. The Côtes bought the present farm of Rosaire Gagnon from a Simard, but they never bought that beach. It was deeded to the village by my grandfather."

"A fact apparent to everyone, I am certain."

The priest rose with his guest and walked to the door with him. When he walked back, he was thoughtful. There were many people on the road above the beach saying the rosary, the Mayor told him, and an artist visitor on the island was on his way to the mainland to inform the newspapers. Matters were getting out of hand, but he would only complicate the affair by taking public notice of it before he had all the facts. He was well aware of the weight of his opinion when he spoke for the Church, and it was a weight that he did not exercise recklessly.

The old jealousy of the Simards and the Gagnons was stirring, too, and that was not a good thing. Rosaire Gagnon owned the farm nearest to the site of the alleged vision, but the pioneer on that land had been a Simard. What a situation that was!

"Alleged vision?"

For the first time in his thinking, Father Bélanger permitted himself the question mark. Wildly incredible though it appeared, suppose that there was truth in this? If the Queen of Heaven had manifested herself on the island this day!

The thought shook him. No man was ever prepared for a manifestation of the supernatural, for a direct revelation from Heaven; no priest and no layman. The stories of Lourdes and of La Salette were stories of doubt and skepticism and outright scoffing, with priests not the least of the offenders.

Lourdes and La Salette and Fátima! In those three places the Blessed Virgin unquestionably appeared, her appearance signalized by miracles which left even unbelievers without answer or argument. Stern and hostile forces had sifted and searched and attacked the evidence that she left behind her and the evidence had withstood all challenges. Lourdes was, even today after a hundred years, a living miracle and a testimony. In what way did these humble places differ from Ile-aux-Erables? Was it less probable that she would appear here than in those other obscure hamlets, unknown to the world until she selected them?

And the timing? The First World War was drawing to a close when she appeared at Fátima. The Second World War was nearly over now. It was finished in Europe and coming to a climax in the Pacific. There was, beyond question, a period of doubt and trial and difficult adjustment facing the world with the coming of peace. Did men ever need a supernatural sign more than now, a reminder that wars are caused by the folly and the greed of men, peace by the grace of God to those earnestly seeking it?

Father Bélanger paced back and forth, asking himself questions for which he had no answers. Suddenly he stopped. He had a swift, dazzling picture of what this vision would mean to him if it was true. He had been a brilliant student at the seminary. There was no self-glorification in that. It was written in the record that he had left behind him. He had dreamed of an important parish after his ordination, or perhaps one of the newly industrialized parishes where he could employ himself in combating the modern heresy of material-ism. It was a disappointment to him when the bishop assigned him to one of the simplest of rural parishes, a parish of simple piety and of resistance to change. He had resigned himself to it, obedient to authority, but now?

The picture in his mind was that of a great shrine. If the Blessed Mother of God had deigned to visit his humble parish, her first visit to Canada, to North America, then that parish would be known through-out the world, known as Lourdes was known; a place of miracles, of healing, of great pilgrimages.

Almost as swiftly as the picture formed, he dismissed it. It was pride and presumption for him to think such a thought, linked as it inevitably was to the personal distinction that would come to himself. He raised his eyes to the crucifix on the wall. Words came into his mind, replacing the picture, words out of the Gospel according to Saint Matthew:

"Again, the devil took him to a very high mountain, and shewed him all the kingdoms of the world, and the glory of them."

The priest continued to stare at the crucifix. So, he thought, there must come such a moment to every man, as it had come to the Saviour Himself, when he was shown the glory of the world that might be his if he renounced Heaven. One could so easily be deceived.

He made the sign of the cross, exorcising ambition, returning to the role that had been entrusted to him. He was the pastor of this parish and he would seek the truth of this matter and seek nothing else.

It did not occur to him then that he was already leaning backward in his resolve not to favor any development that would mean personal distinction. It did not occur to him at all.

The sexton appeared in the doorway. "The children are here, Mon-sieur le Curé," he said. "All of them except the little Rivard girl. Her father will not permit anyone to see her or talk to her.

Father Bélanger nodded grimly. He had all of them, it seemed, except the central figure. Well, from the others, much could be developed.

"I will see them, Benoit," he said. "I will see them at once."

# VI

Antoine Masson had grown to the age of reason, which is seven years, with the knowledge that he had four parents. He had a mother and a father whom he had never seen and who were also named Masson. He had a mother and a father with whom he lived, whom he loved and who loved him. There was also God the Father, Who created him and Who was Almighty, and the Blessed Mother Who was his Mother in Heaven, to whom he prayed. These were realities in his life and he did not understand them, nor try to understand them: he accepted them. Most of the things that he understood frightened him.

He was frightened by personal experience; the rough play of boys who were physically superior to him, the necessity for reciting lessons with others watching him, the greeting of an adult which required a response from him, any venture into the darkness of night away from his familiar surroundings, a rebuke of any kind for a fault committed or a task left undone, the responsibility for carrying any object which might be dropped and broken.

Antoine was ashamed of his own fears because the other children derided them and seemed to be without fear themselves. He did not know what to do about the fears, nor the shame that he felt for them. He could not ask anyone what to do because that was another fear. He was afraid to talk about himself lest someone laugh at what he said.

Sometimes he believed that his mother liked him to be frightened because she was always very kind to him when he was most afraid.

She seemed very happy when she was telling him that he must not be unhappy, and this he did not understand at all.

On the day of the vision, every one of his terrors descended upon him.

He liked and trusted Valérie Rivard because he felt safe with her. She never mocked him nor made fun of him, and it did not disturb him that she always commanded him. He was accustomed to obeying orders. He did little else. When he saw Valérie passing the gate with her basket on her arm, obviously going to collect shells, his liking for her was strong enough to overcome his timidity in the presence of a noisy, boisterous boy like Robert Drolet. He joined her, trying to pretend within himself that Robert was not with them.

He was dismayed when his tongue slipped and he came so close to betraying Valérie's secret about the rosary. Her anger with him set up a wall between them, and he was so eager to atone for his mistake that he was willing to do anything she asked him to do. The talk about hearing silence bewildered him and Valérie's command, when it did come, was a sheer horror. He did not want to chase Robert; he wanted to avoid him. Running was one of the difficult things. He was not accustomed to physical exertion. He ran, and the ease with which the other boy eluded him was discouraging. He was in a panic when he returned to Valérie, in no condition to look at anything strange and unfamiliar, anything that could so change Valérie's voice and make it climb the scale with excitement. Her statement that she saw a lady walking on the water was too much for him. He fled from her and from the beach, then, but when he was alone on the road, he was his own torturer.

He was ashamed as he had so often been ashamed. He knew that he should have been brave, that either he should have refused to chase Robert or, having chased him, he should have caught him. He hadn't really tried to catch him because he was afraid of him.

He should have looked when Valérie called upon him to look and see what she saw. He was a boy and he had run away from the beach where a girl stayed. He looked at himself and he was disgusted, and he did not know that other boys, many other boys, boys like Robert, never saw themselves as they really were and never knew shame at their own failures. He was weak in his own eyes and he wept for his weakness because he wanted to be strong.

His mother asked questions which he did not answer, and she did not care whether he answered them or not. She comforted him because he needed comforting, held him close to her and told him not to worry about anything. That, he knew, was something that she liked to do, but it did not help him.

Terror returned to him with the entry of his father. His father was always strict with him, and he asked questions because he wanted answers. He did not understand that sometimes the answers would not say themselves. Today he was very angry and he wanted to know everything that had happened at the beach. He asked the questions very fast, and the more questions he asked, the less Antoine could remember. It was a very helpless feeling, standing before his father and not being able to answer because he could only tell it the way it had happened and not with answers to questions.

His mother said, "Let him alone, Benoit. He does not know anything." His father was still angry. "He knows enough to answer me," he said. "I will not abide his willfulness. We'll let Monsieur le Curé talk to him. He'll answer then and we will see what we will see."

There was a threat in those words which hung over Antoine in the banishment that followed. He remained in his room, alone with his own thoughts and fears, until he was summoned by his father into the presence of Monsieur le Curé.

Father Bélanger sat in his big chair in the small, spare living room where he talked with those of his parishioners who brought him problems outside of the confessional. There was a plain, dark crucifix on the wall behind his chair. Antoine's father had brought in extra chairs. André Drolet sat in one of them. He was an older boy and Antoine did not know him very well, but, for some reason that he could not explain, he had always liked him. There was something wrong with André's mouth. His lips were swollen and puffed. He was looking at the floor and he did not seem happy at being here. Antoine could understand that better than he could understand the pleased expression on the face of Robert Drolet. Robert *did* like being here.

Father Bélanger made a gesture with his hand to Antoine's father, asking him to stay. Antoine's father sat where Antoine could not see him. Father Bélanger smiled at André.

"You are the eldest, André," he said pleasantly. "Tell us, please, what occurred this afternoon.

André raised his eyes. "I don't know, Father," he said. "I had finished the work I was doing for Rosaire Gagnon and I was going home. I saw Antoine running on the road. He looked frightened. I wondered what had frightened him. When I reached the road I saw Valérie and she was crying."

"Crying?"

"Yes, Father. I spoke to her and she told me that she was crying because she saw a lady in white in the door of the Little Point rock. She said that Robert and Antoine wouldn't look. She said that they ran away and left her and she got frightened and ran, too."

"Did she tell you that the lady was the Blessed Virgin?"

André hesitated. "No, Father. Not then. She said that there was light, like a room behind the door. She said that the lady stepped down and walked on the water and called to her to come to her."

"She heard the voice calling to her and the boys did not hear a voice?"

"No, Father. She said that the lady called her with her hand and that she walked on the water just like it was frozen into ice."

"When did she say that the lady was the Blessed Virgin?"

"She didn't say that."

"She didn't?"

"No, Father. I thought that she should tell somebody. I was taking her home. Then I thought that it sounded like the Blessed Virgin, the way she talked about the lady, and I asked her if it was."

"Ah! So you put that idea into her head?"

André seemed confused. "I don't know, Father. She said that she thought that the lady was an angel. When I said that it might have been the Blessed Virgin, she wanted to go back. She didn't want to be impolite to the Blessed Virgin. She wanted me to go back with her." He paused and frowned at the floor. "We met my mother and she took Valérie with her. So I went in to feed the chickens."

Father Bélanger looked at Robert who was fidgeting in his chair, eager to talk. He smiled at him, too. "Well, Robert, what do you have to say?"

"She didn't see anything, Monsieur le Curé. Valérie didn't see anything. It was a game that she was playing with Antoine."

Antoine felt all the eyes in the room fixed upon himself but he did not raise his eyes to meet them. It was a moment like the dreadful moment in school when he was called upon to answer a question; but there was no question. Robert was still talking, his voice high and excited, full of importance.

"I was going with Valérie to the beach. My mother told me to go. Then Antoine wants to go when we see him. Then he asks Valérie if she is saying the rosary to know how far it is . . ."

"Wait!" Father Bélanger raised his hand. "What does that mean, Robert?"

"I don't know, Father. It is what he says to her and Valérie is angry with him and says it is a secret that he shouldn't tell. And I know it is a game they play with the rosary because they don't answer when I want to know what it is. Then when we reach the birches, Valérie stops and she is praying. I can see she is praying and I ask her about it but she doesn't answer me."

Antoine raised his eyes. Nobody was looking at him now. Everyone was looking at Robert. Father Bélanger was leaning forward in his chair and he seemed to be very interested.

"You say that Valérie stopped to pray at the birches, Robert? Before she went down to the beach? Before she said anything about a vision?"

"Yes, Father. I thought it was part of the game that was a secret with Antoine, so I ran away from them on the beach. Before that she was talking about hearing the silence and silly things like that. Then she told Antoine to catch me and he couldn't do it." There was triumph in Robert's voice. "When I came back she said she heard voices and asked me to listen——"

"Voices?" The priest spoke sharply. "You are certain that she said that, Robert?"

"Yes. She did. She said she heard voices."

"Your brother says that she told him this lady called to her with her hand."

"She said that about the voices before she said she saw somebody on the rock."

"Did you hear anything, Robert? Or see anything?"

Robert laughed. He had a loud laugh. "No. It was something she made up to frighten Antoine. I wasn't frightened. I went home."

Father Bélanger sat back comfortably in his chair. He seemed pleased. Antoine knew that it was his turn to answer questions and terror gripped him. This was worse than answering questions in school.

Everyone was looking at him and his father was seated behind him where he could not see his face.

"Antoine," Father Bélanger said gently. "You have heard what Robert says. Is that what happened, as you remember it?"

Antoine stared at the priest and he could feel his heart leaping and falling. He had never contradicted anyone in his life. He was afraid of Robert. It was almost impossible to say where Robert was wrong, even if he was able to speak out, but Robert *was* wrong. He had to make Monsieur le Curé understand that. There was no escape for him. He clenched his hands tightly.

"It isn't right what he said about the voices, Monsieur le Curé," he said.

His own voice, sounding loud in the room, was more alarming than Robert's frown and the way in which Robert moved forward in his chair. Father Bélanger bent slightly forward.

"Tell me how you remember it?" he said.

"Valérie said she could hear silence. Robert said that she couldn't. He ran away. She sent me away so she could listen to it. When we came back she said that she heard it, the silence, and it was like a voice."

Antoine was breathless with the effort that it took to pump those sentences past his trembling lips, word by word. He gulped for air. "After that she saw the lady. Robert ran away again. He wouldn't look. She asked him to look. He ran away."

"Did you look when she said that she saw somebody on the rock?"

Surprisingly, it was easier to answer now. He was caught up in a memory, reliving it. The fact that there were people in the room no longer seemed important.

"I was afraid," he said.

"Why?"

He could not answer that. He did not know why he was afraid when other boys, or even girls, were not. He looked wordlessly at the priest who seemed to recognize the difficulty.

"Did you—yourself—hear any voice, Antoine? Or see anyone on the rock?"

"No, Father."

The answer was true but there was more that had to be said. He felt that and did not know what to do about it. He plunged desperately.

"I didn't see her, Monsieur le Curé," he said, "but the lady was there."

"How do you know that?"

This was the most terrible question yet because Father Bélanger sounded angry. Antoine saw the priest's face through a haze.

"Valérie was seeing her," he said. "I could tell from her voice. I could tell, Father. She kept asking me to look. There was somebody there to see. I didn't want to see her."

"So!" The priest sat silent for a few seconds and to Antoine that silence was like some great height on which he was suspended, in imminent danger of falling. He gripped the seat of the chair with both hands.

"Suppose you tell us now," Father Bélanger said, "about this game of Valérie's, a game with the rosary? What is the secret that she had with you?"

There was no doubting now that Monsieur le Curé was angry. His voice was stern. Antoine heard a chair creak behind him as his father moved. He stared at the priest.

"I cannot tell that," he said. "It is a secret."

He dropped the words into silence, a dreadful silence; the silence of the frowning priest, the staring Robert, the surprised André. His father's voice literally crashed across that silence.

"Antoine! A secret from Monsieur le Curé? A secret game with the holy rosary? Have I raised you no better than this? Answer immediately!"

Antoine wanted to cry. He wanted to run away. He wanted to surrender and tell them all that they wanted to know, begging them not to be angry with him. He felt hot and cold and he wanted to go to the toilet. There was something within him that would not permit him to escape, a compulsion stronger than terror. The face of the priest floated in a haze before him.

"I can't," he said. "I promised."

It was said and he waited for the heavens to fall, for the silence to be shattered by horrid sounds and for violence to descend upon him. He heard his name explode with the release of his father's pent breath and then, incredibly, Father Bélanger's voice, soft, with no anger in it.

"Peace, Benoit. The boy is right. We respect promises. They are the kindred of vows. It is good for one so young to respect them."

Silence flowed back into the room on the voice of the priest and the haze before Antoine's eyes dissolved. He was looking at everyone in the room, except his father who was behind him, and everyone was looking at him; but he was no longer afraid.

"I will ask you this, Antoine," Father Bélanger said. "Was this game with the rosary anything that you considered wrong, anything of which you are ashamed?"

He could answer that. "No, Father," he said.

"Very well. That is all, Antoine."

The priest rose and looked from one face to the other. "Is there anything else? Anything that anyone remembers about this matter that I should know?"

André raised his eyes. "I believe that Valérie saw the lady, Father."

His voice trembled but he stood before Monsieur le Curé, saying what he said. Antoine thought again that he liked André Drolet very much.

"Why do you believe that?" the priest asked.

"It is like Antoine says. Something in her voice, Father. It was the way she looked. I believed it."

The priest smiled. "She, too, could believe it and yet it might not be so. I will ask each of you—André, Robert, Antoine—to remember only this; that, by your own accounts, you did not witness any miraculous event today. None of you heard or saw anything unusual. You must not bear witness to what you do not know. That is sinful. Until I talk to you again, you must answer questions about the matter by saying that you do not know. Do you understand?"

"Yes, Father."

They answered him in chorus. Antoine stood straight and he was no more afraid to speak than the others. André, as he turned to go, slapped him on the shoulder, and he looked up in surprise. André was moving away from him and did not look back, but there was comradeship and approval in that slap and the younger boy recognized it for what it was, wondering a little but pleased. He had never received a slap like that. His eyes followed André Drolet, then he faced his father.

His father was not angry. His father did not say anything. There was a strange expression in his father's eyes but it was not stern or disapproving or threatening. His father had never looked at him in that way before.

He was to remember that expression on his father's face for many years before he understood what it meant: that, in a baffled and bewildered way, his father was proud of him.

# VII

Father Bélanger stood in the parlor after the departure of the Drolet brothers. Benoit Masson still lingered in the room, having sent Antoine away to his mother. The priest sensed the man's need and the difficulty that Benoit encountered in expressing himself in personal matters. He had known his sexton for many years.

"That Antoine of yours is a fine boy," he said. "He astonished me. It is a rare trait in the very young, that standing upon a principle. He has great possibilities, your Antoine."

The sexton cleared his throat. "He has always been a good boy, Monsieur le Curé. I was disturbed tonight. Indeed I was. It seemed to me that he was disrespectful, of unseemly conduct. But yes. I, too, perceived the matter of principle, the respect of a confidence. But I am bewildered by the affair."

The priest crossed the room and adjusted the wick of the oil lamp on the table. Electricity had not yet brought its benefits to the island.

"It required moral courage for the boy to overcome his customary timidity," he said. "I say 'customary,' Benoit, rather than 'natural,' you comprehend? Timidity in a young boy is not natural. You must permit Antoine more freedom, less concern and caution. He must grow according to his own nature. He is a boy whom you can trust."

"Yes, Monsieur le Curé. But, of course. That was our desire for him, that he should grow naturally into a fine man. We were over-concerned, perhaps. He is all we have. One perceives always that an accident, a wrong step, and he is lost. Our only one!"

Father Bélanger understood. The Massons were rather old for the task when they received their "only one" and he not of their own flesh. The priest had long been aware of the weakness in the boy, the ineffectual qualities; not until tonight had he seen the strength, and a certain beauty that accompanied that strength.

"It is not good at any age, Benoit," he said, "to walk in fear. That is not the way of faith. Take pride in your son's strength, not in the walls that you build around him. Tell Germaine that."

"Yes, Monsieur le Curé. Yes. It is good to hear you say that. Tonight was a revelation to me. We will discuss it. Indeed so. And, you will pardon me. I should not have detained you. Monsieur Mederic Lepage is waiting on the porch to speak to you."

"I was not detained. I detained myself. I will see him presently."

Father Bélanger walked slowly across the room. He stood for a moment beneath the crucifix. The interview with the boys had gone much as he had anticipated. The situation was as he had imagined. There was childish imagination and childish piety intermingled in it. There were a few disturbing elements in the story, factors that did not resolve easily. He regretted that he had not had the opportunity of questioning the little girl. That was going to be difficult.

Louis-Charles Rivard, in his strongheaded way, would fail once more to see that he had common ground with the priest of his parish. He would consider himself opposed and, out of that, much that was awkward would inevitably ensue.

The priest shook his head and walked out onto the porch, into a calm, still night, heavy with the scent of honeysuckle. Mederic Lepage rose from the chair in which he had been sitting.

The material and financial affairs of the parish were handled by a *fabrique*, a corporation consisting of the curé and three church-wardens (*marguilliers*) who served for three years each, a new warden being elected each year, replacing one whose term had expired. Mederic Lepage was one of the *marguilliers*. He was a big man physically and big in terms of influence on the island. He owned one of the mid-island farms but he did not look like a farmer tonight. He looked more like a successful businessman from the mainland, in a gray suit and a soft hat.

"Good evening, Monsieur le Curé," he boomed. "A big evening for you, no doubt. A big evening."

"Reasonably busy, Monsieur Lepage."

Mederic Lepage laughed. He was a hearty man and he had the

manner of a politician. He prided himself on being a modern and considered most of his neighbors old-fashioned. He considered himself young and progressive. He was forty-five.

"I will take only a minute, Father," he said. "This matter of the vision, it engages all of us, *n'est-ce pas?* You more than anyone else. Yes! The Church cannot move in the matter, of course, until all is investigated, but there will be other visits of the Blessed Virgin, no doubt, as at Lourdes. We must be ready for them, must we not?"

Father Bélanger's smile was tight. "We move fast, Monsieur Lepage, if we assume that we have had one visit."

Mederic Lepage laughed again. "Yes. Yes. Of course. Always the caution of the Church. All must be proved. But, attend! I bring my mite of testimony. My sister, Suzanne, was one of the first to hear the story of the little girl. She says that there is no doubt, no doubt at all, that the child saw the Blessed Virgin. She is convinced. Absolutely. And she is a hardheaded woman, Suzanne. Yes. It devolves upon us, always under the guidance of you, Monsieur le Curé, to liberate the little girl from that atheist of a father. She must go again to Anse-Saint-Jean like the blessed Bernadette, since the Holy Mother has chosen her."

The priest reached into his pocket, under the soutane, for his pipe. It was a small thing to clutch in such a deluge of words, but one gripped what one could.

"Monsieur Rivard is not an atheist," he said mildly.

"He is but one step removed from it. A good man of his kind. I have nothing against him. But he has locked up his daughter and has expressed himself most violently against the vision. We must all stand with you, Monsieur le Curé, in bringing him to his senses. No man must be permitted to oppose the Blessed Virgin when she comes to us. *Ma foi!* It is unthinkable."

The priest sighed inwardly but he laid his hand on the arm of Mederic Lepage, steering him without appearing to do so, toward the path which led to the road.

"I know that I can depend upon you," he said. "You are one of the staunch ones. I will call on you in due time."

There was no flattery in that. Mederic Lepage was staunch; a faithful Catholic, a just man. He did what he considered the right thing. If he was not always lovable, or restful to his auditors, that was a mystery of human personality and one accepted it, as one accepted the fact that some just men had axes to grind and ground them.

"But, of course," he said now. "You have your methods. Yes! But time will press us. The world will descend upon us before we are ready if we delay." He broke off suddenly to turn his head, bending toward the priest. "Have Gagnon and Bouchard spoken to you yet?"

Edmond Gagnon and Jacques Bouchard were the other two *marguilliers*. Father Bélanger shook his head. "No. I have not seen them."

"They will call. They will see things as I do. No doubt. Exactly! There is no other way to view the matter. This is a wonderful day. The island shall become a place of miracles. All the world will come here. Nothing must interfere. They will see that as I do."

"Truth is not a matter of vote," the priest said softly. "One deals with what has happened, or that which has not happened."

"But surely?"

Father Bélanger had his man safely pointed toward the road. He stepped backward. "If the Blessed Mother has a message for us," he said, "no man can prevent its delivery. Of that you can be certain."

He raised his hand in a gesture that was like a blessing, or perhaps merely a wave of farewell. He walked back to his porch and his hand gripped his pipe tightly. The motives of people were embarrassingly transparent at times. Looking at those motives, one was inclined to turn his head away.

"Prestige for Nicolas Simard who is old," he thought, "and profit for Mederic Lepage who is young. And Céleste Drolet?"

He thought about Céleste Drolet. Seeking all of her life to be praised for what she is not! *She* would be hostess to the Blessed Mother. The memory of his own temptation was still fresh. His mind, too, had gone straight to the mark of personal advantage. He shook his head.

"If She should come," he thought, "who among us would be worthy to receive Her?"

He heard the hoofs of a horse on the road, the creak of a carriage. A heavy step sounded on the path and a short, stocky, powerfully built man ascended the steps. There was no light save the filtered moonlight that flowed through the poplars, but Father Bélanger recognized Edmond Gagnon and called to him. The man said "good evening" gruffly and sank into a chair beside his pastor without waiting for an invitation. He was wearing his work clothes and muddy boots. The smell of his stables was still on him.

"What is this business of a vision, Monsieur le Curé?" he said.

This was a novelty. Someone had come to inquire rather than to inform. Father Bélanger reached for his tobacco pouch. "You know as much as I, Edmond," he said quietly, "since your knowledge brings you here."

"I know nothing, Father. I have heard that a little girl, the Rivard girl, who is wise beyond her years with her father's talk and his books, has made talk of seeing the Blessed Virgin. I have heard that my sister Céleste, who has less sense than my horse, Badaud, has been spreading the story. It is not a circumstance that gives one confidence."

"I have heard what you have heard. Little more. The small Valérie has not told me her story. It would be awkward if I were to call and ask for it."

"Unthinkable. It would create an issue."

The two men lighted their pipes. There was respect and liking between them, the solid foundation for a friendship that had never needed pledges. Of all his parishioners, Father Bélanger esteemed no man above Edmond Gagnon, who had faults as all men have, but who erred in strength more often than in weakness. In the flare of the match, he saw the man's dark eyes, his seamed and leathery skin, the full mustache, the firm thrusting chin.

Edmond Gagnon was fifty-two. He had eight surviving children out of ten, and he was one of those admirable farmers who had plans for each one of them, with money or land set aside for each. His own life had been difficult, with many of his father's responsibilities thrust upon him too soon, including the duty of providing for his father's younger children as well as his own. He was a hard man because it had been necessary that he be hard in order to survive, a careful man with money because his money had to care for many people.

He cleared his throat now and spat over the rail. "My son, Rosaire, and his wife, are down at the beach praying with many others," he said gruffly. "I can find no fault with a prayer but do you think, Father, that there can be any truth in this story?"

The priest stared into the darkness. "It is not a matter for thinking, is it?" he said. "Rather for seeking the truth through seeking all of the facts. Don't you agree?"

"Yes. Of a certainty. But I cannot believe it. There is no reason."

"We cannot know that. The reason, if there were a reason, would be God's. Our Blessed Lady has appeared on earth before, and to children, and where she was not expected."

"I cannot believe this one. This is not the place for miracles. My farm has been worked by Gagnons for more than two hundred years. There are other farms as old. Miracles here would mean a shrine like Beaupré. There would be no more farms, only parking lots for tourist automobiles. It is insupportable to think of it."

The priest drew thoughtfully on his pipe. It was amazing, the difference in men. Where one saw gain in a miracle, another saw loss. "You cannot mean," he said, "that you would deny the island to the Blessed Mother, if she wanted it, because her coming would convert your farm to Her use rather than yours?"

"No! I would give her my farm. I would give my farm to the Church; but it must be proved to me that the land is needed."

"Yes. I can see that."

They smoked a while longer in silence. Edmond Gagnon was a quiet man in meetings, saying little. With very few people—perhaps only with his wife, Eugénie, and with his pastor—did he trust words to speak for him; to all others he stood on his deeds and his decisions, without explanations or apologies. He cleared his throat again and the priest sensed that there was more on his mind than his resistance to miracles.

"There is another matter," Edmond Gagnon said at length. "My sister, Céleste, is telling everyone that there is a miracle. She thinks only of that now. She will think of other affairs later. The farm of my son, Rosaire, is the only land from which you can see the rock of the Little Point at high tide. I bought that land from the husband of Céleste in 1930, fifteen years ago. There has always been bad feeling about it."

"In what way? It was before my time."

Father Bélanger knew the story in its bare outlines, but there was a need in Edmond Gagnon to tell that story tonight, to tell, perhaps, his own side of it as he would not normally do. The darkness was pressing against the porch, and when he pulled on his pipe, Edmond's face emerged from that darkness, or partially emerged, like an image in a shadowed church, touched by the faint, sputtering illumination of a vigil light.

"Céleste was always my father's favorite," he said. "With good reason. She was a girl and she came to him late. A pretty little thing. He educated her well. Pierre Drolet was not the man for her, but she set her will against the family in the matter and my father gave way to her."

There was shock still in Edmond Gagnon's voice, remembering. He pulled hard on his pipe. "Moreover, Father, my father did what no man can explain. He gave the Côte farm, which he had bought, to Céleste and her husband. To a daughter, mind you."

Father Bélanger nodded. He understood the shock of that. Land always went to the sons of the family and there was never enough land for all.

"My brother, Jean-Pierre, had reason to expect that the Côte farm would be his. He had worked it. There was bitterness in him, Father, and he left home without saying good-by. No such thing had ever occurred with us. He went to the States."

Those last five words hung suspended in the darkness. The priest honored the silence that bound Edmond Gagnon and himself because it spoke of something for which Edmond would never have words, his feeling for his lost brother, Jean-Pierre.

"The husband of Céleste," he said at length, "was no farmer. He did not know how to do our kind of work."

A grudging respect crept into the harsh voice of Edmond Gagnon when he spoke of his sister's husband. The man had tried for three difficult years to be what he could never be, a good farmer; and with little help from his wife, who knew even less about a farm than he.

"A woman of amazing and continuous complaints, Céleste," her brother said.

The climax came in 1930 when Pierre Drolet came to Edmond and offered to sell him the farm. Céleste wanted to live in a smaller village house and she wanted a piano. The thought of that want of hers still stirred anger in the man who sat beside the priest on the porch.

"She valued a piano above land," he said, "land that would support her sons, and the sons of her sons."

"We are all differently made, with different needs," the priest said gently.

"No. I do not believe that," Edmond said grimly. "Our needs are the same. We must eat and have shelter, and feed our children and shelter them and educate them. A piano does none of these things."

His respect for Pierre Drolet did not survive that incident. The man, he believed, should have compelled his wife to go with him to the work that he could do, and the money from the land should have helped to establish him so that he could provide for his children.

"I was thirty-seven then, Father," he said, "with six living children and one ready to be born. It was a difficult time but I could not let the land pass to strangers. I bought it. And Céleste has always said to all who would listen that I cheated her husband, who knew nothing of land."

Father Bélanger straightened in his chair. This was the heart of the affair. This was the reason why a man not given normally to words found language with which to unpack his heart and his memory.

"Is your conscience at peace in the matter?" he said softly.

"It is fifteen years. I was younger. Who can know?"

"The farm was worth more than you paid for it?"

"Yes. He did not bargain with me."

The silence surrounded them again, broken only by the distant chorus of nocturnal insects. "What can I do?" Edmond Gagnon said. "I am more prosperous now than then, but it is not dishonest to pay what a man will accept."

"No. But it seems to me that you accuse yourself."

"If I owe anything, it is owed only in my own mind, not in law or justice."

"Most of us know more about law than about justice."

"Yes. I have thought about this often. Tonight it walks in my brain. But it would set nothing right to place money where it would be wasted. Drolet would be a fool with any sum, and so would she. I owe no debts to foolishness."

"Nor to pianos," the priest said wryly. He tapped his pipe against the heel of his shoe. "They have sons," he said.

Edmond Gagnon's chair creaked as he shifted his weight. "One observes André," he said. "He is not afraid to work, that one. But he will not make a farmer. He has not been raised to it."

"He has a good mind. He is outstanding in the school."

Edmond Gagnon tapped his own pipe and put it in his pocket. "I will pay for the education of André," he said. "He shall have what I give my sons."

"You will not regret that."

"It is a thing I will do. Thank you, Father. You have had much patience."

He rose and stood facing the priest, a short, blocky shadow, darker than the darkness behind him. "I will go now and pray with my son, Rosaire, and his wife," he said. "The Blessed Virgin is there on the Little Point because she is everywhere, but I do not believe that the little Rivard girl saw her."

He turned and strode down the path toward the road where he had tethered his horse. Father Bélanger's "good night" floated after him and then it was quiet again. The priest repacked his pipe. He was in a thoughtful mood. Edmond Gagnon's story had moved him; not so much in the part that was told, but because of so much that had not been mentioned; the little details of a young farmer's long, long struggle with the land while the children came, the illnesses and family crises, the departure of a beloved brother for the States, the problem of buying land that he did not want strangers to have.

Long ago Father Bélanger had discovered that only on the surface is a quiet rural community like Ile-aux-Erables simple and uncomplicated. There were no great scandals, of course, and no monstrous sins such as crowded the pages of modern novels, novels which Father Bélanger received sometimes from his brother in Montreal and read with a sense of wonder and astonishment. People loved and hated on the island, however. People aspired and conspired, struggled and suffered, and doubted and knew desperation. Tonight some strange force, acting like a spiritual magnet, had drawn from ordinary people the emotions and the secret longings that had been hidden under the surfaces of seemingly placid lives.

One could almost believe—but, no! One waited and one weighed facts. To do otherwise would be emotional.

Father Bélanger shook his head. He rose from his chair and put his pipe away. He descended the steps and turned right on the path that led to his church.

# VIII

André Drolet left the presbytery with his brother, Robert, who, for a few minutes at least, was quiet, content to walk without asserting himself. André was vaguely dissatisfied with the meeting in the presbytery parlor and he, too, walked in silence, frowning at the road. He had a conviction that the questions and answers had not been quite right; not the precise questions, perhaps, or not the complete answers to the questions put. The logic born in him with his French blood was at odds with the result. They had all done their best, but he did not believe that they had given Monsieur le Curé all of the facts. There was something missing, something important, but he did not know what it was.

The confusion was probably the fault of Robert, who liked to show off and to be considered important. André did not believe that Robert had lied; Robert just did not know as much as he thought that he knew. Robert never did. He could not talk about it to his brother while they were walking through the village. He would have to wait until they reached home. He hoped that his mother would not be there.

Robert raised his head with a sudden jerk. "Look!" he said. "Here comes the old man!"

He swerved and ran as he had run from the beach. André glanced, startled, at the small shadow losing itself in the massed darkness, then raised his eyes. His father was standing in the road, looking with a puzzled expression on his face, into the shadows that had swallowed Robert.

Pierre Drolet was a huge man, tall and broad and powerful. His hair was thick, black, curly, and very lightly touched with gray. His features were bold, irregular, like the work of a hasty sculptor, and he had large teeth that were startlingly white. He had a black beard, closely cut, shaped to his chin and jaw. His eyes were very dark, almost black. Those eyes probed the darkness, then came back to André.

"What is the matter with him?" he said. "Did I ever hurt him?"

"No."

A single word was enough to answer the second question. André answered the first with a shrug. He could not attempt to explain Robert. Running away from his father was not evidence of physical fear; it was something else. Pierre Drolet had a voice of thunder when he raised it to command obedience, but he had never struck either of his sons.

The big man was balancing himself rather unsteadily with his legs spread far apart, and André knew that he had been drinking, as he often did. Many people drank on the island. Farmers made cider from apples, and brandy from berries and various fruits. They made whiskey from potatoes. On the north shore there was a house where fishermen and laborers sometimes sang and drank all night. That was where his father went. A boy knew such things and accepted them.

"You are not afraid of me?" Pierre Drolet said.

"No."

"Are you afraid of anything?"

It was a difficult question. André looked away from his father, toward the church. It would not be honest to answer "No," but he despaired of explaining himself if he answered "Yes." His fears defied definition.

"I am not afraid of people," he said.

Pierre Drolet laughed. He had a great, booming laugh that sent sound echoing under the arches of the trees. "*Ma foi!*" he said. "You do not know what you say. There is nothing in the world so terrible as people." He shook his head. "*Ça c'est sûr!*"

It did not seem to make sense, but then the talk of men who were drinking seldom made sense. At thirteen, André Drolet knew that much. His father swayed back and forth, his feet anchored to the road as though they had roots.

"You are my son," he said. "My son, André. I do not know if you are a friend of mine. It is a droll thing, that, no? I want to talk to you."

André did not want to talk. He was tired. There was in him, however, a certain shame for his brother who had run away. He could understand how that would seem to his father. There was no reason for it. His father was right about the other matter, too; the matter of friendship. He had never been his father's friend and his father had never been a friend of his.

"I would like to talk to you, too," he said.

"Good!" The big man seemed pleased. He stopped swaying. "We will sit on the fence of the churchyard," he said. "It is a good place. Are you afraid of the cemetery?"

"No!"

André had heard ghost stories all of his life. There were men and women on the island who liked to tell them. He had never seen a ghost and did not expect to see one. The place where people were buried did not frighten him.

"The dead come back sometimes and that is a fact," his father said. "But they never hurt people, I think. It would not be reasonable."

"Did you ever see any?"

"I think so. There is something about that. One cannot be certain of it. Someday I will tell you of these things."

His father was friendly, genial, happy. André did not remember him as ever being like this before. His father was away most of the time and when he came home, he always brought many presents for everyone. He never seemed interested, then, in making friends. All that interested him was the presents, and whether or not everyone liked them. It was frightening and one did not know what to say, even if one liked the presents. It had been that way ever since André was very small. After he gave presents to everyone, Pierre Drolet was only a big stranger in the house. André had never known how to talk to him. This way, the way he was tonight, it was easy to talk to him.

They walked past the church together, the gravel crunching under their feet. His father looked at the church, a solid mass of dark stone with a silvered steeple that was glowing faintly with reflected moonlight. "He is good to us, God," he said unexpectedly. "He gives us more than we suspect. He gives us many things, God. Do not forget it."

André looked at him from the corners of his eyes. How could anyone forget God? He thought, then, that Pierre Drolet was his father and saying words that he thought a father should say to his son. He liked the swift flow of emotion that moved through him at the thought that he was his father's son; that he was not merely someone who resembled Pierre Drolet. He was aware, as he had been many times, of his father's size and strength. He straightened beside him, making himself taller. He thought about his mother.

His mother did not like her husband. She never spoke kindly of him and much that she said was unkind. She had told André many times that until she married she had had a lovely life. She said often to her sons that their father was cruel and that he had caused her great suffering, but André had never seen the cruelty and he did not know what she meant. He had accepted it as fact, however, because his mother said it and because so much else that she said was true.

"Everyone respected the Gagnons," she said often. "Everyone respects them now. Look around you! See for yourself. You can be proud that you have Gagnon blood and you need not concern yourself that no one respects Pierre Drolet."

André had observed for himself. His mother was correct about the Gagnons. They were a highly respected family. She was not right about his father. People respected him, too, but in a different way, a way that André was certain that she did not understand. Many of the men from the farms felt superior to Pierre Drolet because they were good farmers and he had failed as a farmer; but they were afraid of him and a little envious of him. He had traveled far and he told exciting stories of the adventures that he had had. He had been able to hold his own in the lumber camps for many years, where, admittedly, men were tougher than on the farms. André had been certain, when he was younger than Robert was now, that his father would have an easy time with any man on the island in a fight, probably with any two men. André had been proud of that but it was an empty, comfortless pride because he had never felt himself a part of the man who inspired it.

The school was a dark rectangle on their left, a lifeless building in summer, without pupils, abandoned even by the nuns who attended school themselves on the mainland. Pierre Drolet looked at it.

"Are you good with the studies?" he said.

"Yes. Most of them. They are not too difficult."

The man nodded. He seemed to grope for some comment to make.

He raised his hand and the fingers were widely spaced. He dropped it and his shoulders rolled.

"*C'est ça*," he said. "Do you want to be a farmer?"

"I don't know. I don't believe so."

"*Crois bien.* It is a good life but there are other lives. Do not be what you do not want to be. *Ça fait sottise.*"

"Maybe I cannot do anything about that. One does what comes."

The big man frowned. He stooped and picked up a sawed branch that someone, probably Benoit Masson, had dropped when hauling wood for a summer kitchen. He turned it over in his hand.

"That is the holy truth," he said. "One does what comes."

For some reason which he did not understand, André felt closer to his father in that moment than he had ever felt in his life. They walked together on the path that climbed to the cemetery on the hill. The moon was bright in a clear sky, and from the low stone wall that surrounded the churchyard, they could look down upon the glistening surface of the river, the stubby lighthouse northeast of them, blinking its warning to any craft afloat.

André had never seen the river from this point at night. He could see lights on the mainland, the lights of Baie-Saint-Pierre on the north shore. He had seen those lights many times from the dock, but they were different when one viewed them from the hill. Everything was different. Pierre Drolet seated himself on the wall with a grunt.

"Each of these poor fellows has a small farm now," he said. "They don't need much land in this place. That's a fact."

André looked at the grave markers, white and gray in the silvery light; slabs and crosses, wooden markers; nothing elaborate. One prayed for the soul and merely identified the place where the body lay. There was a stone structure in the middle of the churchyard which he had always considered more interesting, by far, than the graves. This was *Chez les Morts*, the house of the dead, where those who died in winter awaited burial until the frost went out of the ground.

"Gagnons!" his father said. "Many Gagnons are in this ground here. Many. They bury Gagnons here more than two hundred years. Your mother, she likes that. They don't bury any Drolets here. You won't find them. Drolets belong someplace else. Many places."

His speech was a form of thinking aloud and André recognized it for what it was. His father was talking to himself, for himself, and required no answers. "That is not, maybe, precise," he said. "Two Drolets came here. Babies! Children of your mother and me, brothers of you; older than you if they lived."

André tried to imagine the two lives that were briefly lived before he was born. His brothers! He could not imagine them nor feel that they were brothers. His father seemed to be thinking of them, too, but they were real to him. There was sadness in his face.

"Babies have no importance in a cemetery," he said. "No one knows them. They have no history."

This mood was beyond André. He felt that his father was slipping away from him again. The sense of intimacy was gone. He wanted that feeling back, the feeling of being one with his father. He sought it in the one way that he knew, the direct way, the sharing of an experience that he could share with no one else.

"Valérie Rivard saw the Blessed Virgin today," he said. "Down at Anse-Saint-Jean, in the doorway of the Little Point."

His father looked at him, his left eyebrow climbing higher than the right. "You think so, eh?"

"It is true. But Monsieur le Curé does not believe it. I could not find the right words to tell him how it was that Valérie told me."

"For something like that, there are no right words. Me, I am not Monsieur le Curé. I will listen with my heart. Tell me of this!"

His father's eyes were fixed intently upon him and the feeling of intimacy was back. He had made no mistake. He could talk to his father. André drew a deep breath.

"I was helping Rosaire Gagnon——"

He started his narrative there, with himself and with what he had been doing. The big man sat hunched on the flat stones of the fence. He had the branch in his hand, the piece of sawed firewood that he had picked up. He had a large knife, too, and he whittled the wood while he listened. André was aware of him, the attitude of his body, the movement of the knife; but he was seeing again, vividly, every moment of the afternoon; the fright in Antoine's face, the tears on Valérie's. Because he was reliving an event, not merely relating incidents, his mind did not censor what he said nor check him when, consciously, he would have checked himself.

". . . so Valérie said to my mother that I would not return with her and my mother hit me in the face."

66

"*Sang de Dieu!* Is this true?"

His father cursed. It was not a loud or angry curse; it had sadness in it.

"I did not mean to tell that part."

"Why not?"

"I am ashamed of it."

His father stared at the branch that he was carving. He seemed to be considering that statement, weighing it, putting a value on it. He nodded his head.

"Yes!" he said. "A man is ashamed when a woman makes him so. Men do not make men ashamed, *n'est-ce pas?* With us it is different, another thing that is not shame."

It was André's turn to nod. He knew what his father meant, without understanding the words in their sequence. The words of the meaning were not so important as the meaning itself. As though he feared that he had been obscure, Pierre laid one big hand on the boy's shoulder.

"It is a bad thing for a man to be hit when he cannot return the blow, no?"

"It is not so bad now, thinking about it."

Pierre concentrated once more upon his carving. One of the blades of his big knife was a file with which he smoothed the edges of the wood. He spoke without raising his eyes.

"It is very interesting, my André," he said softly, "but this little girl did not see the Blessed Virgin, I think."

"She did. I could tell if she was lying about it."

"I do not speak of lying. When you get old like me, you are not so sure about what is lying. *Ma foi,* no! I never speak of it." Pierre turned the wood in his hand. "Once at Jonquière, that's a long way from this place, I knew a man who saw Saint Joseph."

The boy's eyes widened. "Did he really?"

"I do not think so. He was a carpenter, this man. After he sees Saint Joseph, who is the carpenter himself, this feller is a very good carpenter; very careful, very exact, very honest. He thinks Saint Joseph is watching what he does." Pierre shrugged. "Maybe he did see him. Who knows?"

André was frowning. He considered this story disappointing. It did not prove anything. A fact should be, or should not be. He wished that his father knew more about this man and could make it clear about the miracle, one way or another.

"Why don't you believe that Valérie saw the Blessed Virgin?" he said.

Pierre bent over his carving. "This is not much of a place," he said mildly. "Why should She come here? There is no reason for it."

That was the core of the difficulty. André's mind, too, had questioned the idea that the Mother of God should appear on the beach of Anse-Saint-Jean instead of in the church; to one girl instead of to everyone. Considering the matter reasonably, it could not happen; but he liked the wonder of it and he had seen Valérie's face when she told him the story. An event could be unreasonable and still happen.

"I believe that she did see the Blessed Virgin," he said firmly.

"Maybe so. Who knows? Monsieur le Curé will say that it did not happen. The Church must be cautious, but that will be a pity for the little girl, a most unhappy thing. Yes. For you, it can also be unhappy if you say that this is true. It is not something that you *know*."

André recalled suddenly his promise to the priest; that he would not discuss the matter nor answer questions about it. It did not seem to him that he had broken his promise in telling his father, but it was apparent that he could not tell anyone else what he believed; because of the promise, and because he really did not know what Valérie had seen, or had not seen.

"My mother believes that it is true," he said. "She is telling everyone."

Pierre Drolet gave no indication that he heard his son. He turned the figure that he was carving, working carefully with the file, holding the wood close to his face because the light was dim.

"Your mother was the prettiest girl I ever saw," he said gently. "Very pretty. Hair like gold. Bright eyes. Very wide, very blue. She had the lovely voice, too. Sing like a bird."

André was startled. He had discovered the "pretty" quality in his mother for himself; a quality that came and went, that he did not see often. It was odd that his father should speak of it. He knew that his mother disliked his father. He had never thought about his father's feeling for his mother. If he had thought about it, he would have assumed, probably, that his father also disliked his mother. This, obviously, was not true.

"You are too young, my André," his father said, "to know about a woman. If I knew, I could not tell you. It is a knowing that grows in you, or grows not. One thing I tell you sure. A man should not give to a woman everything that she wants. But no! She does not want what she says. It is better if a man gives only what he has and gives with a good heart. This much I tell you sure. It is a thing I did not know when I was young."

He paused a moment, shaking his head. "A man cannot tell a woman what he wants of her," he said. "She has to know."

André sat beside him, silent, trying to understand. This, if he could understand it, might explain why his father was away most of the time. It might explain many things. His father waved his hand toward the river.

"You know what they named the Saint Laurent, the first French? They name that *Le Chemin du Bon Dieu*. The Road of God, they name it. That is one great river, my André. Downstream there, pretty far, not too far, there is Baie-Sainte-Catherine and a place called Tadoussac. I tell you about that place sometime. That is where the Saguenay comes to the Saint Laurent. There is a river you should see."

The man's voice flowed on, a little like a river itself, strong and sure and powerful, then hesitating over a word as the great stream hesitated momentarily when confronted by rocks and islands. Pierre's fingers worked on the wood that he was shaping as he called images out of his memory. He told the boy of the wilderness, of the great silent forests and the men who went into them with axes, of towns carved out of those forests and of logs lashed into mighty rafts. He dropped names that had music in them; Chicoutimi, Rivière-du-Moulin, Kenogami, Saint-Ludger-de-Milot, Mistassini, Rivière-aux-Rats, Descente-des-Femmes.

"Descente-des-Femmes, there's a pretty place," he said. "Everyone there is named Villeneuve. Everyone in the parish is called Villeneuve. You can hardly believe it."

The boy wondered why this was so, as he wondered about many swiftly drawn indistinct pictures that he had of his father's world, but he did not interrupt with questions. He was afraid that, if once he diverted it, the flow of words would stop. Occasionally his father chuckled when some amusing thought struck him.

"You read the newspaper, eh? *Tiens!* What is it, that newspaper?

It is a piece of the forest. First there is the tree, then that tree is chopped down and trimmed. This makes the log. The log is ground up and that is le pulp. From le pulp there comes the paper. You have never smelled the pulp town, no? *Tonnerre!* There is a smell! Before it is the newspaper, that pulp is one big stink, I tell you."

Pierre Drolet knew the forest and the pulp. He knew the swift water and the mighty dams, the hydroelectric plants and the great new plants for making aluminum. He was the intimate of bear and moose and wolf. He had visited them in their own homes. He had known Indians who lived wild and free in the far north and who came down to the settlements once a year to go to confession and to Mass and to have their babies baptized, because they had been converted long ago and remembered always that they were Catholics.

"I talk too much, I think."

He stopped his flowing narrative abruptly, looking at the figure that he had carved. He rolled it between his palms, then kneaded it with his fingers and his thumbs as though it were wax. He held it out to André.

"You know who that is, *hein?*"

The boy saw the figure clearly for the first time. It was amazingly well done, about eight inches high; a powerfully built, broad-shouldered man with strong features and a fringe of beard. The man stood with his chin raised, looking upward, his clenched fists held close to his body, level with his waist, the left hand forward and slightly higher than the right.

"*Bien sur!*" André said. "That's you."

His father laughed. "That feller! No. Look you! He does not have *les bottes sauvages*. He does not have an axe. Not him! No. He has brains, that feller. You bet. He's somebody. That feller, he's *you!*"

André looked again at the figure. It was the image of a man, not of a boy. This was the way his father expected him to be some day, big and strong. He did not know what to say about it.

"*Il se fait tard,*" Pierre Drolet said. He rose from his seat on the wall, stretching his muscles, looking out over the dark water. André rose, too, standing beside him. It was indeed late. The lights of Baie-Saint-Pierre had vanished and there was a great silence pressing down upon the island. The breeze off the river was a touch of moisture on his skin, air that moved without sound. His father hummed a few bars, then opened his voice.

"V'la le bon vent . . . Voila . . ."

He stopped and looked at André. "You know that one?"

"No."

"Then it is no good. We try another." His teeth were white in a wide smile. "I know. One is never too young."

He hummed again and André nodded his head. They turned away from the cemetery then and walked in step toward the village. André felt his father's arm across his shoulders. His father sang and he sang with him:

> Auprès de ma blonde
> Qu'il fait bon, fait bon, fait bon.
> Auprès de ma blonde
> Qu'il fait bon dormir.

They broke the silence into fragments and scattered the fragments down the hill. They passed the church, and the presbytery was just beyond it. Monsieur le Curé would probably be awakened, and le bedeau, Monsieur Masson, and the wife of Monsieur Masson, and Antoine. It was exciting and it was more than a little scandalous and no one could do such a thing alone in the late night when people slept.

> Qu'il fait bon, fait bon,
> Fait bon.

They turned into the village road and the song was suddenly over. Pierre Drolet stood straight. "Your mother will be asleep," he said. "It is not good to awaken her."

"No."

"You know the quiet way to enter, the very quiet way?"

André nodded. "Yes. I do."

"A boy must know such things. I knew such a way in my father's house." The big man hesitated, seeming to grope again for a word that he wanted, reaching for it with his right hand, then letting his hand drop.

"You are thirteen, my André," he said. "It is not too late to do the big thing, you and I. Not too late yet, I think, and we will do it."

He slapped the boy's shoulder, a quiet and awkward gesture, then turned away. He walked down the road and he did not look back. André did not know where his father would sleep and he wasted no thought on it. He gripped the carved figure in his left hand, the image of the man that he would some day be, and he watched his father walk away until the shadows engulfed him. He was not tired. It was the most wonderful night of his life.

# IX

The home of the notary, Louis-Charles Rivard, was one of the newer houses on the island, but built like the old originals and sufficiently weathered to look an age that it could not claim. It had stone walls, three feet thick, faced with wood that protected the mortar from the icy winds of winter. The roof was steeply pitched, extending well beyond the walls to carry the snow free of doors and windows. All of the rooms were on one floor; the library where the notary conducted his business, the small formal parlor, the huge comfortable kitchen-dining room, the three bedrooms.

Valérie had the middle room. She lay in the darkness, knowing that she should be asleep, floating on a current of wakefulness, aware of the voices in the other room but indifferent to the words.

Her father was talking to her aunt, Laure, and his voice was still an angry voice as it had been since he met her on the road and brought her home. She could not understand why he should be angry because she saw the Blessed Virgin, nor why he would not listen to her when she tried to tell him about it. Laure was even more baffling to her. Laure always listened to her, even when her father was not interested in something that she had to say. Today Laure had said: "Hush, child. You must not say such things."

When she had tried to make Laure tell her why she shouldn't say what happened, Laure had said only: "You must eat your supper. You should have been home hours ago."

If she couldn't say anything, she couldn't tell Laure why she wasn't home hours ago and how people wouldn't let her go home. Everybody wanted her to tell about the lady in the doorway of the rock when she did not want to tell about it any more; but when she wanted to tell her father and Laure, they wouldn't let her say anything.

"This is some of your pious foolishness coming home to roost," her father had said to Laure. "This is what happens when you fill a child's head with all kinds of nonsense. Miracles! Visions! Folk tales! Stupid superstitions!"

Laure had been angry, too. "Someone in this house has to teach the child about her religion," she had said, "and set an example for her, if her father won't set one."

"Religion! I'm not talking about religion. I haven't interfered with it. I'm talking about all this pious humbug about little saints, and showers of roses, and angels leading children by the hand. You and Céleste Drolet are two of a kind."

"I will not be compared to Céleste Drolet!"

It was not unusual for Laure and her father to quarrel, and Valérie was never distrubed when they did. Neither of them ever stayed angry very long, and it was easy for Valérie to forget their quarrels when they forgot them easily themselves. Tonight the quarrel was disturbing because it was longer than most quarrels and because she was the cause of it. Her father seemed to be angry not only at her because she saw the Blessed Virgin, but at Laure, too, for the same reason. Laure had nothing to do with it. Laure was not even there. She was not responsible herself. She didn't know when she went to the beach that she would see anyone in the doorway of the rock. She had never seen anyone there before.

She had eaten part of her dinner, even when she had not felt hungry, because Laure had said that she must eat it. After that she had been sick and vomited. Laure had put her to bed and that was strange, too. Laure did not stay to say her prayers with her. Tonight Laure had acted for a minute as if she was going to say them, then she shook her head and said: "You better say your prayers by yourself tonight, Valérie. Be sure to ask God to tell you what to do."

She did not know what Laure meant, but Laure had left the room before she could ask her. She could hear her father's voice, very loud, and she knew that he was walking back and forth while he talked, as he often did.

"Do you realize what this would mean to that child if those fools had their way with her?" he said. "She would be a freak. A holy show!

They would parade her from one end of the country to the other, as that female imbecile did tonight. She would be an exhibition, like those sad Dionne quintuplets, with no life of her own."

"If she did not see the Blessed Virgin, no one will pay any attention to her," Laure said, "and if she did, the matter is out of your hands."

"She's my daughter. You're not going to tell me that she did see a vision down on that miserable beach."

"I never said that she did. That Céleste Drolet is responsible for the whole affair, trying to call attention to herself."

Valérie didn't listen any longer. She buried her head in the pillow so that she could not hear. Her father and Aunt Laure were like Madame Charbonneau. They believed that she had told a lie about the lady.

"I didn't tell a lie," she whispered desperately. "I saw her. I did."

She closed her eyes and tried to see the vision again as she had seen it. All that she could see was the statue of the Blessed Virgin on the side altar in the church, a very beautiful lady in a gown of blue and white who stood with her hands held out, palms upward, smiling, with a halo around her head. That wasn't the way the lady stood nor the way she was dressed, nor the way she looked in the doorway of the rock. She had been all in white, with no blue, and she did not have a halo. That was all that Valérie could remember. She could not remember her face. She could not remember exactly what she did with her hands, except that she was calling to her, wanting her to come closer. The lady stepped down and she was not standing on rock any more. She was standing on the water. She was standing on top of it.

Valérie opened her eyes. She could not see with her eyes closed. She tried, but she could not see with her eyes open, either. She did not know if the lady walked on the water or only stood on it.

"I wasn't polite to her," she said aloud. "I didn't come to her when she wanted me to come and I was wearing my old gray dress with the stains, and my moccasins were dirty and I didn't comb my hair. My hands were dirty, too. I had been working in the garden with Laure and I didn't wash them. I didn't even say a Hail Mary to her."

She cried softly, remembering her own failures. She said the Hail Mary very slowly and solemnly, staring into the half-light of the room, the voices of her father and Laure rumbling in the background. She could see the gracious figure smiling at her as she prayed, but it was the statue in the church again, not the lady on the rock.

"Maybe it wasn't the Blessed Virgin," she thought. "André said that it was, but he didn't know. I thought that she was an angel."

She tried to see the vision again, thinking of her as an angel, but when she thought that, all that she could see were the two angels on either side of the high altar in the church, brightly colored angels.

Valérie was suddenly tired. She wondered how she could be like the Dionne quintuplets when they were five and she was only one. She wondered why André's mother hit him in the face and why she didn't like her husband and what Monsieur Drolet came home to do.

"*Il ne vient à la maison que juste le temps de me rendre enciente.*"

That was what Madame Drolet had said. Robert repeated it that way. It was a very baffling sentence. She wanted to ask Madame Drolet what it meant but Madame Drolet only wanted to talk about the Blessed Virgin.

"I did see her," she whispered. "I saw a lady. I did."

She yawned. Her eyes were very heavy. Laure and her father were still talking in the other room. The voices went on and on while she drifted away from them.

# II
## THE AFTERMATH

# I

On the last day of July 1945, a horde of strangers invaded Ile-aux-Erables. The visiting artist who had carried the news of the vision to the mainland on the night before had done his work well. He had phoned to radio stations, which put his report on the air, and to newspapers, which sent reporters and photographers to cover later developments. He was a well-known artist and his word carried weight.

Vacationists from resort towns on the north shore landed on the island in the morning from a great variety of river craft, seeking novelty and excitement after hearing the broadcasts. Many interested, or curious, citizens of the Province of Quebec discovered with astonishment that a well-populated island, easily accessible on the Saint Lawrence, lacked telephones and that they must go to the island for information if they were not satisfied to wait for the newspaper or to depend upon the mail.

Paul Charbonneau, who prided himself on his hotel, operated in conjunction with the post office and the general store, registered a record crowd of eight guests and was able to accommodate that many only through the process of doubling up. He was momentarily grateful that he was not faced with the problem of housing a woman, but the women arrived later, some of them accompanied by husbands, and he was pained at the necessity for turning them away.

A few of the village people co-operated in the emergency by turning over spare bedrooms to pleading strangers. Nicolas Simard, the mayor, who lived quietly with his wife in a house large enough to accommodate a normal Canadien family of ten or twelve people, did not yield to any appeals until late afternoon. He was confronted then by a courteous gentleman from Toronto who described himself as a journalist. This man, so obviously a personage, was assigned to the largest guest room and assured that there could be no question of payment, that the house was honored by his presence.

Monsieur le Maire did not discover until time for the evening rosary that his guest was a Protestant. It was a very great shock to him.

The mayor was only one man of many on the island who found the day bewildering. Ile-aux-Erables had never attracted tourists and was not accustomed to them. Few people on the island spoke English or understood it, and no one on the island ever tolerated interruptions in the rhythm of work, apart from Sundays and the solidly established feast days which were always anticipated.

Family gardens were heavy with beans, carrots, onions, and peas. The sun was bright in the sky and farmers were watching for the first breath of a northwest wind as the signal to start cutting hay. It was Tuesday, practically the beginning of a working week. Men and women had all that they could do.

Into this world of reason and of order came an invasion of people who had nothing better to do with their time than to spend it in asking questions. They expected to be understood when they spoke in their foreign tongue, and they expected the work of all men to stop because they, the questioners, were not working. It was insupportable.

The natural courtesy of the people who lived on Ile-aux-Erables was subjected to a strain, but it did not break. From Télesphore Turcotte, the blacksmith, who considered English a very amusing language, to the smallest child in the village, *les insulaires* did their best to make the unwanted visitors comfortable. The natural exceptions were Louis-Charles Rivard and Monsieur le Curé.

The home of the notary was under siege early in the day. Everyone who came to the island wanted to see the little girl who claimed to have seen a miraculous vision. Louis-Charles was in a murderous temper, and when the people who trampled his garden and took up positions all around his home refused to go away, he barricaded his door—a door that, like the others on the island, had never before been locked—refusing to answer to demands or inquiries. The newspapermen from Quebec City were, of course, the most persistent. They were Canadien, French-speaking, Catholic, and they knew what they wanted. They took pictures of the house, called to him through doors and windows, and tried to prevail upon him to accept the notes of inquiry and lists of questions which they tacked to his door.

Father Bélanger was in a more difficult position. He was a target of only slightly less importance and interest than Valérie Rivard. He was the man whose "Yes" or "No" might make or break the story. The dignity of his position as pastor did not permit him either evasion or escape. He said his morning Mass as usual and he faced the newspapermen with the laconic statement that he had neither information nor comment to offer them.

When strangers presented themselves at the presbytery, as they did all through the day, he talked to them in his little parlor, refusing to discuss the vision, expressing the hope that they would enjoy their visit to the island and his regret that limited accommodations would make their stay necessarily short. There was humor in his politely worded statement for those who had humor; not everyone had.

Conspicuously absent from the roll call of visitors to the island was a group which had, certainly, a greater interest in the events and a greater curiosity about the outcome than any other. There were no priests. Individually and collectively, they decided that the Church might be embarrassed by any premature clerical interest in a rumor of miraculous occurrences; or, if the Church were not, the local pastor well might be. Prudently, they stayed at home, leaving the field to laymen who might indulge curiosity without assuming responsibility.

No one succeeded in eliciting a statement from Benoit Masson, *le bedeau*, and few of the visitors, of course, knew anything about the presence of Antoine on the beach. Antoine was kept discreetly indoors and out of sight. Not so Robert Drolet.

Robert was available to all seekers; tireless, voluble, and acquisitive. He guided strangers to the beach and he showed them the door in the rock. When the tide was out, he showed them where Valérie had stood and described what she had done. His native shrewdness informed him early that belief in the vision was more popular than unbelief, the seeking for wonder more compelling than doubt. He became a believer, himself, when he sensed the prevailing wind, and he changed his story to fit the expectations of the people he guided.

"I ran away because I thought that Valérie was playing a joke on me," he told them. He managed to look sorrowful and full of regret.

"If only I had looked I would have seen the Blessed Virgin, too."

Robert collected money from all of the people he guided, but his regret that he ran away was, in several instances, productive of extra offerings from women. He was co-operative in posing for pictures and this, too, was profitable. He led all of his tourists, ultimately, to his own home after telling them that his mother was the first person who spoke to Valérie after Valérie had seen the Blessed Virgin. He had no lack of customers through a long day because the ferry from the north shore made an unprecedented number of trips to accommodate the curious and the thrill seekers who came from the summer resorts and from Beaupré, the famous shrine, which was always thronged in summer with seekers after the miraculous. When the visitors realized that there was no place to stay, no restaurants or hot dog establishments, they tried to see as much as possible within a very short time. Robert was the high point of an otherwise drab experience.

Céleste Drolet was too busy to give any thought to Robert. The dream of her life had come true. People from the large world outside, many of them from the fabulous United States, had come to the island and sought her out. She sat in her own parlor, the formal parlor that was never used except on extraordinary occasions, and talked to them. Many of her visitors spoke only English, but she had studied English in the convent and had taught it during one year of teaching school, so she did not concede the fact that years without practice in speaking it had robbed her of proficiency. By dint of many gestures, verging on sign language, she made out very well in maintaining her own illusion that she was bilingual. The majority of those who came spoke French and with them she was truly impressive. She described Valérie Rivard and told the story of her life, describing in great detail the meeting on the road when the child confided in her the fact that she had seen the Blessed Virgin. With a nice feeling for drama, she showed her visitiors the piano on which she gave music lessons to Valérie. She exhibited to them, too, some of her own petit-point embroidery, done years ago before she was married. The praise of the women recaptured for her some of the magic of the past, the past when she was so often praised and for so many reasons.

There was no cupidity in Céleste, as there was in her son. To the strangers who hesitantly suggested leaving an offering, her refusal was dignified but firm.

"I consider myself very fortunate that I have been able to tell you of Valérie," she said. "I am greatly blessed that I am so close to the child, that I was the first person in whom she confided."

The visitors were impressed with Céleste Drolet and her starved soul expanded under the warmth of their approval. She had always been quite certain that there were qualities in herself that were wasted on the island and on the people she knew, qualities which could only be appreciated by people of the outside world, people of education and of culture. She was proud of the piano which was, in itself, a symbol of culture. She was proud, too, of her bookcase and the books in it, the overflow of books which she had arranged artfully on a table.

There was one disconcerting moment when one of the male visitors took one of her books in his hands and discovered the pages still uncut. She experienced a moment of dread that he would examine others.

Céleste had gone through a period of book buying, of sending away for books, waiting with a sense of excitement for their arrival, picking them up importantly at the post office. She had intended to read them, but the impulse to possess a book seemed to be satisfied by possession. Today she regretted that she had not, at least, cut the pages, but the regret was momentary. Her day was very full.

Not since she was a child, led out proudly by her father and ordered to sing or to recite for company, had she received so many compliments. Only the newspapermen, of all her guests, disappointed her, and she had expected more from them than from all of the rest. As writers, they should have been cultured, witty, interesting conversationalists with sensitive intuitions to inform them that in her they had found a kindred spirit. Actually, they were curt, abrupt, in a hurry, and interested only in the answers to very ordinary questions. If there had been no one else, they would have been destroyers of the dream, but there were many others. The newspapermen were a minority group that she could, regretfully but decisively, wave away. Céleste Drolet needed them less than they needed her. She was the bridge that they must cross to the vision which had brought them to the island.

In all of that day, neither Céleste nor Robert mentioned either Pierre or André. Pierre left the island, without farewells, on the return trip of the ferry which brought the first visitors. He was headed back to his beloved Saguenay, but his going was not an event. There was no one to note it or be concerned.

André, as usual, was working for Rosaire Gagnon. He went to his work before the first contingent of visitors arrived, and he worked the vegetable patch far from the road, so he was not aware of the problems which beset the villagers, nor of the sudden prominence of his brother Robert.

Shortly after ten o'clock, Marguerite Gagnon asked him to bring Rosaire in from the big field. An excited Rosaire sent him for the midwife. André saw the horde of strangers in the village then, but he had no time for them. He had to get Madame Lafleche back to the house in a hurry, and he did.

A daughter was born to Rosaire and Marguerite Gagnon on the stroke of noon. She arrived three weeks before she was expected and if newborn babies hear anything, the first sound that she heard on earth was the ringing of the Angelus from the tower of Saint-Thomas-Apôtre.

André knelt in prayer with Rosaire. There were tears on the young farmer's face and he could scarcely pray. He was a lean, loose-limbed, awkward youth with gaunt features and blond hair as coarse as straw, untidily cut. He worked his calloused hands together as he prayed, and after he made the sign of the cross which followed the "Amen" he stumbled to his feet.

"The Blessed Mother has given her to us, this baby," he said huskily. "She was not to come so soon. She is the first miracle. I will call her Valérie-Marie. She was born on my land. From this land one sees the place where the Blessed Mother stood. Last night Marguerite and me, we said the rosary in sight of it, the fifteen decades. She is the answer to that, my daughter."

As matters developed, the birth of a baby, a commonplace event on Ile-aux-Erables, was the big news of the day.

The vision story, with no one but Céleste Drolet and Robert to keep it rolling, was losing momentum by the time the midwife returned to the village. Madame Lafleche was a tight-mouthed, discreet woman when circumstances warranted discretion, but she exercised no Spartan restraints upon herself when she saw no reason for them. Within five minutes after her return she was telling her neighbors about the miracle baby who was to be named "Valérie-Marie." Within a half hour, two hitherto bored and frustrated newapapermen from Quebec were talking to her. Miracle or no miracle, she was a delight to them.

Antoinette Lafleche was no ordinary midwife. She was a squarely built, gray-haired, level-eyed woman of sixty-three who had qualified as a registered nurse many years ago in Quebec before her marriage. A widow for over twenty years, living on an island which did not support a doctor, she was an expert bonesetter, a practitioner in healing herbs, and a woman of infinite resource. Twice, she told the fascinated reporters, when winter isolated the island, she had successfully performed appendectomies.

"Isn't that practicing medicine without a license?" one of the men asked.

Madame Lafleche met his eyes without blinking. "It certainly is, young man," she said. "But both of those men are alive today. They would not be if I had waited to obtain a license."

She refused to be drawn into support of the vision. "I know nothing about it except what I've heard," she said, "and one may hear anything. Rosaire Gagnon believes in it, of a certainty, and on this island there are many Gagnons."

The journalist from Toronto, arriving late on the island, had a difficult time. He was sent on his long journey because of one piquant and tantalizing statement in the first reports of the vision out of Baie-Saint-Pierre; "Valérie Rivard, whose father is reputedly an atheist——"

"If the key arch to this miraculous occurrence is the daughter of the village atheist, it should be diverting to watch the Roman Catholics try to build another shrine on it," the editor said. "Let's get the atheist point of view."

Hugh MacWhirter tried. He had no more success at the house of Louis-Charles Rivard than the others who preceded him. His next reasonable step was to talk to the man's neighbors. He assumed logically that the post office would provide him with a cross-section of public opinion, so he stationed himself in the large room that provided a comfortable buffer space between the Charbonneau general store and the Charbonneau hotel. Paul Charbonneau, himself, was the first disappointment.

"But no, monsieur," he said. "There are no atheists on this island. It would be unthinkable. There have never been atheists here, if one excepts the Iroquois who came here only to kill the Catholic Hurons. Everyone on the island is Catholic."

"I have been given to understand that this man, Louis-Charles Rivard is not."

"*C'est dommage!* Someone has, to make a poor joke for himself, perhaps, pulled your leg. Monsieur Rivard is assuredly a Catholic."

He could obtain no other answer from any of those he interrogated. Some of them were curt in answering, and some of them were amused, but all were agreed upon one fact: that he had been misinformed, that Monsieur Rivard was of the Faith and greatly respected.

In answering as they did, neither Paul Charbonneau nor the others were in a conspiracy to lie about the matter or to conceal truth. They were all aware of Louis-Charles Rivard's scornful and often shocking statements about religion and the Church. They were aware, too, that he did not go to Mass or to the Sacraments. To their minds, this was a temporary condition in which the man found himself, as had many before him. He was still *un des nôtres*, and his neighbors were confident that he would return on his deathbed, if not before, and that he would enjoy a good toasting some day in Purgatory for his derelictions. They did not take his philosophical departures at all seriously.

"It is not a matter of belief with him," they agreed. "He has carried a heavy priest on his back at some time or another and he has not yet recovered from it."

All of which was a subtle affair, involving neighbors who had lived together all of their lives in one place. It was not a question that could be discussed intelligently with anyone named MacWhirter—and it wasn't.

Nor were the newspapermen from Quebec any more successful in penetrating the life and the thinking of Ile-aux-Erables. They were *pas insulaires*, off-islanders, no less than MacWhirter, to be treated with courtesy but not to be entrusted with facts, thoughts, or impressions which did not concern them. They sent their stories to the mainland for transmission on the last ferry, and they gathered in the big room of Paul Charbonneau's hotel to listen to the news of a wider world over his massive battery-powered console radio.

Field Marshal Sir Harold R. L. G. Alexander had just been appointed by King George VI as Governor-General of Canada, succeeding the Earl of Athlone. President Truman of the United States,

Premier Stalin, and Prime Minister Atlee, who had replaced Winston Churchill, were preparing to confer on vital problems in Berlin. A long list of French politicians, in eclipse since they fled France during, and after, the fall were seeking the headlines once more with denunciations of Marshal Petain.

Those islanders who were accustomed to dropping in at Charbonneau's for the evening newscast were silent because there were strangers present, but they listened with grim, set faces. They understood Petain and they did not have anything in common with his enemies.

They were men of the land, these islanders, and if Canada were invaded and conquered, they would stay on their land while they could, and work it and care for it; only the itinerant and the man without true roots, could flee from the conquerors. The French of Canada had been conquered once by the English, but they had stayed on the land and preserved their language and their Faith under their own leaders, men like Petain who stayed with the people. As now, there had been "Free French" in those ancient days, leaders who had fled before the English and returned to live in luxury in France, but they were not honored in Quebec.

This question of Petain and the charges of collaboration had been argued many times in Charbonneau's.

The newspapermen cared little, one way or another, on the Petain question. They listened to the broadcast passively. There had been many like it of late, many newspaper front pages that differed little from this one of today which was in the making. It was quite evident that something was lacking in the prosaic march of events across the face of this last day in July 1945. Something was needed as a relief from politics, from the scurrying of little men trying to appear great now that danger was past, from the drabness of victory which had dimmed so swiftly the tinsel glory of war.

The news needed, perhaps, a small girl and a glimpse of wonder, a breath of Faith.

"If I could take a picture of the little Rivard," a photographer said. "I would like to have one of those white cats in it. Did you ever see a place with so many white cats?"

Paul Charbonneau took his pipe from his mouth and gestured with

87

it. "Attend!" he said. "I will tell you of those cats. You will scarcely believe it."

He told them at great length. White cats, it seemed, were mentioned by the earliest chroniclers of island history; white cats only, no other color. There were other cats now, of course, all colors, shades, and mixtures, but the pure white streak persisted; no one knew how. Certainly no one had the time or the inclination to concern himself with the breeding of cats. But no! The cats, however, were a necessity. They made the island impossible for rodents. In the summer the cats belonged to no one and lived as they pleased, but in the winter they found the hospitality of homes or lived in barns.

"One asks," Paul Charbonneau said dramatically, "how it is that these cats do not become too numerous for the island to contain, eh?"

No one asked. Charbonneau held his pause of inquiry embarrassingly long. One of the Quebec reporters shrugged. "It is, perhaps, that they are English cats," he said, "with a small sex life and few children."

The man from Toronto made a polite sound of protest. "That is hardly fair," he said. "An aspersion."

"Monsieur will, perhaps, inform us on the sex life of the English?"

The Quebec reporter assumed an expression of courteous inquiry. Paul Charbonneau looked from one man to the other. He liked argument and debate among those he knew well, when the outcome was predictable, but not among strangers in his house. He laughed, ignoring the byplay.

"But no," he said. "Our cats are Canadien and most assuredly French. Of a certainty! There is another explanation."

The explanation, it seemed, lay in the struggle between cats and climate, a contest which always resulted in a tie, neither antagonist winning. There was a high cat-infant mortality, but the total number of surviving cats remained constant, with no appreciable increase or decrease from year to year.

Charbonneau made quite a narrative of it. The newspapermen stared at him. This innkeeper, they thought, was a bigger bore than his monstrous radio, but the cocktails that he prepared from local ingredients had a soothing effect, and Madame Charbonneau was preparing a dinner which could be anticipated by the nostrils.

There might not be miracles in this cat-wonderland, but there were compensations.

Other women, down the ten-mile length of the island, had already served dinner to their families or were engaged in serving it. There was an uneasy awareness throughout the entire island that an extraordinary event had occurred or had, at least, possibly occurred. There were many visits made to the numerous outdoor shrines and much discussion among those who made them.

The six o'clock newscast was heard on farm radios, and at seven o'clock a station in Quebec broadcasted prayers, as it did every night. The first program belonged to the world of events in which the people lived and the second belonged to the world of their belief which was no less real to them. They were a devout people, a people who prayed in grief and in illness, in gratitude and in thanksgiving, more often in pure worship, lifting their minds and hearts to God, asking nothing.

When the prayers were said and the evening chores were done, the Gagnons hitched their horses to rigs and wagons. There were the parents of Rosaire, the uncles and the aunts, the sisters and brothers and cousins. There were, too, the Hamels, the family of Marguerite Gagnon. A new child had been born of these families and the child was linked to the story of a miracle. A cavalcade rose to welcome her to the world, and ultimately, whether they accepted the story of Valérie Rivard or not, most of those who rode to Rosaire Gagnon's farm would linger to pray with Rosaire within sight of the shrine.

Father Bélanger dined alone, and later, in his study, he paced restlessly. He heard the horses, the creaking of wagons, the many voices, when the Gagnons and the Hamels drove in. The birth of a baby, particularly a girl, seldom created as much interest as this one. There was material for thought in that. The baby was a fact, but the legend that surrounded her now, that might conceivably always surround her, was quite possibly a momentary delusion. He raised his eyes to the wood carving of the Blessed Virgin, standing in a niche among the shelves of books that lined the study wall. Possibly a delusion? Yes! Probably so! Yet, possibly not.

Patience was a simple virtue. The practice of patience could, however, be difficult indeed. He had to wait and mark time. In prudence, he could do nothing else.

# II

Louis-Charles Rivard did not endure the siege of his home stoically. He was a man with a low boiling point and he erupted sometimes to small provocation. On the day of visitors, the provocation was great. Why in the name of all the devils did not people mind their own small and petty business? By what right did strangers hammer on his door and stand in his flower bed shouting questions at him? He paced his study, railing at them, but while he paced and ranted the quiet, unexcited, sardonic monitor within him kept asking, "Why should they not?"

He listened to that inner voice ultimately when he wearied of exploding energy at invisible targets. He threw himself down in his swivel chair and the chair groaned in protest against his weight as it always did. He was a man of impressive stomach and heavy shoulders and short legs, an ugly man if one took note only of his broad face, fleshy nose, and wide mouth, but a man of compelling interest when one met his eyes. Those eyes were large and full of life under bushy brows. They were eyes of many eloquent moods; commanding, shrewd, angry, or as gently compassionate as the eyes of one of the milder saints. He wore a mustache and a fringe beard, which were always carefully trimmed, and the trimming of his beard was another index to his character. He was careful of his clothes and of his person. There was pride in him and a dignity that survived his explosive rages. Living a life of its own, independent of his temper, he had a questioning, reasoning, well-informed mind.

His intelligence took command when his fury was spent. "See here," it said, "these strangers are merely people. You have been dealing with people all of your life. They are curious. They have a right to be curious. There is a bit of religious hysteria involved, too. Your daughter is concerned in that. The whole situation is abnormal. How can you expect people to react to it with indifference?"

He sat for a while in his chair, brooding. His daughter, Valérie, was, in truth, at the heart, the very center, of all this madness, and he would give anything that he possessed if this were not so. He had no word of blame for her. In her innocence, she spoke, no doubt, from some impulse of her heart. How many adults understood the innocence of a child or could communicate with it? There could be no fault ascribed to Valérie in this sorry affair that had developed. He told himself that and yet he was afraid for her. The mind of a child was a delicate film on which adults wrote, and often recklessly. Damn adults!

He had not asked a single question of the child. There had been too much of that before he found her. That Céleste Drolet, *l'espèce d'idiot*, had dragged her around like a doll, putting words in her mouth, tiring her to exhaustion. The child had been trembling and wild-eyed when he rescued her, like a little animal that has been the sport of boys.

His sister, Laure, tapped on the door of his office and followed her tap into the room without waiting for his invitation. She was no longer young, Laure, but today she appeared older than her years, her heavy flesh sagging, her eyes worried.

"Louis-Charles, you must take some action," she said. "We cannot live like this. The house is a prison."

"Our ancestors lived like this, but the people outside were Iroquois. It was permitted to shoot them."

"I do not ask that you shoot anyone. I do not ask anything for myself. But this is a bad experience for Valérie."

"What of her? You have not been nagging her about this matter?"

"I have not mentioned it. She is listless, like one who is sick, and why not? She cannot go out-of-doors. She knows that there are people all around the house and that they seek her. It is a terror to her. She sits in her room and looks at a book which she does not read. What are we to do?"

"What would you have me do?"

Laure had been standing, but she sought a chair now and sank into it. "Louis-Charles, it is in my mind and I cannot help it. Suppose that it is true? Suppose that that little innocent one has been blessed by God with a vision of the Virgin?"

Louis-Charles stared at her. His lower lip protruded. "You should be outside shouting for a look at her with all of the other fools," he said.

"It is often the fool who calls others fools. You have closed your mind. You have not talked to her, or heard her, as a judge would hear even a stranger and a thief."

"Have you?"

"No. Out of respect for you. You are her father."

Louis-Charles tapped his desk with his fingers. He had been unable to feel anger toward Laure today, not even the anger of exasperation which she so often aroused. They were companions now in a dilemma and she had been prudent.

"It is best for the child not to discuss it, believe me," he said. "It would be like asking her to relive a bad fright, a horrifying experience, to ask a nightmare to return to her for our inspection. In principle it is the same thing. This is an emotional mood, built into shock by stupid women."

Laure shook her head. "It would be better to have it out. It is bottled inside the child."

"It will be easier for her to forget if we do not give it importance. We must not make it an issue."

"Louis-Charles, you should see Monsieur le Curé. He should talk to her. That would settle the matter."

"No. It is impossible."

Laure rose. "Will you have lunch with us?"

"I will take mine here. I will come out for dinner."

The man sat for a long time after his sister left him, his head down, his chin against his chest. He could build any position of his into invincibility with words, but when he was alone, the doubts infiltrated. He could not quite banish that question of Laure's: "Suppose that it is true?"

He had a deeply rooted prejudice against all reported visions and private revelations. He abhorred the big shrines which built simplicity into spectacle, and the pilgrimages which seemed to have less affinity with worship than they had with the herding of sheep. He could build no belief in the random interventions of spiritual beings in the material affairs of men.

"She could not have seen anything," he said.

He was uneasy. His prejudices were strong but he had had a normal Catholic boyhood in a mainland town as staunchly Catholic as this island. He had not been much older than Valérie when he served the Mass as an altar boy. He could remember now, in the quiet of this room, the moments of awe that he had felt, the exaltation of spirit. There was peace, even in this troubled hour, in the remembering; the shadowed hush of the church in early morning, the distinctive fragrance of heated wax as the tiny flames danced on the candles, the sonority of Latin, the tingling of his nerves in tune with the Sanctus bell.

The calm certainty of the Catholic Church invested all of the ritual with meaning, with a soul-shaking solemnity that reduced the wall between the worlds to tissue thinness. One felt the supernatural only a breath away when one surrendered oneself to it.

The mind of the man had turned to other paths from those simplicities of childhood, but he had not denied them to his daughter. It was not merely that she must live and grow in a community of unfaltering faith, but because he wanted the beauty of it in her life; the Christ Child in the household of Nazareth, with Joseph, the carpenter, teaching Him his skills; the Blessed Mother, fated to tragedy but lovely and gracious in the suffering that she shared with all mankind, as she was lovely and gracious in her joy.

Yes! He had wanted that for a little girl growing up, and the feeling for saints as friendly, invisible helpers in difficulty, belief in the guardian angel, the shining companion of her soul. It was good for her to know faith and beauty, and to grow in the knowledge that she must be worthy of the friendship of the invisible, as she must be worthy of the best qualities in people around her if she would call those qualities forth from others.

He could not have given her all of that alone.

But perhaps it had gone too far. One could be hurt at any age by surrendering oneself to fantasy. Faith was faith, but credulity was the whiskey of fools, which made them drunk with superstition.

Laure brought his lunch and he ate it without knowing what it was.

In the afternoon, that phrase of Laure's—"Suppose that it is true?"—

came back to haunt him in another guise. If he was wrong in all that his reason assured him was right, then what destiny awaited a child who had been permitted a glimpse of Heaven, who had been chosen as a messenger?

He was familiar with the story of Bernadette of Lourdes. She had been interrogated, browbeaten, doubted, humiliated, accused of falsehood, by both civil and religious authorities. She had been subjected to every test that the mind of man could devise, seeking for flaws and inconsistencies in the story that she told over and over. She had been robbed of her childhood. Her sole refuge from a world that would accept her only as a freak, never as a normal human being, had been a convent.

Louis-Charles Rivard clenched and unclenched his fists. He would not have it. He would not surrender Valérie to it. The fact that Bernadette found in her bitter path the straight road to sainthood left him untouched. It was an abstraction with which he would not contend. He had only one child. He would never have another. For that one he wanted the fullness of a normal life on earth, more happiness than he, himself, had had, children of her own, who would give to her what she had given him.

It was a bad afternoon, but he tried to be gay at the dinner table, aware that his own voice echoed in the closed house, mocking him. Louis watched Valérie anxiously and Valérie, of all impossible things, seemed afraid of him. He had never brought fear into her life, or let it in where he could bar the door. *C'était insupportable!* Between himself and his daughter, no shadow should ever fall.

When they left the table he crossed the room to the bookshelves beside the great open fireplace, cold now but retaining its memories of brave, roaring defiance to winter. He selected a book and turned, holding it in his hand.

"Come, *petite*," he said. "I will read you a story."

"Yes, Papa."

There was a momentary flash of the accustomed eagerness in Valérie's face but it was only momentary, a brief light swiftly extinguished. Louis-Charles seated himself in the big rocker and took the small, sturdy body onto his ample lap. He held the warmth and the softness of her close to him as he turned the pages. This was an old book that had served them many years. Valérie read, herself, books that were far more advanced, but no child ever outgrew the books that were early discovered, early loved. Louis-Charles cleared his throat. There was an actor lost somewhere in all else that he was and had been, an actor who found release only in the telling, or the reading, of stories to a little girl.

"*Dans la Bretagne, il y avait autrefois la noble famille des Barons Kerver,*" he read. "*Le Baron, qui était aussi brave que bon, avait douze enfants, six fils, grand et forts comme lui, et six filles, belles comme le jour et vraiment adorables.*"

The story had always been a favorite of Valérie's and the large family of the Baron interested her greatly because she was surrounded by large families of children into which she entered only as a visitor, someone from the outside. The large families of a story belonged to her. This was something that Louis-Charles understood very well and he had used the medium of stories often to supply for her the brother and sister feeling that she would never know in actuality. Tonight she was quiet in his arms, with no exclamations about "*les six fils et les six filles,*" no comment of her own to make the story live.

Louis-Charles was troubled, but he read on. Before the story was finished he felt her heavy in his arms and he knew that she was asleep. He carried her into her room and laid her gently on her bed. She did not awaken.

Laure was washing the dishes. She paused and laid a cup aside, drying her hands nervously on her apron. "Louis-Charles!"

He waved a heavy hand. "I know what you are about to say. I am not without perception."

He walked heavily into his office and seated himself in his swivel chair which protested futilely. He packed and lighted his pipe and in the quiet room, surrounded by his books and the symbols of his daily occupation, he fought a long, lonely battle with his pride.

In the morning he shaved, dressed with care, and stood for a moment staring at his front door before he opened it and stepped out into the sunlight. It was cooler in the house, behind walls of three-foot thickness, than it was out-of-doors. A solitary newspaperman, keeping watch for all of the others, became instantly alert.

"Monsieur Rivard!"

Louis-Charles brushed him aside and walked grimly down the village road, ignoring the people who greeted him or called to him. The air was fragrant with a dozen scents and the wind was from the northwest. The farmers would be cutting their hay. A white cat sat in the middle of the road and stared at him insolently, knowing that he would walk around her, as he did. Observations and impressions hovered briefly on the surface of his mind, like the summer insects which touched his skin, then flew away. He turned from the road and walked in the shade of the poplars to the porch of the presbytery.

Germaine Masson opened the door and there was no surprise in her face, no expression of any kind. "I will tell Monsieur le Curé that you are here, Monsieur le Notaire," she said.

"Merci."

This, Louis-Charles thought, as he had often thought before, is an admirable woman and a paragon of discretion; or else she is an empty barrel containing nothing that can be disturbed. It was a thought as fleeting as an observation on the weather. He stood in the small, bare parlor with its desk and two chairs, the crucifix on the bare wall.

"Bon jour, Monsieur le Notaire."

Father Bélanger entered the room quietly. His face was perfectly composed, but his eyes were animated. Louis-Charles bowed to him, stiffly.

"Bon jour, Monsieur le Curé."

They were polite, formal, taking the measure of each other as though they had never met before. "He has the advantage," Louis-Charles thought, "because I have come to him." Aloud he said, "I have come to invite you to my home that you may speak to my daughter."

"I will be delighted. Won't you be seated first. A few minutes. We so seldom have an opportunity to speak to each other."

Louis-Charles seated himself in the visitor's chair and watched the priest who sat in the chair behind the desk. "We have nothing to talk about, you and I," he said gruffly.

"Or much. I was hoping, at any rate, that you would come today."

"You knew that I would have to come. You did not come to me. You could afford to wait."

The eyes of the priest became still, intent. "Would it have been good for you, or for the little Valérie," he said softly, "if I had allowed myself to become a part of the excitement of the village?"

"No. Probably not." Louis-Charles conceded the point reluctantly.

"But it is difficult to see how the situation could be much worse. We are deprived of our freedom."

"I can see that. And the little Valérie? How is she?"

"How would she be? She is in terror. That is why I am here."

"Terror?" Father Bélanger's eyebrows rose in interrogation. "I would not expect that. Does she maintain still that she was the witness of a vision?"

"That I do not know. I have never discussed it with her."

The priest leaned forward, concern in his face. "Surely, monsieur, you or her aunt must have sought her confidence."

"Neither of us. There was too much of that. She was driven to hysteria, to vomiting, by the questions of stupid women. We did not subject her to more."

Father Bélanger rose. "And you are inviting me to question her?"

"I want the matter settled. Definitely settled! I do not want my child hunted like an animal by morbidly curious people. You are the only one who can settle it, and I cannot hope that you would do so without talking to her."

"Nor hope that I *could!*" The priest looked thoughtful. "You have no idea what she will tell me?"

"I have already answered that."

"We will go then."

They went out of the presbytery and, as Louis-Charles had anticipated, a large group of people waited for them. All of the newspapermen were there and the photographers took pictures of the priest and the notary together. It was, Louis-Charles thought grimly, like the climactic scenes of a sensational trial, when the fate of the criminal hangs in balance. He drew his own lips tight and permitted the priest to silence the questioners. For once the newspapermen were not persistent. They recognized this for what it was, the first contact of the Church with the alleged vision, the making or breaking of the story. They were content to follow along and to wait, and the villagers followed to wait with them.

Within sight of his own home, Louis-Charles was assailed by the first doubt. Perhaps it would have been better if he had talked to Valérie himself before going to the curé. He should, at least, have told Laure of his intention, so that she might be prepared. But, no! Laure could not have refrained from talking to Valérie if she had known that the priest was coming. It was better to tell the story, once more, and only once. His step faltered.

"*Mon père,*" he said. "You will be gentle with her?"

The priest broke stride, surprised, then laid his hand upon the man's shoulder. "But, certainly!" he said. "How could you doubt it?"

They entered the house. Laure was playing checkers with Valérie. In spite of her bulk she literally leaped to her feet at sight of the priest. The checkerboard overturned and checkers rolled wildly, wheels without wagons, across the floor. Louis-Charles had no eyes for Laure. He was looking at his daughter. The pallor in her face alarmed him.

"Valérie, my little one," he said softly. "Monsieur le Curé has come with me because he would like to talk to you."

He knew then, in that moment, that he had made a mistake. There was desperate appeal in the eyes of the little girl, an appeal that he could not answer because it came too late. She could have talked to him, had wanted to talk to him. He knew that now as he knew that she was afraid to talk to the priest.

"Valérie and I are old friends," Father Bélanger said lightly. "I gave you a medal in the school when the term was finished, did I not?"

"*Oui, mon père.*"

Valérie curtsied, her eyes fixed upon the face of the priest. Father Bélanger seated himself. He looked at the checkerboard, then smiled at the little girl.

"We seem to have lost our checkers," he said, "so we will not play. No. But maybe you will be so kind as to sit at this board and talk to me."

Louis-Charles stood without moving. He had delivered his daughter up to this and now he had to stand helplessly by, like a spectator at a play, not knowing what would happen. He saw Valérie seat herself, her wide eyes still focused upon the priest. Father Bélanger picked up one of the surviving checkers and turned it in his hand.

"Valérie," he said. "I have talked to Antoine and to Robert and they have told me a most interesting story about what happened at the beach, but they do not know everything that happened, so I came to ask you."

"They ran away," Valérie said.

"Yes. But you stayed. Tell me what happened after they ran away, what you heard or saw."

"I don't know."

"Well, tell me what you remember."

"I don't remember."

Valérie's face was white and strained. Louis-Charles drew a deep breath. He sank slowly to his knees so that he could bring his head to the level of hers. "Valérie, *chérie*," he said. "Tell Monsieur le Curé what you told all the ladies of the village."

She looked at him, then looked away. "I forget," she said.

The priest watched her face. "What of the light in the rock and the lady?"

Valérie's lips trembled. She shook her head. "I didn't see anything," she said. "I forget."

"The boys did not forget. You asked them to look, remember? To look at what?"

"They ran away."

"Was it a game that you were playing, Valérie?" the priest said softly. "A game of make-believe?"

"No. Antoine doesn't play games and Robert is too noisy."

"Wasn't there a game with the rosary?"

Valérie straightened in her chair. "It wasn't a game. It was a secret."

"That is what Antoine said. And he would not tell me about it. Nor his father."

Valérie's eyes came to life. "What did you do to him?"

"Nothing. Nothing at all, child. We admired him because he kept his word." The priest paused. "It is your secret. Will you tell me what it is?"

"Maybe it is a sin. I know how far it is from one place to another place because I know how much rosary it takes to get there." The wide eyes were anxious. "Is that a sin, Father?"

The priest shook his head slowly. He smiled. "No. Most surely not. If your prayers, or the thought of them, go with you from place to place, no harm will ever come to you. You stopped to pray before you went down to the beach, Robert says."

"That wasn't the rosary. That was an Act of Contrition. I said it for Robert."

"For Robert. Why?"

"Maybe that is a secret, too. Robert's secret."

Watching his daughter, some of the tension went out of Louis-

Charles. She was relaxed and natural now and she seemed to have put fear behind her. He was astonished at this new glimpse that he had into a child's mind that he had been certain that he knew and understood. There was a curious expression on Valérie's face and she was making an odd gesture with her finger, a circle in the air.

"He did not say that it was a secret," she said. "I said the Act of Contrition for Robert because he does not like his father."

She hesitated as though about to say more. Her finger described another circle. The priest looked startled at the statement about Robert and her prayer for him.

"I tried and tried to remember," she said. "When I was in bed, I tried and tried. All that I could see was the statue of the Blessed Mother in the church."

Father Bélanger leaned forward. "You were praying for Robert and then you thought of the statue of the Blessed Mother in the church? And you thought that you saw her on the rock. Is that it?"

Valérie looked distressed. "No. I tried and tried. I can't remember."

"But you remember the statue in the church when you think about it?"

"Yes. It wasn't the statue but—I don't know any more."

Louis-Charles rose to his feet. "I believe that that is enough, Monsieur le Curé," he said.

Father Bélanger looked thoughtfully at the checker in his hand, then laid it on the board. "Can you think of anything else, Valérie," he said, "anything at all that you want to tell me?"

Valérie sat motionless, her eyes on his face. There was a struggle going on inside of her, a struggle for the command of words, perhaps, or a more grave conflict than that. Her father saw it and was afraid for her. He reverted to the thought that he had had when he had taken her from Céleste Drolet, the analogy of the small, helpless animal tormented by boys. There would be no more of that.

"You have been answered, Monsieur le Curé," he said curtly. "Amply and enough."

The priest rose reluctantly. "Yes," he said. "It seems clear." He patted the child on the head. "You are a good little girl, Valérie," he said. "May God bless you all of your life."

Louis-Charles walked to the door. The priest followed him slowly as though loath to leave. The notary was impatient.

"It leaps to the eye, *mon père*," he said. "The child has been steeped in piety. My sister Laure, that driveling Drolet woman, the school, the church, everything. She cannot measure a foot by a foot; it must be a prayer."

"Do you believe that it has hurt her, the presence of God in her life, or hurt the woman she must be?"

"It has fixed a statue in her eyes so that she sees it in the rocks. I would have her see a rock where God placed a rock—and nothing else."

Father Bélanger passed a thumb across his lower lip. His eyes were thoughtful. "We cannot, unfortunately, read what carelessness has erased," he said. He raised his eyes to Louis-Charles. "As for your rock that would be a rock? Since God made it, His image is in it. It might be good for you, Monsieur le Notaire, and good for me, if our eyes were the eyes of children and could perceive the truth of rocks which is hidden from us."

He opened the door and the newspapermen were around him. He raised his hand. "There has been no miraculous visitation, as we understand the term," he said. "Neither has there been any deception or untruth. A child of innocence and great beauty of mind saw the reflection of her own prayers and talked of them. It is not her fault that she was misunderstood."

"Then the Blessed Virgin did not appear on this island?" a voice challenged.

Father Bélanger stood straight. "If you mean in the sense of Lourdes or Fátima, the answer is 'No,'" he said, "but the Blessed Virgin is always present on this island so long as innocent children see her in their prayers."

"But the little Rivard girl did not see her on the rock of Anse-Saint-Jean?"

"In actual presence, no."

"She has admitted that?"

"She has explained the matter."

Standing inside his door, Louis-Charles heard the voice of the priest, the questions that were asked of him. He turned away and walked into the other room. Valérie looked up at him, half fearfully, and he swept her into his arms, holding her against him.

"Valérie, baby, my little one, are you all right?" he said. "You are not frightened any more?"

"No, Papa."

Her head rested against his shoulder and he could feel the vibration of her muffled sobbing as it coursed through her body. He patted her gently, helplessly.

# III

"It is all a hoax, a great imposture. The little Rivard girl lied about seeing the Blessed Virgin. She has confessed all to Monsieur le Curé."

"Small wonder that she is as she is, with a father who does not go to church."

The word sped swiftly through the village and almost as swiftly from one farm to the next. On Ile-aux-Erables, as in all the Province of Quebec, the transmission of news has always been, since Indian days, simple and direct. The farms are long and narrow, running back from the road, and though a farm may be a couple of miles in depth, the farmhouse is only a short distance from the houses on either side of it. The pattern worked well when pioneers depended upon one another in case of attack, and it still serves the cause of neighborliness and parish cohesion, of which gossip is merely a by-product.

Father Bélanger had tried to phrase his statement carefully, sparing the child, but he was not directly quoted. The interpretation that his listeners put upon his words had a greater survival value than the words themselves.

The news reached Suzanne Lepage while she was putting up the hair of one of the Bouchard girls. After a blank moment of consternation, she tightened her thin lips.

"It does not surprise me," she said. "I never liked or trusted that Rivard child. She has always had a sly way about her." She paused for a calculating moment, then laughed. "And what of Céleste Drolet?" she said. "Sitting on her throne and receiving all of those strangers! What of her, *hein?*"

Jeanne Charbonneau shrugged the denouement from her heavy shoulders indifferently. "*C'est ça!*" she said. "I never believed that there was any truth in it. It will go hard now with the little one, however. It was not her fault. Céleste Drolet should have let her alone with her childish imaginings."

Nicolas Simard was sitting alone on his porch when the word reached him. He was obviously disappointed and he made a ceremony out of relighting his pipe. He looked southward where the heat haze hung above the beach of Anse-Saint-Jean.

"Nothing to it, eh? Nothing to it. Well! Well!" He shook his head. "I am sorry this is so, but it takes a fall out of the Gagnons, does it not? They were riding high and fast in the matter, trying to make a Gagnon miracle out of it. No good came of that."

To Céleste Drolet the message arrived late. The day had started auspiciously, as had the previous day. Robert had brought her two distinguished visitors from the United States, a professor on the faculty of a great university, the name of which she could not pronounce, and his very charming wife. They spoke French—with a horrid American accent, naturally—and she could comprehend them. They had visited France and they knew of Perche from whence the first ancestor of the Gagnons had come to Quebec. They were, assuredly, people of culture and they accorded her great respect. Céleste showed them, as she had not shown any other visitors, the medal that she had received at the convent for her knowledge of literature, and the program of the pageant in which she had played a leading role. They praised her and they praised her house. They told her that it was very interesting about Valérie but that if there was no Valérie, they were content with their journey because they had met her.

It was an enchanting experience. All of her life, Céleste had dreamed of meeting people like these Americans. She had known that it would require a miracle to bring such an event to pass and she had prayed for that miracle. The experience was hers now and richer than her imagining of it. When her visitors left, she went into her own room and looked at herself in the mirror. There was a strange warmth in her body such as she had not experienced in years, a flushed feeling along the surface of her skin.

She looked at her own reflection and all of the years fell away, like a dropped shawl. The eyes looking back at her were sparkling with youth. Her mouth looked soft. She smiled, parting her lips slightly. Assuredly, she was not, and did not appear to be, the same woman who had endured so many humiliations before the miracle happened. She raised her hand, touching her hair gently. She had had no time to spend on the curling of her hair in the shop of Yvonne Côte and Suzanne Lepage, but she liked the effect that she had achieved herself. Her hair was still very light, Gagnon hair, and she had made it a soft frame for her face. Her green cotton dress was unpretentious but she wore green well.

Robert's voice carried clearly to her from the path which led to the house. He was bringing more visitors. There was understanding in Robert, and thoughtfulness, such as André would never possess. Céleste turned from the mirror reluctantly, but with excitement stirring in her again. It was an adventure, meeting people, people of education, intelligence, and discernment. She walked to the door expectantly.

This second group of the day had five people in it; English-speaking people, Protestants, who did not believe in miracles or visions but who were interested in them. They were from Hamilton and Ottawa and were having a holiday at the great resort of Murray Bay, which Céleste had never visited but of which she spoke familiarly. These people, too, were very polite and respectful. It surprised them that she had a knowledge of music and had given piano lessons to Valérie Rivard. They admired the rosewood chair in the parlor and the catalogne, her woven rag rug. She did not tell them that her mother had loomed it since they seemed happy in their belief that she had done so.

The next visitors were very difficult. They were Canadiens from Saint-Adèle-en-Haut, and they had not achieved a financial standing which supported vacation trips to resorts through innocence, credulity, or blind trust in human nature. The husband was a man of business and he had come to Ile-aux-Erables from a comfortable hotel on the mainland only because his wife had insisted upon coming. He had not liked the ferry and he did not admire the island and he had considered the trip to the beach with Robert very dull, very hot, and too much walking. His wife had bright, inquisitive eyes, she asked many questions, and her manner was grimly determined. The treasures of Céleste were a commonplace to her and she was dissatisfied that Céleste could tell her so little of what she wanted to know. She did not care about the past history of either Céleste or Valérie; she wanted to know if Valérie would return to the beach and if another vision was expected if she did. She was interested, too, in the morals of Valérie's father, who was not, she understood, a good Catholic.

Into this unsatisfactory situation, Robert came like something blown by the wind. He addressed himself to his mother, ignoring the visitors, and his voice had a loud, shattering quality.

"Valérie didn't see the Blessed Virgin," he shouted. "She didn't see anything. It is as I told you. She has admitted it to Monsieur le Curé. She has told him that she did not see anything."

Céleste felt as though an earthquake had moved the flooring of the room under her chair. She gripped the arms tightly, and it seemed to her that everything and everybody in the room trembled with the same shock.

"What is this you say?"

Her voice was high and thin, a weak carrier of meaningless words. It was a palpable absurdity to request repetition from Robert, who included repetition always in his first telling, but Robert was given no opportunity to answer her. The man from Saint-Adèle-en-Haut was on his feet, a stout, angry, belligerent figure.

"What am I hearing?" he demanded. "It is a fraud, this miracle? I have come to this abominable place for nothing? I have walked to that *sacré maudit* beach to see nonsense, a hole in a rock? Is it that you think me a monkey of which fun is to be made?"

He was hurling his unanswerable questions at Céleste and she was too stunned to comprehend them. She could only raise her hands in a futile gesture of self-defense.

"There is some mistake, Monsieur," she said, "of that I am certain."

She looked for Robert, but Robert had remembered that this bad-tempered man had paid him very reluctantly for his services as a guide. Robert was gone, risking no demands for repayment. The determined-looking woman, evidently aware that she had an unhappy day ahead of her, was already moving toward the door. She shifted as much of the blame as she could before she left.

"I must say that you have imposed upon us shamefully," she said.

Her husband threw a parting glare at Céleste and followed her. They left behind them a silence that still shuddered to the memory of sound and fury, a vibrating silence in which Céleste Drolet heard the broken rhythm of her own heartbeat.

"It can't be so," she whispered. "Dear God, it can't be so!"

It was incredible that Monsieur le Curé could have gone to the Rivards, or the Rivards to Monsieur le Curé, without her knowing of it. It was necessary that they pass her house. If it were not for the bend in the road and the four old maples, she would be able to see the Rivard house from her window. No event so shattering to her happiness could occur within so short a distance and leave her unaware.

"*C'est impossible!*" she said.

She rocked slowly back and forth, lacking the will that would command herself to rise. She hoped that Robert would return so that she might question him; in the same instant, she hoped that he would not. She did not want to hear Robert say again what he had said to her in the presence of strangers. So long as he did not return, she could tell herself that she had not heard him clearly, or that he was a child who spoke without thinking and without knowing what he said.

That was it. Robert was a child and without responsibility. It was unthinkable that Monsieur le Curé would confide in him. Robert had merely repeated some stupid remark that he had not understood, some spiteful word of Jeanne Charbonneau's, perhaps. André should be here to tell her what was happening in the village. He was never with her when she needed him. And Pierre? Where was Pierre? For the first time in two days she thought about her husband and wondered about him. He, too, should be here.

The house was suddenly a lonely place, the house that had sparkled with the presence of so many people. Distinguished people had sought her out and had talked with her. They had understood her and they had discerned in her the qualities which set her apart from her unfortunate environment. Now they were gone.

Céleste rose swiftly and walked to the window as though she could, in motion, dispel the loneliness and banish the memory of her last two visitors, the voice of Robert, the words that she refused to hear or to recall having heard, the terror that was coiling inside of her.

She looked out of the window toward the village road, with the sense of seeing it for the first time that day. Reality moved slowly, relentlessly in on her. She *was* seeing the road for the first time today. She had been entertaining visitors. She had been very busy. She had gone into her room to look at herself in the mirror. She did not know who passed her house, who went to the Rivards or who left. She had permitted her miracle to escape from her. It had come to the testing point and she had not been present.

She remembered Robert's words now. They rang as clearly in the room as when they were first uttered: "Valérie did not see the Blessed Virgin. She didn't see anything. It is as I told you. She has admitted it to Monsieur le Curé. She has told him that she did not see anything."

The hands of Céleste moved to her throat. There was a scream trapped there and she could not release it. Her lips moved, forming words, but there was no breath to propel them outward into sound. She clutched at her throat, pressing it and then releasing it. Her breath flowed weakly, a mere trickle of breath.

"The liar!" she whispered. "The deceitful, scheming little liar! She has destroyed me."

Hatred swelled in her, a great black wave of hatred that lifted itself high and hung suspended, tons and tons of hatred, timeless, a wave without a beach on which to break, needing no beach, not compelled to fall or to break or to complete the cycle of any law, living in suspension until her mind released it.

"The liar," she whispered again. "The treacherous, vicious little liar. Valérie Rivard! God will punish her and all belonging to her!"

Never in her life had she felt such hatred as this, not against her husband, Pierre, who had wasted her life, nor her brother, Edmond, who had defrauded her, nor Jeanne Charbonneau who criticized her to her face. No! Never before had she hated like this. She had put her trust in the false story of a shameless little show-off who was seeking notoriety, and she had stood with her against everyone.

"My own daughter! I called her my own daughter!"

Tears rolled down her cheeks and beside her nose, silent tears that flowed without sobs to pump them; the tears of enmity which are not of weeping. She trembled, then suddenly the trembling stopped.

The gate latch clicked and there was a step upon her path. She blinked and brushed the tears away, leaning forward. The woman who was coming to call walked slowly. There was a half-smile on her face, her thin, hatchet face. Céleste Drolet straightened and something within her turned hard and cold.

"This," she thought, "is the first one. There will be others. But they won't gloat over me! I'll give as good as I get. I owe nothing to any of them."

She dabbed hastily at her eyes with a handkerchief, the little lace handkerchief that she had exhibited to the people from the United States. She straightened her thin shoulders and opened the door for Suzanne Lepage.

# IV

Father Bélanger returned to the presbytery after his brief announcement to the press and to the people assembled before the home of Louis-Charles Rivard. He was dissatisfied with his interrogation of Valérie without knowing exactly why he was dissatisfied. He was convinced that there had been no actual vision. That much was established. Some other factor, however, had eluded him. If he knew what it was, he might be able to stand between the child and future unhappiness.

There was, of course, in the mind of any child much that remained beyond the reach of even the most sympathetic adult. This little girl, unfortunately, had sustained a series of rude shocks before he had had an opportunity to question her. She had retreated within herself, taking with her the memory of those vital minutes when she had called upon the two boys to look upon a vision which was not to be seen if they had looked. There was a baffling mystery in that certainty which called for witnesses. The experience must have been, if only in imagination, momentarily intense, an experience in which the child believed. If one could only return with her to that moment of certainty! But, no. That was impossible. She had lost the experience, whatever it was, in the repeated telling of it.

"The sources of the vision idea, at least, are obvious," the priest said.

He paced back and forth, considering those sources. A combination of circumstances had built a mood of religious intensity in the child; the measuring of distance in terms of rosary time, the prayer for a playmate who disliked his father, the discussion about the sound of silence. One could not ignore the fact, either, that she was a girl accompanied by two boys. Even if she did not comprehend the desire herself, the desire to impress or awe her companions was probably present.

There was still a missing element.

Valérie remembered now the image of the Blessed Virgin in the church, and that image had probably been in her mind when she prayed on the road before she went down the path to the beach. But how was one to account for her original narrative and the detail of the lady walking on the water? Or the fact that she did not think of the Blessed Virgin in connection with the vision until it was suggested to her? If her imagination projected the image in the church, why hadn't she recognized it and named it instead of speaking vaguely in terms of an angel or a lady.

"If I could have talked with her immediately?"

Father Bélanger continued to pace. He had faced many problems in his parish, problems that were graver by far than this little idyl of children on a beach, and disposed of them with less soul searching or unease of spirit than that which he had experienced today. That fact, in itself, disturbed him.

He raised his eyes to the wood carving of the Virgin, standing serene above his books, and he was assailed suddenly by a sense of loss, of loneliness, of vast regret. If it had been true, if his parish had been so honored, if Quebec had been so favored? How much it would have meant to so many! Not to the inevitable opportunists, but to those who sought their rewards from life in spiritual coin!

He knew the faults of his people and he did not minimize them; the pettiness, the meanness here and there, the jealousies, the occasional malice, the blind, perverse stubbornness. He knew, too, their patient piety, their acceptance of hardship and suffering in the name of God, their loyalty to the Church, the beautiful simplicities of their lives. They knew how to pray, his people, and they would have opened their hearts in welcome if this, like Lourdes, had been a real visitation.

He made a dismissing gesture with his right hand. Such thoughts were fruitless. "It will be very difficult for the child, Valérie," he said. "We must endeavor to help her."

He worked to that end through the days of the week that remained, careful in his speech lest he plant the thought that he sought to counteract. He talked to many people without seeking out those to whom he spoke. On Sunday, he faced all of the people of the island at his two Masses. He had no eloquence nor fine gifts of oratory. He spoke to them as he always spoke, in simple, direct language. He reminded them that Christ gathered little children about him and proclaimed that theirs was the Kingdom of Heaven.

"They see more clearly than do we, the children who are raised in the knowledge of God," he said. "They are without guile. They have the pure vision of unspotted souls. When they attempt to tell us what they have seen, we misunderstand. We are accustomed to seeing only physical things, material things, and we strive to make their vision one with our own."

He tried valiantly in his pulpit to banish the idea that there had been any conscious deception, that there had been untruth in Valérie's story of the vision. He did not mention her by name but he made her the symbol of all children. He saw comprehension in many of the eyes raised to him, and nods of approval. These people had children of their own.

"It is not necessary," he said, "that the Blessed Mother manifest herself physically. She is close to you in your own homes when you pray to her, closer than she was to the Blessed Bernadette who knelt upon the ground and looked up at her. Every human heart into which she is invited is her miraculous shrine."

Father Bélanger had never in his life put forth more effort in a pulpit, nor striven more fervently to reach his people. Never before had he felt the same urgency, nor preached with the feeling that he had one opportunity, and one only, to set straight a matter that might well confuse, to the point of spiritual danger, a number of those whose souls were charged to his care. Yet, even as he spoke, looking into the many faces, some upturned and some turned away, he knew that there were minds closed against him, minds that he could not reach.

Rosaire Gagnon sat grimly in his pew, his eyes fixed on the altar, not looking at the priest. Rosaire clung stubbornly and tenaciously to the belief that the vision had been real and actual, a miraculous visitation, and that the pastor had acted hastily in deciding otherwise. He had openly stated his belief. His infant daughter would be baptized in the afternoon with the name of Valérie-Marie.

There was no fault in Rosaire, nor any menace to the normal childhood of Valérie Rivard unless, in his stubbornness, he exalted her too greatly. Nor was there danger in the boy, André Drolet, who believed as did Rosaire and who stared now with puzzled eyes at the image of the Blessed Virgin.

Suzanne Lepage and her sister, Yvonne Côte, were another matter. They sat straight and unyielding in their pew, symbols, both, of the type of woman who knows what she knows and who cannot be persuaded. It was easy to understand them, to have compassion for them and still to fear their capacity for evil, for the causing of trouble.

Suzanne, like many of the island girls, had failed to attract a young man who inherited land or a means of livelihood on the island. Too few of the youths who sought careers elsewhere returned to claim brides. It was unfortunate, but there were lonely, warmhearted unmarried women who had learned to adjust to life where Suzanne had not. Suzanne had grown to womanhood with the envy of other women in her heart, envy which was the begetter of spite and bitterness. Her sister, with whom she lived and worked, had been tragically widowed at nineteen. She had no children and she, too, lived with bitterness.

Happiness did not flow from either of these women, nor true kindness. Their interest in other people was tinged with morbidity and morbidity mothered gossip. Words of counsel never pierced the armor of their self-esteem. Because they observed the outward forms and did not sin consciously in the flesh, they were invincible in their conviction of righteousness.

A priest faced no more baffling problem than this. Unless?

From his pulpit, Father Bélanger could see Céleste Drolet, sitting in her pew, flanked by her two sons. She looked straight ahead of her, her features as sharply etched as though they had been carved by an angry sculptor from one of the harder woods. No words of his would reach Céleste Drolet whom, more than any other person in his congregation, he strove to reach. He had never been able to reach her. He had tried many times through the years when her own happiness was at stake. It was hoping for too much, perhaps, to appeal to her in behalf of another.

Céleste lived in her own picture of the world, a flat surface of improbability without dimension. She willed the impossible to happen and she had no awareness of the possible, or of the inevitable. She did not believe in cause and effect; she believed, rather, in vague rewards for vaguer virtues, pitying herself that the rewards were denied to her. She was in constant rebellion against the realities with which all human flesh lived, twisting even the precepts of religion into shapes of her own desiring.

Not a bad woman, Céleste. Certainly not! But a woman of tragic misdirection. Her will propelled her into isolation, where her heart found only loneliness, and she would not turn back, nor follow any counsel but her own. Today she was hating the little Valérie. That hatred was carved in her face as he spoke from the pulpit above her, and she would not heed the Voice of which his own was but a feeble echo, the Voice that counseled her not to let the sun set upon her anger. She would not call her own emotion "anger." She would find a righteous, self-justifying name for it. And the sun would set.

The hatred of a woman for a child could be an evil beyond the measuring, the creator of terrible consequences, but on what ground did one meet and combat it? It was easier for a priest to talk to a drunkard or an adulterer, who would know himself for what he was, and know shame, than to talk to a woman with hatred in her heart and no sense of wrongdoing, no regret, no self-admission of fault.

Father Bélanger finished his sermon and stood for a moment, looking out over the heads of his parishioners. He was conscious of the forces that had been released, as forces are always released, by any extraordinary event which involves the hopes, aspirations, fears, or frustrations of human beings. His sermon had failed. He had reached only those who needed least what he tried to say, and he had not reached those who could hold the unleashed forces in check. In time, if God spared him in this parish, he would deal with those unleashed forces again and again in different forms and he knew it. He was Monsieur le Curé to whom all problems came ultimately. He could pray that they would come before the fashioners of problems grew weary of fashioning them and sought solutions, but that was seldom the way of it.

He made the sign of the cross and returned to the altar. He left behind him the echo of his own poor words in French and lifted his voice in the language of the Universal Church: "*Credo in unum deum* (I believe in one God) . . ."

In that there was a calm certainty. He that created, alone, had the wisdom to read the hearts of men and women, to find truth in the chaotic mass of human error, to balance right and wrong, to know the purpose of events. "*Et iterum venturus est cum gloria, Judicare vivos, et mortuos* (And He shall come again in glory to judge the living and the dead)."

Valérie Rivard sat beside her aunt, Laure, with her hands clasped tightly around the small prayer book on her lap. She listened to the words of the sermon and she knew that Monsieur le Curé was speaking about her, even though he did not mention her name. She knew, too, that he was kind and that he was her friend and that he did not believe that she had lied, even if he did not believe that she had seen the Blessed Virgin. There was a mystery in that, as in so many mysteries of religion, which one had to believe even if one did not understand; the mystery that she said that she saw the Blessed Virgin, and that she did not, and that it was not a lie.

She wished, as she had wished so many times since it happened, that she could remember exactly how it had been and what she had seen. She could not even remember what she told people. She could remember telling them and telling them, but she could only remember her own voice and not the words; which was very strange.

Monsieur le Curé was explaining to everyone how a child can see something and yet not see it, but she did not understand the explanation. That was not a mystery, it was merely something that happened all the time. She knew many things which she could not tell her father or Laure or Monsieur le Curé because none of the words that she knew would say what she wanted to say. It was different with them. They knew too many words. She could not always think in the words that they spoke; so there were times when she did not know what they were thinking or what they were trying to say to her.

In a way, maybe that was a mystery after all. Like the Trinity! Even if the Saint Maurice was not like God and she was not supposed to say that it was, she liked to think of it in that way; one river that was three rivers when it flowed into the Saint Lawrence. She could see that in her mind and believe it, even when it seemed odd to say it.

"Trois Rivières where I was born."

Without turning her head, Valérie could see several of the boys and girls who were in her class in school. They had all looked at her strangely when she saw them in front of the church and they did not speak or act as they usually did. The dark knowledge came to her now that never again would she be quite as she used to be in the company of other children. She had had an experience beyond their ken. She had been discussed by adults as they would never be discussed. This she sensed, without the necessity for putting words to knowledge. Something had happened to her.

She could see André and Robert with their mother. Madame Drolet had not spoken to her when they met this morning but there was a terrible look in her eyes. Madame Drolet had hugged her and told her that she loved her, that she was like her own daughter. She remembered. She had tried to do everything that Madame Drolet asked her to do, but Madame Drolet did not like her today. She could not understand it, and it frightened her because she liked Madame Drolet and she did not know what she had done that was wrong, or what she could do now that would be right.

She could not see or sense or guess the days, the weeks, the years ahead of her.

In the passing of time the large Gagnon family would be stirred to loyalty because Céleste Drolet, who was a Gagnon, awakened their sympathy. Because others criticized her, they would overlook the fact that they considered her silly and vain and inept. They would be kind and invite her to their many homes. Wherever she went, and as often as she went, she would make remarks or allusive comments on the slyness, the deceitfulness, the deceptiveness of the Rivard child. They would pay little attention at first and then, being simple people, they would accept what they heard so often as a truth. They would view with misgiving, or outright disapproval, any close friendship between their children and the Rivard girl.

· Valérie Rivard was to grow up with that.

The busy tongues in the beauty shop of Suzanne Lepage and Yvonne Côte would not be friendly to Céleste Drolet, nor kind. They would find the choicest material for criticism and mockery in her assumption of importance during the days of the alleged vision. Valérie, a child, and of too little importance in herself for gossip, would be unfavorably presented as a minor character in the drama of an unpopular woman. The unfavorable impression of her would remain in the minds of many women who would not remember how or where they received the impression of her. They would credit it, in time, to their own observation and opinion, viewing her with subconscious distrust.

Valérie Rivard would live with that, too.

The sermon was over and the priest was at the altar. The drama of the Mass moved solemnly on to the ringing of the Sanctus bell, the hushed moments of the Consecration, then the *"Domine non sum dignus."* It was the time for Communion and Valérie felt the nervousness of Laure as they rose to go down to the Communion rail. She felt the eyes of people and she understood why Laure was nervous. People believed that she had lied about seeing the Blessed Virgin and one had to be in the state of grace to receive Holy Communion. She could not tell them that she was in the state of grace and that Monsieur le Curé had told her so.

She wished fervently that her father was with her. She wished that he would walk up the aisle with her. Her father would not be nervous about people as Laure was. Never!

The future was yet to be. It would be months before that wish of Valérie's would be fulfilled. Suddenly, unexpectedly, Louis-Charles Rivard would attend Mass. He would sit grimly beside his daughter in the pew and people would stare and whisper. He would behave perfectly, following the Mass, beyond the criticism of anyone, and yet there would be some who would say that his presence in the church was a scandal, considering some of the opinions that he had openly expressed.

Father Bélanger, moving along the Communion rail with the Chalice, could not see into the months ahead either, but the forces that he had felt in the pulpit were to bring Louis-Charles Rivard ultimately to the presbytery.

"You have seen me now three Sundays at Mass, Monsieur le Curé. I wish to return to the Church."

"Why?"

"It has occurred to me that I am a better Catholic than those who frequent the church habitually and who treat my daughter with spite."

"It is a bad reason for a good decision."

"If I had a better reason, I might be a pious soul. Your pious souls treat a child of eight, because she carried holy pictures in her imagination, like a fallen woman."

"It is not that blunt. This is a small community. Small communities magnify small events because they lack large ones. Your own unorthodoxy played a part in the matter."

"I will be orthodox. I will stand beside my daughter. If there are better Catholics than we, they must prove it."

"To you or to God? No! It won't do. You cannot return to God to shame your neighbor. To worship God you must love Him. To love Him, you must love them."

"And they?"

"Each man and woman stands alone before God. Let be! Ask questions of your own soul. You are not permitted to question theirs."

"You will not permit me to return?"

"In another mood and for another reason! We could talk well to each other, you and I. We have much in common, more than you have ever granted."

"We could not converse amicably. I can be a Catholic, but I cannot maintain patience with nonsense."

"Nor can I. You quote Voltaire frequently, I understand. Look! You will find him on my bookshelves."

"We read him with different eyes, discovering different meanings."

"Not necessarily so. We are educated men. We read. Voltaire is the gentleman who, when their King abandoned our ancestors on this soil to the mercy of the English, congratulated him that he was rid of his 'acres of snow.' Those acres of snow have nourished you and me, and those who bred us. Voltaire knew as little of the supernatural as he knew of Canada, but he robed his ignorance in the raiment of wit. We could discuss that, perhaps."

"Yes. We could discuss that. Again, not always amicably."

"The discussion, at least, we would have in common. Minds are not stimulated by heads nodding in agreement."

The words would not be spoken for many months. The future held the meeting of Monsieur le Curé and Louis-Charles Rivard in suspension among the events that were yet to be.

Valérie returned from the Communion rail with her eyes downcast. So, too, did André Drolet. The boy buried his face in his hands, feeling the miracle within him, the union of himself and God. This was, for him, always, an awesome and wonderful moment when he found his place again in the pew after Communion. It was the moment when he voiced silently his gratitude for all that he had, his special requests, his supplication for any help that he needed.

Today he had only one prayer. He prayed for his father. He could not understand why his father had gone away, without speaking to him first, without telling him when he was going. They had been so close to each other that night on the cemetery wall and he had been looking forward to the big things that they would do together. Then his father left and did not say good-by.

He could not know, but there would be monthly notes to him from Pierre Drolet for more than a year; awkward, scrawled notes telling nothing of his father's life or work but lightened occasionally by a joking phrase, a piece of rough humor. There would be a post-office money order for him in each of the letters, separate and apart from the money orders that would come regularly to his mother. André would divide the checks with Robert because it seemed the fair thing to do, although his father ignored Robert. He would deposit his own share with Monsieur le Notaire so that he would have it when his father returned.

The future hid all of that behind its veil, as it hid the shattering shock of Pierre Drolet's death near Arvida on the Saguenay in the late September of 1946. After the Requiem Mass for his father, André was to have a memorable interview with Edmond Gagnon, stiffly uncomfortable in his Sunday clothes and embarrassed at the necessity for speaking at some length. He was to feel the kindness behind the grim hard personality of his uncle, the gruff shyness, and to learn for the first time that Edmond Gagnon planned to pay for his education in the field of his own choosing. He would believe for a time that he wanted to be a priest and he would remember always the older man's slow, studied comment.

"Be a priest if you can. A man can do no better, but it isn't in every man. Whatever you do, use your education honorably. The money that pays for it comes from the land. Never work for the English or the Americans as your father did. They will use you up and throw you away like an old bucket. Work for your own kind, and speak your own language, and never take advantage of a man with less education than your own."

The boy knelt in the pew and all of that was a year away from him. Father Bélanger turned to the congregation and raised his hand in blessing before moving to the side of the altar for the reading of the last gospel. They were all on their knees before him, men, women and children, who would play out a complicated drama that would not be drama at all if there were no human errors, conflicts, prejudices, passions, and perversities. He blessed them and the blessing carried his hope for them, the hope of the Church for them, that their deeds, too, might be blessed; but the deeds were their own to perform in the free exercise of their free will. They were many people with many wills.

It was Sunday, August 5, 1945, in the Province of Quebec, and before the day was over it was August 6 in Japan, ten time belts away. On that day an American plane dropped the first atom bomb on Hiroshima, the Pacific War moved into its final phase, and a new era in world history dawned.

At Fort Lewis, near Tacoma, Washington, a slender, rangy young man of eighteen, hammered a typewriter through most of that day. His name was Keller Barkley and he was the son of a great newspaper editor in the Middle West. He had been drafted into the infantry when he graduated from high school and he was a foot soldier, but news was in his blood and he wrote for the post paper on his own time. He whistled while he typed, a trait that other people considered annoying, and always would consider annoying.

Keller Barkley had never heard of Ile-aux-Erables, but he would hear of it. He would, ultimately, bring to a climax the affair of the vision on the beach of Anse-Saint-Jean, but not immediately. It was to take him twelve years.

# III

THE UNBELIEVER
1957

# I

It was August in the Province of Quebec, and when the sunlight was not standing naked in the fields, it sported in diaphanous robes of mist along the river. Keller Barkley watched it from the window of the train which carried him from Montreal to Quebec. The fields were flat and cut into long narrow strips by the fence lines. Glimpses of the river were few, but there were houses on every narrow farm strip; Breton and Norman types of houses with small windows and steeply pitched roofs. There were thin, silver church spires every few miles and villages of gaily colored houses and narrow streets. It was all very much like France and Barkley's memories of France were bitter. He doodled with a ball-point pen on a pad braced against his knee. It was a practice of his that he had once described as a defense against thinking, but he did a lot of his thinking in terms of symbols on paper.

The pad was crisscrossed with tiny sketches of houses, church steeples, and square, utilitarian railroad stations, some of the sketches overlapping. It had words written on it, too, a few descriptive words, occasional French phrases, the names of towns. Towns along this right of way, so close to the United States, bore names like "Saint Vincent de Paul," "Cabane Ronde," "L'Epiphanie." There was one wonderfully named town in the timetable, on a spur line out of Trois Rivières. It was called "Grand'Mère." Keller Barkley had copied the name on his pad in block letters. It stuck in his mind.

"Imagine anyone in the United States naming a town 'Grandma'!"

The train, which had passed unconcernedly the stations of many small towns, slowed almost to a stop with no town immediately in sight. Put Bigelow, in the chair on Barkley's right, awakened with a

123

snorting sound that was like an interrupted snore. He was a big man, forty pounds too fat, and he traveled with his jacket in the luggage rack and his shirt collar open. He blinked at the window.

"Hot, isn't it?" he said.

"You're looking at it, not feeling it."

"I feel it when I look at it."

For some reason known only to the engineer, the train came to a full stop. The window framed one of the inevitable farms. There was a man in a field with two horses and a piece of equipment doing some incomprehensible job; incomprehensible, at least, to Keller Barkley who did not know one growing thing from another.

"If you were out there, Put," he said, "you'd have something to complain about. That character is *hot*."

"I wouldn't be out there. I believe in farming by absentee ownership, American style, billing the government for the stuff I don't raise. These people live in the Middle Ages."

"I've seen work being done in Iowa and Kansas."

"So have I. With machinery. Some of these people still use oxen in the fields. They're an anachronism. They go to church and pray that the modern world will go away and stop confusing them. And they pray in French! Nearly five million of them up here in this Province speaking French, with the United States and English Canada all around them!"

Barkley watched the man in the field, who was turning the animals, reversing his direction, the sun beating mercilessly down on him. "All right," he said. "They speak French. That citizen out there just told his horses something. They understood it. Why should he speak English?"

"They don't all talk to horses. Some of them have to ask Americans or English-speaking Canucks for a job. Then it makes a difference."

The train resumed its journey. Keller Barkley made little marks on his pad. As he feared, Putnam Bigelow, once awake and launched on a subject, became talkative. He was a man with a poor opinion of the French Canadians. He was making this trip on a survey of the American invasion of Quebec, an invasion of capital which exploited the resources it found and used the labor available. To Bigelow it was an exciting story, this awakening of Rip van Winkle from his long sleep and putting the old loafer to work. It was a story of rivers harnessed to electric power, electric power harnessed to big industrial plants; of aluminum, pulp mills, mineral exploration, and oil.

"We are giving them package towns," he said, "that are better than anything they've ever been able to build for themselves; paved streets, hotels, movie houses, air conditioning, modern homes, drug stores, parks, recreation centers."

Keller Barkley yawned. "And not one of them named 'Grandma,'" he said.

"What do you mean, none of them named 'Grandma'?"

"A little item that we've overlooked. You can't love a package town, or an air conditioner, or a supermarket."

"Who in hell wants to love them? We use them. They're a standard of living."

"Okay."

Keller Barkley slid down in his chair, one foot braced against the window sill. He was one inch shorter and many pounds lighter than his father, who was a burly six footer, but he always gave the impression that he was thinner than he actually was. The bone structure of his face was prominent; cheekbones that jutted slightly, a clearly defined jaw line, a firm chin. He wore his dark hair clipped short in a brush cut and his eyes were a smoky blue that very often appeared to be gray.

He was annoyed at himself for challenging Put Bigelow. There was no point to it. He was no more enamored of French Canada than Bigelow was, and his own mission to Quebec was not friendly. The forces of habit were pretty strong, however.

Some combative spirit within him always sought for the flaw in any smug, self-satisfied picture, and usually found it. Put Bigelow was, and always had been, a genius at painting smug, self-satisfied, self-righteous pictures in prose. He was a popular critic because he had no personal convictions strong enough to influence him. It made no difference to him if he wrote about Republicans, Democrats, Big Business, or Labor Unions; they all came out of the Bigelow typewriter sounding alike. He called his technique "the positive approach" and a great many people liked it. Keller Barkley had crossed swords with him many times in print when he was writing a column of his own for a competing newspaper syndicate; but that was all over.

Today he did not mind listening to Put. It brought a little of the atmosphere of the life he had left into a dull journey. The meeting with Put Bigelow in Montreal had been a surprise, a happy coincidence. He had been alone with his own thoughts too much and it wasn't good; not the way his thoughts ran lately.

"You haven't changed, Kel," Bigelow said genially. "Same old formula! When you see a head, you hit it. I should have remembered."

His eyes were speculative, and Barkley saw the inevitable question building up behind the other man's none too subtle face. He turned it deftly before it was launched.

"I read your series on the Nickerson court-martial," he said. "You did a good job."

"Did you? Say, that was a deal! There's more to this missile business than anybody will talk about. Nickerson was right and he wasn't. As I see it——"

Put was off to the races, talking about himself and his ideas. It was safe conversational territory in the heat of noon and Keller Barkley was content. Later, much later, in the dim dignity of the Château Frontenac cocktail lounge, when the sun had set and the massive chairs were comfortable, when the scotch glowed in a man's veins, the situation was different. Put Bigelow moved from a mood of heavy humor to a mood of medium-weight brotherhood and solicitude.

"Y'know, Kel," he said. "I always admired you. Always did. Never wanted to admit it. You were a pretty young squirt to have a column of your own, but you were awfully damn good. Different! Of course, you got a terrific break when Arthur Drake cracked up. His column fell right in your lap."

"Not in my lap, Put. I had to run a little and catch it. Give me that much."

Kel was relaxed. He wouldn't fight anyone to establish the facts, but he wouldn't admit that he was the darling of the gods, either. He had worked two summers of his college years on his father's paper, and two years in a Washington press bureau. He had been Arthur Drake's leg man in 1950 and Drake was a drunk. Somebody had to put Drake's column together for him half of the time. In 1952 Drake had gone to a sanitarium with a breakdown and Keller Barkley had done the column under the Drake name for a year until Arthur Drake died. The syndicate had given him his own by-line then on the column.

He was twenty-five and a Washington columnist of note. It was phenomenal, but it was not blind luck.

Put Bigelow was feeling his drinks. There was a wet shine in his eyes. "Another thing, Kel! I never said anything to you about it. Me, I can play for laughs but I don't know how to handle some things. I felt awfully damned bad about Sally."

Kel stared at his glass. He lifted it and took a deep swallow. "Thanks," he said.

"I knew her before you did. When she was doing society for the Washington *Press-Dispatch*. She was wasted on a job like society, with the talent she had."

"She was damned good at it."

Keller Barkley wanted to get up and walk away. There was no sense in that. He could never walk away from it; it followed him. Sally was doing society when he met her at a party in the Cuban Embassy. He didn't know then that she was doing anything except drinking champagne, which she didn't understand. That was 1954. He was already a big name. She was blond and small, in a simple white evening dress, sitting on a white marble bench to the right of the white marble staircase. The effect was dazzling. She had a champagne glass in her hand and she was drinking in quick, determined sips, her eyes tightly closed. Kel frowned at her.

"You should never drink champagne alone," he said. "It gives you a headache unless you have someone to keep you company."

The girl did not look up. "Everybody tries to give me advice," she said plaintively. "Somebody else told me that if I stopped drinking champagne once I got started, I'd be drunk. I don't want to be drunk."

He sat down and talked to her. She had a light, funny little voice that defied all of the laws of rhythm and she seemed to be talking from some never-never land of her own, far away from where they sat. "You are not real, of course," he told her. "You came out of a bottle like somebody in *Arabian Nights*. But I wish you really existed."

That was the beginning. It was a shock to discover that she was a newspaper girl with a story to write. In his bigness and self-confidence, Kel had assured her that he would write it for her, whatever it was; but he hadn't written it. Her story was the clothes worn by prominent women at the party. She dictated it to him, half asleep, in his apartment, without notes to aid her, remembering all of the women, all of the gowns, all of the jewelry. He typed it for her from her dictation.

She wasn't always like that, but she was never like anyone else, either.

Keller Barkley came back to the awareness of a fresh drink in his hand, Quebec's Château Frontenac all around him; the broad, white, glistening face of Putnam Bigelow across the table. Bigelow had obviously been talking at length about Sally. Kel was glad that he had missed it. He did not want a Putnam Bigelow version of Sally. A man like Put could never know.

"It was easy to understand why your column went all to hell after she got smashed up in that plane accident," Bigelow said, "but I couldn't figure out why you gave it to Alan Corbin."

"It's the way I got it. He was doing the work."

"The syndicate would have carried you." Bigelow leaned forward, his weight jolting the table, his fingers curled tighty around his glass. There was a trace of awe in his voice, or maybe only morbidity.

"She died at Lourdes, didn't she?"

Keller Barkley swallowed the drink in his glass at one toss. "Yes, Put," he said savagely, "she died at Lourdes. A poor little Protestant who never went to her own church—bounced all around in a lot of Catholic voodoo and mumbo jumbo, trying to believe in it."

He slapped his glass down so hard upon the table top that a cube of ice bounced out and spun crazily. "Now, for God's sake," he said. "Let's skip it."

The evening blurred for him at that point. He did not recall whether they had another drink or not. He had only a confused impression of the dining room, no memory of dinner. Incongruously, he did remember the three musicians in seventeenth-century costumes, in white wigs, a woman at the piano in a voluminous gown, the violinist and cellist in lace and ruffles and knee breeches. The cellist looked like pictures of Papa Haydn. That was something else that he owed to Sally, music. He had been strictly a mouth-organ man, with a slight side interest in juke boxes, before he met Sally. He didn't know much more now. She had had only a year in which to work on him.

Somewhere, somehow, he lost Put Bigelow. When he went to the desk for his key, he asked for it in French and he was feeling so dignified and courteous that he knew that he must be drunk. He was opposed to drinking without gaiety and he could recall no gaiety. The situation seemed out of hand.

His room number was 2323. In the United States, a number like that would be on the twenty-third floor; in Quebec, for no imaginable reason, it was on the third. It was a large room, and once he had doused his face with cold water, it was the loneliest room in the world. The conversation with Put Bigelow had brought back all of the devils that had ridden him since his return from France, the devils that had made it impossible for him to handle even a simple routine news beat in Washington. He was content to be alone again, free from the necessity for talking, but not to be alone in a hotel room. He went downstairs and his head was clear. He could observe and he could think, which was not, perhaps, a blessing.

The hotel was crowded with the summer throngs and the voices in the lobby spattered sentences around in French and English. Outside, on the Place d'Armes, a line of calèches, with weary horses, waited, the drivers watching patiently for the mad tourists who were willing to ride aimlessly around at any hour of the night. Keller Barkley circled the towering hotel to the Dufferin Terrace, the long boardwalk that looked down upon the Saint Lawrence. Like every place else in Quebec during August, it was crowded, families, individual strollers, couples, guests of the hotel, and people from the town. A slight breeze moved across it. It had been like this, a place of promenade, before the English came. He walked to the rail and looked down on the roofs of the lower town. Some of those houses were a couple of centuries old at least.

He thought then of Put Bigelow's proud boast about the American invasion of Quebec. Some of that invasion flowed up and down the terrace, Americans made welcome for the money that they brought and spent. A young man and a girl were seated on one of the cannons which commanded the river and the slope that led down to it; a preposterous piece of armament in 1957, hardly big enough to fire a decent firecracker. In 1776, these guns on which tourists perched now had been sufficiently lethal to repel another American invasion. General Montgomery had died on the slope under the fire of one of them, and an atom bomb could have been no more decisive as far as he was concerned. Benedict Arnold had been wounded in the same futile charge. The guns remained, and the steep slope, and the walled City of Quebec; but the men were gone.

Keller Barkley had a sense of vast time, standing there with his hands gripping the railing. He had taken one of the standard tourist tours in the afternoon, shortly after he and Put Bigelow arrived from Montreal. He had seen some of a city's surface and had absorbed some of its mood. Quebec did not belong in North America; it belonged on another continent and in another century. He watched a ferryboat on the river below him, half the way across to Lévis, a scattering of lights upon the hilly south shore.

"Bluebonnet would have loved this, all of it," he said.

It was one of the things that they had planned to do. They had planned to explore cities together, preferably the very old ones. They had both grown up in cities and would not have known how to explore anything else. He stood silent and straight, blocking out of his mind the shuffle of feet and the click of heels on the boards, the sound of voices. Sally seemed very close to him on Dufferin Terrace, teeming with ghosts of its own.

He had called her "Bluebonnet" when he discovered that she was from Texas. It had not meant much at first but it had gathered about it a special significance. No one else had ever heard him call her that. It was not a nickname; it was the name of a mood rather than of a woman, the mood of the night on which they met, a place of magic that they created together and to which they returned often, never by conscious planning. No one who knew them in Washington ever knew them at all. They had not known themselves until they met and merged.

Their honeymoon had been a time of wonder. They had had only three days and they had so much to discover about each other, so many memories to build, so many plans. It had been a time of great gentleness, of absurd solemnities. Sally had lain in his arms on the last night of it. She had seemed so very small, so defenseless; she wasn't that, but it was the illusion that she created and Kel had felt big and defending because of it.

"I will have to keep my job, Kel," she told him gravely. "I am going to need it in order to keep my mind in step with yours. You would grow tired of Bluebonnet, Kel, if she could be summoned like a genie out of a lamp, or if she were always hanging around. You could not always be the man who makes Bluebonnet possible, either. I would not want you to be. If we have two selves, we are lucky; but we need both of those selves if we are going to live together."

He kissed her before he laughed at her. "You are too mental," he said. "If you were just Sally Ferris I'd be afraid to be in the same room with you."

She had been right, of course. They lived their jobs to the hilt and they respected the privacies of each other, but they lived a love story like no other love story they had ever read of, or heard of, a marriage unique among marriages. They had lamps to rub and genies to summon, magic carpets to ride. They were not, they assured each other, sentimentalists; they were realists with an escape hatch.

It had been pretty damned wonderful.

Sally had always wanted to do feature and personality articles. When she got a chance, she took it. She had a remarkable gift for discovering extraordinary things about ordinary people, but she handled any story that came along. She was doing a routine story about private flying when disaster struck. Her pilot cracked up his landing and they took Sally out of the wreckage with a broken back.

Keller Barkley stood staring down at the Saint Lawrence, at the lighted ferry which was nearing the Lévis side.

They had done a lot with the grim months of surgeons and hospitals. They hadn't quit. She was Bluebonnet on some of the darkest days and she had thought about him when any other woman would have thought only of herself.

"You are wonderful in what you do, Kel," she said. "Nobody is any better. But it isn't your best writing self. If you would only put the Keller Barkley that I know into the books you could write, you would be the greatest writer in the world."

He did not contradict her in anything that she wanted to believe, anything that it helped her to believe, but he had no illusions about himself. He was a grandstand umpire, a second-guesser in the audience. He could put his finger on flaws, weaknesses, stupidities. He could ask pertinent questions. He could write with vehemence and punch. He stayed within his limitations.

Sally did not drop the subject. Nor did she concede her hope that she would live, that she would be whole again. She read a book about

Lourdes and it made her thoughtful. "I need a miracle, Kel," she said. "I want to go there."

If she wanted anything, she could have it. They went to Lourdes, the shrine of mercy and of miracles, and Sally did not come back.

The memory of her surrounded him. He could hear, faintly, the odd, offbeat, little voice, inhale again the subtle scent she wore. He ached with the awareness of her and the knowledge that she was not.

"So, I am writing your book for you, Bluebonnet," he said. "It's the kind of a book that I can write. I am going to tell the truth about these miracle factories and about the wonder kids who see visions, the ones who admitted that they were liars and the ones who didn't. It is the only thing in the world that interests me now. I hope you know."

The Château Frontenac loomed above him. In room 2323 there was a manuscript on which he had spent many long hours of research and of writing. He had a chapter that he planned to write in Quebec, a chapter on one of the admitted frauds. He had photostats of clippings from Quebec, Montreal, and Toronto newspapers, and he was going to the island where the affair occurred only a dozen years ago. Most of the principals should still be living. When he had living people to confront, he knew how to uncover facts. Hostility or evasion would not disturb him.

He felt Sally very close to him always when he thought about writing a book. It was something that she had wanted and he was going to give it to her.

## II

The morning was bright. Keller Barkley's head ached. He had a tight feeling in his throat and his body felt heavy. Not even the shower that he took, reluctantly, completely awakened him and breakfast held no appeal. He tried to tell himself that he was hung over, but he could not make himself believe it. He had had nothing to drink after dinner and he had been captain of his own ship when he finally decided to go to bed, with no haziness and no unsteadiness.

"A damned cold, probably," he said. "The sensible thing, I suppose, would be to put in a call for the house doctor and climb into bed for the day."

He was opposed to sensible things when they interfered with plans or schedules. There was a note in his box from Put Bigelow with a copy of his itinerary, the list of places at which he would stop on his epic survey of the American invasion. That decided him. He no longer had a job, but nothing that Putnam Bigelow had to do was more important than what he planned to do himself. Put was already on his way.

The route to Ile-aux-Erables was via ferry from Baie-Saint-Pierre, but there was no train until the afternoon and he was warned that, since it stopped at Beaupré, it would be crowded with tourists and pilgrims en route to the shrine of Sainte Anne. That, Keller Barkley said, in French, was insupportable.

He hired a driver and a car. The driver's name was Fernand Jobin. He was a short, slight man of perhaps fifty, with alert brown eyes, deep furrows in his face, and gray hair clipped short. He spoke English with a very slight accent. He was delighted, however, when he discovered that his passenger spoke French.

"It is a rare thing," he said. "One seldom encounters it. Sometimes there is a person who speaks in French a few words. These they keep repeating and it becomes a trial of the nerves. For one who is English, or from the States, to speak it truly, that is a matter for astonishment."

Keller Barkley shrugged. He took no credit for his mastery of French. His father was strong in his conviction that every educated American should speak one language other than English, that America's role in the world since the First World War demanded it. Kel had grown up with French and had carried French courses in high school and college. His father took him to his first Alliance Française meeting when he was twelve.

"So I speak French," he thought, "and wouldn't I be damned stupid if I didn't? After all of that!"

He was aware, of course, that he had an American accent and always would have, but he had encountered worse accents among the French in France and there were probably worse in Quebec, too.

His head ached abominably and he tried to escape from the ache by concentration on the informative lecture which Fernand Jobin included with the trip. The effort at concentration was not a success. The old seigneury of Beauport merged in confusion with the parish of Gifford and the Beaupré coast. The falls of Montmorency were a hundred feet higher than Niagara, he was told. When he looked at them without enthusiasm, his driver was immediately on the defensive.

"In the spring there is more water," he said, "but they are very beautiful."

"No doubt."

Fernand Jobin was baffled. He explained that he had taken this route because it wound through the old Quebec of farmhouses that were centuries old, outdoor ovens where women still baked quantities of bread at a single baking, wayside shrines where neighbors still said their evening prayers together.

"There is a faster way, the new highway beside the river," he said, "but one sees nothing."

"I like this better."

The man glanced sharply at him. "You are sick, Monsieur?"

"I'm afraid so. Let's stop somewhere and get some aspirin."

They pulled off the road and drove up a gentle slope to an old house that bore a sign with the legend: "Henri Trudelle—Marchand

Général." The interior was a combination grocery store, five-and-ten-cent store, cut-rate drug store, and rummage sale. Merchandise of every conceivable size and description crowded the walls, the shelves, the cases, and the floor. The proprietor procured a bottle of aspirin tablets from a lower shelf, looked at Barkley, and shook his head.

The aspirin tablets would do no good, he said. The man should go to bed and sweat. He should take a mixture of pine gum, whiskey, and maple syrup. The driver had a few ideas of his own. Camomile tea was mentioned and a few other remedies. Keller Barkley swallowed two aspirin tablets and walked out. He had a stubborn determination then to prove that aspirin was all that he needed and that he was feeling fine. He insisted upon stopping at the next roadside shrine and on getting out of the car to look at it.

The shrine was a stone shelter, doorless and windowless, open on the side facing the road. It contained four life-size figures; the Christ on the cross, the sorrowing Mother, and two kneeling women. There was a plaque which proclaimed that this particular shrine was a memorial. Keller Barkley blinked his eyes and read it.

JOSEPH MASSE GRAVEL

1641

*Ses Fils Reconnaissants*

1941

"His grateful sons," he repeated huskily. "Why?"

"He was their first ancestor, Monsieur," Fernand Jobin said. "He came from France to this place in 1641. After three hundred years, his descendants come from all over Canada, some from the United States, to do him honor. They are very many, the Gravels. They had outdoor Masses here, said by Gravels who are priests, and they made this monument. It is a happy thing, no?"

"Yes," Keller Barkley agreed. "It is a happy thing."

He walked back to the car and it was very nearly his last effort. He could no longer deceive himself that two aspirins were all that he needed. He sank down in the seat and watched the road apathetically. There were a great many signs: *"Cabins—A. Simard," "Chemin Privé," "Cabins à votre droite."* There were a great many vehicles and they progressed slowly. They were in a town, larger than the

135

villages through which they had passed, and on either side of the street there were stores and booths with signs shrieking for trade. This was Beaupré, home of the shrine, and one could buy statues, pictures, postcards, pennants, and stickers for one's automobile, anything at all. The backwaters of piety were filled with fancy debris and all for sale.

The shrine of Sainte Anne itself loomed up before them, a huge Romanesque basilica of white granite, with two lofty belfries, octagonal spires rising out of square towers. It was shockingly incongruous to Barkley after the drive through the quiet charm of the countryside, the simple churches, the roadside shrines, the old houses. Before it and around it, great masses of people moved and maneuvered. At least three processions, with banners held high, were trying to make their way to the basilica through the milling herd of unorganized humans who belonged to no procession.

"You would like to visit Sainte Anne, monsieur?"

The voice of the driver seemed to come from far away. Keller Barkley sank lower in the seat. "No. I would not," he said.

"It is a beautiful place. Many miracles happen there. The cripple comes with his crutch. He stands on his feet. He walks away. *Pas des béquilles!* It happens often. Many serious sicknesses go away. To cure your headache would be a simple matter for the good Sainte Anne, *m'sieu*, if you but ask her."

The man was almost pleading. There was reverence in his voice. There was no shock to him in the sight of all these people. He considered the basilica beautiful.

"I'll stick to aspirin," Barkley said.

They made their slow way through the town to the road again. It wound and it climbed. Barkley closed his eyes. It seemed to take an incredible time to reach another town. The driver brought the car to a sudden stop and Barkley blinked. There were no crowds here. This was a sleepy village. The church looked old and it had the clean, unpretentious lines of Quebec country churches, a mellowness, a quiet dignity.

"You would like better to visit this church, perhaps!" the driver said. "It is the church of Saint Joachim."

"Who is that?"

"The father of the Blessed Virgin. He is a very good saint, him. You would make a visit and a request?"

There was a wistful note in the man's voice. "He likes to visit churches," Barkley thought. "I am a disappointment to him." It was regrettable. Fernand Jobin was a kind, solicitous companion, but he had the wrong tourist today, a tourist who had gone to the Virgin Mary at Lourdes but who did not come to Quebec to visit her relatives.

"I think not," he said. "Sorry."

He added the "sorry" out of consideration for the feelings of a sincere man, but he was not sorry. Churches, and particularly Catholic churches, did not attract him, in sickness or in health. He settled down to enduring the trip, to using up the time which the car translated into miles. They rolled into Baie-Saint-Pierre and made the discovery that the ferry waited for the train which Barkley had scorned, a train not due for an hour.

"How about hiring a boat?" Barkley said.

"It is possible, but not wise." Fernand Jobin seemed worried. "Monsieur, permit me to drive you to Murribé. There is a fine hotel. Everything nice. A good doctor. On Ile-aux-Erables, there is nothing."

Barkley's hazing mind made a note that Murray Bay sounded more musical as one French word than it did as two English words, but it meant nothing to him. His objective was fixed in his mind and he had not suffered the day to go elsewhere.

"No," he said.

"Then you must have food, m'sieu."

Barkley did not believe so, but his driver was adamant. A man did nothing well, he insisted, on an empty stomach. He could not be strongly well, nor decently sick, nor even manage to die nobly. "Not that you will die of it, m'sieu, but you are not a well man."

Fernand Jobin found a quiet restaurant but he would not share the table and the meal. There was a code covering that. A driver-guide did not do it. It was a flattery that his company was esteemed, but one did not do what was not done. *Voilà ce que c'est!*

That was virtually the last clear memory that Barkley retained of him. Fernand Jobin returned to take him to the ferry but by that time every image was blurred. The boat and the trip to the island were shadowy elements in an experience that had no reality. He had an impression of people talking to him and of his own insistence that he be taken to the hotel, that walking was out of the question. It seemed to be a matter for debate, but ultimately he was taken on a rough ride in some sort of vehicle. A voice said: "*Voilà! L'hôtel*," and he said, "*Merci.*"

He walked with an effort, holding his shoulders back. Someone carried his bag and typewriter. He fumbled in his pocket for change and a rough voice told him that money was unnecessary. A broad face, draped with walrus mustaches, swam into his vision, and some instinct told him that this was the proprietor of the hotel.

"I desire a room," he said, "and a doctor will, perhaps, be necessary."

"But yes, monsieur. Most certainly."

He had done all that he had willed to do. He had reached Ile-aux-Erables and he had made his wants known. He no longer had to hold himself together or keep moving. The face disappeared and the room which he could not see was revolving slowly. Keller Barkley reached out for something solid that his hands might grip, and the hands of strangers reached him first. He sank into a vast blackness and there was no bottom to it.

He swam up out of the darkness to a brief awareness of people talking, of being dressed or undressed, moved around. There was a woman's voice. It faded, grew fainter, and vanished into silence. He came back to awareness and a voice was addressing "Monsieur le Docteur." A deep, grave voice spoke, a man's voice, and he could not distinguish the words. He was rolled on his side and he felt a sharp stab in his hip. He recognized that, indifferently, as a hypo. The voices were pitched low and there was solemnity in them. He had the idea then that he was dying.

His mind came out of the mist of indifference to contemplate that idea. There was momentary shock in it. He had selected this place for another reason. He would not have come here to die. Bluebonnet! He wouldn't write her book. Bluebonnet was gone. This, too, was France.

He drifted away from the voices. If there was an eternity, some place to go out of life, Bluebonnet was there and that was where he wanted to be. If there was no eternity? *Eh, bien. Voilà tout!*

It took him longer the next time that he swam up through the blackness. Something was happening. The voices were different. There was a cadence that made the sound of the voices terrifying. He forced his eyes part way open. He was in a bed. There were two little sparks of flame that danced at the foot of the bed. Voices rose and fell, not in conversation, not in chant. He struggled very hard for consciousness, concentrating first upon the dancing sparks. *"Les chandelles,"* his mind said. That was it. Candles! The voices were a hum, a rise and fall; a monotony, a broken rhythm. Prayer! People were praying for him. Catholic prayers! The rosary! Nothing else sounded quite like that, nothing at all.

The sound ceased almost in the second of his recognition of it. He heard the rumbling, slithering, thumping sound of people rising from their knees to their feet, the scrape of a chair, a woman's voice.

"Monsieur le Curé."

The effort of opening his eyes again was enormous, and while he exerted that effort, Barkley was unable to hear the words that were spoken in the room. He turned toward the sound of the words and he saw the black soutane, the hands of the priest, the face shrouded in mist. The strength went out of him and he fell back, his eyes closing. The priest bent over him and asked a question. The inflection of the words told him that it was a question but he could not distinguish the words themselves. He had no voice of his own. He felt a hand clasp his hand and the voice called to him. It did not matter that he could not answer. He did not want to answer. He had nothing to say to priests. The voice spoke to him again, close to his ear. He took a perverse pleasure in floating away from it in the Stygian darkness.

There was silence, a vast silence, then he heard the deep voice once more, but it was no longer questioning him nor calling him; it was intoning great majestic sounds. There was harmony in this single voice, a steady rhythm, not broken or uneven like the rosary sound. Keller Barkley roused slightly out of indifference. There was something puzzling, challenging, about the voice. It was not the sound of French or of English, distinctive series of sounds even when one did not unravel the words. This was different. His body twitched with shock. Latin!

He was dying on a priest's prayer, a Catholic rite.

Frantic danger signals sounded through all of his being. It could not be like that. It must not be like that. Blind instinct rebelled and he fought against the comfort of the enfolding darkness, the soft nothingness on which he rested. He forced one hand to lift in protest and he moaned with effort. A sharp voice that was not the voice of the priest spoke and the words lost themselves in space. Barkley concentrated on following them, lifting himself high. They were French words, and if he could follow them, they represented an escape from the Latin. He felt sweat on his body and he knew that his mouth was opening and closing. Someone poured liquid on his tongue from a spoon. It was neither hot nor cold and it had no taste.

He swam into a gray world out of the blackness and he could not rest in it. He was very tired but he forced himself on. He did not know where he was, but there was a place to which he was committed, a place he must reach. He was no longer aware of anyone else in the world but himself. He was alone and there was danger threatening him, some frightful experience awaiting him if he stopped to rest.

At his bedside, Doctor Leon Norbert was closing his black bag. "I have hopes for him," he said. "He has regained his will to live. He had none of it at all. I could not command effort from him."

"It was Monsieur le Curé that commanded it," Jeanne Charbonneau said. "It is so often true. The Last Sacrament brings strength to the body as well as to the soul."

Father Bélanger shook his head. "We can say that God helped him, certainly, and the skill of our good friend, the doctor, which comes also from God. I could not administer the Last Sacrament. There is no evidence that this stranger is a Catholic."

"But he speaks French, Monsieur le Curé. Even in his delirium he speaks French."

The priest smiled. "The Devil speaks it, too, no doubt, Madame Charbonneau, as well as he speaks English. I gave the young man conditional absolution, and now we must pray for him and for Monsieur le Docteur who is wiser than we in the needs of a sick body."

The man on the bed did not hear the voices. He slept, breathing heavily.

# III

Keller Barkley returned to the world through a series of visual impressions which preceded any sensation of bodily comfort or discomfort. He stared upward at the heavy beams, dark with age, then turned his eyes to the source of light, the window which framed a small section of pale blue sky and a single cloud that was shaped like a reclining sheep. He raised his body, bracing himself on his elbows, and he could see a wide stretch of the Saint Lawrence, sparkling water more deeply blue than the sky. He had the vague impression that he was in a cabin on a ship and he settled back to ponder that.

He became aware of the walls, as brightly yellow as the sunshine at first glance, then not quite yellow. There was a pattern. A boy and a girl and a dog ran beside a stream toward a gray stone Norman windmill. Once he was aware of it, the windmill dominated his view for long minutes, the children and the dog fading into insignificance. The windmill seemed to repeat itself to infinity, becoming a whole series of windmills on all the walls. He became aware that it was a sunny day in the history of the windmill and the yellow sunlight emerged once more from the wallpaper.

There was a stone chimney that came out of the floor and thrust upward through the beams, an immense affair that seemed a dozen feet wide. His bed was huge, too, wide enough for three or four boon companions to sleep side by side. There was a crucifix in the direct line of his vision on the far wall that was right-angled to his bed. He stared at the crucifix, wondering, and fragments of memory returned to him. He was trying to reach a hotel when all sensible impressions dissolved into chaos. Was this a hotel? With a crucifix on the wall? In Quebec, the answer was, "Yes. Probably so."

A short, stout, cheerful woman bustled into the room without knocking. She clasped her hands together and uttered a cry of delight when she saw that he was awake.

"Why, monsieur!" she said. "This is the wonderful surprise. You are better today. You have decided that you will come back to us."

Keller Barkley would have sworn, when this woman entered the room, that he had never seen her before, but he remembered her suddenly, moving through a number of scenes that reproduced badly on the memory screen. He remembered her voice, her solicitude, her bullying of him, moving him around in the bed as though he were a doll, forcing liquids on him. He remembered her name.

"You are Madame Charbonneau," he said.

"Oh-ho, monsieur! You are the fox, the sly one. You know more than we credit, eh? You have not always been asleep, not you! You remember Madame Charbonneau, who forgets sometimes that you are not one of her sons."

She came close, clucking over him, straightening his pillows. He was embarrassed in the realization of his helplessness, of all that she must have done for him, but there was no awareness of his embarrassment in Madame Charbonneau. He had been dying one night, she told him, and out of his head for two days, very quiet for a day and a night. Luckily, she added, her daughter who lived in Rivière-du-Loup was visiting her and had helped to take care of him. She went to the door and called "Catherine!"

Catherine was a shy young woman, with a full figure, not yet as heavy as her mother. Paul Charbonneau came, too, a bluff, hearty, rotund individual with walrus mustaches and a florid complexion. It was, he assured Barkley, an occasion of great joy to the household that their guest had overcome his infirmity. The joy was genuine. It was written in the faces of the three people in the room. There was no adequate response that a man could make to it.

When he was alone, after he had eaten some very remarkable soup which Madame Charbonneau brought to him, Keller Barkley tried to organize his own thoughts. He remembered Fernand Jobin and a horrible day of travel, his glimpse of Paul Charbonneau's face before he collapsed. He remembered dimly, too, that a priest had prayed over him and that a doctor had jabbed him with a needle. It was not the way that he had planned to arrive on Ile-aux-Erables. In a sense, he was disarmed.

He had been enveloped in solicitude and friendliness and he had not come in friendship. He wondered how these people would feel if they knew why he had come and what he planned to do. They would have to know, of course, ultimately.

For a weak moment, he considered the possibility that he could write his book without the planned chapter on this island. Almost immediately he rejected it.

This chapter was perfect for his purpose. He had read and re-read many times the newspaper accounts of the affair on Ile-aux-Erables and he was satisfied that it contained the basic elements of Lourdes, Fátima, and La Salette, differing from them only in the fact that it was an admitted hoax. He could not talk to Bernadette of Lourdes, or the children of the other apparitions, or the people who knew them, but here he should be able to face the story in its entirety. He had notes and clippings on other pretended visions, other fakes, but none of them were as close in detail as this one to the visions that had been accepted as genuine.

His jaw tightened. This might prove to be the most difficult assignment that he had ever undertaken, but there could be no question of abandoning the book. He was writing it for Sally and no one else mattered.

The arrival of the doctor broke his reflection. Doctor Leon Norbert was too perfectly the man of medicine—short, strong, capable-looking, with narrow eyes and a carefully trimmed Vandyke; but like the Charbonneaus, he was warmly, genuinely, happy that his patient had recovered.

"You arrived on the ferry and tried immediately to leave on angel wings," he said jocularly. "It was unreasonable of you."

"I am often unreasonable, but I doubt the angel wings. What was the matter with me?"

"Climactically, Asian flu. You were our first case on the island. I feared that you had brought it to us. Seemingly not. We are a hardy people and the Charbonneaus, who took the greatest risks, were without fear of it."

"I am deeply in their debt."

"A debt of the heart, yes; of the purse, no. They would be sensitive about that."

"Thank you. I'll remember. Why did you say 'climactically' in connection with my Asian flu?"

"Because I am convinced that you paved the way for it, probably through poor eating and sleeping habits, plus tension, worry, and a few other modern complications which are practically unknown on this island. I know nothing of your plans, affairs, or circumstances, but if you can afford to stay here a few weeks, you may count your profit, ultimately, in terms of years."

The doctor was young, in his thirties. He looked and sounded more like Montreal than like a rural community. There had been no doctor on the island in 1945, according to the clippings. There had been a midwife, a salty character evidently, who practiced not only medicine but surgery. Twelve years had wrought changes. What had those years done to the girl who invented the vision, to the boys and the rest of them?

Barkley's mind was clear, but his body was weak. He rebelled savagely against that weakness, against the whole chain of circumstances that made friends for him where he wanted no friends, that made him a helpless dependent in a place where he needed freedom of action. He thought about his stubborn, unreasoning struggle to reach this island when he could have remained a while in Quebec or stopped at Murray Bay.

"It was a gallant charge," he said. "I led it nobly. But I fell off my horse."

Self-mockery carried him only a short distance. He found a focus for his antagonism in the two framed pictures which faced each other across his bed from the north and south walls. They were horrible examples of Catholic lithography; a mild, prettified Christ pointing to his exposed heart, and a vapid, magazine-cover Virgin Mary pointing to her heart. The hearts looked like valentines.

"I can't do anything about them," Barkley said grimly, "but I've got to get back on my feet and get out of here. I've got work to do."

Getting back on his feet was not easy. He spent two days rebuilding his strength and not trying to do anything else; two days of fabulous Charbonneau meals, of listening to Paul Charbonneau, who was a prodigious talker, of meeting awkward, ill-at-ease, friendly men who came to the Charbonneaus in the evening to play checkers or cards or to watch television. TV on the island was a shock to him.

"Only three years ago, the electric line came and before that the telephone," he was told. "To us they are new things but the television is not popular. The people do not believe what they see on it. The people on the television speak French but the things that they do and say are incomprehensible."

There was a wealth of material for a book in the life going on around him, a strange way of life according to all of the standards by which he had lived, but it wasn't the book that Keller Barkley had come to write. The individuals in whom he was interested were not mentioned in conversation and he asked no questions about them. The Charbonneaus were not to be faced with that. He had to face the man who was certain to oppose him, but who was, himself, a key figure in the affair of a dozen years ago. Any other approach would be oblique, crafty, a form of detective work lacking in honesty or dignity. He waited for his vitality, which returned to him slowly.

On Friday, Keller Barkley located Anse-Saint-Jean on a map of the island and walked the road that led to it. It was high tide. He stood at the edge of a small path, shadowed by graceful birches, and the river rolled almost to his feet. A high angry rock stood tall and commanding on his right, and a low, black spire protruded from the water on his left. It was a hazy day and the river was indefinitely wide, with a false horizon of mist in the south, like a shading line in white chalk.

He was vaguely disappointed.

On Saturday morning he returned when the tide was out and this was another picture. He was astonished at the wide stretch of beach that spread itself before him. The river was clear and sparkling, with gulls wheeling above it, sweeping low to ride the ripples and taking off again. He could see a town on the south shore, with a church spire that looked like a spear of silver in the sun. He descended the path to the beach and three little girls, with baskets in their hands, paused in their task of gathering shells to watch him.

He looked toward the black rock on the east side of the cove. It stood high above the water when the tide was out and it created the illusion that it was bending toward the observer. Imagination might conjure many images out of that rock. It was a cowled monk, bent in humility, or an old woman in a shawl bent with toil. The bending was probably not an illusion but a reality. Some freak of the winds had hollowed the west face of the rock and there was a depression in it that was like the entrance to a cave, taller than most cave entrances, doorway high and fashioned like a doorway. There was no cave. He could see the solid rock out of which the portal had been carved, like the backing of a mock doorway in a stage set.

"It looks like a niche designed to hold an image," Keller Barkley thought. "I can see how one would get the idea. It seems unfinished without an image . . ."

He nodded his head. His eyes had seen and his imagination had embellished. He was ready for Monsieur le Curé.

He walked back slowly on the village road. Ile-aux-Erables was a place of quiet and of fragrance. He could not identify the many individual scents that blended into the perfume of the place but the blending was marvelously done and a man's nostrils could take joy in it. He had mentioned that to his host and Paul Charbonneau had laughed loudly.

"It is not always so, nor everywhere so," he said. "You should smell the fields when they spread on them *l'éperlan*, the small fish, for fertilizing. Or the breeze when they slaughter the hogs. There are many perfumes here, m'sieu."

Barkley shrugged. "The thorns on roses, the hang-overs in gay bottles, the climb uphill after coasting down. Why not?"

"Why not, indeed?" said Charbonneau. "There is more joy in a good chair when the feet ache, *n'est-ce pas?*"

It was easy to get along with Charbonneau. He was one of the fellows of infinite jest, sometimes heavy but always good-natured. There was no gloom in him.

Keller Barkley walked up the path between the two rows of sentinel poplars to the presbytery. The woman who opened the door was tall and heavy. She looked at him with round expressionless eyes, then invited him into a bare, bleak little room with two chairs that faced each other across a narrow desk. The inevitable crucifix hung on the wall where a visitor must look at it. Barkley remained standing and electric currents of anticipation ran through his nerves. This was his best moment on the island. He felt like himself once more, standing free of the shackles of obligation. He owed Monsieur le Curé nothing save candor.

146

The priest did not keep him waiting. He came into the room with a soft step, a half smile on his face. "*Bon jour,* monsieur," he said. "I am happy to see you well again."

"Thank you, Monsieur le Curé. I had good care."

"You did indeed, and needed it."

"I understand that I had your prayers."

"You had many prayers besides mine. You are not of our Faith?"

"No."

"I was fairly certain of it."

"How could you be when I was unconscious?"

The priest smiled again. He gestured to Barkley, inviting him to be seated, and seated himself in the chair behind the desk. He was a short, dark-skinned man of indeterminate age, compactly built. He had brown eyes and a wide mouth. His hair had retreated to three small islands, over his ears and low on the back of his skull; the little that was left was still black with only a trace of gray. He was thin-lipped but there was no severity in his countenance. He had, perhaps, been stricter with himself than with others. He conveyed no disapproval of the fact that his guest was not a Catholic. His attitude seemed to be the same as that which Barkley had felt in the Charbonneaus; polite regret, even sympathy, the attitude that one might have to another who was crippled or maimed or incapacitated. It could be an infuriating attitude, yet, strangely, was not. There was a gentleness that redeemed it.

"I came to this island because I am writing a book, Monsieur le Curé," Keller Barkley said. "It is not a book that you will approve, I am certain, but I feel compelled to write it. An incident which occurred here is a vital chapter in the plan of my book. A girl named Valérie Rivard claimed that she saw a vision of the Virgin Mary, then admitted that she had engaged in a deception and had seen nothing."

Father Bélanger's facial muscles were still. His eyes were intent. "Deception is a harsh word in this instance," he said. "It was a slight incident, not of sufficient importance to be included in a book. The child was eight years old, of a lovely imagination and quite innocent. Of what interest could she be in your book, monsieur?"

"Because she was probably exactly like the others, the children who made similar claims and never retracted them."

"Ah! This book, then, is to be an attack on the Catholic Church? On its veneration of the Mother of God?"

"No! I am not interested in attacking your Church or anything that it teaches. I am interested in Truth. There is a Protestant chapter in my book. The children of Salem, Massachusetts, were imaginative children, too. They did not see visions of the Virgin; they saw visions of witches, because witches were part of their folklore and their environment. A great evil came out of their imaginations because adults took them too seriously. I don't believe that they were essentially different from your Bernadette, or your Valérie of this island, or any other little girl who claims that she sees visions. And, by the way, it is interesting that these witnesses of wonders are invariably girls."

Father Bélanger's eyes were fixed unblinkingly on Barkley's face. "You are willing to ignore, while seeking Truth, the miraculous spring that came out of the ground to Bernadette at Lourdes and the miracles that have been wrought there?"

"I have been to Lourdes, Monsieur le Curé."

The silence was tense between the two men. The priest, at length, broke it. "You sought a favor at Lourdes and it was not granted?"

"My wife died there."

Father Bélanger looked unhappy. He took a short, black pipe from his pocket and carefully packed it. "For such a loss, there is no solace," he said. "Have you children?"

"No."

"What do you want from me?"

"I would like, if you will give it to me, your account of what happened here, your opinion of the child who claimed that she saw the vision, and your explanation, if you have one, as to why she made the claim."

"That is impossible."

"Why?"

"You have paid me the courtesy of speaking French. I appreciate it. On this subject we cannot communicate, in French or in English. Words do not have the same meaning for us."

"I cannot accept that. I have written stories involving Catholics and Catholicism. I had no trouble understanding the vocabulary of your Faith. Belief is another matter."

148

Father Bélanger lighted the pipe that he had packed so carefully. He passed the flame of the match back and forth across the bowl, taking his time. Keller Barkley could feel hostility in him now. It was polite, controlled hostility, but it was there.

"*Eh, bien!*" he said. "Let us examine your situation. You never sought Our Lady at home, yet you demanded her favors abroad. What did you bring to her? Love? Devotion? Faith?"

"We brought our need. As far as I ever heard, that was the idea. We had a desperate need and we were there."

"God knows our needs better than we do, monsieur. The future is His. What He gives is often greater than what we asked, but we are too blind to see or to understand. The soul of your wife found, perhaps, what her body did not."

"We were not talking about God, Monsieur le Curé. We were talking about the vision of a girl named Bernadette, the vision which is now known as Our Lady of Lourdes. My wife did not read of a shrine to God where miracles were supposed to happen; she read of a shrine to the Virgin Mary."

All of the bitterness of that bleak, rainy day on which Sally died welled up in Keller Barkley. It was in his voice, in all of his being. The priest shook his head sadly.

"An ocean of misunderstanding separates us, monsieur," he said. "The Blessed Virgin is one of us, born of our flesh. She is the mediatrix. She stands between us and Heaven, more easily comprehensible to our poor minds than the eternity of God, but she is not God. She does not work miracles upon the flesh, nor forgive sins. It was not she who turned water into wine at Cana, but she requested it."

"Put it any way you will. Regard the Virgin Mary any way you will. I still do not believe that Bernadette, or any child, ever saw her. There is an explanation for the claims that these children made. The key to that explanation may lie here, in the girl who admitted what the others did not. That key is what I am seeking, only that."

There was no antagonism in Father Bélanger now. As Keller Barkley's anger swelled, the priest seemed to retreat. He was not a combative man but he had strength. Barkley did not underestimate that strength.

"The purpose that you seek to serve is small," the priest said quietly, "and the hurt that you inflict could be grave. The child who was eight years old at the time of the incident that interests you is now a girl of twenty. Her life has not been easy. Many of her difficulties grew out of that incident."

"I deny that my purpose is small. I am interested in those difficulties that are linked to that pretended vision."

"She does not, I assure you, deserve more difficulty."

Barkley's jaw tightened. "I won't discuss with you the deserving of difficulties. That is another bypath, a digression. I didn't come here to hurt that girl or to hurt anyone. Perhaps I can save many people from hurt by what I write. I am going to try. More people have been hurt by a belief in miracles than by a disbelief in them."

The priest puffed slowly, thoughtfully, on his pipe. "You are honest. You have faced me with this. I keep reminding myself of the fact. Will you discuss with me the many sound reasons why you should abandon this unhappy book?"

"Absolutely not!"

"*Eh, bien!* Then I will save my breath for a prayer that you will stay with us long enough to find the Truth that you seek. I will make only one request."

Barkley waited. He had learned long ago to be wary of "Jesuitical cunning." This priest was not a Jesuit, but there were depths in him. "Whatever he is planning," he thought, "it's a mousetrap. All that the poor damn mouse can see is the cheese; then bang!"

"Do not tell anyone, as you so frankly told me, the shape of this book of yours or its purpose," the priest said slowly. "There are people on the island who are quick of temper and capable of violence. This book is something that they would not comprehend. They would be outraged and they are as strong in hatred, unfortunately, as in friendship, loyalty, or hospitality."

"I have never hidden from anyone. Since you, too, are outraged, you should not be concerned if your people try to prevent me from writing my book."

"It does not solve the problems of a priest to have his people fall into sin. You are seeking Truth. To know people, you must know them in friendship. There is no other way."

Someone at the door pressed a button and chimes echoed through the presbytery. Father Bélanger tapped the ash from his pipe into a tray on the desk and put the pipe away.

"That is, unquestionably, Mademoiselle Rivard, who has come to help me with some correspondence," he said. "I will suggest to her that she take you to meet her father, who is gravely ill and starved for such conversation as you can provide. You will, thus, meet her happily and through her the others who interest you."

Keller Barkley rose. He stood looking into the eyes of the priest. It had all been too easy, and he mistrusted easy victories. He was slightly uncomfortable in the knowledge that he had been more forthright than polite.

"I do not pretend to understand you, Monsieur le Curé," he said, "but I appreciate your attitude and the introduction to Mademoiselle Rivard. I am sorry that I cannot let myself be committed to secrecy on the purpose of my book."

The housekeeper had opened the door and was speaking to the girl whom she had admitted. "I cannot commit any man to a course of action, monsieur," Father Bélanger said. "Each man commits himself. I will pray for you."

# IV

There had never been a clear picture of Valérie Rivard in Keller Barkley's mind. He had thought about her as a type, as a child linked to a long tradition of precocious children. He could imagine, up to a point, the child who would be capable of facing adults with the claim that she had witnessed some marvel which no one else had seen. He had met Elizabeth Parris and Ann Putnam, who saw witches in their visions, on the pages of the carefully chronicled Salem witchcraft trials, and he believed that he understood them. They were, he thought, merely childishly hysterical, vain, young exhibitionists, seeking to draw attention to themselves by creating visions out of the superstitious elements in their environment. The wave of adult hysteria, which they unwittingly released, carried them further than they would have dared to go.

He found the same elements present in the careers of those children who claimed supernatural visions of a less mischievous type; in Bernadette of Lourdes, whom he visualized as in rebellion against her physical and economic inferiority, longing for respect and attention, probably as vain and hysterical in her deepest being as the children of Salem, but creating a milder vision out of softer superstitious elements.

Physically, he conceived of such a girl as probably a wan, listless type, moody, brooding, indrawn, given to excesses of piety or of morbidity; a whiner or complainer, possibly, or a sullen peasant, or a self-conscious nonentity. He did not believe that she would change for the better with the passing of the years since she would be more apt to develop the neurotic qualities in her personality than to cor-

152

rect them. When the priest mentioned that Valérie Rivard had not had an easy life, that she had encountered many difficulties, Keller Barkley was certain that he knew what to expect.

He met Valérie Rivard in the bleak little visitor's room of the presbytery.

She was a smiling young woman with extraordinary brown eyes; large, widely-spaced, candid eyes that lighted with interest, and perhaps a flash of curiosity, when she was introduced to him. She wore her dark hair short in what might have been described as a home-cut page-boy bob, and her skin was a rich golden tan. His first, startled impression of her was that she was a vital, vivid personality. When she turned her head to speak to Monsieur le Curé, the impression vanished and she was a very ordinary girl, neither beautiful nor pretty.

She had a short, concave nose that dipped at the bridge and rose to a rounded tip, a large mouth, a round face and a soft jaw line. She was a short girl, five foot three at a guess, and she was strongly built but without heaviness. She wore a simple blue cotton dress, a print that suggested a shower of snowshoes. It had no particular lines of its own, but her chest was deep and her breasts were fully rounded under it. She wore flat-heeled slippers that barely missed being moccasins.

Keller Barkley had seconds in which to photograph her mentally while Father Bélanger was telling her that the letters would not suffer through a slight delay, an hour if necessary.

"Your father will enjoy meeting Monsieur Barkley, I am positive," he said, "and it may be that you can tell him much of the island yourself since this is his first visit."

He extended his hand to Barkley. There was a faint smile on his lips. "I hope that you will extend your visit, monsieur," he said, "and that we will have other discussions."

The handclasp was like a truce between them, a waiting truce. "He looks as though he has just pulled a large rabbit out of a small hat," Barkley thought. "He knows that the girl is not as I anticipated. But I am not buying his rabbit yet." A faint hostility to both priest and girl stirred in him. "We'll see how she adds up."

They walked down the aisle of poplars together and there was a tension between them that held back speech. They were young and strange to each other and the island was a place where, apart from a saving humor and a surface lightness, the forces of life and living were taken seriously; religion, work, politics, love, marriage, children, chance encounters. As they neared the road, Barkley shook his shoulders impatiently, seeking to banish a mood that was unwelcome.

"Is it far to your home, mademoiselle?"

"Oh, no, monsieur." She raised her head, turning to look upward into his face. "I know that you have been very ill. If walking distresses you, we will walk very slowly."

He laughed. "I was not thinking of that. I am entirely well. I can probably walk as far as you can. I was hoping that your home would be at a distance. Monsieur le Curé said that you have an hour."

"Oh!" She smiled at him briefly and looked away. "As to that, there are many ways of arriving anywhere. Only a straight line is the short distance."

"We will not walk a straight line," he said.

They turned right on the road and he was aware once more of the rich fragrance all around him. The hot sun of August made a mist out of clover and honeysuckle, of a dozen varieties of flowers, of many growing things that he could not name, and the lazily moving breeze from the river stirred the mist, blending the perfume. There were buttercups and daisies beside the road, roses on all the fences. The road curved gracefully toward the church and the cleared gravel space designed obviously for the vehicles which brought the faithful to Sunday Mass. There were groups and clusters of trees, standing, themselves, like parishioners between the main road and the church itself, and to either side of it. The straight line between the rear door of the presbytery and the side entrance to the church was a very short line compared to the route of the road.

"Have you seen the view from the cemetery, monsieur?" the girl asked.

"No."

"You will like it, I think."

He did not tell her that he avoided cemeteries, that he had always disliked them, and now more than ever. Today he was committed to whatever she selected. It was the only way that he could learn what she was like. She was still shy with him. After a half dozen steps on the path that circled the church, she stopped suddenly.

"You do not have a hat," she said. "The sun is very strong where there is no shade."

154

Her own hat did not command attention, a small straw soup plate of Navy blue which fitted tightly to her skull, offering no shade to her face. Barkley took from his pocket the dark blue beret which Paul Charbonneau had insisted upon selling him for the protection of his brain from the sun. He did not ordinarily wear a hat and he felt sheepish about the beret. Valérie Rivard laughed as he put it on.

"You are not accustomed to the beret," she said. "I can tell. But it is better for an artist than the big hat of the farmer or the black straw hat of Monsieur le Curé."

"I am not an artist."

"I think so." She was walking beside him again. The path had widened and it climbed steeply. "I have known artists who paint pictures. Sometimes they come here. Never have I known an artist who writes. I have read many books and envy those who write them."

"I don't write books."

"I have heard that you are a very famous writer."

"How?"

"And that you are a Protestant," she said gravely. "I have never known a Protestant."

Keller Barkley frowned. It seemed incredible that one could be the age of this girl and know only Catholics. Maybe not. It was all around him; in everything, coloring everything. He was aware that the girl was looking up at him. He met her incredible eyes. She was smiling.

"Madame Charbonneau is of the family Bouchard," she said, "who live on the other end of the island. We have a party-line telephone system, twelve phones on one line. I have not listened to Madame Charbonneau but people who listen are also talkers."

"And a man who is sick does not have much privacy."

"Nobody has much privacy, monsieur. If you were of the island, you would know many things of me, of all of us."

Keller Barkley thought about that. A newspaperman was in a poor position to make a point about privacy. It was a party-line profession, publicizing privacies under the name of "News." He had not come to Ile-aux-Erables with any idea of respecting the secrets or the private life of Valérie Rivard.

"I would like to know more about you," he said, "but not from the telephone."

She did not answer him. They had reached the crest of the hill and

155

she paused there, her head held high, letting the scene speak for itself. There was a cemetery with a jumble of stones, but Barkley's eyes passed over it to the incredible blue and the astonishing width of the Saint Lawrence. Colorful marker buoys bobbed in the current. There was a large freighter laboring upstream in the south channel and smaller craft hugging the north shore, a single white sail. Baie-Saint-Pierre was a miniature movie set in three dimensions, bright with sunlight; behind it the serrated line of North America's oldest mountains, the Laurentians.

"I am glad that you brought me here," he said.

"It is a place of many pictures."

She moved around, showing him her pictures with the manner of an exhibitor possessed of camera and screen. She was far away from him as a person and close to the scenes that she presented, so apparently she forgot him. Her eyes were alive and there was a fluidity of expression in her face. She gestured naturally, gracefully, with eloquent hands.

From a spot south of the cemetery wall, they looked down upon a square, modern building. This, she told him, was the *fromagerie* of Jacques LePage, whose brother owned a farm and whose two sisters owned the village beauty shop. There were two trucks standing beside the building, one in the process of being loaded.

"They ship cheese everywhere," the girl said, "even to the United States. They would like to start a canning factory."

From the north wall of the cemetery, they looked down upon the long ferry dock, which also handled most of the other island shipping. Twenty thousand barrels of apples and fifty thousand bags of potatoes were harvested and shipped from the island each year, she said casually. The dock was managed by two sons of Mederic Lepage. There was another modern building near the dock. This was La Coopérative Agricole, which marketed many of the smaller island crops and handicraft work on a co-operative basis.

"Which Lepage runs that?"

The girl laughed. "But no! It employs a Gagnon and a Simard. Roland Lepage, who is a son of Jacques is, however, now the notary since my father has been ill. Everyone calls him Monsieur Lepage and they still call my father 'Monsieur le Notaire.'"

Keller Barkley had been deploring to himself a newly born pacifist attitude, a difficulty in bringing his forces of hostility and opposition to honest focus. Those forces had sizzled in the past few minutes and thrown off sparks. Without knowing any of them, he felt an active dislike for the Lepages. "One of those go-getter families," he thought, "always getting themselves elected to committees and running everything in sight." It was, of course, illogical and unreasonable for him to resent that, since it was in the natural order of life as he knew it, but today he did.

"Your father, then, is gravely ill?" he said.

"Very gravely ill." Valérie's eyes clouded, then she smiled. "He will admit that, monsieur, but he will accept no sympathy. He says that he had a most grave and difficult birth, too, and that nobody sympathized with him." Her smile was gentle. "He is very tough, my father, with a loud bark."

Mention of her father was the signal for the termination of the tour and they both knew it. Valérie stood at the summit of the path once more, but she was facing west now. The gay old houses with roofs of blue, red, yellow, and green were glimpses of color through the trees, and the ridge which ran the length of the island was plainly visible, like the spire of some giant, prehistoric lizard. It was an arbitrary ridge, which apportioned the long, sheltered, high-ground farms to the south, and the shallow, short, exposed farms to the north.

The Saint Lawrence was two great rivers when viewed in this direction, one on either side of the island, but the coves were hidden by the greenery and the slope of the ground.

"I walked to Anse-Saint-Jean this morning," Barkley said.

If the name stirred memories and associations in the girl's mind, as it must, she gave no sign. "It is the prettiest beach," she said. "Anse-Saint-Luc is larger and deeper. Anse-Saint-Marc and Anse-Saint-Mathieu, on the north shore, are mud flats at low tide. Anse-Saint-Mathieu was once a place of bootleggers."

She smiled when she mentioned the bootleggers, but it was a remote, impersonal smile. She was suddenly more guide than girl and there was no tension between them. "How old is thirty when one is twenty?" Barkley thought. "Very ancient, no doubt."

He rebelled inwardly against being relegated to the company of old men and he was not interested in mere guides. He wanted more than a glimpse of the girl who was a chapter in his book. She was moving ahead of him on the path, a graceful girl who moved lightly like a dancer, imposing no weight upon the earth.

"Have you always lived on this island?" he asked.

Valérie looked back, then slowed her pace to permit him to walk beside her. "I went away to school, to a convent where I boarded, on the south shore," she said. "A small place. I went to the business school in Quebec for a fall, a winter, and a spring." She paused for a moment, seeming to hold her breath. "I was born in Trois Rivières."

"Oh, were you? I remember Trois Rivières. The train stopped there on the way to Quebec and I got out to stretch."

"What did you see?"

Valérie was as interested as if he had started on a good story. She stood quietly on the path, her eyes fixed intently upon his face. He made an apologetic gesture.

"Hardly anything, I'm afraid. Let's see! I walked down the platform to the station; a rather small, ordinary station. I don't recall anything special about it. I bought a Trois Rivières newspaper, *La Nouvelliste*. I remember that because it is a damned odd name for a newspaper. I bought some postcards because I'm a type who does that in strange towns. I never mail them to anyone, so I still have them somewhere."

He stretched the incident out because he had her attention and because even small facts about one's home, he knew, are often interesting out of all proportion to reason or common sense.

"Oh, yes! I remember another bit. There is a wire mesh, or iron mesh, screen between the station platform and the streets. The ones that I saw were narrow streets. The houses are built right up to the station screen. The nearest one had a circular outside staircase, one of those wrought-iron affairs, and there were two little girls playing on it. They are so accustomed to trains and to the people who ride them that they did not spare us a glance; they kept right on playing. There were two small girls and only one doll."

Valérie Rivard was nodding her head as though she liked the bit about the two oblivious children and the one doll. She waited expectantly and Keller Barkley searched his mind in vain for another detail. He spread his hands helplessly.

"Did you see the Saint Maurice?" she asked.

"The Saint Maurice? Oh, yes. That's the river, isn't it? I saw it. We passed over the bridge slowly. It was practically choked with logs, or rather, log rafts. The logs were lashed together."

"Did you see where it flows into the Saint Lawrence?"

"No. I don't believe one can see that from the train." He spread his hands wide again. "I am sorry that I did not see any of the really beautiful sections of your town, Valérie. There must be many that you remember."

He used her name, Valérie, instinctively, without a thought, although first names, except under conditions of intimacy, were not the custom of the country. She did not seem to notice. She shook her head.

"I left Trois Rivières when I was a baby."

"And you have never been back? Not even when you were in Quebec? It can't be far from there, seventy-five miles or so."

"That was far to me when I was in school. There were difficulties." She smiled faintly. "And I do not want to see it. You will not understand this, monsieur, and I cannot explain it. I love to hear about Trois Rivières from anyone who has seen it, and I read about it, but I never plan to see it. Never."

"I believe that I could understand that if I tried."

"Do you?"

"Yes."

"Try! Then tell me sometime of your understanding."

"I will."

Valérie resumed the walk again, down the path, and he felt tall beside her. He had had more than a glimpse of her in those few moments. A veil had blown aside and it had not revealed any of the dark traits that he had associated with the girl who fabricated a miracle. There was something appealing in her attitude toward Trois Rivières. If he could get to the bottom of it, he felt that he would understand much about her.

They emerged from the narrowing of the path beside the church to the solemn congregation of trees. A group of four barefooted children walked in the grass beside the road, following an older girl who wore moccasins. They stopped walking and straightened their bodies like small soldiers when they saw the two adults.

"*Bon jour*, Mademoiselle Valérie."

"*Bon jour*, monsieur."

It was a common occurrence. There were children everywhere one

walked on the island and, invariably, even when he was alone, Barkley
received the same polite salute from any that he encountered. It had
never happened to him anywhere else. The older girl was smiling
expectantly at Valérie. Valérie turned slightly.

"Monsieur Barkley," she said. "I would like to present someone who
is special to me because she was named for me, Valérie-Marie Gagnon."

Keller Barkley stepped forward and held out his hand to the awkward, embarrassed youngster of twelve who curtsied to him. He was
remembering the newspaper clippings, the so-called miracle baby who
was born three weeks too soon on the night of the pretended miracle.
He had a strange feeling of unreality, standing beside Valérie Rivard
and touching the hand of this child who was a living memorial to
something that did not happen.

"How do you do, Valérie-Marie," he said.

He met the other children then, Rita, Marthe, Marc, and Lygette;
a few, a mere sampling, of the children of Rosaire Gagnon, who was,
himself, only one of many Gagnons. The sheer mathematics of
Canadien virility staggered one. He said so when they resumed their
walk and Valérie Rivard shook her head.

"It is very wonderful," she said, "and sad to be only one child, without brothers or sisters."

"Do you mean that you would *want* so many?"

Her eyes widened. "But, of course."

He did not believe it, but he was given no time to voice his disbelief.
The village road was a thoroughfare and they had to walk in the grass
that paralleled it as did the children. There was a duckboard walk
in the neighborhood of the hotel, but not here. Two horse-drawn
buggies passed them and a light Ford truck with the name "Turcotte"
and much advertising copy on the side panel. A sauntering youth in a
green beret, sports shirt, and flannel slacks stopped when he saw
Valérie and stood with his hands in his pockets barring their way. He
was nearly as tall as Barkley and looked like an athlete rather than like
a farm youth. There was strength and grace in him, and arrogance,
more arrogance than any man needed. His eyes were insolent.

"This is how one works for Monsieur le Curé?" he said. The question mark hung suspended on the end of the sentence.

Valérie had stiffened when she saw him. Barkley could feel, without touching her, the tensing of her body. She ignored the question, as he was certain that she would not have ignored it if she had been alone.

"Monsieur Barkley," she said, "this is Robert Drolet."

The young man's eyes moved slowly, lazily, to Barkley. He was even more deliberate in removing his right hand from his pocket. "I have heard of you, monsieur," he said. "You are a novelty here. I meet many Americans. I live in Montreal."

Keller Barkley shook his hand reluctantly but with something of the same feeling that he had experienced in meeting the little Gagnon girl. This character, too, had stepped out of his clipping file.

"I hope that your meeting with Americans in Montreal is pleasant," he said dryly.

The blue-green eyes measured him without friendliness. "Not always," he said. "There are Americans and Americans."

He shrugged, waved his hand mockingly to Valérie and strolled on, his hands in his pockets once more. Valérie's lips were tight and there was anger in her eyes, in the poise of her body, in the way that she walked. Barkley did not intrude upon her silence. He could understand her anger, without knowing what had triggered the conflict, because Robert Drolet was easy to dislike, but he was less interested in understanding her anger than in observing it. The soft-voiced, pleasant guide, the absorbed listener to trivia about Trois Rivières, had fire and submerged passion in her. She controlled it, but the emotion behind her eyes when she looked at Robert Drolet was no meek thing, and no such transient thing as temper; it was deeper, stronger and more abiding; it was hatred.

She paused when she opened the gate in a fence that was heavily hung with roses. Her face was pale, despite the overlay of tan, and the fire had gone out of her eyes. She bit her lower lip before she spoke to him.

"Monsieur," she said. "I regret that incident."

"You need not. It wasn't your incident. To paraphrase an expression, there are Canadiens and Canadiens."

She led the way into the house. Barkley felt the heat of the day fall away from him like a dropped load. The stone walls of three-foot thickness, which guarded against the winter, provided summer comfort beyond the capacity of air conditioners. There was a large room, lined with bookshelves on the right, and two men intent upon a checkerboard. They looked up and accepted, with seeming reluctance, Valérie's introduction of Keller Barkley.

Louis-Charles Rivard was a huge, fleshy man with skin that looked like moist lard, large mustache, raggedly trimmed beard. He merely grunted and waved his hand.

The other man, André Drolet, was young, possibly in his late twenties. He had the appearance of a tall man, even when seated behind a table. His shoulders were wide and there were long ridges of muscle in his forearms. He was long-headed, with strongly carved nose and chin. His dark hair was untidy and there was curl to it. He had beautifully shaped, even teeth, as Valérie had, and there was warmth in his smile. He did not rise for Valérie or for the introduction.

"The world must await the outcome of our war," he said.

The two men concentrated grimly on the game. When André Drolet finally conceded, his two kings trapped by Louis-Charles' five, he shook his head. "I am humiliated," he said.

"The presence of my daughter in the room is bad for your wits," the older man said. He looked at Barkley. "Do you play chess, monsieur?"

"No. I'm sorry."

"Nobody on this island plays chess except Monsieur le Curé, who does not have the mind for it." His eyes shifted to André. "And few play checkers well."

"One uses the mind that one possesses, even if it is a poor thing."

The younger man reached behind him for an aluminum crutch. He swung it around deftly and rose, never for a moment off balance. He had only one leg. His right leg had been amputated above the knee and the leg of his trousers was pinned up around the stump. He extended his hand to Barkley.

"I meet you and I must immediately leave," he said. "I am sorry."

"I, too, regret it."

"We must talk some time. I read your column when you wrote one, monsieur. It was as I would have liked to write if I could do it."

He gave Barkley no opportunity to answer him. He was already moving toward the door, leaving behind him no answer to the question of the column. Valérie walked with him to the door and they conversed in low tones. Barkley heard her ask solicitously:

"What happened? You are not wearing your leg."

"It is nothing. A clumsy fall! The leg is uncomfortable for a day or two, so I must be a stork."

The door closed and the voices were gone. Louis-Charles Rivard was half-reclining in a chaise longue, pillows propped at his back. He had compelling eyes and they were fixed upon Barkley's face. He inclined his head slightly in the direction of the departing André Drolet.

"He is a damn fool, that one, as most men are," he said. "What, monsieur, is your weakness?"

# V

The coming of the American to Ile-aux-Erables introduced one more disturbing element into the already disturbed life of Valérie Rivard. After their first meeting, it seemed to her that she saw him everywhere she went. Because she was fluently bilingual and could write letters in English she worked often for the co-operative, for the *fromagerie*, and for others on the island who were developing interests which brought them into correspondence with Americans or English Canadians. These people, of course, never attempted to write in French even when they were making inquiries of French-speaking people in a solidly French province. On her walks from one place to the other, she frequently encountered Keller Barkley or saw him at a distance. When she encountered him he walked with her to her destination, or if she was going home, he accompanied her and visited her father.

She sensed early a rather intense interest in herself on the part of Keller Barkley and it puzzled her. It was a man-woman interest and her instincts were too sound, too logical, too thoroughly French, to blink at the obvious, but there was more than that to it, something that she could not define. She could not be certain that he himself recognized any other interest in her than the vague one that eluded her. He was not like the other men she knew.

"I wish that you would call me Kel," he said once. "It seems absurd for you to call me 'Monsieur' and I do not think of you as 'Mademoiselle'; I think of you as Valérie."

He did not understand either island custom or island etiquette, but there was a sincerity in him that she could not offend.

"It is very difficult to speak your name, Keller Barkley, in French," she said. "Would you like me to speak to you in English?"

He had laughed at that. "No. Just forget the 'Monsieur.' 'Kel' is not too difficult to say and I have been thinking in French since I have been here, so I would rather speak it."

She had never lived where it was required of her to think in English and that was one of the great gulfs between them. He belonged to a large world and she belonged to a small one. One night with her father and herself he looked at pictures in the picture books of American cities which they had long treasured and in which they did their traveling. He was very pleasant and interesting. He tried to answer all of their questions and he did not realize that he destroyed places that had a fond reality for them.

It seemed that the pictures were very old. There were no more elevated tracks in New York and many of the buildings were no longer there. There were other buildings. It was the same with Boston and Washington and Chicago, with everything changed. He did not know Detroit, Cleveland, or Buffalo well, but it was difficult to believe in those cities when the others no longer existed as she knew them.

"I will send you some guides and postcards when I return to the States," Keller Barkley said.

They thanked him gravely but they could not tell him that the new pictures would have no meaning. Valérie would risk no journey to Trois Rivières because she loved it as she imagined it and would not have it changed. No new version of New York, or any other American city, could replace the wonderful, exciting picture cities to which she had traveled with her father since she was a little girl. Her father would never see those postcards or guides that the American promised, and that was another cruel fact of this summer.

Life was running out on Louis-Charles Rivard. He knew it and made jokes about it. Valérie laughed with him because he needed laughter, but neither of them laughed inside. They were acceptors of the inevitable. Valérie would not have held him to life if she could. The load of pain that he carried so gallantly was heavy and he had earned the right to lay it down before it broke his courage or his pride. Her world would be a lonely place without him, but she would carry loneliness if he could lay down pain. There was so little else that she could do for him.

The American could not know these secret things, yet for some odd reason of his own, he seemed to be seeking knowledge of her life. He did not know Laure and how could anyone tell him of Laure? What possible reason could he have for wanting to know?

Laure, her aunt, had died too soon. Laure would have found strength and a will to live in her brother's need of her, if he had needed her while she lived as he needed her now. His pride would not permit his daughter to do for him the many tasks of his sickroom, nor place upon her his embarrassing dependence. He had hired Madame Lafleche, very old now, but grimly competent still, the midwife who had faced all human ills on the island before the doctor came. He abused her scandalously, but she never misunderstood him.

"This ancient *accoucheuse* is too old to learn new tricks," he said. "Because I am big of belly, she is hopeful that she will deliver me of something. She watches me with an obscene eye."

Madame Lafleche inhaled a pinch of snuff without blinking or changing expression. "I've delivered better than you of more than you could carry," she said, "and I'd learn a new trick, too, if you had the need of it."

There were many such exchanges between them. The American saw only the surface of things, but on that surface, he was good for Louis-Charles Rivard. He asked questions about the Canadien inheritance pattern and about farming and industrialization and politics. He argued and debated and he had a good mind. Louis-Charles was delighted with him.

"A fine mind, that, for large affairs," he said, "with no understanding of small ones. One sharpens ones brain on such a grindstone."

"He does not sharpen my brain," Valérie said. "What does he want of me?"

Her father smiled broadly. "He wants an excuse to visit *me*. What else?"

Valérie did not rise to raillery. "That is what I want to know. His attitude is most curious."

"He is young."

"He is thirty."

"An American is younger at thirty than a Canadien of twenty-five."

"In some ways."

166

"You are twenty and a woman. The odds are against a man. This man is more baffled than baffling, and you probably know it."

"You are not so wise as you sound," she said, "and you are of no help to me."

There was amusement in her father's eyes and she knew that he considered the American's interest as romantic, and that the thought did not displease him. He might change his mind if he considered the matter serious, but he was not thinking of that now. There were so many things that her father did not know and that she could not tell him.

"I'm going to walk as far as the church," she said. "I'll stop at Charbonneau's if you need anything."

"Nothing." Her father waved his hand. "Convey my respects to Saint Joachim. My regrets that I have not called."

He still made jests about matters religious, but no one who knew him took them as seriously as they did once. The image of Saint Joachim was a new one in the church and the idea amused him because he knew the history of it, the man who commissioned the carving of it and his motive. It was a funny story for another day. She might tell it to the American some time since the American liked to walk with a girl and ask questions about her childhood and questions about religion, as no other man would dream of doing. She returned the wave of a hand and walked out into the late afternoon.

She was twenty, her father said, and he had probably forgotten much of what that meant, if he had ever really known. It was so different for a man.

This summer of 1957 was a time of restlessness in the life of Valérie Rivard, of impatience and of a nameless frustration. The wheel of human destiny on Ile-aux-Erables was completing another full turn and she felt herself standing apart, a spectator, feeling the rhythm of Nature in her nerves, in her blood, in her emotional being; forced on the surface of her life to ignore the vibration in the air around her, walking decorously, innocent in deed if not in knowledge. It had been thus in the summer that she reached eighteen and again at nineteen, but twenty was urgent and there was a disturbing conflict within herself that she could not ignore nor pretend into nonexistence.

This was August, and the island throbbed with the fierce hot life of growing things; peas, beans, carrots and onions in the household gardens, corn and grain in the fields, fruit on the trees, potatoes in the earth, berries in the brûle. Men strained their muscles in a race against Time, women worked in the gardens and in the kitchens, canning and preserving against the needs of winter, children poured into the berry patches with their pails and baskets.

It was a time of work, intense and feverish, with September only the turn of a calendar leaf away, and no relaxing of the pace. The apple crop would be ready and the big barrels waiting, then the potatoes, which must be dug from the soil, and dozens of other seasonal tasks and chores depending upon the character of the individual farm. The dark would bring weariness, a pleasant lassitude, a joy in small talk, small relaxations, a little music. Sunday meant the solemnity of the Mass, a rest from labor, visiting and pairing off in front of the church, special guests at the family dinner, an easy day and the tensing of muscles to meet another week.

In all of this, men and women shared, knowing the need of the land for them, the need of each for the other. They were drawn close together in the common lot, in their work and in their weariness, their sense of accomplishment, and in their pride of doing well what must be done.

Valérie Rivard merely witnessed it, and felt it; she was not a part of it. She had never been a part of it except for brief intervals. Belonging to a farming community, she lacked farm skills. A girl grew on a farm as a tree grew, or any other living thing, knowing her place in the life around her, learning to play her part and to do her own work, sharing her future husband's life before she knew him.

For one who did not belong, the after-time was the most difficult, the days of fall when the sun no longer exerted a blazing pressure, when the wind off the river had a breath of the north in it, and the earth cooled. There was a lazy, languorous period after the fall plowing when men whistled as they did odd jobs around their homes, the splitting of firewood, the mending of fences, the repair of this and that, the leaning against a fence with a neighbor to share a pipe, watching the great geese flying overhead.

This was the time when women did their mending and their sewing, the working out of designs for hooked rugs or catalogne, usually in chatty, gossiping groups. The ruthless winds were gathering in the north then for their winter invasion, rounding up the snow packs, and everyone was aware of them, thinking of how snug and warm the house would be when living and working moved indoors. It was the time of marriages.

Nearly everyone on the island had been born in July or in August.

A woman felt the rhythm of the seasons when she was twenty. There was a great surge of masculine seeking when the heavy work of the year was over and done, a need for gentleness and kindness and the softer sharing after the companionship of toil and struggle, a need for fulfillment when one had reached the age for it.

A woman felt that surge as a beach must feel the strong tide rolling in. There was excitement in it and a wild beauty. A woman felt it in all of her body, in the swift flicker of images across her mind, in the yearning of her soul. There was chastity and a woman burned candles to it in faith and in fidelity, but she knew when she was ready to be sought and she knew when she no longer wanted to wait to give life back to life.

Thus Valérie Rivard, walking in the drowsy heat of the afternoon.

There were two men and they bore the same name, a name linked to most of the unhappiness that she had known.

André Drolet stood tall in her life. He was kind. He had understanding, such as few men have, for the moods, the bewilderments, the self-contradictions, the little personal privacies that no one was capable of putting into words. He anticipated a need for sympathy and his scorn was often the only sympathy that was needed; he never offered, or accepted, pity. He had a mind in which one might wander indefinitely without boredom, and a fierce, questing spirit that sought for beauty and for meaning in life. He was strong and masculine and there were hot fires banked within him, but he did not seek her as a man should seek a woman. He was imprisoned within a wall of his own building and it was not the way of happiness for her to scale that wall. She had tried to show him the way out, she had shared many experiences with him, and she had built memories with him; but the beach did not go to the tide, and could not.

Then there was Robert.

Valérie had known him all of her life and she had no illusions about him. He was selfish and had always been selfish. He cared for no one but himself and he had no loyalties. He did have charm and magnetism, an animal quality that was not all animal. There was a physical attraction that he exerted, that she felt, and that she despised herself for feeling. Until this summer he had been away from the island for three years. Valérie's curiosity had been tantalized by those three years, by the discovery of traits and habits that were strange in someone who was familiar. Being as he was, Robert was swift to sense her interest in him and to magnify it.

She had invited trouble and she knew it. There was no sense or fairness in blaming anyone else.

Robert was of the island, but he was no longer like anyone else on the island. He was aware of the strong feeling between men and women which ripened in the months of the hot sun, but what everyone knew and held as right and natural and inevitable, Robert treated as a discovery of his own, to be reduced to sly, insinuating words. He laughed at the normal island climax because it was simple, direct, and uncomplicated, the mating of two people in marriage under the laws of the Church and of Quebec Province, which permitted no divorce. In Robert's new environment, among the people he knew, one did not necessarily pledge anything; one acquired a certain knowledge and one laid siege to a woman's instincts, indifferent to her affections or to her emotions, amused at the very word, "love."

Her knowledge of the new Robert did not come all at once. She did not immediately understand him. He was boastful, but he had always been so, and vain and a show-off. He wore clothes that were spectacular and bizarre on Ile-aux-Erables but he wore them well and he was not self-conscious about them. They were part of the strangeness that made him exciting.

"You should come to Montreal," he said. "You are bilingual and you can earn a lot of money there. I could show you around. I know people."

He told her a little of his life in Montreal, where he sold sports equipment and instructed winter tourists in skiing. He talked well and she had always been interested in the places that she knew only in books, the places she had never seen. He flattered her and she was not accustomed to flattery. Even knowing it for what it was, she liked it. He tried to make love to her and he repelled her. He wanted her, but there was contempt for her in his wanting. He was interested only in that which she held in common with all women and not in anything that set her apart as one woman. There was no such factor as marriage in the equation of his wanting.

All of this Valérie Rivard could see and understand and evaluate, but discussion of it was impossible. There was no one with whom she would discuss it. She tried to avoid Robert Drolet, but the island was too small and it amused him when he discovered that she was trying to avoid him. She began to hate him then.

She hated Robert Drolet, not for anything that he was, himself, because he could be anything that he chose to be without affecting her; she hated him because he reduced her to something less than she was, because he put thoughts into her mind which she had forcibly to eject, because he showed her ugliness where she had always seen beauty.

Whenever they met, his eyes claimed a knowledge of her that he did not have, and when others were present, he always managed to convey the impression that there was some secret understanding between them. She could not quarrel with him, or lose her temper, without playing into his hands and providing fresh entertainment for him. Her only weapon was indifference and it was a weak sword, because she was not indifferent.

Robert was at his arrogant worst when the American was present and Keller Barkley did not like him. She considered that thoughtfully, then shook her head. She had reached the church and she walked into the cool hush of it, the half-light. The sanctuary lamp glowed before the shadowy altar and the massive oil painting of Christ and Saint Thomas was completely lost in the shadow. Jeanne Charbonneau was kneeling before the image of the Blessed Virgin. She was often there. She had children for whom to pray, children who lived in widely separated places. Before the Saint Joseph altar an old man knelt. She did not know which of the old men it was. There were a few in the village who could no longer work even at light tasks when the work was heavy in August. It was very sad for them.

Valérie slipped into the last pew, but she did not pray. Prayer had deserted her. She stared at the altar. It was so difficult to come, as one was commanded to do, with love for one's neighbor, with no ill feeling toward anyone. It was difficult to know, in the presence of God, what one wanted. One was free to choose from so many alternatives and it was a frightening freedom. She could pray for guidance but it was a prayer that froze in her throat. She feared that she would be guided into some destiny that she was not ready to accept, and that, of course, was wrong, a failure of love and a failure of faith. She sat staring at the altar and then, after a long time, she rose, genuflected, and left.

A tall shadow detached itself from the deeper shadow beneath the trees and moved into the thinning sunlight of late afternoon. Keller Barkley stood across her path and she looked up into his face. It was a strong face and, she thought, a handsome face. The tragic quality which she had marked in him before was more apparent today. There was a troubled expression in his eyes.

"Valérie," he said. "There is something that I would like to tell you. Could we walk to some place where we can talk, the cemetery or Anse-Saint-Jean?"

She considered, wavered, rejected, all in one tick of an invisible clock. She did not want to hear what Keller Barkley wanted to say to her. She was no more in a mood for it than she was for prayer.

"You may walk home with me," she said.

He gestured his dissent with one swing of his hand through a short arc. "I cannot talk to you while walking through the village."

"You have before."

"Not today." He looked at his wrist watch. "Do you have twenty minutes?"

"No, I'm sorry. I have an appointment."

She felt suddenly hostile toward him and she did not understand her own hostility. He was polite, as he always was, and patient; but his eyes had narrowed.

"It is important," he said. "Take my word for it. When can I talk to you, alone and uninterrupted, for twenty minutes?"

"Not tonight," she said. "Tomorrow will be Sunday, when everyone visits." She spread her hands. "Shall we leave it to chance?"

He stood very straight, looking at her, then he turned and strode away. "I don't believe in chance," he said.

She watched him for a moment and she remembered her father

saying that an American of thirty was younger than a Canadien of twenty-five. Her father had a strange wisdom. She walked toward home, but she was not going home. She had had only one destination through all of this hot afternoon, but she had chosen not to follow a straight line.

# VI

There was a gate in the fence of the Rivard property that opened on the path leading to the house. If one passed the gate and walked to the end of the fence line, there was another path which led to an old stone structure which was the workshop of André Drolet. It was on the Rivard property and it had been there when Louis-Charles purchased the place, probably a survival from the old regime before the original farms were cut up into village properties. Valérie's father had never found a use for it and he had been delighted when he discovered that André needed an atelier. Characteristically, he hid his delight, as he hid his benevolence, under gruffness.

"You will rid it of its porcine phantoms," he said. "I have always suspected that the place was a morgue for pigs."

The idea amused André and the first work that he did there was the carving of two signs, in simulation of street signs. He placed them at right angles to each other on one corner of the structure: "RUE MORGUE" and "PLACE DES COCHONS MORTS."

"I not only have an atelier, I have an address," he said. "It is most elegant."

That was in 1955, when André returned to the island, with Korea behind him, and many hospitals, and much study under the disabled veterans' rehabilitation program. Valérie was eighteen and he was twenty-three. He had lost a leg in a war that no one on the island approved. His uncle, Edmond Gagnon, refused to speak to him because he left college to serve in that war. It was a bad time for André, a very bad time. Those who did not disapprove of him to the point of hostility were sympathetic to the point of pity—and one was as bad as the other.

Valérie considered André a hero and she was dazzled by all the places that he had visited and the strange sights that he had seen. They cleaned and scrubbed and polished the interior of the old stone structure together. When he found it difficult to perform some task while wearing his artificial leg, or difficult to maintain balance with his crutch, she found work to do which kept her back turned to him. She never helped him with any task unless he asked for help. As he developed confidence in her, it no longer embarrassed him to ask. He was able, then, to make jokes about his own clumsiness. When it seemed natural to laugh at him, she laughed.

It was one of the happiest periods of her life, in spite of all that Madame Drolet did to complicate it.

Valérie walked down the little path now and the street signs were still in place. The door to André's atelier had more dignity. A muscular hand, carved from dark wood, held his name plate:

ANDRÉ DROLET
graveur sur bois

There was a knocker but Valérie entered without knocking, as she always did. André was working on his statue of Saint Paul, with a spotlight in place upon the floor, the beam focused on his work. He was wearing a blue sports shirt which was dark with perspiration between the shoulder blades and molded to the outlines of his powerful chest. His duck trousers had once been white but they were streaked with paint, stain, shellac, and a dozen nameless elements. He was molding and massaging the face of the image with his fingers, as he always did when he was in the final stages. He whistled as he worked: no particular melody, merely a low, cheerful sound.

André did not hear her enter and Valérie stood in the doorway watching him. He had recovered from his fall and he was wearing his leg. It was remarkable how many things he had learned to do on that leg since those first uncertain days when he returned to the island. He had broad, powerful shoulders and hands of astonishing strength, long-fingered hands. He worked with rapt concentration, loving the work that he did.

"May I enter for a small fee?" Valérie asked.

André lifted his head and turned slowly to face her. "How small is this fee?"

"Miserable. I am tired of my own company, which I find very dreary today. I want to give it to somebody."

"A poor gift." His eyes narrowed. "What is the matter with you?"

"Nothing. I am merely being a woman."

André shrugged. "There is no cure for that. The fee is not enough. What else have you?"

"Appreciation."

"No. Have you critical faculties?"

"Yes. A few small ones."

He nodded his head gravely. "Accepted! What do you think of Saint Paul?"

There was always a lot of nonsense and make-believe on the surface of her relationship to André. It seemed to belong to this atmosphere of careless disorder, of carved figures finished and unfinished, of blocks of wood that would some day have features and personalities because a man willed it so. There was a taint of varnish in the air but it was subordinated to the clean fragrance of many woods, the distinctive scent of balsam.

Valérie walked slowly across the room to the figure of Saint Paul, which was one of three images for a church in a new industrial town on the lower Saint Lawrence, a commission which meant much to André and to his career.

The image was five feet tall and it had a dynamic quality in it, as did all of André's work in wood. He did not follow the tradition of passive saints. There was life and inner stress and a feeling of emotion in his human figures as there was in this Saint Paul, who leaned forward slightly, one hand raised, arrested forever in midsentence as he preached. Valérie studied the face intently, her head on one side, frowning. This study of character in faces was something that André had taught her to do when he discovered that she had an aptitude for it. She had very quickly reached the point where she could discuss with him at length the character behind a face in a painting or an illustration in a book. She moved around the Saint Paul, then moved away. She raised her eyes to the intent eyes of André.

"He looks mean," she said.

"Mean?" André lunged forward, startled. "Impossible!"

"Mean! And avaricious."

"You are mad."

She stood facing him, conceding nothing. "How did you feel him?"

André reached into the breast pocket of his shirt for a cigarette. He extracted it from the package with two fingers and rolled it around in his hand.

"Saul of Tarsus!" he said thoughtfully. "A hard character. Intolerant. Eloquent. Uncompromising. Tactless. Courageous. Tough enough to swallow his own medicine. But, mean? No! Avaricious? Certainly not!"

"Look at him!"

André hung the cigarette on his lip and rolled it to the corner of his mouth. He gripped the image in both hands, tipping it backward so that he could look into the face. He turned it one way and then another. He took the cigarette from his mouth and passed it to Valérie without speaking. He whistled softly as he picked up one tool and then another, selecting the one that he wanted. He went to work, then, on the face, his blade seeming barely to touch the wood. He concentrated upon the eyes and upon the wrinkles that radiated from them. He touched the corner of the mouth, the two lines beside the bold, prominent nose.

Valérie held her breath. He worked swiftly, silently, without pausing to study what he was doing. When he laid the tool aside, he pressed his fingers on the wood, seemingly into it, the muscles ridging in his forearms. He relaxed his grip and massaged the face gently. He studied the image with narrowed eyes, then stretched out his hand for his cigarette.

"Now?" he said.

Valérie studied the face again. It was like looking into a completely different face. She had seen this miracle happen before but it was no less a miracle the second time, or the third, or the fourth time that it happened.

"That's it," she said enthusiastically. "That is what you wanted! The meanness is gone. He is strong. Not patient, but wise. I think that is what I want to say. I don't believe I would like him, but I would have confidence in him."

"I don't imagine that very many people liked him, but they believed him."

André lighted his cigarette. He sat on the tall stool beside the bench and his entire body relaxed. "It is easy to slip into the weakness of strength," he said. "So many strong qualities become weaknesses if they grow too strong. They show in the face. Sometimes it is only in the shading of a line; or two fine lines as against one bold one. It is always a challenge."

He looked thoughtfully again at the image. "I did not hold all of his qualities in mind. I may have permitted myself to think of Paul as a bigot. He was not that. Not quite! But he had the strength of a bigot. That is where the meanness came from. I could perceive it when you indicated it. I cannot explain the avarice. I did not see that."

"It may not have been there. I saw something that I did not like and that is the name that I gave to it."

"I needed your eyes. I was too close to it."

Valérie sat on a low stool, hugging her skirt around her knees. This was one of the wonderful moments when all of the normal, everyday problems, big and small, seemed unimportant, when she felt herself a part of André and of his work, a participant in the awesome process of creation. This image of Saint Paul would be finished and stained and received by a distant church that she would never see. It would be blessed and placed in a niche. Countless people would look at it and pray before it. They would think of the great epistles and of the tireless man who traveled far and suffered much and converted so many. The image would age and mellow and remain in its niche after all of her own story was told, after she was gone. Through all of the years it would have a little of herself in it because she had been honest with André as she had always been honest with him. It would be only a little of herself and very much of André, but she would be there.

"You will be finished soon," she said.

"Another week, or less. I will take them to the church then."

"It will be good for you to have the trip."

"I will like it. I have never seen one of these towns that the big companies build."

"They must be ugly."

"Yes. But what is beauty? Many people consider my carving ugly. They would prefer a plaster horror from Rue Saint-Sulpice in Montreal. I will not go to this town, Valérie, looking for what is ugly in it."

Neither of them heard the door open and they were not aware of the woman who entered and who stood, as Valérie had stood, outside of the circle of light, watching them. They were startled when she spoke, but only slightly so, interrupted in mid-conversation but not astonished. It had happened before and in the same manner.

"I suppose that I can wait again with your dinner until you are ready to come, as I have waited often, and for your father before you."

The voice of Céleste Drolet was cold, uninflected, but there was a world of hostility in it, glacial hostility that had no spark of anger or human passion to warm it. She advanced slowly into the room and the light was harsh to her.

Céleste was only fifty but there were women of seventy on the island who looked younger. She was thin and wiry and her hair was gray, with streaks, or tints, of lighter color through it, like silver that is neglected and unpolished. She wore it pulled back severely into a bun. Her features were thin and sharp, her mouth a pale, straight line. Her pride of appearance survived only in the clothing that she wore. Her dark green dress was old but freshly ironed, her apron stiff and gleaming white. André rose, balancing himself momentarily with the tips of his fingers resting on the bench.

"You never have to wait long," he said gently. His eyes lifted to the clock on the wall. "It is not time yet. Not for a half hour."

Céleste looked at, and through, Valérie. She had not spoken to her in years. Her darting glance returned to her son. "If your work is done, I have work enough with which I would be glad of a little help," she said. "And if you have time for talking, you might think of your mother." She turned away, walking stiffly. "But I am not interesting enough for you, I suppose."

She slammed the door behind her and the echo from the second room of the studio, beyond, was like muffled thunder. André drew one last inhalation from his cigarette and, by his expression, he found it bitter. He crushed the stub in the bottom third of a tin can that he had fashioned into an ash tray. His hatred of scenes was in his face, and his humiliation at being confronted in the presence of another person with a situation which he could not control or change.

Valérie did not intrude upon the interval of silence which she knew that he needed. This incident, one of so many similar incidents, illumined painfully in André the strength of which he spoke, the quality which grows strong to the point of weakness. His patience and his gentleness to his mother deserved another name, one that Valérie could not find in her vocabulary. He was in slavery to her. It was worse, in a way, seeing him like this than watching him when he was learning to do his work on one leg. He made sacrifices that were without meaning and he accepted a dominance that was without intelligence, which led him in futile circles to no accomplishment, to no conceivable happiness. Valérie's hands clenched into fists. She could not turn her back and pretend that she did not notice.

André's mother had no interest in his work. She either ignored it or belittled it. Her tongue was never kind to him, and often cruel. She accepted support from André, contemptuous of him that he had little, boastful of Robert's alleged successes in Montreal, which Robert never shared with her.

Valérie looked at the image of Saint Paul. She thought of the deep lines in the face of Céleste. If only André could work in flesh as he worked in wood! It would probably take no more time or effort than he had expended on this image tonight to soften those rigid lines, those tight distortions, to change the strength of hatred into love, self-pity into resignation, scorn into kindness, cruelty into compassion. He couldn't do it, of course. No one could. Human flesh resisted change more than did the hardest of woods.

The silence was suddenly intolerable. "What is the matter with Robert?" she said. "Why doesn't he help with the work since he does nothing? Or provide companionship if that is what is needed?"

Her doubt was in her voice. No one had more relatives on the island, nor more roads to escape from loneliness than a daughter of the Gagnons. André raised his head to meet her eyes.

"She has convinced herself that Robert will take her to Montreal with him when he leaves. She talks about meeting all of the people whom he knows, the English and the Americans."

Valérie drew her breath in sharply. "He hasn't promised her anything like that, has he?"

"Of course not. It is all in her own mind."

André spoke softly. There was pity in his voice, and in his eyes.

He offered pity—the least of the gifts that he, or anyone else, had to offer—to no one but his mother. There was sadness in that. It was the quality that she commanded.

Valérie tried to close her mind to the thought of Céleste Drolet building, against all reason, another hurt, another disappointment, for herself. Céleste had to know, if she let herself think at all, that Robert would not take her to Montreal, nor do anything for her that would call for effort or sacrifice on his part. She would not let herself know.

It was difficult to look at the man across the room. They were sharing now, she and André, the foreknowledge of future unhappiness that was not of their making. They had so much else to share, so much that was worth the sharing, but the way seemed forever blocked, needlessly blocked.

She rose abruptly and crossed to the figure of John the Baptist which André had completed before he had started the Saint Paul. She looked at it with misty eyes and waited for the mist to clear. André's John was strongly built, but his features were cleanly, delicately carved. This was a man who would be hard to break, but not a fighter. He was standing with his chin held high. There was an odd expression in his mouth and eyes, an expression difficult to interpret. He seemed to be facing an experience that he dreaded, something that frightened him, but before which he would not give way.

There was drama in the pose and she had asked André if this was the moment when John the Baptist faced his sentence of death from the lips of Herod. André had shrugged and said: "It could be. All I know is that I saw him like that."

An artist could make such statements but André rarely did. She turned to him now.

"Has Antoine Masson seen this yet, André?"

He came back slowly from wherever his thoughts had taken him. "No. Why should he?"

"Because anyone who sees it will recognize Antoine."

"The people of this new parish have never seen Antoine."

"It would disturb him to hear of it. It would be better if you showed it to him."

"I may do so." André looked thoughtfully at his own handiwork.

"I have embarrassed neither John the Baptist nor Antoine, Valérie," he said slowly. "I have paid them both honor."

He spoke solemnly, seriously, and the depth of some feeling that he had for Antoine Masson was in his voice, a feeling that she had never quite understood. She parted her lips to speak and there was a sharp click from the clock that signaled the completion of an hour. She turned expectantly, as she always did.

The clock had been, once, a mere cuckoo clock, but now it was like no other clock in the world. André had replaced the small, plain door of the cuckoo with a door that he had carved himself, the door of an habitant's house. It opened and the habitant himself emerged; a bent old farmer with his toque, his long coat, his pipe and tobacco pouch, his big muddy boots. No cuckoo sound accompanied him. He coughed six times to announce the hour and retired. Valérie shook her head.

"His cough sounds worse," she said. "When is Polycarpe going to stop smoking?"

"What would you? If he quit tobacco, we would never know what time it is."

Their eyes met and laughed together. André had an affection for his own creation and there were long hours when Polycarpe of the clock was his only companion. They had shared many small jokes at the expense of Polycarpe before this, but laughter was short tonight.

André bent to turn off the lamp and Valérie hesitated before she walked to the door. It was the dinner hour, *Chez* Drolet, and Céleste must not be kept waiting. It would be good, Valérie thought, if life were as simple as a joke, if Polycarpe could be deprived of his tobacco pouch and time would cease to be. She felt the presence of André close behind her and she turned slowly to stand facing him in the shadow of a spreading maple.

She looked up into his face, into his eyes. The heat of August weighted the air and the throb of life and growth was in the ground beneath them. André looked tired, haggard, and Valérie knew with certainty the struggle between André, the man, and André, the son of a mother who was pitiable. She would not have helped him if she could, but she sensed his moving away from her while they still faced each other, less than a foot apart. He seemed to grow taller as he withdrew within himself. He touched her shoulder with his fingers, a brushing touch. There was affection in the gesture, but what was that?

"Good night, Valérie," he said.

He turned down the path toward his home and she stood motionless for a moment, willing him to turn back, but he did not do so. She knew the arguments, the weary thoughts, in his mind. He could seek her on only one leg, carrying on his back a woman who hated her. He permitted himself to stop there. He was a man. A man had to seek a woman as he was, bringing with him what he had; the woman could always escape him if she wished to do so, but she could not pursue, not a woman who was woman. He was very blind, André——

She walked slowly back to the fence line and a stately, dignified white cat joined her, one of the males. He had the air of bestowing his company rather than of accepting hers, so she did not stoop to the banality of petting him or playing with him. When they reached her own gate, he sat in the middle of the road, watching her solemnly, his eyes like small yellow flames.

"Good night, Monsieur le Chat," she said.

She mocked André with mimicry, but it was an empty performance. André was not present to hear her, so she mocked only herself. The white cat sat in the road, indifferent, absorbed in an inner, secret life of his own, watching her open the gate which, at the moment, had no interest for him.

There was supper, *Chez* Rivard, also, and Valérie prepared it. but the clock did not command her. She made a point of that to herself, knowing that it was a childish point. Her household was not a normal one. Most women obeyed clocks. She sat with her father, after the dishes were washed, and sipped wine to keep him company while he drank island brandy diluted with water in a highball. He ate little and drank little now, but this was an interval that he loved, whether he spent it with her or with someone else who would talk with him. She wanted to talk about André's Saint Paul, so she talked about Keller Barkley.

"What do you think of the American now?" she said.

"A good man, but young. There is a tragedy in him somewhere that has derailed him. I can feel another man inside of him. Can you?"

"Yes. That is true."

Valérie had not put words to her own impressions, but she nodded quickly, recognizing in her father's summation an unvoiced thought of her own. Her mind moved into that thought. The idea of another man within the man she knew was intriguing.

"It is not easy for him here," her father said. "He is a writer of big affairs, which are often ridiculous. In those affairs, a farmer is a statistic. This young man has met his statistic vis-à-vis and he does not recognize him."

Valérie waited. Her father liked to discuss people and theorize about them. This analysis tonight was oddly similar to her own analysis of André's Saint Paul.

"The Catholic Church is an abstraction to him," Louis-Charles said. "He has regarded it as something that the people had before they had science, something that bears the same relationship to his world of affairs as does the privy to modern plumbing."

"That is a crude comparison."

"It is exact. He is crudely civilized. Suddenly the Catholic Church is all around him. It unnerves him."

"He did not seem unnerved to me."

"Nevertheless, he is. He has a purpose on the island. I do not know it, nor care. It is his concern. He cannot accomplish it. He understands facts and does not comprehend the truth behind facts. That limits him."

Louis-Charles Rivard was suddenly drowsy, as he so often was with this evening drink. "This American conceives truth to be a liquid," he said sleepily, "which one pours into the jug of the mind. His mind is a good jug, but truth will not take the shape of his container because it has a form of its own."

He blinked and nodded, then opened his eyes wide. "On the other hand," he said. "I like this American. He is honest—I respect his mind."

His eyes closed again. Valérie sat quietly for five minutes. When she was certain that her father was asleep, she rearranged the pillows behind his head and dimmed the light. She walked to the door and stood looking at the stars. They were very bright tonight and they seemed to be concentrated above the island in a low sky. The cricket chorus was harsh, unmusical, a distant rise and fall of sound. Nearby, *le rossignol* sang. He wasn't actually a nightingale; he was a white-throated sparrow. One name or another, his voice was an added touch of loveliness to night.

She wished that she had walked with Keller Barkley and listened to what he had to say, instead of going to the atelier of André Drolet.

# VII

It was Saturday night at Charbonneau's. The people who came in
from the distant farms were making purchases at the store, visiting,
laughing, talking. It was a big, sprawling place, Charbonneau's, with so
many additions and wings built onto it that one could not tell where
the original farmhouse began or ended.

The store held everything: groceries, canned goods, cosmetics,
patent medicines, shoes, boots, articles of clothing, hardware, baby
bottles and nipples, radio tubes, candy and chewing gum, cigarettes
and tobacco, a new spinning wheel. Keller Barkley had always associated spinning wheels with antique shops and it had startled him
to discover that they were still manufactured, that one could buy them
new.

"Why not?" Paul Charbonneau said. "The young girls starting
out do not always inherit them. Not all of them want spinning wheels,
of course. Times are changing. But?"

He shrugged eloquently. Times were changing, but had not yet
changed. In addition to his stock on hand, he had the catalog of
Dupuis Frères on the counter. Dupuis Frères of Montreal was to
Quebec Province what Sears Roebuck and Montgomery Ward were
to the rural United States. In a special room of her own, Madame
Charbonneau worked with the catalog, also. Young women consulted
solemnly with her, turning the pages of dresses, hats, handbags, shoes,
costume jewelry. She advised and she measured, and she could always
tell a girl if someone else in her own circle had ordered a dress like the
one that she had in mind. Women who could have ordered direct, out
of the catalogs in their homes, preferred to order from Jeanne

Charbonneau and pay a little more for the added thrill of shopping. She was their Fifth Avenue.

Madame Charbonneau saw nothing paradoxical in the fact that spinning wheels and ready-made clothing were sold under the same roof and to the same people. "But, certainly, monsieur," she said, "we can all sew, and weave, and make our own thread from island flax, but we are women. If one is fortunate, there should be some article in the mode for each season, *n'est-ce pas?*"

So, men and women came to the store on Saturday night, many of them on their way to, or from, confession. Women gathered in their own secret rendezvous with Jeanne Charbonneau, and another group, all men, occupied the chairs in the big room that opened off the store. They played checkers or cards, or they sat in tight, argumentative circles. There was a TV set but no one turned it on. The entertainment which TV brought to them was alien and they were capable of providing entertainment which was their own.

At another time, and in another mood, Keller Barkley would have enjoyed a place on the fringes of this company, where his presence could be ignored. This was the cracker-box forum of Quebec and men spoke freely, many different types of men. Some of them came directly from their work, bringing with them the sweat of the day and the odors of the barn, lending force to Paul Charbonneau's amused comment that not all of the island air was perfumed. Some of them, too, were prodigious spitters and the room was liberally equipped with cuspidors. There were rough, coarse, belligerent men and men with fine, tranquil faces and intelligent eyes.

Tonight there was less argument and more of indignant agreement. As Barkley understood the issue, English-Canadian management, always referred to as "English" in this company, had sent in German immigrants to break a strike of Canadien workers at Murdochville on the Gaspé. It was part of a larger pattern, the forum was convinced, whereby the wealthy English Protestants of Toronto proposed to offset superior French virility by importing workers from non-Catholic, anti-French sections of Europe to compete with Canadien workers on projects which were looting the resources of Quebec to fill English and American pockets.

"They begrudge to us even the niggardly workman's share of the treasure they are taking from our soil," one voice said.

Keller Barkley's combative spirit was stirred. Without knowing anything about the subject at issue, he knew that the situation was not as simple as they made it. Nothing was ever that simple. It was tragic for Canada, all of Canada, that such mistrust existed between two elements of the population. He hesitated, listening to the voices, remembering a conversation that he had had with Louis-Charles Rivard.

"We are a stubborn people, a difficult people, and a trial, no question of it, to the English, who blame us for division in the country," Louis-Charles said. "But look you, monsieur! When does Toronto have its biggest parade? It is to celebrate the Battle of the Boyne River in Ireland. They carry a statue of England's King William the Third, in that parade, they who deride the statues in our churches! When he was King of England, the history of Canada was completely French. So why do they honor him in Toronto? Because, my friend, he defeated a combination of French and Irish Catholics at that battle of the Boyne in 1690, a battle which had nothing to do with Canada. We are not the only stubborn and difficult ones dividing Canada, m'sieu."

Keller Barkley had only the one version of that parade and its significance. Again, the matter was probably not as simple as Louis-Charles Rivard made it, but any cleavage between the two races who lived together, and governed together, in Canada was worth thinking about. He had made a note to look up the other side of the question.

Paul Charbonneau hailed him as he turned away from the big room and walked toward the stairs. "Hé, monsieur! You are, perhaps, thirsty. You will share with us *un p'tit coup?*"

The broad face was lighted by a smile, the slightly protruding eyes gleamed with friendliness. Barkley hesitated again. A drink would be good, the conversation incidental to the drink would be even better. There were so many facts, ideas, and viewpoints here that fascinated and challenged him. He shook his head regretfully.

"I would like it very much. But not tonight. I have work that I must do."

"But yes. One understands that, m'sieu."

Before he mounted the stairs, Barkley could hear the voice of Paul Charbonneau explaining that the American could not take time for pleasantry. "This writing of a book is like the marrying of a young wife," he said. "One does not go out at night. No?"

Monsieur Charbonneau had no idea of the nature of his guest's book, but he was proud beyond all measure that a book was being written under his roof. It was, he said many times, a great honor to his house. He did not read books but he conceived of a book, any book, as belonging to the main stream of literature. He thought of no minor figures when he thought of literature, only of great names. The sound of Keller Barkley's typewriter was like sacred music to him. All of which was highly embarrassing.

Keller Barkley stood in the middle of his own room and lighted a cigarette. By the mere act of closing a door he shut out the island, the Province of Quebec, and all of it pieties and its problems. He had grown accustomed to the room, almost fond of it; the massive bed, the ancient beams above his head, the profusion of windmills and children and dogs and running water in the wallpaper. He had even grown accustomed to the crucifix, which was a symbol of the place in which he found himself, a symbol of vast and awe-inspiring dignity. He had blocked out of his mind the two exposed hearts which faced each other across the room, and he was seldom aware of them. He looked at the pile of manuscript beside his portable typewriter.

The book had grown in the past week. He had worked hard, grimly hard, but he was not satisfied with what he had accomplished. He had done his best chapter on the alleged vision at La Salette because he disliked the children involved and he had notes on their later lives which seemed to support his thesis. He was having a more difficult problem with Bernadette of Lourdes, but he did not consider it insurmountable. On the simplest chapter of all, the chapter of an admitted hoax, with the people involved and with all the associations around him, he had made no progress. He had failed, he told himself, because he had not faced the issue head-on, which was the only way that he knew how to face anything.

He had sought Valérie today with the intention of laying his intents and purposes before her, asking the questions that he had to ask and getting on with the task that he had come here to accomplish. She had been as remote as the stars and she had neatly evaded him. She would not give him twenty minutes, now or in future time.

"Let us leave it to chance," she said.

She did not know what he wanted to say, of course, but it had not made any difference to her. She had been indifferent even beyond the point of curiosity.

"And maybe it is better that way," he said.

He could move along his own lines now, freed from any idea that he was being unfair to her in seeking, from any source, the truth of what had happened on the day that she claimed that she had a vision. The advice of the priest had cost him a week. He had gained nothing but a knowledge of many irrelevancies through the method of meeting and knowing people. The straight line to what he wanted was the asking of questions. He had known that from the beginning and he was a fool for permitting himself to be diverted.

He had a momentary vision of Valérie's dark eyes, the white flash of her smile, the touching earnestness in her expression when she was trying to explain something, the intent way in which she listened when she was interested, listening with her whole body. He had seen so many of her moods, most of them charming, then today she had been cold and aloof. A man learned nothing from a woman's projected idea of herself.

He seated himself at the typewriter and picked up a sandwich of paper, a white sheet and a yellow sheet with carbon paper between them. This was the moment that brought Sally close, the moment when he settled down to work on the book, but it worried him that she seemed to be leaving him, that it was more difficult every day to feel her presence beside him as he had felt it when he had started to write. The island was partly responsible and the room. Sally would not have liked the island. When he had tried once to see the room through her eyes rather than his own, it had looked shabby, crude, assembled without taste, unbalanced in color and in the distribution of the heavy objects that furnished it. He and Sally would not have come here, of course; he was here because he had lost her.

As he rolled the paper into his machine, he saw her again as he had seen her that first night, a small, blonde girl in a white gown against all of that white marble in the Cuban Embassy. He saw her, flushed with champagne and half asleep, in his apartment, dictating her story. He closed his eyes and he could hear her funny little offbeat voice. He could still recall a few phrases, meaningless to him at the time, meaningless yet. They ran around in his mind to the uneven rhythm of the well-remembered voice.

"Burnt sugar crepe—girdle of gold—circular bodice—panniers——"

It was a long, long way to Washington, to the big embassy parties, to the world that he and Sally had known. There were many, many miles between the women downstairs, selecting their dresses and accessories from the catalog of Dupuis Frères and the women whose gowns Sally had photographed at a glance and remembered. He frowned, dissatisfied with his own conclusion. The women might, after all, be more alike than different, women who were expressing themselves in clothes. It made no difference.

Where, he wondered, did these women of Ile-aux-Erables wear the clothes that they selected so carefully? There were no public places; no cafés or theaters, cocktail lounges or restaurants, or big hotels; no place to dance, or, as on Dufferin Terrace in Quebec, to promenade. He had mentioned that to Valérie and she had laughed softly.

"There are many things that we do," she said, "but this is a season of work. No one has time to play. Stay on the island until the work is done and you will learn many things."

She would not elaborate on that statement. It was one of her secrets and she kept secrets well. Invariably he left her with the baffled feeling that a conversation had been merely started. He had only snatched moments with her, walking to, or from, the astonishing number of places where she worked, and he met very few of the island people during the long days. He seemed to be the only one on the island who had no work to do.

He frowned at the white sheet of paper in his machine. That was not true. He did have work to do. He was writing a book.

The island was in the book, but he did not know the island. Day after day it was the same, with scarcely any change in the weather. What was it like when the deep snows blanketed down? Or in the springtime? He remembered his driver on the day when he traveled through the fogs of fever. "Let me take you to Murribé," the man had said. "There is nothing on the island." How long would it take a man to learn all there was to know about nothing? Valérie——

He snapped his fingers. Damn Valérie! He did not want to think about her. He knew what winter was like in Washington. Damned disagreeable sometimes, but one got around. He and Sally used to dance at the Shoreham Terrace when they were feeling festive. They were invited to a lot of big parties. They attended a number of parties at the White House, among other places. They stayed home and worked. Sometimes their two typewriters would beat out a duet and they would not speak to each other for hours. There was an odd comfort in the companionship of another typewriter when your own was singing. Sometimes one of them had work to do and did it while the other read or did some doodling thing. When the work was done, they ate anything that was in the refrigerator and washed it down with coffee, and it made no difference what time it happened to be. They laughed at people who were kept awake by coffee.

In the spring Washington was a garden. One could not talk about it without sounding like a sentimentalist; one looked at it, smelled it, felt it. He and Sally would sit in their car and look at the river and talk about life and about themselves. The Potomac might look like a creek if one were accustomed to looking at the Saint Lawrence, but it had its own beauty. When they were not feeling famous, or important, or elegant, he and Sally would cross over to the Virginia side, to a drive-in called The Hot Shoppe and look at the river backwards, with the old red buildings of Georgetown University on the hill and all that terrific panorama of the monuments and public buildings, the Washington Monument spire, and the Capitol, spread out and sparkling in the sun. Sally often made odd remarks that were strangely memorable even when the meaning, if any, was obscure.

"Beauty frightens me," she said once. "I always have the feeling that I have no right to look at it."

She had introduced him to good music and even made him understand a little of it; and to ballet, which repelled him at first and which he learned to enjoy. He took her to baseball games, where she was ignorant but willing, as he was with music.

How, he wondered, did they develop baseball players in Quebec when all the heavy work demand coincided with baseball weather? The answer was that they didn't. They imported baseball players and raised their own hockey players, the best in the world, and their own skiers. He was here in the wrong season, but it was in summer that Valérie claimed that she saw the vision, so summer was the season that he had to experience.

He made an impatient gesture, brushing the island out of his life.

He tapped the space bar of the typewriter, staring at the white sheet. He had to get the work rolling.

He saw Sally in that tiny room that they had had at Lourdes, with that awful desperation in her eyes. He had made a fool of himself at Lourdes, and a nuisance. He was Keller Barkley and he wanted a miracle and he needed it in a hurry. He had talked to doctors, priests, anybody and everybody, but there were so many people and so many logical, orderly, French procedures which stood between them and the healing waters. When they had got through all the paper work and the rest of it, nothing had happened. They had to try again, with the frightened feeling that the miracles, if any, would go to the insiders; to the people who knew what was going on in all of the rituals and ceremonies and processions, as they certainly did not.

Sally had never conceded. She never said "if"; she said "when."

"When I am better, Kel," she said, "when I feel stronger, I have an idea for a novel that we have got to do. You'll have to do most of it because you write better, but some of it I have clear in my own mind. Maybe I'll dictate that part to you, like I did that first night, remember?"

He sat beside her, holding her hand, keeping alive the hope that they both had to have. "You will probably have to dictate most of it if it's a novel," he said, "or type it yourself. I can't use words to paint portraits or landscapes; all that I can do is draw cartoons with them."

"You're wonderful," she said, "and we will do our novel together. It will be a child, Kel. Yours and mine. It may be the only kind of a child that I can ever give you, but it will be ours."

He patted her hand until he could bring his voice back out of silence, past the hard, tight obstruction in his throat. When it did come back, it was husky with the words that he could not say.

"We'll have a lot of them, Bluebonnet," he said, "and we are the only ones who will know their true names."

That was their last night. Sally died the next day in that miserable French town, with the rain beating down and the wind playing a dirge on the chimney tops.

Keller Barkley sat motionless, staring at the paper. The sound of voices floated in through his open window, voices raised in argument downstairs.

He swore softly. A child might lie and build up phantoms or visions to make herself important, and it would make no difference to anyone unless adults, who should know better, or who wanted to be important themselves, took the childish lie and built it bigger. It made a difference then. It mattered when it resulted in the raising of a heartbreaking hope, when desperate people brought their belief and laid it trustingly at the feet of a lie, as Sally had done.

His fingers started to move on the keys. He wrote grimly, savagely, oblivious of the world around him. He wrote for hours, without even a pause for a cigarette; then suddenly, he stopped, at the end of his line, written out. He did not read what he had written, but he was excited about it.

Tonight he had found the key to this whole fraudulent business. The children were always in the forefront of these miracle and vision legends, because children disarmed suspicion; but behind the scenes there was an adult, or adults, stage-managing the whole production. There had to be. Once the hoax was perpetrated and acceptance won for it, the children were whisked off the stage to a vague, shadowy area of holiness while the adults took over. Without adults to exploit their imaginative falsehoods, the children would grow up as Valérie had, no longer giving a thought to the wild tales that they had told when they were very young.

He had roughed the idea out in detail, drawing on all of the cases that he had studied, working without referring to his notes, remembering without effort the incidents that he needed to illustrate his point. He had stopped when he reached the end of the adult section. He could not get inside the children as children. He did not know any children intimately and the years of his own childhood had a tendency to run together in his memory. When an event stood out sharply, he could remember the circumstances of the moment and recall how old he had been at the time of the event, but he could not actually get back into the boy that he had been.

He had made friends, after a fashion, of the children he met on his walks. They were the most polite, and possibly the most handsome, children he had ever known, but he did not have the knack of conversing with them on their own level. He could not imagine Valérie as a child of eight. He had never known Sally as a child, of course, and neither he nor Sally had ever engaged in childhood reminiscences. They had lived in the moment that they had until she had been so badly hurt. After that, the future had been important to them, but not the past.

The sound of voices floated in through his window, no longer raised in argument or noisy discussion; a monotonous, droning sound now, a rising and falling of voices in irregular cadence. In spite of his antagonism and deeply rooted prejudice, he listened with a feeling of awe. These men who assembled at Charbonneau's had spent their evening at checkers or cards, drinking beer, debating the events of the day, telling stories, and now they were preparing to go home. Before they parted, they knelt down to say the rosary together, praying for one another and for their families.

It was unbelievable. It was incredible. It belonged to the innocence of the world before Evil came. Yet, there it was!

Some of these same people had knelt, intoning that same chain of prayer, in this room, praying for Keller Barkley, a stranger, whom they believed to be dying. Not even the bitter memory of rosaries being said in dozens of languages at Lourdes was strong enough to make Barkley forget that. Men whom one did not know made one a gift out of their simple faith and vast sincerity. One could not forget it. Prayer on Ile-aux-Erables was not, as he had always regarded it, a mere superstitious practice; it was something that the people had to give to each other, to anyone who needed it. Moreover, it was a gift that the most humble could offer to the most exalted. There was an odd kind of democracy in it.

The tempo of the voices quickened and the listener knew that the five decades were finished and that the prayers of conclusion would not take long. He listened then to the good nights that were being said, shook his shoulders to ease the tension that had built in him, and went downstairs. It was late, but he could not permit himself to be stopped against a wall. Sleep would not come to him if he did.

The space below was strangely still and deserted. Keller Barkley could hear Monsieur Charbonneau in the store, noisily putting away items of stock, closing up for the night. Madame Charbonneau was probably in her fitting room. He sat in a big, heavily padded chair to wait for them and picked up a newspaper that someone had left. It was folded to the comics page, and they were the same comics that he had read in the United States; the same, yet different, as all things here were different.

Here were characters whom he knew: Mickey Finn, Joe Palooka, Dennis the Menace, Mickey Mouse. In the Province of Quebec, these characters not only spoke French, but were French, emerging as Michel Finaud, Joseph Bras-de-Fer, Ignace la Menace, La Souris Miquette. Strangest of all was "Blondie" who was "La Famille TeteBeche."

Paul Charbonneau came bustling in from the other room and stopped when he saw Barkley ."Ah, monsieur," he said. "You arrive late, when everyone has gone. The ant works long while the foolish grasshoppers play, n'est-ce pas?"

Barkley smiled. "I think that grasshoppers are smart."

"Perhaps now Monsieur would like a little refreshment?"

Madame Charbonneau had entered the room from the other direction. She looked at him expectantly. She was tired, but she would cook him a meal if he desired it. Barkley shook his head. "No, thank you. I have one question to ask, with an apology for asking it at the end of the day."

He paused, reading reserve in the two faces before him. The French instinct was to be on guard against an announced question. He should have thought of that.

"A dozen years ago," he said, "there was a lot of excitement here over a supposed vision. Do you mind telling me what you know about it and about the girl who claimed the vision? What kind of a little girl was she?"

Paul Charbonneau puffed out his fat cheeks. His slightly protruding eyes protruded a little more than normally, then retreated behind heavy lids. He threw up his arms in a gesture of helplessness.

"A small matter, that, monsieur! One scarcely remembers. It came to nothing. It is of no importance."

"Possibly not. But it interests me. And it must have seemed of great importance here at the time."

Madame Charbonneau seated herself heavily in one of the chairs. "That is true, monsieur. Briefly, there was excitement. Newspaper writers came here. They stopped in our house. They complained of many inconveniences that they found. They were very great complainers. We learned from them what we should have. Before that, we did not know. So few people came that we were a joke to our neighbors because we had a hotel. It was, you comprehend, before we had electricity on the island, or telephones, and we had no plumbing."

Barkley seated himself, facing her. One had to let people reach a subject in the way that suited them, or they never reached it. He had learned much about the Charbonneaus. They had literally farmed on their few village acres that the island considered a mere vegetable garden. They had operated the store with the aid of their children and an aged uncle of Jeanne Charbonneau's. They had raised and educated ten children, who were all off the island now and whom they visited in the winter months. They owned a hotel and they were a success story. Paul Charbonneau stood while his wife was speaking. He looked unhappy.

"Monsieur must understand that this excitement was nothing," he said. "A game of children. There was no vision. Monsieur has met the child who is now a woman, Mademoiselle Valérie, the daughter of Monsieur le Notaire."

"I have met the woman. I never knew the child. What was she like? And how did this game that you mention attract so much attention that newspapermen came here?"

Monsieur Charbonneau looked appealingly at his wife. She frowned slightly. "The little Valérie was a good child," she said. "It was unfortunate that she did not have a mother, or brothers and sisters. A child who is much alone develops fancies and imaginings. She was not a favorite of mine among children so I cannot tell you much of her."

"Why wasn't she a favorite of yours?"

"One does not know, m'sieu. One like greatly, or little, or not at all: voilà tout."

"Do you mind telling me if you disliked her? I am asking only because I want to know what she was like when she claimed the vision."

Madame Charbonneau's lips tightened. "I am not certain, monsieur, that she ever did claim a vision."

Keller Barkley was startled. "What do you mean, Madame Charbonneau?"

"It is as I said. I talked to that child within the hour, or maybe the half hour, after she played with two boys on the beach at Anse-Saint-

Jean. They ran away and left her and she was crying about it, as little ones do. The tears were still on her cheeks."

"What did she say?"

"What she said matters little. It made no impression on me. It sounded as though she recited something that she had been told. There was a woman with her who talked to her before I did and who stayed beside her, putting words in her mouth."

"Who was the woman?"

Madame Charbonneau made the sign of the cross. "God forbid that I should name her, or speak evil of her, or judge her, monsieur, when I have been to confession today and hope to receive the good Lord in Communion tomorrow; but it is as I said. The little one did not seem to know what she was saying."

Paul Charbonneau cleared his throat. "That is all there is to it, monsieur," he said. "There was much excitement, and careless talk, because who would not want the Mother of God as a visitor to his village? But there was nothing! When Monsieur le Curé talked to the little girl she could remember nothing, not even that she said this-or-the-other that was attributed to her. There is no importance in the incident, monsieur, and it would be an absurdity in a book."

Keller Barkley rose. "I am grateful to you both," he said. "One is intrigued with these little mysteries."

"But, of course." Madame Charbonneau smiled in obvious relief. "One lifts the lid of the pot to discover what is cooking."

"And discovers that it is only cabbage."

Charbonneau too was smiling. Barkley said good night and climbed the stairs to his room. He looked at his manuscript and felt excitement racing in his nerves. His instinct had been sound when he released it from the leash. There *was* an adult author of these childish visions. At least, there had been in this case, and this case was his test, the laboratory in which he measured and weighed all others. It made no difference that Madame Charbonneau scrupled to name a name. He had his copies of the newspaper accounts and they contained the name of the woman who first spoke to Valérie Rivard on the day that she claimed the vision.

Tomorrow he would interview Madame Céleste Drolet.

# VIII

The calendar leaf turned over in the night and it was suddenly September. The sky and the land and the river were oblivious to the passing of one month or the arrival of another. The first breath of day was hot and the heat increased as the sun climbed out of the east.

The people of Ile-aux-Erables drove in from the farms to Mass in a wide variety of horse-drawn vehicles. They gathered before the church in groups and clusters, men visiting with men, women with women. There was a brightness, a cheerfulness about them, with no hint that the work of the week had been heavy. They were not quaint, nor were they picturesque. The men were dressed as similar groups of men would dress in Montreal or Quebec. Despite the heat, no man was in shirt sleeves. They wore suits, or, in the case of younger men, jackets and slacks.

The women wore color. Like the houses of the province, they combined colors daringly, but the clash that one expected did not occur. They had the French gift with hats and even the older women wore them pertly. There was nothing about the women who were assembled before the church of Saint-Thomas-Apôtre that suggested the peasant women of Normandy and Brittany although they too were creatures of the land. Some of them were heavy, most of them were strong, but the majority appeared slender. Blondes and brunettes seemed to be fairly evenly divided.

According to Monsieur Charbonneau, the blondes showed the Breton strain and the brunettes the Gascon. Keller Barkley, who doubted all simplifications, doubted that one. After hundreds of years of fierce French fertility in Canada, he thought, some people were light and some were dark but it was a long road back to the Bretons and the Gascons.

There were two Masses. Keller Barkley did not attend either of them.

Madame Charbonneau was dismayed. "Everyone knows that you are not *un des nôtres*, monsieur," she said, "but we would be happy if you shared our prayers, or said the prayers that are your own during the Mass." She paused before adding the clinching remark. "It would, doubtless, please the good God if you would do so."

Keller Barkley shook his head. "I am sorry, Madame Charbonneau."

He was not sorry, actually, save in the polite sense of the term. He could not explain to Madame Charbonneau how he regarded Catholicism; nor, for that matter, how he regarded Protestantism. It was unfortunate for the Protestants that he was regarded as their representative on Ile-aux-Erables because he could not fairly represent them. He had no formal affiliation with any faith and had never cared particularly. In that, he followed his father.

Stephen Barkley was a great newspaper editor and he prided himself on his objectivity, on the complete freedom of his mind. He took a positive stand on any issue when he was convinced that he was right, and he made a point of the fact that he was able to do so only because he accepted no opinions imposed upon him from the outside. He lived in relative peace with the divers elements of his own community, at peace with his conscience, and, by his own expressed conviction, at peace with God. He served amicably on committees which included rabbis, ministers, and Catholic priests. At Christmas, Easter, or when he felt some impulse stir, he attended church services and took his family with him. The church that he selected was usually Episcopalian, Presbyterian, or Methodist and the doctrinal divergence of the three faiths interested him not at all.

"It doesn't make much difference to me which church I attend," he said, "and I don't believe it makes any difference to God. I can come as close to Him outside of a church as I can inside of one; but some people cannot. I can respect their need without following their example."

Keller Barkley had grown up in the acceptance of the fact that he was a created being and that there is a God. The lectures in college, the bull sessions and the arguments, had no effect on that acceptance, quite possibly because it was not sufficiently a part of himself to involve him in a life-and-death struggle as it seemed to involve others. Oddly enough he accepted from his father, too, a belief that, as he discovered later, was a matter of doubt and debate among religious people, even among ministers: the divinity of Jesus Christ.

"If He wasn't God," Stephen Barkley said, "then God was in Him in some manner that we can't understand. Look at the facts! Hundreds of men, thousands probably, died on crosses, crucified. It was one of man's favorite barbarisms over a long period of time. Nobody knows anything about any of them except the One. This was no obscure death, even though it occurred in an obscure place. The whole world was destined to know about it, and did, and does. The world changed, and is still changing, because of it. No man ever made such a mark on history. Jesus Christ wasn't an ordinary man and He didn't speak with an ordinary, human tongue."

Keller Barkley heard statements like that often in his home when he was growing up. He learned, in time, to question many things, including his father's convictions; but Stephen Barkley was sincere and honest and courageous. He said that a man should keep his word and live decently and try to leave the world a little better than he found it. He believed in the Ten Commandments as a guide to conduct. He had his faults and he fell short of his goals often, but he was not a hypocrite.

Stephen Barkley's son was more like him than unlike him. Kel had covered big Catholic stories and Protestant stories as a reporter, trying conscientiously to get his facts straight, but no more involved personally than if he had been writing of Elks, Odd Fellows, or Nobles of the Mystic Shrine.

There was nothing in such a background that would make sense to Madame Charbonneau or anyone else on the island. Here, Roman Catholicism was an overwhelming fact of life; bigger than birth and death, of greater importance than the weather, which controlled crops, towering high above the individual life, which it reduced to humility. Keller Barkley was astonished by it, awed by it, more impressed than he willed to be, but aloof from it and apart. He had no interest in the Mass, not even the interest of curiosity. He had not entered the Church of Saint-Thomas-Apôtre since he had been on the island. The people, however, did interest him, whatever they did.

He had a pair of very fine binoculars, which Paul Charbonneau had loaned him on the first day of his convalescence and which he had neglected to return. From one of the windows of his room, he had a clear view of about three quarters of the visiting area before the church. It became a small stage for him, which he watched, unseen. Strange actors and actresses appeared on that stage, the people whom he did not see during the busy weekdays when the work of the farms held them close. There were a great many older people at the first Mass; not so many of the younger ones or their children. Barkley watched them until they went inside, then lowered the binoculars.

He had not seen Céleste Drolet, the woman for whom he was watching.

He did not know Madame Drolet by sight, but he did know both of her sons. He was banking on the fact that one or the other of her sons would accompany her to the church. He would know then, without asking questions, when she would be home. Allowing her time to have her breakfast after she left the church, since he understood that most Catholics went to Mass fasting, he would call on her.

Valérie had not attended the first Mass, either.

He dismissed the thought of Valérie as swiftly as it came. Any meeting with Valérie, or any conversation with her, would depend upon Chance, which was the way she wanted it.

It was quiet in his room and he was aware of unrest in himself, a feeling akin to loneliness, and that was strange. His life had accustomed him to being alone. Writing was a lonely occupation. He turned the glasses once more upon the clearing. Two large dogs were moving around aimlessly and he could see another asleep in the shade. There were several of the inevitable cats, two of them white, who sat widely separated in a semicircle, seemingly watching the dogs, but dignified, aloof, superior. The people were all gone, drawn as by some powerful magnet inside the church.

Keller Barkley lowered the binoculars again and glanced at the crucifix on the wall of his room. There were elements in the religion of these people which were not contained in his father's philosophy or his own. There was worship. He could not imagine worshiping the unseen, the unknown, the infinitely distant. He could go along passively with the idea that there was a God, that there must be, and he could accept the possibility that Jesus Christ was God made manifest;

but he could not unite the two in his own mind and bow his head in worship. It was a relationship that his mind could not grasp.

He could not understand the element of penance, either. He regretted many acts of his life and he had known shame. He despised weakness in himself and there had been moments when he had held himself in contempt. He had made mistakes which he had not repeated. When he was made aware that he had hurt others, he had done his best to repair the damage. He could not accept the label of "sin" upon any of his acts, nor could he imagine accepting disciplines or deprivations in atonement for those acts. If the idea of God were a stronger reality in his life, he might be able to think in such terms; maybe not. Sacrifice was in the same category. Deliberately depriving himself of something that he wanted as an appeasement of the Unseen was an absurdity that his reason rejected.

Then there was prayer. The atmosphere of this island was saturated with it. People had prayed for him. It was incomprehensible. He had tried to believe in it when Sally needed a miracle so desperately, but he could not believe, even then, that there was any invisible being who would hear him if he spoke a prayer, or sent one winging into space upon a thought. He could not kneel as these people did and speak to silence, or petition silence, or thank silence. He couldn't do it.

"I guess that I am not even a good pagan," he said. "If I were, I would have a dozen gods and believe in all of them."

He watched the people again when they left the church. He thought of Put Bigelow, who would be very much amused at this horse-and-buggy cavalcade. The horse-and-buggy had been made the symbol of everything backward and old-fashioned and out of date by an eloquent American politician, and that concept coincided with Put's opinion of the French Canadians. How smart would it be for these people to own expensive automobiles when the longest trip on the island was less than ten miles? As for tractors? There were a few on the island, according to Charbonneau, who took a dim view of them.

"A farmer cannot raise the food a tractor eats," he said, "and in winter it is useless. A horse can earn his living all year round. You should see the sleighs when the deep snows come, monsieur."

"These people live in the Middle Ages," Put Bigelow had said derisively. "Some of them still use oxen in the fields."

Keller Barkley asked Paul Charbonneau about that. Charbonneau shrugged. "But, of course! Some of the farmers on the north shore farms of the island use them. There is nothing the equal of oxen on low, wet ground, monsieur."

A cosmic columnist with several million readers did not know everything.

Keller Barkley paced around his room. He smoked cigarettes. He riffled the pages of his manuscript with a sense of wonder at himself that he had written so much copy on a single subject. He was geared to writing a column which ran to four typewritten pages, double-spaced. It had taken something bigger than himself to drive him into this sustained effort—his love for Sally. It wasn't his book; it was hers.

The time seemed endless till the second Mass. The people assembled as for the first Mass, but the average of the adults was much younger and there were many children. Groups of women made bright, colorful patterns in the clearing that was crossed by bands of sunlight and shadow. Barkley identified Céleste Drolet immediately. He could not miss the identification. She came with both of her sons, one on either side of her. As the other groups did upon arrival, this group of three broke up immediately, the men drifting to men, Madame Drolet joining a circle of women. Keller Barkley held her in the binocular field, studying her.

She was a trim, slender woman. She wore a small flat hat with a flower in it. Her features were sharp. She seemed to be accepted with genuine friendliness by the women she joined. She moved right into their conversation. Barkley shifted the binoculars to follow her two sons. They had joined two different groups. André was talking to two men older than himself; Robert's group looked younger than he was.

Valérie walked into the clearing alone. She hesitated briefly, then took a course that avoided Céleste Drolet and the women with whom she was talking. There were groups of younger women laughing and chatting. Some of them waved to Valérie or spoke to her and she waved back, saying something in reply. Barkley followed her with puzzled intentness. The girls who greeted her did so casually and she, obviously, was not expected to join them. Nor did she move confidently into the company of the girls as Madame Drolet did into the company of the women.

"There is something wrong, deep-down wrong, with a woman who is not liked by other women," Sally said once. As a rule, that seemed to work out, but it was a generality and not the law and the prophets. There could be circumstances which would change the equation.

"Her life has not been easy. Many of her difficulties grew out of the incident," Monsieur le Curé had said of Valérie. "She does not deserve more difficulty."

Could this be one of the difficulties? Keller Barkley shook his head. It was fantastic. He could not believe it. The girl of twenty would not be isolated, on the outside of friendly groups, because the child of eight had claimed a vision that she had not seen. Something, however, was wrong; either with the girl or her contemporaries.

For just a moment, Valérie was facing him and he had her, full-face, in the binoculars. She did not look like someone who would lack friends. There was nothing withdrawn or sad or self-pitying in her face. Her remarkable eyes were lighted up and he had the same impression that he had had when he first saw her, of a vital, vivid personality; then she turned away to greet the children who surrounded her.

There were six young girls, ten or twelve perhaps, and Barkley recognized in one of them, Valérie-Marie Gagnon, the miracle baby, the child who was named for her. If there was doubt about the attitude of the older girls, there was no doubting the warmth of liking for Valérie Rivard on the part of the children. It was an odd situation.

The bells rang and the church drew the people in. Keller Barkley laid the binoculars aside and resigned himself to another long wait. He tilted his chair back, braced a pad on his knee and doodled, drawing tiny figures at random, church spires, running children, cats, Disney-like figures, a woman's head. He frowned at the pad, not actually seeing what he drew.

Valérie Rivard was in his mind now and he did not attempt to drive her out. Seeing her with the children stirred a nameless emotion in him. On the first day that he had walked with her, she said that she wanted many children. He had doubted her then and the doubt remained. It was not credible.

None of the women whom he knew had any desire for large

families; most of them shrank from the idea of a single child, or considered a single child, if they achieved one, a lifetime contribution to the race. He had never quarreled with that point of view. There were many arguments to support it.

The island was different. There were children everywhere. That did not change the basic situation for the individual girl. A big family meant pain, discomfort, and danger, oft-repeated. It meant work, and more work. It was a trap which held a girl to one place, to one monotonous round of duty until her youth was gone. How could she want it?

He could understand a girl wanting marriage and risking children as part of the marriage, wanting a man and reckless in her love for him; but wanting children as children, many of them, with all that bearing them entailed? No! He could not understand that at all.

The pencil stopped drawing, poised in suspension above the pad. It was possible that Valérie was honest on that question, that she really did want many children, even if he could not understand it. It was in her tradition, her environment, the custom of her country.

"Let's look at that," he said to the silent pencil. "Maybe the smart world from which I came is going at everything backward. Maybe the way to get rid of fear, frustrations, and inhibitions is to accept responsibility not to evade it. The people who do exactly what they want to do, the people who are always freely expressing their drives and personalities, obeying no rules, are the ones who are always mixed up and racing from one psychiatrist to another for help. The fewer disciplines they accept, the more mixed-up they become. Their system doesn't work for them. How about that?"

He made a series of question marks on the paper before him. There was a subconscious, or perhaps conscious, revolt going on in the United States against butterfly living, too. He had never looked at it in such a light before because he had written of it as a social and political phenomenon, or a new economic factor, without breaking it down into its lowest common denominator, the human being.

The baby crop since the Second World War was tremendous. Most of the subdivisions which sprawled over the landscape on the fringes of the cities were, in many respects, like Ile-aux-Erables, islands in a sense, on which there were many babies born, on which many simplicities of living were necessarily introduced because of the babies, many sacrifices made, many disciplines accepted.

"I don't know," he said.

He was prepared to knock down the picture that he had drawn, to demolish it as swiftly as he had built it. There were arguments on the other side. He did not voice them, nor frame them in his mind. He stared out of the window, suddenly tense.

What would it be like to be married to a woman who wanted children, many children?

Heat moved in him and he could feel the swelling of his body at the thought. There was excitement in it and desire; not the mere sex wanting of a body for a body, but something deeper, stronger——

To live with a woman who wanted children, many children; wanting them oneself! There would be no fear, no doubt, no holding back, no restraint. One would be swept into the swift, strong current of life, tossed by it, carried by it. The sex play of bodies passing in the night, bringing no destiny to each other, was a mere dancing of shadows on a wall compared to it. The flame would leap higher because it would be truly a living thing, and two bodies would know their own season, their own high hour, if they were bodies from which other bodies would flow into life, willed and wanted.

Keller Barkley had never known that.

A man could know no such fulfillment with a woman who feared, or who surrendered herself merely to an act and not to its purpose; nor any such fulfillment if he, himself, feared or strove to withhold effect from cause. It had to be all or nothing, the wanting of each other and the wanting of the children that their bodies sought with the same hot instinct that drove them to each other. All else was a thwarting, a limiting, a restless emptiness.

"I'm crazy," he said huskily. "There is beauty and I have known that. A lusting clod of a peasant can bring children into the world, many of them, without imagination, without ever glimpsing beauty."

That was another one of the lesser things. If two people loved beauty, if their minds soared, if they mated in the trinity of body, mind, and spirit, knowing and accepting consequence, proud that their love had purpose; that would be fulfillment. A man could endure all else in life if he knew love on those terms, and lived it, sharing it.

"Impossible!" he said. "Life isn't like that. Not for anyone."

He could feel sweat on his body. A trickle of it ran down his chest. There was an ache in his groin. He came back to the room, the island, the purpose of the moment, with a sense of shock.

The Mass was over and the people were deployed around the clearing in groups again, men and women mingling now. He brought the binoculars to focus and centered Valérie in the lens. She had her back turned to him, walking away. André Drolet walked beside her, bending toward her. He limped slightly but he did not have a crutch or a cane. He was tall and Valérie had to tilt her head to look up at him even when he bent to her. They seemed absorbed in each other. Barkley followed them with the glass until they moved off stage where the willows set a boundary to vision.

Keller Barkley remembered the first night at Valérie's home when he had met André Drolet. Valérie had left with André and they had seemed close to each other then too, apart from everyone else. The many children that she wanted would be André Drolet's children probably. How could the man support her, and them, in this island world of intense physical effort? A man with one leg?

Barkley's body was still uncomfortable. He experienced a sensation that translated itself into personal loss; which was absurd. Valérie Rivard was nothing to him, nor André Drolet, nor any of these people.

The binoculars swept back. Céleste Drolet was leaving a group with which she had been visiting. She walked purposefully across the clearing in the direction taken by her son and Valérie. Barkley could not see Robert Drolet anywhere. He followed Madame Drolet until she, too, moved off stage. On a hunch, then, he held the glass on the spot where she disappeared. He did not have to hold it long.

Céleste Drolet marched triumphantly back and she had her son with her. Even at a distance, with binoculars, that triumphant attitude was apparent. André seemed glum. He voiced something that looked like protest, his left hand thrown out in a gesture that seemed to minimize whatever she said. Robert Drolet emerged from nowhere, cutting across the clearing behind his mother and his brother, unseen by either of them. He, too, moved out of the binocular field in the direction originally taken by Valérie and André.

Madame Drolet continued her march till she reached the group that she had left, four women and two men. She spoke with animation, using her hands for emphasis, indicating André who seemed embarrassed. The scene was like an introduction, the chairman of the meeting introducing the speaker of the day. The audience did not seem too interested.

"Phony!" Barkley thought. "She invented some subterfuge to bring her son back, and it isn't too convincing to these people, or to André either."

It was a fascinating bit of drama and it took him out of himself. All that it needed was sound: dialogue, some sense of what was being said. Madame Drolet obviously had not liked it when her son had walked away from the clearing with Valérie. Or she wanted to demonstrate publicly her own command over him, despite his interest in the girl. If that was her object, she had succeeded. It was an odd slant on André Drolet. He did not look like a man who would be mother-dominated, or tied to apron strings.

The various groups in the clearing were breaking up. Madame Drolet left with her son who walked silently beside her. He moved with a certain practiced precision. They walked in the direction of the road and were lost to the glasses in the deep shadows under the trees.

Keller Barkley continued to watch while people made adieux. Monsieur le Curé was talking to a large group which included six small babies in arms; the weekly crop for baptism, Barkley guessed. He swung the binoculars around once more.

Valérie had not returned, and neither had Robert Drolet.

# IX

Keller Barkley was ushered into the formal parlor of Céleste Drolet's small house, and that, he knew, was an honor and a compliment on Ile-aux-Erables. Formal parlors were to be admired, not to be entered save perhaps by Monsieur le Curé, not to be used save for the laying out of the dead. The parlor of Madame Drolet contained too much furniture, too many family portraits, too much bric-a-brac, and yet, with all these handicaps, it achieved a certain distinction. It was an interesting room.

"I was disappointed, monsieur, that you did not call on me earlier."

Céleste Drolet uttered her rebuke with the air of one privileged to utter rebukes, but Barkley sensed uneasiness beneath the glacial calm. He had an idea that if he were to say "Boo!" to her, the whole structure of cold superiority would collapse. It would, however, be difficult to say "Boo" to Madame Drolet. She was a severe-looking woman, with eyes that were peculiarly fixed and still, a tight mouth bracketed with deep lines, a thin nose and sharp chin.

"I regret your disappointment," he said. "I was ill when I reached the island and I have not been good company for anyone."

"Nevertheless, you sought out others, monsieur."

Céleste Drolet seated herself on a small sofa and indicated by a gesture of her hand that he should be seated in the handsome rosewood chair, which competed with the piano for dominance of the room. She was only slightly less formidable seated than when standing.

"There was a time," she said, "when important visitors called on me as soon as they arrived. Many journalists and writers have visited me and people of culture and education, professors and their wives from the United States. I taught school before my marriage and these people knew that in my home they would find a congenial atmosphere. I am, of course, bilingual. Would you prefer that I spoke to you in English, monsieur?"

"I am quite comfortable speaking French, thank you. Unless you prefer to speak English?"

"No. It makes no difference."

She watched his face with eyes no longer still, eyes that had come to life with sharp suspicion. "At any rate, you are here. You have heard no good of me, I imagine, from Jeanne Charbonneau."

"I have never heard Madame Charbonneau say an unkind word about you."

"*Peut-être que non !* I would not expect you to tell me. Nevertheless, unkind words have been spoken and many a word that is untrue. God will judge them in His time. There is always jealousy in a small place and a lack of understanding for cultural pursuits, as Monsieur has, no doubt, perceived in his own experience."

"That is true, Madame Drolet, of many places, although I have not encountered it personally on this island," Barkley said gently.

He was surprised that this woman inspired gentleness in him. He had been prepared to dislike her, and nothing that she had said, or done, thus far was likable, but her very aggressiveness had a certain appeal. She was a pretender, fiercely defending pretense, and that made her tragic. It was a defense that was never victorious. His eyes took a quick inventory of the room, seeking a subject of conversation that would please her. The piano was obviously the central point of pride, an old mahogany upright with yellow keys.

"I have been admiring your piano," he said.

The grim face lighted surprisingly. "It is a very fine piano, as Monsieur, who is from the United States, will readily appreciate. My father, who arranged for my education in a convent, with the study of music a requirement, always wanted me to have a fine piano."

"Do you still play?"

There was a moment of hesitation, then an unexpected smile. "Only for my own satisfaction. I no longer play in public. My life has been hard, monsieur, and I have had little opportunity."

As though discussion of the piano had opened some tightly locked compartment of her personality, Céleste Drolet became suddenly animated. She rose from the sofa and moved swiftly across the room, eager to impress and making no secret of it.

"Since you are a writer, monsieur, you will be interested in this." She displayed a small case which, when opened, exposed a silver medal. "It was awarded to me in the convent for my knowledge of literature."

She stood before him, watching his face while he examined the medal, then gestured with elaborate casualness to her bookcase. "I have always been, as you will note, a lover of books."

The bookcase was small but the shelves were neatly filled with the familiar paper-bound French editions. Barkley had no opportunity to examine the books or to comment on them. Céleste Drolet had another treasure to offer for his inspection. It was the program of a pageant in which she had enacted a role long ago. The program itself was a slender two-leaf affair of four pages, but it had been carefully bound between two wooden covers on which characters from the pageant were skillfully carved. Keller Barkley was more impressed by the carved binder than by the program and that was a mistake. Céleste took it from his hands and put it away.

"My son, André, made that," she said. "He is handy with tools and likes to make objects of wood."

She had other objects that were not of wood to which she directed his attention. She was very proud of her petit point, her catalogne, her woven rag rugs, and she spoke of them with the naïveté of a child as she exhibited them.

"It is in the French tradition that we make such things, monsieur. The ladies of the courts had such skills and the first gentlewomen of New France. Those of us who are educated are taught in the convent *la science des ouvrages*, to create beauty for our homes."

The treasures of Céleste were old, obviously old, with no new objects of beauty to indicate a continuing interest. There had been, during all of the past week, an exhibition of island handicrafts in the assembly hall of the school building. Keller Barkley had attended one evening at the insistence of Madame Charbonneau. The latest designs from island looms were being judged, embroidery and all kinds of fine needlework, a bewildering array of feminine creativeness from clothing for children to elaborate petit point. Madame Drolet had not been represented and he had a doubt now that her hands had created the objects that she showed him. It did not really matter. The woman did matter.

She seemed to have shed years in the short time that he had been in her home. Her eyes were bright and there was color in her cheeks. Her hands trembled as she folded a piece of very fine lace into tissue-paper wrapping.

"The rosewood chair in which you are seated, monsieur, came to me from my grandmother. I am a Gagnon and we are a very old family, as anyone of the island can tell you. You must see the shrine beside the farm of my brother, Edmond, and the inscription in bronze. It is one of the sights of the island."

"I will make it a point to see it, Madame Drolet."

Barkley decided that it was time to press the object of his visit. "I met a young girl of the Gagnon family in the village," he said casually. "She is Valérie-Marie Gagnon and she was linked, I believe, to an occurrence which proved to be other than miraculous."

Céleste Drolet's body straightened and stiffened as he spoke. If she had been a child in the pride of her own possessions, she was a child no longer. Her face contorted and malevolence looked from her eyes.

"If you know that, monsieur, you know more than that," she said. "The child of Rosaire Gagnon is unfortunately named for a sly, deceitful girl, who lied treacherously to me and betrayed my trust. She is today as she was then, and she will wrap you around her finger as she has done with others if you commit the folly of listening to her."

"That is enough! Don't tell him anymore!"

Robert Drolet stood in the doorway. He wore a yellow sports shirt and green slacks. His light hair had a tousled look, as though he had just arisen from a nap. There was a contemptuous superiority in his expression as he looked at Barkley.

"I have been waiting," he said, "to see how long Monsieur l'Améri-cain would flatter you before he revealed his purpose. He is, Maman, a writer. He would sell for a good price in the United States what you would tell him for nothing."

"That is not true," Barkley said quietly.

He had not thought of money in connection with his book. He was not writing it for money. People exaggerated, in their own minds, the wages of writers. A man might spend a year on the writing of a book that would sell less than a hundred copies. There was a sneer on

Robert's full lips. He was a handsome youth in physical terms despite the unpleasant qualities of his personality.

"You are not wasting your time, monsieur," he said. "That you cannot make me believe. Ça va! If you wish to know of this matter concerning Valérie Rivard and the Virgin, I can tell you. I was there. I was interrogated by le curé. I know all there is to know. It will cost you a hundred dollars."

Barkley felt the strong current of antagonism that was flowing between Robert Drolet and himself, a current that did not flow one way. It would satisfy his own pride to have his relationship to Robert on a basis of money paid and accepted. That same pride would not consent to the other man's terms. He drew his wallet from his inside pocket and slowly counted out twenty-five dollars. He placed the bills upon the small table beside his chair and rested his hand flat upon them.

"I will pay twenty-five," he said.

"Fifty."

"Twenty-five and no more."

Robert had his eyes fixed upon the money. He shrugged. "You know the value of your own work," he said. "There are Americans who can afford to pay more than that for a lesson on the skis."

Barkley ignored the thrust. "What do you know?" he said.

Robert leaned against the slot into which the sliding doors recessed when the formal parlor was open. It was a position which compelled Barkley to turn in his chair and look up at him.

"The vision was a fake," he said. "Valérie knew what she was doing. I warned my mother and she would not listen. She believed Valérie and it made much trouble for her."

"It was the greatest heartache of my life," Céleste Drolet said.

Barkley did not look at her. He concentrated his attention on Robert. "How do you know that it was a fake?"

"I was there. Antoine Masson was with us. He was a sissy. Every one teased him or made fun of him. Valérie made him do anything that she wanted. She gave him an old broken shell down on the beach and told him to chase me and give it to me. The poor fool did it and he could not catch me."

"What about the vision?"

"There wasn't any vision. She had some kind of a prayer game with him. She used it to scare him. She started to talk about hearing voices and about silence making sound and he was so frightened that he tried to bury his head in the sand. Then she thought of something else. She said that there was someone up in the door of the rock."

"Did you look when she said that?"

Robert laughed. "I wasn't Valérie's fool. I went away and left them there."

"If you didn't look, you don't know whether there was anyone on the rock or not."

"I knew that there wasn't. Later she admitted it."

"As I heard it, she merely said that she could not remember."

Robert's eyes narrowed. "Your interest in this incident runs deep, monsieur. Have it as you will. It is easier to say that one does not remember than to admit that one is a liar."

"What else do you know?"

"There is no more to know. I have told you what I told Monsieur le Curé. No one could tell him more. There was nothing else, as my mother will assure you."

"It is as my son says. There was nothing to the affair but lies, brazen lies." Céleste Drolet's voice was dull, flat, lifeless. "If I had listened to Robert I would have been spared much suffering."

Barkley nodded and rose to his feet. He handed the money to Robert and turned toward Céleste Drolet. She was not looking at him. She had her eyes fixed in dismay upon the bills which Robert was counting. There was an agony of shame and embarrassment in her face and Keller Barkley regretted the payment of money then. The pretense that Madame Drolet's house was a mecca for the cultured, in which celebrities felt at home, was shattered by the payment of twenty-five dollars to her son. She had confirmed what he said and included herself in the transaction that was concluded in her formal parlor. She looked up suddenly to meet Barkley's eyes and her pride rallied.

"My son is a man of affairs in Montreal," she said defensively, "and accustomed to the ways of cities as are you, no doubt, monsieur."

Barkley ignored the statement because he had to ignore it. It meant no more to the woman than it meant to him. There was nothing to say except what he could say sincerely.

"I enjoyed my visit with you, Madame Drolet," he said, "and all of the lovely things that you shared with me. It was a very pleasant experience."

Her lips trembled. No one had said "Boo!" to her but the right to rebuke was gone from her, and the superior attitude; and, sadly, the pretense. "I will be happy, monsieur, if you will come again," she said.

She knew that he would not, and he knew it. Robert had returned to the room from which he had come, and Keller Barkley went out into the smothering heat of the afternoon. He shook his shoulders impatiently to rid himself of thoughts that he did not welcome. Apart from the unhappy aspects, much that he wanted to know had developed from his visit to the Drolets.

Like him or not, Robert had not impressed him as a liar. His story had been straight, backed up by small details. It might not be exact, or even true, but it was as he remembered it and as he believed the facts to be. The picture of a small girl enjoying her dominance over a boy, and inventing new ways of frightening him, was convincing. It was a reasonable explanation of an otherwise unreasonable event.

Robert had been plausible, too, in saying that it is easier to forget than to admit that one had lied. He was a contemporary of Valérie's at the time and less likely to be deceived or impressed by her than an adult would be.

All of which added up to a picture of Valérie Rivard that Keller Barkley, the man, wanted to reject; that Keller Barkley, the writer of a book on visions, found perfect for his purpose.

Madame Drolet had contributed no evidence at all, unless her extreme dislike and resentment of Valérie, her bitter characterization of Valérie, could be considered as evidence of sorts; on the contention that Valérie, through her own actions, had earned the older woman's antagonism.

Be that one way or another, a new character, one whom Barkley had not met, emerged from this Drolet visit as essential to a fuller understanding of what had happened twelve years ago at Anse-Saint-Jean.

He had to meet Antoine Masson.

He was thinking of that boy who had been a "sissy" and "the fool of Valérie" as he opened the gate to the main road. A cheerful voice, with a surprised note in it, hailed him. André Drolet had stopped in the middle of the road. He wore a gray shirt, open at the throat, and army slacks. There was friendliness in his dark eyes.

"You have never visited me, monsieur," he said, "and I prided myself that I had lured you with attractive bait."

"You did! I have wondered where and how you read my column."

"Come along then and discover! 'Mad dogs and Englishmen,' they say, 'stay out in the noonday sun.' We are, thank God, neither."

André reversed his direction deftly. He had an uneven gait, rolling slightly as he walked on the rough road, but one who did not know would not suspect that he did not have two legs of his own. Barkley looked at him curiously. This, obviously, was his day for Drolets. There were contrasts in the family. This member of it did not seem to belong with the other two.

"I wouldn't have figured you as a hater of the English," he said.

"I am not. But one should not anticipate that any Canadien will love them. It asks much of human nature."

They passed the Rivard house and both men looked at it, each aware that the other did. André led the way to a small path which angled to the left at the end of the fence line. There was a low stone structure with a heavy door at the end of the path. A carved hand on the door held a name plate. André opened the door and they stepped into the cool interior.

Light flowed into a large room from rectangular-shaped windows high in the walls. Barkley looked at the three images carved from wood: a conventional Virgin Mary with her hands dropped to waist level, palms upward; a compelling, bearded figure in biblical robes, who seemed to leap at the beholder with argument on his lips; a young man with a fine head and courageous stance, wearing the brief prophet's tunic of goat or camel's skin.

"Those are impressive figures," he said.

"Thank you."

André had a chair near his workbench, taller than the ordinary chair, with a slightly tilted bucket seat into which he slid easily. There were leather loops at various points above the bench and a structure on wheels that looked like a miniature crane, about five feet high; silent witnesses to his handicap and to the ingenuity with which he had met it in doing his work and handling weight. He noticed Barkley's interest in his apparatus and smiled faintly, offering no comment.

"*Eh, bien!*" he said. "To explode my small mystery. I subscribed to a Chicago paper when I returned to the island. I had seen some of the

United States and, for a while, I considered living there. The paper carried your column."

"I wondered. I am still astonished that you remembered the column and my name."

"That, too, is easy. As I told you, I liked your writing. Then there was a story about you in one issue. It told me that you had been in the infantry and stationed at Fort Lewis in 1945. I, too, was in the infantry and at Fort Lewis in 1950. It was a bond."

"It certainly is. I don't suppose that the place changed much in five years, or that Tacoma did."

"Probably not. Tacoma knew how to get the soldier's dollar."

"It did in my day, too."

They laughed together, sharing reminiscences. André had trained at Fort Lewis from November till April 1950, as a private in the famous French-Canadian regiment, the Vingt-Deux, known to English Canadians as the "Van-Doos." He had anecdotes of his first contacts with American soldiers and there was humor in him. It was easy to like André Drolet.

"Why did you enlist?" Barkley said. "It is none of my business, but I'm interested. Quebec is rather famous for opposing conscription and war service of any kind."

André lighted a cigarette. "You are opening a big subject, a hornet's nest of a subject."

"That is all right. Let's open it."

"*Ainsi soit-il!* I enlisted. I was eighteen and a college student with very big opinions. It hurt my pride that there were reflections made on French courage. I considered my uncles and the people of my island narrow-minded and wrong when they maintained that the English made wars out of habit and incompetence, and that their diplomatic stupidities around the world should not involve Canada or its people in faraway fighting for obscure objectives."

"Events proved your people wrong, didn't they?"

André smiled. He had beautiful teeth and his eyes smiled with his lips. "Consider!" he said. "I was not old enough to be conscripted to fight Germans and Japanese as the ally of Russians and Chinese, which the English said was essential for the defense of Canada and the existence of a free world. I was old enough to be convinced that by fighting Chinese Communists, with friendly Japanese bases and

Japanese hospitals behind me, I was defending Canada and the existence of a free world.

"You may have been."

"Maybe," André gestured wearily. "But the people who are always right in their absurdity will be using the same arguments for conscription again when it becomes necessary, for the identical reasons, to become the allies of Germans and Japanese in a war against the Russians and Chinese." He paused. "So now, when I am older, I do not believe that events have proved my people wrong."

André Drolet spoke softly, but there was tension in the air. Barkley had experienced it in the United States where there was not the same racial cleavage as in Canada, nor any conflict of languages. He had known senators and congressmen and cabinet members in Washington who could be whipped into blind fury on these issues of foreign policy, and alliances, and war in their own time. He did not believe that English Canadians were all of one mind, either, nor French Canadians; nor that Wisdom dwelt exclusively in either of their houses.

"The English Canadians are in the same boat that you are," he said, "and in the same mad world."

André frowned at his own right hand which clenched into a fist, opened, closed again. "That is true," he said reluctantly. "But we are a bilingual country. We always have been. The English do not teach their children the other language of Canada. Only three per cent of them speak French, but they want to lead the whole country, of which we are forty per cent."

Some memory was moving in him, or some emotion that he was striving to repress. His eyes came up to meet Barkley's and Barkley remembered Monsieur le Curé's statement that there were violent men on the island, dangerous men, who would not abide his book. Here, for the first time, he had the feeling that he was looking at one of those men. There was, for the unguarded moment, a fierce, ruthless, savage fighting man facing him in this quiet room that was fragrant with the scent of many woods.

"I speak good English. I speak it as a courtesy when among the English, as you speak French among us. But in the uniform of the Vingt-Deux, a regiment which has won glory for Canada, speaking my own language with a friend, I have been told in a public place, in a Canadian city, to speak *white*."

The angry memory glowed hot, then the flame went out. André Drolet snapped his fingers.

"But they are not all like that! We, of the Vingt-Deux, relieved the Princess Pats when we went into action in Korea. They were good troops. We were friendly allies, all from the same country."

The hot flame glowed again for an instant in André's eyes. "If all of us spoke Canada's two languages, we would have been *comrades*."

André rose from his chair with an easy, twisting motion and stood erect. "I told you that we were attacking a hornet's nest," he said. "Shall I get you some beer?"

"By all means."

There was an arched doorway leading into the room beyond. André passed under the arch and disappeared behind the dividing wall. Barkley rose from his own chair and moved restlessly around the studio. André's emotion was contagious. He found himself picked up and carried along with it. That wouldn't do. He had to remind himself that there was another side, that there were always two sides. A man with a prejudice, or a bias, dwelt upon the incident which supported the bias and ignored the many incidents which contradicted it.

He moved around the silent figures of wood. He was not in a mood for images of the Virgin, or of the saints, and he found it easy to ignore them. The part of his mind which he had tried to put to sleep was wide awake and clamoring for a chance to work. There was so much that he could do with the many issues which the voice of André Drolet had barely touched in passing. It was not in the nature, or the training, of Keller Barkley to argue or debate with people like André, nor to join forces with them. He could take joy in talking, as he had talked today, with many people like André, of many conflicting convictions from all sections of Canada; then, in sitting alone at a typewriter and putting it all together, or tearing it all apart.

He was, in a sense, a farmer of ideas; not originating them so much as cultivating them in others, gathering them, threshing them, winnowing them, making a harvest of them. He paced and the ideas were all around him, like the crops of the island. The destinies of the United States and Canada were linked. How much of all this confusion of tongues did Americans know or understand? He made an impatient gesture. It wasn't any of his business. Let Put Bigelow write about it!

He paused, frowning. Put Bigelow couldn't write it. Put Bigelow had a mind that was furnished like a wall mirror, filled with seemingly solid things that were merely reflections from without.

"To hell with it!" he said.

He had paused in his pacing beside the workbench of André Drolet. There were tools of various sizes and shapes, small blocks of wood, shavings, a flat board with a pencil sketch of a face on it. There were shelves rising from the back of the bench, against the wall. On two of the shelves there were small carved figures in specially made niches that set them apart. One of them was the image of a man and the other was the image of a small girl, no more than seven or eight inches in height. Barkley leaned forward, suddenly intent.

The child was kneeling, with a basket on the ground beside her. Her head was raised and she was looking at something above and beyond her, awe and wonder in her face. She was a sturdy, stocky little girl and she had her hands clasped. Barkley, who had tried in vain to imagine Valérie Rivard as a child of eight was suddenly seeing that child, seeing her on the beach of Anse-Saint-Jean with the vision in her eyes.

He turned away reluctantly from the bench when André came back into the room with two cans of beer. André glanced swiftly at the carving of Valérie, then at Barkley, his face expressionless. He held out one of the cans. It was already punctured and the tin was cold.

"You have seen the ads," he said. "*La bière robuste pour les gars robustes*. Let us flatter ourselves."

"*Absolument! A votre santé!*"

The two cans touched and they sat again, facing each other. They measured each other as they drank, under no compulsion to speak. This André, Barkley thought, was different from his brother in every way, even in appearance. He was not handsome, as Robert was; he had more rugged features, roughly carved features. His eyes were better, though; warm eyes with intensity behind them. He would be a dangerous enemy, and for all of his crippling injury, he was a powerful man physically. He finished his beer and tossed the can accurately into a tall wastebasket across the room.

"You were interested in the little figure of Valérie?" he said.

"Yes. I recognized her, of course."

"I would expect that. Examine it more closely if you like."

André leaned back in his chair and Barkley was aware of the man's eyes following him as he crossed the room and lifted the small figure from its niche. It was not as smoothly, as professionally, carved as the large figures and he had an idea that it represented the earlier, much earlier, work of André Drolet; but the little girl was wonderfully alive and the reverent awe in her face was remarkably portrayed. The woman was there in the child. One could not fail to recognize her.

"For some reason of your own, you are curious about Valérie's vision, it seems."

André's voice contained a hint of hostility. Barkley lifted his eyes from the image. "I am. How did you know?"

"I saw you leaving my mother's house. I have watched you while you examined that small carving. You knew what it represented."

Barkley shrugged. "I have heard your mother's version of it," he said, "and your brother's. It is a curious event. What do you know about it?"

"I know more than anyone else knows. Everyone but Valérie has forgotten that I was the first person to hear her story."

Barkley's interest quickened. "I did not know that. What was her story?"

"I have told you. All of it. My version, if you want to call it that, is in that piece of wood that you hold in your hand."

"The expression on her face would indicate that she actually did witness a vision, or believed that she did. Is that what you mean?"

"She saw the Blessed Virgin."

André's voice was calm, uninflected, but there was conviction behind the words. His eyes were slightly narrowed.

"But she repudiated it," Barkley said.

"She never repudiated anything. She told the truth. She said that she could not remember."

"Would it be possible to forget? An experience like that?"

"It would be—because she did forget."

André Drolet propelled himself to his feet and there was not even a momentary pause for balance as he moved across the room. He touched his image of an old man preaching.

"Look at my work for a moment! I am not satisfied to portray disembodied saints. I strive for people. We are not idolaters. No one will worship these pieces of wood that I carve. These images will deserve their place in a church only if they remind the people who pray there that the saints were not born saints, that they were human beings. I study the kind of men and women they were, and I try, in my medium, to make them more real than the portrait of an ancestor in the parlor."

"You succeed damned well."

Keller Barkley did not know where this was leading, but he was fascinated by the fire in the other man, the sudden aggressiveness. André turned to his figure of the young man.

"That one, or this!" he said. "I had my concept. Now, regard the Blessed Virgin that I made."

Barkley looked at the quiet, calm, youthful figure, seeming to smile yet not quite smiling. He knew nothing about sculpture, in wood or any other substance. "It is a lovely concept," he said.

"It is not a concept at all. It is not mine. It is conventional. It is like a thousand others. Do you know why?"

"I wouldn't know. I could only guess that you did not feel free with her, believing as you believe; that she was, perhaps, beyond you."

"No! She has never held herself aloof from humanity. She is *un des nôtres*. That is why she reveals herself as God permits. I would carve her as she is, if I could know. Which brings us back to Valérie."

André crossed the room again and seated himself in the chair. "Valérie does not remember the experience," he said, the sudden calm in his voice contrasting oddly with the passion of the few previous seconds, "but she knows that she had an experience. She does not recall seeing the Blessed Virgin, so she cannot describe her, but neither can she accept any picture or image that she has ever seen as like her, or even remotely like her."

Barkley stared at him, baffled. "I don't understand."

"No one could. That is why she has never discussed the matter with people who were merely curious. I made a trip to Quebec and borrowed books of art from the library at Laval. I have showed her all of the great concepts of the Mother of God, and the ordinary ones, and the mediocre ones. She knows when she looks at a picture that it is not right, but she does not know how she knows, nor what is wrong."

"I will have to think about that," Keller Barkley said.

He was remembering, without wanting to remember, that the brother of André Drolet, who was on the beach with Valérie when André was not, was equally positive in his statement that Valérie had seen nothing and that the alleged vision was part of a game, the teasing of a boy named Antoine. He was remembering Madame Drolet, the mother of these two men, who did not compromise in calling Valérie, "today as she was then," sly and deceitful, lying treacherously. There was Madame Charbonneau, with her staunch conscience and cheerful good will, who stated that Valérie was not one of her favorite children. Could this business of rejecting the art of the centuries on the basis of a forgotten experience be a game with the man, André, comparable to the game with the boy, Antoine?

André lighted a cigarette and the striking of the match was an explosive sound in the deep quiet of the room.

"Think well," he said. "It will be many years before you have thought as long on the subject as have I."

Barkley was suddenly aware that, through all of the discussion, he had been holding the little image of Valérie in his hand. He looked at it again, then walked to the shelves and replaced it. His attention was held by the figure of a man in the other niche. He lifted it from its place and looked at it. This was cruder work than the other image, primitive work, but strangely eloquent. The man was tall, strong, muscular, triumphant over somebody or something. The face suggested André. Barkley turned with the question in his eyes. André looked gravely at the wooden figure.

"That is my father," he said. "He carved it himself."

The door opened before Barkley could reply. Valérie entered, then stopped short when she saw that André was not alone. She seemed disconcerted, but beneath that, Barkley felt that she was disturbed about something, that she had hurried here to André with some problem.

"I am sorry," she said. "I didn't know——"

André smiled, a brief flicker of a smile. "You intrude upon our revels," he said.

Valérie returned the smile. "Revels should be noisy," she said, "so a person could know." She turned to Barkley. "How are you, monsieur?"

"Fine." Barkley was standing beside his chair. "I was about to leave."

"Don't! Wait for a few minutes." She looked again at André. "Marguerite's work was awarded the prize. She submitted so much, and such variety, and such beautiful work. I'm so happy for her."

André's face lighted. "And I! That is wonderful!" He addressed himself to Barkley. "She is the wife of our good friend, Rosaire Gagnon," he said. "No one deserves praise, a little recognition, more than she."

"Then I am happy for her, too."

It was not difficult to place this Marguerite. She would be, of course, the mother of Valérie-Marie, the miracle baby. It was odd how their lives intertwined, the lives of people who were involved, one way or another, with the miracle that had not happened. Or, perhaps, it was not odd at all. The island was small and all lives touched.

"She has eight children," Valérie said. "One cannot imagine how she finds time to do the things that she does."

She turned back to André. "She has been chosen to go to Quebec tomorrow with our exhibit to Les Cercles de Fermières at L'Exposition Provinciale. She has asked me to accompany her."

"That will be good for you," André said, "and good for her."

"Is there any chance? Would you?"

Valérie was asking her question more with her eyes than with her voice. André answered in kind. "I have to finish the work on these, the little details."

"It is only one day. It would be good for you, too."

"Doubtless. I would enjoy it. But——"

"But you will be making your other trip soon."

There was disappointment in Valérie's voice, a note of protest, perhaps of anger. It was difficult to tell. These two people, Barkley thought, would probably have no need of speech at all to communicate if speech became impossible. He felt excluded, outside of the circle of intimacy, not even a spectator since he did not follow the sense of what they were saying, nor understand the conflict which he could sense beneath the surface. Valérie turned suddenly to him and he was aware of nothing save her eyes: clear, warm, friendly.

"Kel," she said, "would you like to ride to Quebec with us? We will go in the station wagon of the Coopérative."

She had always found it difficult to call him "Kel" but she used the diminutive of his name easily now. Barkley felt his heart beating unevenly. He had had so little time with Valérie Rivard. A day in Quebec?

"I would be delighted to go," he said. "I cannot imagine anything that I would like better."

"Good!" Valérie clapped her hands together. "We will not start until 7:30, but we will return very late. You will call for me at my home at 7:15?"

"On the dot."

"It is arranged then and I am happy."

She turned to André and Barkley knew that it was time to go, that between Valérie and André there was much yet to be said.

"I will go along now," he said. He extended his hand to André. "I enjoyed the 'revels' more than I can tell you."

André shook hands with him but he did not smile. They were in that moment of parting a little less than allies, not quite comrades.

"We have discovered much in common," André said. "More perhaps than we anticipated, n'est-ce pas?"

# X

"My daughter looks like Jeanne d'Arc," said Louis-Charles Rivard.

There was both pride and amusement in his eyes. Valérie had made her entrance and pirouetted to model what was obviously a special-occasion dress. It was a simply cut navy, with a white collar that formed two triangles meeting in a V just below her throat. Her hat was a small helmet with a single red feather like a regimental badge. A matching handkerchief of red protruded slightly from one of the two pockets in her skirt.

"She does look moderately belligerent," Keller Barkley said.

Valérie wrinkled her nose. She knew that she had made an impressive entrance and her eyes sparkled. "One of you is wrong," she said. "Jeanne d'Arc was not belligerent. She was a saint."

Louis-Charles snorted. "I withhold comment! She was a heroine. You look as a heroine should look, and absurdly military. This affair in Quebec, which glorifies agriculture, will be impressed."

Barkley was already impressed. This was a Valérie that he had not seen, a Valérie of another mood. The beauty operators of Ile-aux-Erables, he thought, must keep the hours of farmers, who start the day at dawn. Valérie's hair was cut and restyled, straight and uncurled, with bangs and a softly sloping line below her invisible ears. Her father was right. She did suggest Jeanne d'Arc. The dress, with three buttons on either side below the white collar, was mock military, as was the little navy helmet.

"I have been admired, after a fashion, and I am happy," Valérie said.

She stood before her father and the levity faded from her face. "Are you all right?" she said. "Can I trust you for a day?"

Louis-Charles looked no better, and no worse, than on the day when Barkley first had seen him. He was very white and all of his vitality seemed to be concentrated within his huge body as a separate entity rather than as a part of it.

"If this charming crone who delights my days will elope with me," he said, "you will come home to a stepmother."

In the background, Madame Lafleche smiled grimly, but her eyes twinkled. Her humor consisted mainly in inward laughter which had little need for speech.

"I will take care of him," she said.

The morning was blue and gold, with a bright sky, and sunlight that reflected from every object, even those that were not notably reflectors. Keller Barkley was glad that he had worn his best sports jacket and a practically new pair of gray flannels. He had not thought in terms of dressing up to Valérie, but that is the way it had turned out. She looked fresh and lovely, spectacularly young. She made him feel young. He had not been feeling young lately.

"You are wearing lipstick," he said.

"I always do. Nearly always. This is a new shade."

He walked beside her, not knowing what to say, reflecting on the fact that when he did speak, he said something ridiculous. He had noticed the lipstick. It was the first time that he had been aware of it if she had worn it before. He looked at her out of the corners of his eyes. She did not, he was certain, wear make-up. Her skin was richly tanned, a golden tan.

"I hope that you enjoy the exposition," she said. "I have never been to one, but I know that they have rides and games and many things besides the exhibits. It won't be like New York, or any place in the United States, probably, but——"

"Life in the United States is not just one big picture in technicolor, Valérie," he said. "People enjoy the same things there as here. And when I can't enjoy myself with the prettiest girl in town, senility will have me in its bony claw."

"You have not seen many girls lately. But one loves even the compliment that one does not believe."

It was fun walking with her. They walked one of the many surprising minor roads of what was loosely called the village, groves of trees concealing it from the main road, garden patches along the course of it, a low stone fence. It widened into a clearing and Barkley recognized the light truck that he had seen several times, remarkable because motor vehicles on the island were so few. It was parked near a gasoline pump which stood before one of three grouped buildings. Barkley stopped walking.

Here, deep in the seclusion of a hidden road, was a remarkable series of signs, proudly advertising the business conducted in the three structures. The building in the middle was of the familiar heavy stone, with wide barn doors thrown open. Its function was so obvious that it needed no sign, and the sign above the doors was new, evidence of pride rather than of a need for identification. It was a blacksmith shop, a forge, and the sign was a redundancy—"*Télesphore Turcotte, Forgeron.*"

The two flanking buildings were of brick. The one on the right had a sign that identified it as "*T. Turcotte et Fils,*" with a listing of services below the name: "*Garage. Réparations génerales. Service Texaco. Pneus et Batteries.*" The building on the left was also "*T. Turcotte et Fils,*" with another list of services: "*Plomberie. Electricité. Chauffage. Gaz-Propane.*"

"The girl is, *tout à coup*, less interesting than a building," Valérie said.

"My apologies. It is a bad habit of mine. I made my living once by noticing things." Barkley gestured to the signs. "These fascinate me. The Turcottes seem to be branching out."

Valérie laughed. "It was a joke to people that Monsieur Turcotte and his sons should do so many odd things, but we have much electricity, much plumbing, and other things now, so people say that he was wise to send his sons to the mainland to learn such skills. Still, there is not so much business for them as it would seem from all this advertising."

Barkley nodded. It was not in the mood of the day to discuss the Turcottes, but he had seen more in the signs than Valérie, or the people who laughed. Télesphore Turcotte probably had a house filled with children, sons with children, or sons who would have children, many of them. All these different services would not remain under three roofs indefinitely. Ultimately there would be a plumber, or two, doing nothing else, electricians, auto mechanics, heating or refrigeration experts. Trees would go down, garden patches would be flattened out, to make space for the new business establishments, and this obscure road would become a street. The farms, which supported families adequately and happily now, might not support all of these new services which the people on the farms would want. There would be dissatisfaction. It was all there, the promise of it, in those three signs. He glanced at Valérie.

She did not know. None of them knew. Change had already started on its march through Ile-aux-Erables. It would flatten many familiar things on that march and replace them with other things. People would hardly be aware that it was happening; they were not aware now.

"It is like being a witness to the beginning of growth," he thought. "This same process occurred in the United States. There is no stopping it."

He shook his shoulders, dismissing the picture which was as clear as a photograph in his mind, swearing inwardly at the kind of mind that he had, which would entertain such thought on such a morning, with such a girl beside him.

Within fifty yards of the Turcotte establishment, the small road joined the big one, and they were within sight of the modern white building which looked like a warehouse and which was the headquarters of La Coopérative Agricole. A young man in a white shirt and dark trousers was helping another man in coveralls to load cardboard cartons into the back of an old station wagon. Robert Drolet, in a yellow shirt and green slacks, stood in the shade of the building overhang, smoking a cigarette. He stiffened to attention when he saw Valérie and Keller Barkley, then walked toward them, his shoulders rolling aggressively. His eyes concentrated upon Valérie, ignoring Barkley.

"I told you that I was coming," he said. "What is *he* doing here?"

"Why not ask me?"

Barkley threw the question in ahead of anything that Valérie might say. Robert turned his head only slightly. "Because you do not know the answer," he said.

Barkley tensed, but Valérie laid her hand on his arm. "He is right," she said. "It is my question." She took one short step toward Robert, her body straight. "I ask whom I wish to come with me. I have no control over who chooses to go to Quebec."

Robert took her reply as he would take a blow, coming to a full stop, crouching slightly, then straightening again. He was a lithe, pantherish youth. It was easy to imagine him on skis, or on a tennis court, doing anything that required speed of reflexes, balance, physical competence. Barkley had felt once that Valérie hated Robert and he felt something very close to hatred in Robert now.

"You choose nothing!" he said. "You are not as wise as you believe, nor as safe. Ask Monsieur l'Américain, if he will tell you, how much he paid for you."

His eyes swung to Barkley and his chin was thrust forward. "And you, monsieur," he said, "will discover how Valérie plays games. You and Antoine Masson, both of you! It should be very amusing."

He swung on his heel and strode away, his fists clenched, and the air in the place where he had been standing seemed to vibrate with his anger. The young man in the white shirt, who had been helping to load the station wagon, left his task at the sound of argument. He was tall, dark-haired, taller than Robert and heavier, with wide shoulders. His features were finely molded.

"What is the trouble, Valérie?" he said.

Valérie appeared shaken. Her lips trembled slightly but she made a dismissing gesture with her right hand. "It is nothing, Antoine. Robert was being Robert. Have you met Monsieur Keller Barkley?"

"But no! I have wished to meet him." There was friendly interest in Antoine's eyes. "How do you do, Monsieur Barkley."

"I've heard of you, too," Barkley said.

They spoke in generalities, in the seemingly inevitable clichés of people meeting for the first time, until Valérie said, "Marguerite will be waiting for us. Are you ready to leave, Antoine?"

"All loaded and ready."

Antoine was the driver of the station wagon. "I can be so easily spared," he said with a half-smile. "Everyone else on the island is indispensable to the heavy work of the week."

Valérie climbed into the back seat and Barkley sat beside Antoine. He had a puzzled impression that he had met Antoine before, knowing that he had not. Antoine put the car in gear and raised his chin, checking to see that the road was clear.

Barkley remembered him then. Antoine Masson was the young man in the prophet's tunic, the image in André Drolet's atelier. And how damned well André had done him!

He thought about that briefly as the station wagon moved slowly along the main road through the village. André had made a point of the fact that he studied the characters and the careers of his saints before he tried to express them in wood. Then why did he do a portrait of a living person in wood and put a saint's name on it?

The puzzle did not hold him long. Valérie was talking to both of them, talking about the trip and her anticipation of it. What she said, or they said, mattered little. She was probably wondering what Robert meant by his statement that Barkley had bought her. She wouldn't be human if she didn't wonder. For his own part, Barkley was thinking about Robert's references to games and his linking of Antoine to himself; Antoine, whom he had called "Valérie's fool."

The day was no longer quite as bright as it had seemed. Valérie, obviously, had wanted André to take this trip with her. There was less compliment than convenience in her invitation to Barkley. It was her way of thwarting Robert. In such ways as this, she confirmed Robert's characterization of her—and if Robert was correct, Barkley should be delighted. His book would be strong on such a foundation. A girl who deceived, and who knew what she was doing, appearing invincibly innocent to all the beholders! Such a girl might be Bernadette of Lourdes, Mélanie of La Salette, Jeanne d'Arc!

It was strange that he had not thought of Jeanne d'Arc before in connection with his book. She, too, was a girl who claimed visions. He had not thought of her until Louis-Charles Rivard had said that Valérie looked like her. Valérie did! As one imagined that the Maid of Orléans looked anyway. He had not thought of Jeanne d'Arc probably because she seemed less a historical figure to him than a creation of George Bernard Shaw.

"I'm a hell of a historian," he thought, "and I kid myself. I have no damned idea what Jeanne d'Arc looked like. I am wrapping Valérie in every legend that I find, whether it fits her or not."

The station wagon swung into the private road of Rosaire Gagnon. Marguerite was waiting for them, with five of her children around her, four girls and a very small boy. She was blonde, taller than Valérie and heavier, full-bodied rather than fat, strong with the work demanded of her and pretty, surprisingly pretty. She had shy eyes, very blue, and she seemed happy at meeting Barkley, as she was happy about everything this day. She, too, had a new dress, sand-colored, with green arrows at the throat line, a green hat, and a green handkerchief in her pocket.

They were all in the road for a few minutes, and Valérie was telling Marguerite how lovely she looked, and the children were being kissed good-by, and Valérie-Marie, awkward and gangling and freckled but oddly charming, too, was taking her mother's place for the day.

"It is delightful, isn't it, that she has this honor," Antoine said to Barkley. "She has never been to Quebec."

"Why not?"

Antoine shrugged. "Many of the older people have never been even to Baie-Saint-Pierre. They do not want to go there."

It seemed incredible. Baie-Saint-Pierre was only four miles away, across the north channel. Quebec was not a long journey. Barkley watched with interest as Antoine drove past the Coopérative and onto the dock. He had no memory of the ferry ride that had brought him here. It was high tide and the ferry was waiting for them. The Saint Lawrence was simultaneously water and light in motion, blue-green today, streaked with long lines of gold and silver. The houses and the gleaming church spires of Baie-Saint-Pierre were floating in sunlight.

Suddenly, startlingly, frighteningly, Keller Barkley understood how islanders could spend their lives where they were and never see Quebec. He had been only a short while on the island, yet all of his instincts were in rebellion against leaving it. The mainland, and all that it represented, seemed remote from him, infinitely complicated, not worth the effort required to reach it. The same mood was on his companions, stilling conversation as though a switch had been thrown to shut off the current which animated them. The spell lasted for a minute, perhaps a minute and a half, then it lifted.

They left the station wagon and stood on the deck with a light breeze plucking at their clothing, talking for the sake of talking, laughing at nothing at all, watching a collier struggling upstream and waving to two deck hands who waved at them, seeing Baie-Saint-Pierre grow larger before their eyes, the gulls wheeling and dipping low.

Antoine chose the new coast highway because they were people going to Quebec, not tourists viewing old towns, and this was the fast way to go. Valérie and Marguerite were excited merely at the idea of riding in an automobile, and the license plates of other cars fascinated them, the plates of Canada and of so many legendary places in the fabulous "States."

"It is almost like visiting places to see the people who come from them," Valérie said. "But they don't seem real."

Barkley had the sense of unreality himself. He belonged in one of those cars that were passing, making tourist comments in English; not in this one, speaking French. He listened for Valérie's voice while he carried on a conversation with Antoine. The intensity with which she was living this simple experience made an adventure of it, and he wanted to share that adventure; it made no difference where they went. He no longer ascribed any significance to the fact that Valérie had invited him to thwart Robert. If she had not done so, Robert would be sharing all of this, and not he. She had chosen him to share it.

He made excuses to comment on the passing scene so that he could turn in the seat and look at her. He liked the excitement in her eyes, the soft parting of her lips over her perfect teeth when she smiled. It amused him when he became aware that his personal interest was apparent to her and that it disconcerted her. She did not remain disconcerted for long.

"Antoine will not talk about himself unless one demands it of him," she said lightly, "but he is a character for a book that you could write."

Antoine laughed self-consciously. "It is a joke of Valérie's," he said. "The book has already been written."

Barkley transferred his attention, reluctantly, to the youth beside him. "I don't understand," he said. "What book?"

"It is called *Maria Chapdelaine*. It is a novel of Louis Hémon. It tells of *les anciens Canadiens* who made land out of forests and farmed that land."

"I remember it vaguely," Barkley said. "I read it years ago."

"Ah, then you know! It is our great book, I think. A classic of our land and life." Antoine was pleased, obviously, that Barkley had read the book that he valued so highly. "We are doing today what the colonists did in those days," he said, "but we must go further north and we must know many new things to live on the land where summers are short."

234

He was a student at the seminary, studying for the priesthood, and he knew, at nineteen, the kind of priest that he wanted to be. He wanted to go out into the wilderness with a group of colonists, to carve farming land out of forest, to establish a parish where there was nothing.

"The Federal government and the Provincial government encourage young families with grants of cash and deeds to the land they clear," he said, "but there must be fifty families in a group, so that no one will be alone. There must be labor sufficient for any emergency. With each group, the Church sends a priest."

There was a lift in his voice when he talked of his dream that he would be one of those priests. He had much study ahead of him: logic, ontology, cosmology, psychology, theodicy, ethics, philosophy, Latin, Greek. In addition to the subjects which are a preparation for the priesthood, Antoine would be allowed time for the study of animal husbandry, the chemistry of the soil, and other subjects related to modern agriculture. He was permitted to return home in summer to work on farms and to gain practical experience, later to work with lumber crews, felling trees.

"A priest in a new community must do his share of the physical work," he said. "There can be no idle hands."

Barkley looked at him curiously. He was a powerful young man with a richly tanned skin and a profile that a young actor would envy. He seemed happy about all of the terrific study load ahead of him, which would lead in the end to what? To loneliness, utter and complete; probably the greatest loneliness imaginable. All those young Canadiens—and they would have to be young—would have wives with them. The dark at the end of the day's work would enclose them in companionship, love, children, the begetting of children. Only one man in the community would be alone when night came down. He wouldn't even have a contemporary, another priest, with whom to discuss his problems.

"And he wants it!" Barkley marveled. "He is dreaming about it."

Antoine broke off his narrative as they came within sight of the shrine of Sainte-Anne-de-Beaupré. There was reverence in his voice as he called attention to it. The voices in the back of the station wagon were stilled and Barkley had an uneasy feeling that silent prayers were being said. He had been moved by Antoine's discussion of his own aspirations, but the shrine did not move him. Its principal virtue to him was that from this new road it was remote and impersonal; one did not have to run the gauntlet of curio shops and tourist traps. Maybe the shops were an illusion and only the shrine was real—or vice versa. He did not know.

They put it behind them and the traffic on the road was heavier. Antoine drove at a constant speed, making easy work of it. He called Barkley's attention to the eel traps. It was the season for the eels and the catch along the shores of the Saint Lawrence was enormous. An eel trap, it seemed, exploited the ego of the eel. It appealed to his reason by offering him an obvious method of escape once he glided into it with the current. The eel took the logical escape route and there was no turning back. When the tide went out, the eel did not.

Antoine made a droll story of it. He had a flair for that kind of humor and a nice turn of phrase.

They came into Quebec far to the north of the walled city, on Eighteenth Street (18*me* Rue). Barkley regretted that the most interesting part of the city was lost to Valérie and Marguerite on this route, but he waved off the regret unvoiced. They were impressed by everything that they saw, and Le Parc de l'Exposition, when they reached it, was a city in itself; a place of many buildings, of gay, fluttering pennants, of life and movement, noise and excitement. Valérie and Barkley stood for a moment alone after Antoine parked the station wagon near their objective, the Pavillon des Arts Domestiques.

"I must be with Marguerite for three hours, maybe four," she said, "then I would like to see much of this with you if that is agreeable."

He smiled down into the solemn face, the serious eyes. "It is very agreeable," he said. "I will go and I will return—eagerly."

She nodded her head and her eyes were no longer serious; there was laughter in them. "It will be more fun if you are eager," she said, "Yes."

She left him then and, in a little while, he drove downtown with Antoine, who would spend the afternoon in registering for a new term at the university and conferring on his courses. Antoine was a cheerful companion, but Barkley was not at ease with him as he was with André. He did not know whether it was Antoine's youth, or the shadow of the priesthood, or something in himself; but there was a gulf between them. He had this one chance, one only, of seeking

Antoine Masson's version of the affair at Anse-Saint-Jean and he found it difficult to ask the direct question. That difficulty made him impatient with himself and more blunt than he would ordinarily be.

"What do you remember of that alleged vision of Valérie's?" he said.

Antoine stiffened slightly. His jaw tightened, then relaxed. His eyes were fixed on the traffic ahead of him. "We were very small children," he said. "It was a brief incident. There is not much for one to remember."

"Aren't you minimizing it a little? Brief or not, the incident seems to have affected many people."

"Yes. That is true," Antoine said. He frowned at the road, then his frown lifted and he laughed. "If you have talked of this to others, as is obvious, you have learned that I was of no value as a witness. I was more timid than a rabbit at that time, absurd in my timidity, too frightened to observe, to relate, to form judgment. I cannot even say of myself that I was meek, because meekness is a virtue; I was too timid even to be virtuous."

Barkley looked at him thoughtfully. Whatever Antoine, the boy, had been, the man was strong and secure in his own strength; he had to be in order to laugh at his weakness.

"If you were frightened, something frightened you," he said.

"No! One may be frightened by the unknown, and so sheltered that everything beyond one's doorstep is unknown."

"You were not afraid to go to the beach. The fright came after you reached it. I have heard the theory expressed that Valérie frightened you, as part of a game."

"You have been listening to Robert. That isn't so. There was no game. Valérie didn't try to frighten me. As I said, we were very young and we were not developed in all ways, even as children are developed. My lack was experience, even childish experience; Robert's lack was understanding."

Listening to this discourse, it was difficult for Barkley to believe that Antoine was not yet twenty, until the obvious explanation presented itself. However he might try to make light of it, the incident of Anse-Saint-Jean loomed large in Antoine's memory. He had thought about it and wondered about it and sought explanations for it through the years of his growing. His answers today were not spur-of-the-moment answers.

"Good enough," Barkley said. "You've told me what you lacked and what Robert lacked. What did Valérie lack?"

Antoine frowned at the road again, his features tightened in concentration. It obviously had not occurred to him that Valérie lacked any quality that she should have; but he was stuck with his own premise.

"She lacked reality," he said at length.

"How?"

"She had more experience than either Robert or I because she was not afraid, as I was, and she had the experience of many books, which neither of us had, and she had understanding. She did not know what was real and what was not, because she had imagination and did not know that she had it."

"She asked you to look at the rock. She said that there was someone there. Did you look, even briefly?"

"No."

"Did you believe then that she actually saw someone there?"

"Yes. I was a child. She said that she saw somebody, so I believed her. Naturally."

"But you don't believe now that she saw anybody on the rock?"

Antoine smiled, his eyes still fixed upon the flow of traffic. "I knew that you were leading up to that. It is a difficult area of the mind, the area of belief and unbelief. I can't answer you because we may be thinking in different terms. There is a vast literature dealing with visions. The Church recognizes three types of visions: the sensible vision, the imaginative vision, and the intellectual——"

Keller Barkley closed his eyes, letting the words enter his mind and releasing them again to the open air. Antoine was a sincere and earnest young man. His thinking was like his driving; even-paced, within the legal limits, neither spurting ahead nor dropping back, covering ground with no sense of strain or effort. All of which was admirable. He thought clearly as he drove well. He had been well instructed.

Antoine was correct in stating that he was of no value as a witness. He was a witness now merely to theory and to nothing else.

Antoine had read all of the books, and he was an authority on everything relating to his experience with Valérie at Anse-Saint-Jean, but he had lost the experience itself.

Keller Barkley left him at the entrance to Laval University, where students were offering themselves to tourists as guides to the city. It was a short two blocks to the Place d' Armes and the Château Frontenac. On an impulse, he inquired at the hotel desk for Put Bigelow. He did not have sufficient faith in coincidence to believe that Bigelow would be registered, but he was vaguely disappointed that he was not. Listening to Put Bigelow talk for a while would be an excellent way of getting back into the trees, away from the grass roots.

He strolled into the shop off the lobby promenade, where magazines and newspapers were sold. There were a number of American newspapers, and it was a mild shock to discover that they were still being printed, that they carried headlines written in English. He read those headlines with interest. The lid seemed to have blown off in Little Rock on the issue of segregation, with violence and the calling out of troops. The United States, obviously, did not have all the answers to the problems of living either.

On the point of buying the New York *Times*, he changed his mind. He was not ready for that yet. It was another world. He bought a copy of a Quebec paper. Little Rock was in the headlines here, too; in French headlines. The paper made quite a story of it. While he was eating lunch in the Terrace Café downstairs, he turned to the sports page.

"*Les Cardinaux s'approchent des Braves de Milwaukee,*" he read. That was brighter news than any on the front page. He had fond memories of the St. Louis Cardinals. His eye rested on a smaller headline and he chuckled.

"*Mickey et Yogi prennent du mieux.*"

He had a mental picture of Yogi Berra of the Yankees. Yogi would never know that he "*prennent du mieux.*" Hell, he would not even suspect it! Nor Mickey Mantle, either.

He paid his check and looked at his watch. "Eagerly" had been a mere word when he had used it, speaking to Valérie, at best a mild flattery. It was very real now. He was willing to add another word to it, watching the second hand loaf its way around the dial—"impatiently."

# XI

Valérie Rivard had no need of a watch or a clock to record the passing of time. There were so many things to do, and so few minutes. The Pavillon des Arts Domestiques was only one of many buildings, and the second floor only a small part of that building; but there was enough to hold one's interest on that single floor through all of the afternoon. Women from every section of the Province had sent the best of their work to be displayed there, the work of long winter evenings with the embroidery needles, the knitting needles, and the loom. If a woman had imagination, even though she lacked such skills herself, she could guess which of these unknown women had imagination, too, and which had only skilled fingers.

There was a big board at the end of the long room which carried the names of the parishes from which the work had come. There were parishes of which Valérie had never heard: Saint-Pascal, Kamouraska; Sainte-Germaine, Dorchester; Sainte-Clotilde, Athabaska; Saint-Octave, Matane; Saint-Damase, Matapédia. The magic of faraway place names enthralled her, but from the fairgrounds there was the sound of music which floated in through the open windows, reminding her that she had barely time to glimpse in passing the magic of the place that was close at hand.

Several Gagnon and Hamel relatives of Marguerite's, who lived in Quebec, came to see her, and Valérie accompanied them on a round of the exhibition buildings. When they were approaching the most exciting section, she left them with polite regrets. There were some experiences that a girl shared with a man, if she had a man to share them.

She did not have long to wait for Keller Barkley.

He came striding into the long room of Les Cercles de Fermiéres, seeming strangely out of place, as no Quebec man seemed out of place. He looked taller than he actually was, thinner than he actually was. In the time that he had spent in Quebec, he had had his hair cut. She noted that immediately, disapproving the brush cut. His hair had grown shaggy on the island, but it was dark hair with possibilities. His face looked bony, the features too large, without the softening effect of hair. He saw her and his eyes lighted. He *was* eager. He had not been merely gallant.

"How long have you been alone?" he said.

"Five minutes."

"Five minutes of my life wasted."

"We will ask one of these pretty girls to give you five minutes," she said. "And you will have them back."

He did not give the pretty girls a look, although two of the girls, at least, were very pretty, and they were watching him.

"We will go out immediately and start spending *our* minutes," he said.

The lovely work of skilled fingers from Nicolet and Saint-Jean, from Kamouraska, Lotbiniére, and L'Islet was no longer interesting. It was the work of women, which, like the talk of women, has its time and its season in another woman's life. Valérie walked with Keller Barkley, and the air throbbed with music, a military band close by and the hurdy-gurdy music of *Carnaval* farther away.

"I want to see the model home," she said. "I may own it."

"I have a ticket, too. I may own it myself."

That was one of the exciting things. "LE CLUB KINSMEN DE QUEBEC PRESENTE AVEC FIERTE LA MAISON FAMILIALE? VALEUR DE $35,000.00." Such signs were everywhere. One had a ticket, and if one's number was drawn from a box, one would possess the house. Valérie wanted to see the house which was supposed to have such a preposterous value. She could not imagine it.

LA MAISON FAMILIALE stood near the entrance of the grounds. There was a long line waiting to enter it and she joined that line with Keller Barkley. The people ahead of them and behind them were all French-speaking. There were no tourist voices speaking English. These were not expensively dressed people, but they were well-dressed, well-mannered. She glanced upward at Keller Barkley. Even one who was from the United States must be impressed with them. So much that was written was untrue and made the Canadien seem odd. Keller was not thinking of them at all, obviously.

"What will you do with this house when you win it?" he said.

"How can I tell? I can see only the outside, which does not look like a house."

The roof had a very slight slope, not enough to rid itself of a heavy snow, and there was only one floor. There were windows instead of walls. She had seen such buildings in magazines and on the television set that she had bought for her father, but like many other things that she saw, they were remote from her. This was a home that she might own. She could think of this one in relation to herself.

They were inside at last. She stared at the large living room with its tiny fireplace, its thin-legged, weak-looking furniture, its odd-shaped lamps. It was bright and clean and new, but it was not solid and strong and secure. The formal parlor beyond was even less real, with draperies of incredible length and width covering the window. The spindly furniture looked lost in the room. There was no wall space on which to hang the pictures of parents or grandparents, no warmth; it looked cold and bare, not as a formal parlor should look.

"What, no comment?" Keller said.

She shook her head. "Not yet."

*La chambre des parents* was interesting; a large double bed with a crucifix on the wall above it, a gay coverlet, three modern chests of drawers, and miles more of drapery to cover the window where a wall should be. *La chambre des filles* had beds for two daughters, a gay and happy room with a small image of the Blessed Virgin on a little wall shelf between the beds. *La chambre de garçon* had only one bed but two small boys might occupy it. There were no more bedrooms.

"One must have a very small family," she said.

Keller looked at her curiously. "Four is a good score."

They moved into *la salle de famille*, and this was ridiculous; a small enameled table with four queer metal chairs and no room for more. Beyond was *la cuisine*, an expanse of white enamel; sink and stove and refrigerator and cabinets, with many switches and knobs, a place of machinery and not a kitchen at all.

It was all very beautiful, but it was not real.

Valérie walked out into the warmth of the afternoon again. She looked at her ticket. It was number 25818. "I do not want to win it," she said.

"Why not?"

"It is in Quebec and my life is on Ile-aux-Erables. I am not married."

"What is the other reason, the important one?"

"I cannot answer because I do not live in Quebec and I do not know what a husband in the city requires of a wife. In that house I could give him very little. I would feel useless."

"I don't understand."

She looked up into the man's face. His eyes were serious. He really did not understand. She made a gesture of helplessness. It was so difficult to explain.

"You are of the city," she said. "If you were married, what would you ask of your wife?"

"I might be able to answer that," Keller Barkley said. "I have been married, Valérie."

She felt an abrupt pause in the beating of her heart, then a racing to compensate for the pause. This was a fact that had never occurred to her. There were benches beside the path which led to La Place de Concerts et Démonstrations Militaires. She seated herself on one of the benches.

"What happened?" she said.

Keller Barkley hesitated; then, with apparent reluctance, seated himself beside her. "I should not have mentioned that," he said. "She died."

"Oh!" The exclamation floated out on Valérie's held breath. She had not realized that she was holding it. The word that she feared that she would hear was "divorce." She did not know why "divorce," which left a person living in the world, was more terrible to her than "death," which was finality; but it was. "I am sorry for you," she said.

"I did not tell you for that reason. I wanted to answer your question. It was a good question."

"But won't it hurt you to speak of it?"

"The fact cannot be changed by keeping silence, Valérie. I asked of my wife, more than anything else, companionship."

She nodded her head. She could follow that. There had been companionship in cleaning the studio with André and in many other shared experiences; it was a need of a man and a woman. There was, however, much else.

"Would she be happy, your wife," she said slowly, "in that house we have seen?"

"Probably not. She would consider it too much house."

"Too much?"

"Yes. You see, we lived in an apartment, a few rooms. Sally wrote for a newspaper, too. We both worked. That was part of our companionship. There wasn't time for a lot of housekeeping. We ate when we felt like eating. Sometimes we cooked whatever we had in the house, sometimes—often, in fact—we went out to a restaurant. There were always many places to eat. It was simpler to go out for dinner and we had more time when we did."

"Time to do what?"

"To write if we wished, or to read, to visit friends."

Valérie realized that she was betraying her bewilderment in her expression when Keller smiled at her. "It was a different way of life in a different place, Valérie," he said softly, "and I cannot explain it very well, but we were happy with it, very happy."

Valérie looked away from him, remembering that the woman was dead. It would be sad to be very happy with someone, and then to be dead. She still did not understand such happiness, but it was difficult to voice her own thought. When she spoke, it was, therefore, of the least consequential matter.

"It was expensive to live in such a manner," she said. "Extravagant."

"Probably so. If it is extravagant to seek beauty from life in one's own way instead of accepting dullness?"

Something within Valérie rebelled at the word, "dullness." By such a standard as this, her own life was dull, and all that she knew, and all that she did; but she could not admit that her life was without beauty, that she did not know beauty.

"You have tried to answer my question," she said, "but I am without understanding of the answer. You did not ask anything of your wife, as I understand you, except that she be alive and that she be with you."

She read shock in his face. "You have to be more than merely alive to give companionship," he said.

"But certainly!"

244

She rested her chin in the palm of her hand, her elbow on her knee, looking across the fairgrounds, where people laughed and talked, where pennants fluttered, seeing none of it clearly. This discussion had become for her a matter of great significance. She was on the threshold of her own life, the part of her life that was not a mere preparation, that involved all of the years that were given to her and all that was in her to give back to the world. No one could understand life. One could only cling to what one believed, or learn new truths. If Keller Barkley had a truth to tell her, she wanted to hear it.

"I would try to give to the man I married the companionship of which you speak," she said, "and if I could learn, I would be the companion that he wanted me to be and not just myself. I could not love a man who did not have work to do in the world. If his work supported me, I would be ashamed, and a beggar, if I did not offer my work to him; if I did not cook for him, and sew for him, and care for him as he needed me."

Keller Barkley's voice was soft, with a note of patience in it. "We were speaking of the same things in different words. Sally did little cooking or sewing or the rest of it because she worked as I did; but her money went with mine to buy those things we needed or wanted. That, too, was giving."

They were *not* speaking of the same things. Valérie could not accept that. Nor could she challenge directly the woman who was dead. She could speak only for herself and for the marriage that she did not have, for convictions that were clear in her own mind, blurred when translated into words.

"That house, *valeur de* 35,000 dollars," she said, "requires a fortune of a man, or a debt of his whole life, and there is not even a vegetable garden to put food on his table. The house says that he must have four children, no more, and the house is not God."

"Four children is twice the number of people who have the children," Keller said. "It doubles the population."

Valérie turned to look at him. There was so much that she wanted to say to that, but there was no point. "My father was the youngest child of nine," she said. "If his parents had four children I would not be here talking of this matter with you."

He looked at her gravely. "I am one of two children. If I were one of nine, I might not be here talking to you."

She drew her breath in sharply. There was an answer to that. She thought of the children of Rosaire and Marguerite Gagnon. This man had met them and talked to them, but he did not know them. If he knew those children, as she did, which four of the eight would he choose to live and which four would he turn back to God? She shook her head. She could not ask him that, but it was in her mind.

There was a sudden blare of music from La Place de Concerts et Démonstrations Militaires. She and Keller Barkley turned simultaneously on the bench to see the proud parade of a dozen Scotch bagpipers in full kilt regalia. The wild, exciting music of the pipes drowned out every other sound, and Valérie took her reprieve gladly from a conversation that was on the verge of becoming unhappy.

"Oh," she said. "We are not seeing anything. We must hurry."

They hurried. The square was a veritable armed camp, with tanks, airplanes, and military equipment of all kinds; signs proclaiming the values and the virtues of "*Votre Marine*," "*Votre Armée*," "*Votre Aviation*." Other signs directed them to Le Palais de l' Agriculture on their left, but that was too much like home. Straight ahead was Le Colisée, its huge posters advertising the entertainment within; "*Le Spectacle magique et musical, Sim-Sala-Bim*."

Valérie came to a breathless halt. She had taken the urge to hurry too literally. She felt the touch of Keller Barkley's hand on her own, but she did not look at him. This was a type of entertainment that she had encountered in books, and only in books. The posters, and the clusters of photographs below them, portrayed girls in very brief costumes and bare legs. It was a magician's show but there was a chorus line of girls—and one girl, in what appeared to be a black negligee, looking astonished at some feat that the magician was performing. It was all very intriguing, and it called to the part of herself that went adventuring in imagination, that had come in actuality to the fair.

She would like to see this show, to see the actual people who did such things. The posters indicated that it was slightly immoral but, this being Quebec, one knew that it could not be immoral since it was presented to the public. It would be fun to be a part of something scandalous, even if one were only in the audience, anticipating something shocking and knowing that it would not happen. Keller Barkley's hand tightened on hers.

"Would you like to go in?" he said. "It is half over, I imagine, but we could see part of it."

Valérie said "No" regretfully. "There is too much else. I could not sit still."

She flashed her eyes upward, surprising an expression of amusement on his face. He was amused, she knew, because he misunderstood her. That, in turn, amused her.

"Would you like to see the girls?" she said.

"Yes."

"So would I. And I would have more fun. Part of the time I would watch the girls and part of the time I would watch you looking at the girls."

"And that would be fun?"

"Yes. Of course."

Keller Barkley laughed and she joined his laughter. She felt him close to her again. There had been a gulf of distance between them while they were side by side on that small bench, but now it was as it had been in the beginning. She could share this exciting experience with him, an experience that could never come to her again in her lifetime, not in this same way. Step by step, her feet were taking her to *la zone du Carnaval*, the ultimate goal of this journey since first she had learned that she would accompany Marguerite to l'Exposition.

*Carnaval!* It was a word of so many pictures. Harlequin and Columbine and the Clown! Masks and merriment and music! Pierrot and Pierrette!

She had encountered the word so many times in books and the scenes connected with it were always thrilling. It belonged in the ancient times of jesters in caps and bells, to all make-believe, to love that kissed and ran away, to the bright moment before the dark, to Mardi gras, which was the eve of Lent. It meant always escape from oneself, from all baffling realities, a flight to another brief existence as a masked mystery whom no one knew.

With Keller Barkley's fingers gripping hers, Valérie Rivard entered *la zone du Carnaval*, and the music that beat in her ears was right and true, the music of her pictures. It had a rhythm that suggested a broken rocking chair, mockery music that laughed at all real music, creating excitement out of that laughter. Her heart beat a little faster and her eyes darted eagerly from one side of the promenade to the other. No one was masked, of course. It was too much to expect. They were ordinary people, these strollers among the booths, as she was and Keller was, but she suspected that the masks were there. She was wearing a mask herself, an invisible mask. One could not be one's ordinary, everyday self in *la zone du Carnaval*.

She watched people playing games; tossing rings at objects, rolling balls into indentations on a board, spinning wheels. There were prizes that one could win through skill or luck.

"Want to try?"

Keller jingled coins in his pocket. She shook her head. She could not spend money in that way, and the prizes were merely amusing, not anything that she wanted.

"How about this, then?"

He led her across the promenade. A signboard carried the legend: "*Le Toboggan*." The sled had evidently just come to a stop. Young men and women were disembarking from it, laughing, some of them a trifle unsteady on their feet.

"Yes," she said.

A sled without snow fulfilled her idea of the nonsensical, the fantastic, the bizarre. Keller purchased tickets and they climbed a wooden ramp to the long toboggan which seated many people, far more than any real one that she had ever seen. Most of the other couples seemed to be competing for seats in the rear but Valérie sought the front seat. There was laughter in Keller's eyes when he helped her in.

"It doesn't go any faster in the front," he said.

"I know. I don't want to see other people. I want to pretend that we are alone on it."

"You've got a point there," he said.

The toboggan was set on the perimeter of a huge wheel. It was like a wheel from a giant auto, with the tracks where the tire would be. The center was a slightly convex shell, resembling a hubcap, painted a dull gray. There was a metal bar that rested upon her knees and Keller's. She rested her hands on it lightly. He spoke to her but she did not know what he said. She was waiting tensely.

A bell rang and there was a slight whirring sound. The gray center of the wheel started to revolve. It revolved counterclockwise, moving toward them. That was the first swift impression, then her hands tightened on the metal bar. She knew that the toboggan was motionless, but all of her senses insisted that it was plunging down, picking up speed. It was going faster and faster without moving at all, the gray disk a blur. Valérie's breath caught in her throat.

There was a click and the toboggan actually did plunge down now, racing in the track of the angled and tilted wheel, moving clockwise. The sensation of great speed was all but unbelievable. Keller's arm was around her, holding her tight, and she moved close into its protection, clinging still to the bar. She heard girls shrieking behind her as the toboggan climbed the perimeter of the wheel like a rocket heading for outer space, then plunged down toward the fairgrounds and the watching crowd, which vanished in an instant.

Valérie did not cry out, but her shoulders pressed hard against the back of the seat, which gave way under the pressure. She was wholly within the curve of Keller's arm, her left cheek against his chest, both of them lying back, almost flat, the illusion of fantastic speed tearing the breath out of them, a vast roaring in their ears.

She did not know how long the mad race from nowhere to nowhere continued. Seconds? Minutes? Hours? It seemed like hours; like forever. There was neither thought nor language, only physical sensation, a sort of wrenching ecstasy. She did not believe that she could endure it, yet she wanted to endure it.

There was a jolt, a click, a diminution of sound. They no longer climbed and plunged and rocked. This was a languor, a slowing down. They still seemed to be moving fast, with a gliding speed, but Valérie no longer pressed with her shoulders against the back of the seat. The seat straightened as she did, and she became aware of Keller's encircling arm. She moved her head away from the cushion of his chest. The gray disk was visible again as a mere disk, then motion ceased.

There was a dazed moment of return to the world. She looked up into Keller's flushed face, then away.

"Again?" he said.

"No."

She wanted to add that it was wonderful, too wonderful for immediate repetition, but she was oddly self-conscious. She could not talk about it nor look at the man with whom she had shared it. He held her hand in his as he helped her from the toboggan and maintained the pressure of his fingers on hers as they descended the sloping ramp. His hand was very warm but she felt secure in the support that he offered her, the guiding.

He seemed bemused, as she was, not feeling any need for speech. The people around them did not matter; neither the people who had also ridden the toboggan nor the mere spectators, nor the other strollers on the promenade. Valérie was indifferently aware that the light of day was fading and that the lights were coming on in *la zone du Carnaval*. The mad, rocking-chair rhythm of hurdy-gurdy music was in time with her unsteady pulse. She had found her street of masks. No one had features or expressions. She moved without thought in a world of feeling.

They stopped before another ride and her eyes cleared, focusing on it. This, too, was a wheel that revolved, but the people who rode in it were standing in little partitioned cubicles. There was a flow of understanding between Keller and herself. He did not ask her if she wanted to ride on it. A few yards farther on and they stopped again to watch tiny carts bearing shouting children as they ran around on an up-and-down track. The sign stated unnecessarily that there was a *divertissement pour les jeunes*. Certainly it was that, a sport for children!

They were nearing the end of the promenade and the music was fading into the noise ahead of them. Someone was pounding on a drum and there was a loud, brassy voice exhorting people to come forward and witness some wonder. Keller's grip on her hand released and she disengaged it.

"You are very quiet," he said.

"One should be quiet at *Carnaval*," she said. "It is an enchantment."

He laughed at that. "No! *Carnaval* is gaiety, a bit of lunacy. It is never quiet. Quiet is for thinking."

"I must seem gauche to you. I have never seen anything like this before."

The toboggan was behind them, safely behind them now, and Valérie could talk of "seeing," even think of seeing, and not of feeling.

"You are anything but gauche, Valérie," Keller said gently. "Never think it. You are very charming, and you are right. *Carnaval*, with you to share it, is an enchantment."

The drum boomed loudly and they looked toward the platform which stood before a huge tent. This was the tent of freaks and wonders. The man with the loud voice was telling the people who were grouped around the platform about a slender young man in light gray slacks and a brightly patterned jacket. He was *le grand Richiardi, avaleur de sabres*, who would swallow the displayed swords at the performance scheduled to begin in a few minutes. The swords were scabbarded in a large shield and they were of many sizes and shapes. Valérie shuddered.

"Is it a trick?" she said.

"Not exactly. He knows how to pass them down his gullet without cutting himself. At least some of them do."

The sword swallower bowed and retired behind a curtained entrance to the tent. Two girls dressed like the girls in the posters of *Sim-Sala-Bim*, in brief ballerina skirts and long, sheer, mesh stockings, emerged from behind the curtain. They were carrying a basket. Valérie looked at them with interest, wondering about them, but she made no jokes about them to Keller Barkley. They set the basket down, and a man's head appeared above the basket edge, a well-shaped head. The eyes looked at the people down below and the lips smiled.

Valérie stared in horror. The barker announced that this was *Le Crapaud*, who had the head of a man and the body of a toad. He, too, might be viewed inside the tent by those who paid the admittance fee. The head nodded and smiled. The basket was small and the two girls had carried it without effort. The body beneath that head would be a terrible thing to see.

Valérie turned swiftly and walked away, blindly, without a word to Keller Barkley. He caught up with her in a few strides. "What is the matter?" he said.

"I had forgotten. There is always that, too, about *Carnaval*. The hunchback!"

"He is not a hunchback."

"*N'importe*. He is the afflicted, the unfortunate! It is cruel for people to stare at him. It would be worse to go inside and look at his body. How he must feel!"

"Not as you would feel. He is as he is. Because people come to look at him, he can earn his living. He has no other way."

"It is horrible!"

This was one of the facts of living that one could face and accept when one encountered it in books; vis-à-vis, it was insupportable. This was the inexplicable inequality, the human dilemma beyond the reach of philosophy, the doubt cast upon Divine Justice, the challenge to Faith. One could not dwell upon it.

"I will pray for him," Valérie said.

"How? You don't know him. You don't know his name."

"I will pray for *Monsieur le Crapaud du Carnaval*. When anything in my life seems difficult or unreasonable, I will remember him. I will thank *le bon Dieu* that He has given me such simple problems and such easy crosses to carry."

Keller Barkley sighed audibly. "What you need is food," he said. "Fasting at *Carnaval* raises specters, ghosts, and all manner of goblins."

"I'm not hungry."

"Of course you are. Look! Smell them?"

The sign read, "*Chiens chauds*," and the fragrance of frying frank-furters was irresistible. The place that served them was a kiosk in the middle of the promenade, four-sided, with a counter on each of the sides. Valérie breathed deep.

"I was not remembering hot dogs when I said that I was not hungry."

"I did not think you were. It is the food of the bacchanales and of gay abandon."

"Like nectar? The hearts of flowers?"

"Well!" Keller Barkley laughed. "Let's not push it too far."

They stood at the counter and they spread mustard on *les chiens chauds* and they drank coffee out of paper cups. They were packed so tightly in the hungry crowd that their bodies touched. Two girls be-side them were sharing a single man and they were both talking, telling cute stories about themselves. Neither of the girls paid any attention to the other and the man did not seem to be paying any attention to either of them. It was very amusing.

"Have another?"

"Yes. Thank you."

They walked away from the counter with their second hot dogs, and away from *la zone du Carnaval*. The actual place no longer mattered. There was a bench just beyond Le Palais Central, and although it was only dusk the many-colored fountain, *la fontaine lumineuse*, was a living, splashing rainbow in the middle of the square. Valérie was quiet again, looking at it. It was very beautiful. When Keller lighted a cigarette, she roused herself.

"What did Robert mean," she said, "when he remarked that you had bought me?"

Keller held the match for a second before throwing it away. "I have been waiting all day for you to ask that question," he said.

"It was a curious remark."

"It was. Not quite accurate, either." Keller was watching the fountain, or seemed to be. "Since he raised the issue, I will tell you about it. I asked his mother to tell me her version of your adventure on Anse-Saint-Jean beach. Robert would not let her answer until I paid him for his version. That was not buying you, was it?"

Valérie bit her lip. "What did you pay him? Thirty pieces of silver?"

"Hardly. There was no question of betraying you."

"No? Then why did you not come to me and ask?"

"I did. Before I asked anyone else! I wanted twenty minutes from you on Saturday, or any time that you would set. Remember?"

"Yes."

She had wondered many times about that urgent and important matter that Keller had mentioned on Saturday, but she had not guessed even close to the truth.

"Why is it important to you? Why do you want to know?"

"That is difficult to answer, here and now. I was writing a book before I met you, Valérie. I do not believe that any of the girls who claimed miraculous visions saw what they claimed. I came here because you were one girl who admitted what the others did not admit. I felt that I could understand them if I understood you."

Valérie's body stiffened. "And so you went to Madame Drolet and Robert for your understanding?"

"No. Only for whatever they had to say, which I did not have to accept. I did try to know and understand you."

"Like a scientist tries to know and understand a butterfly that he puts on a pin."

"That is not fair either." He turned on the bench to meet her eyes. "Have I treated you like that?"

"How do I know how you have treated me? I did not know your motive for treating me in any fashion until now."

"You were never as I imagined that you would be."

"But, still, I am a character in your book of liars."

"It isn't that."

"It is how you describe it." She drew a swift, deep breath. "If you have the Blessed Bernadette in your book, I am honored to be included with her, no matter how you write it, but I do not deserve the honor. She saw the Blessed Virgin and neither you, nor anyone else, can change that nor make her less than she is." She shuddered slightly. "As for me, I told the truth. I did not remember what they asked me to remember."

"And never since?"

"No."

Keller Barkley flipped his cigarette away. His hand sought hers, and when she tried to pull away, his fingers tightened. "Don't treat me as a villain, Valérie," he said. "I'm not that. Maybe I would be happier if I could believe as you do, maybe not. We are as we are, and as many circumstances have made us. I have to write my book because it is a pledge that I cannot recall. You may be right in saying that I cannot change Bernadette. If she was like you, even a little like you, in your sweetness and your candor, your honesty and your concern for others, I have a difficulty with the book that I never anticipated."

"It is a bad book."

"No. An honest doubt is not bad because it is a doubt. Suppose Bernadette was like you, and involved in excitement as you were, and forgot but did not admit it? Suppose that you had not admitted that you forgot?"

"I had to admit it. I did."

"What do you *believe*, leaving out the question of remembering or forgetting? Did you have a vision that day, or didn't you?"

She rose swiftly to her feet. "Sometime I may tell you," she said. "Probably not."

He rose more slowly, standing tall beside her. "Don't hate me, Valérie," he said. "I'll be remembering this day forever and I do not want to remember your hating me at the end of it."

She looked up into his face, then looked away, half frightened by what she read in it. She gave her hand back to him. "I do not hate you, Kel," she said. "I, too, will remember always."

They walked past the fountain and neither of them spoke until they were only a few yards away from Le Pavillon des Arts Domestiques. Keller stopped abruptly.

"Hey!" he said. "We don't want to join anyone yet. There are too many places we haven't seen."

"We have to go home. Antoine will be waiting."

"But you said that we would be out very late. The night hasn't started yet."

She smiled at his earnestness. "On the island it grows late early," she said, "and to return to the island we must catch the tide. At low tide the dock is too high for the ferry."

He was so obviously disappointed that she forgave him his book. If he felt that he had to write it, what did it matter? No one ever succeeded in putting another person in a book as that person actually was. She would be herself, living her life, after the character bearing her name was imprisoned between covers; not her real self at all, merely a shadow of herself which had passed through a man's mind.

She stood for a moment looking back the way that they had come, the bright lights in her eyes, the music in her ears, a memory stirring her senses. She had visited another planet and it hadn't disappointed her. It had all been exciting and right and beautiful. André could have come with her. He could have left his work for one day. Keller had been kind. He had understanding. He was not André, but André had not come.

She rode home in the back seat of the station wagon, living the day again in her mind, watching Keller Barkley's profile when he turned to speak to Antoine. He did not speak very often. Antoine carried the burden of conversation in the front seat, as Marguerite did in the back. They were both stimulated to speech by all that they had seen and experienced. She and Keller were different. There were experiences that one held close and relived in silence. Today was hers. Because she had lived it, she had it forever. She could return to it as one would reopen a beloved book. When she was very old she would still be able to return to it and walk the promenade of *la zone du Carnaval* with Keller Barkley, as young as she was this night.

She was drowsy with motion and the sound of voices by the time they reached the island, but she was awake and alert when Antoine stopped the station wagon in the road near her gate. Marguerite overcame her timidity and her awe of Keller for a moment as the good nights were being said.

"Monsieur Barkley," she said. "We are having a party for Antoine on Saturday night, before he returns to the seminary. We would be honored if you would attend it."

Keller hesitated a brief second and looked toward Valérie, then he laughed. "You honor me," he said. "I will be delighted to attend a party. A party at your house, and for Antoine, is irresistible."

It was the right note. There were, Valérie thought, such sure instincts in Keller. He complimented Marguerite and put her at her ease, without saying too much. Antoine was pleased too.

"After today, we are all comrades, no?" he said.

There was a single light burning *Chez Rivard*, in the room of Louis-Charles. Keller Barkley walked with Valérie into the dense shadows that gathered around her door. He took both of her hands in his.

"I am grateful, Valérie," he said.

"And I."

She knew that he wanted to kiss her and the emotion of the day welled in her. She moved slightly toward him and his arms went around her. His lips pressed down on hers and it was the recaptured moment of the toboggan's starting. She felt herself moving fast, very fast, in a great blur. The desperate hunger in him brought her back to herself when she was feeling the seat moving backward with the pressure of her shoulder blades. She brought her hands up inside of his and forced his arms apart. She was stronger than he knew.

The toboggan stopped then and she was facing him for a misty moment, seeing his face as a white mask. She brushed her fingers across his cheek.

"I am sorry, Kel," she said. "So very sorry. I have been unfair."

She opened her door and slipped through it, leaning against it when it was closed, her fingers against her lips.

# XII

Keller Barkley walked from the doorstep of Valérie Rivard to the birches above Anse-Saint-Jean. He walked without thought or a conscious objective, pitting physical activity against the futile clamoring of his body for the release that it could not have. It was not the first time in his life that he had walked thus, for the same reason. It was the only remedy that he knew.

He was surprised when he realized where he was. He could hear the river before he saw it. The tide was still high, but going out. He could see about one third of the beach, a black emptiness that contrasted with the faint glow of the river, which picked up the reflection of the stars. There was a boulder, roughly the shape of a sleeping seal, to the left of the path that went down to the sand. He sat on the boulder and there was a rest of sorts for his back. He reached down and scraped up a handful of pebbles, slightly larger than aspirin tablets.

He could still feel the softness of Valérie's lips on his own, the curve of her body in the arms that had held it briefly. His flesh was not so urgent now. He could think about her. The want of her was no sudden thing. It had been building in him for hours.

"I have been unfair," she said.

He flipped a pebble into the darkness. A man could interpret a statement like that in many different ways; but, coming from Valérie, it was best to take it as a simple, direct, uncomplicated statement without guile in it.

She had been herself, fulfilling herself, through the time that they had had together; sincerely, unaffectedly, completely herself. She had met an experience that she wanted, an adventure of which she had

257

dreamed, but he had been merely incidental to it. Not until the end did she realize that she had stirred a want in him that she was unready, unwilling, unable to meet. She had not been frightened by that want, nor scornful of it; she had been compassionate to it, regretting that she could not satisfy and quiet it. Her innocence did not walk blindfolded, but it was still innocence. He had not realized that there was such innocence in women, in any woman.

He had known women who anticipated thoughts and desires that a man did not have in order to show their alleged sophistication. He had known women who tantalized and teased the animal in a man so that they could parade their self-conscious virtue through a routine of hypocritical indignation at the animal. He had known women who walked blindfolded, and women as stupid as Potiphar's wife, who assumed that a man had no choice if a woman was willing. He had not known any women like Valérie Rivard.

He flipped three pebbles, one after the other, into the darkness, listening to hear them hit. It was a form of doodling without a pencil or pad and it helped him to think. Something had happened to him that his body could not shake off, nor his mind reason away.

He was thirty and he had not lived in safe harbors, but he had walked the promenade of a French-Canuck Carney today, holding hands with a girl who prayed for the creatures of the freak tent. His mind, steeped and pickled in newspaper brine and in the cynicism of politics, had not protested. Valérie had evoked high magic out of the word *Carnaval*, and ringed it with romance. It was still a "carney," the lowest rung on the shabby ladder of show business, but she touched the tawdry thing with her idealism, her shining imagination. Incredibly, it responded. He had seen it respond. It had become what she dreamed that it was, and she had not been disillusioned. He had been picked up and carried along on the current that carried her. She called it "enchantment" and it was. She had within her what he had always sought for himself, but she did not know that, or even suspect it, because she had not seen him once through all of the day, until the final moment, as a person; he was merely the sharer of a dream.

"She wanted André," he said, "and he should have been there, not I. What in hell is the matter with that guy?"

The thought of Sally came like a puff of wind off the river, soft and unobtrusive, bringing with it no pain. To Sally he had been more than a mere extension of herself. She had seen in him, whether it was there or not, much of the same offbeat quality that he saw in Valérie.

"Deep down, you are a romantic, Kel," she told him. "You are always looking for wonder. This so-called savagery of yours is merely indignation because there is so little that is marvelous in the world and so much that is mediocre. If you would only leave the damned world alone and write a book the way you talk to Bluebonnet!"

He had talked a lot of nonsense to Bluebonnet, Sally's occasional self, but there was nothing extraordinary about that. He had an idea that most men talked out of reason and out of character to the women they loved. It wasn't anything that a man could put in a book. There was irony, though, in the fact that the book he was writing for Sally was not as she had always imagined a book that he wrote would be. It was, in fact, anti-romantic, anti-wonder, anti-marvel. It had to be!

"But one thing does not have to be," he said grimly. "I am not going to fall in love with a character who stepped out of that book. That would be too damned much."

He flipped six more pebbles into the shadows and rose. Today was today, and it was over. Tomorrow would be different, very different. He looked out over Anse-Saint-Jean, where a miracle had not happened. It was black dark with not a spark to light it. He threw the rest of his pebbles away and went home. His body obeyed him quietly.

The morrow, however, was not as simple as it had seemed in prospect.

The morning was cloudy, the first of his mornings on the island that was without sun. He chained himself to his typewriter, banging the keys emphatically, rewriting when his mind found nothing new to put on paper, writing in detail his memory of Robert's statement, and Céleste Drolet's and Antoine's. He told himself when he settled down to work that he would put Valérie out of his mind.

"Let's face it," he said. "She is in love with André Drolet. That is the way that it was meant to be."

It was a poor method of forgetting a woman, to spend a day writing about her.

"If it wasn't for that damned party on Saturday night," he said once, when he stopped for a cigarette, "I would pull out now."

He stared into the smoke cloud that floated lazily above his typewriter, knowing that if he left the island the party would go on without him, that he had taken no vow, that he had only to pack a bag, put his typewriter in its case, and go.

"It's part of the picture that I am trying to get," he said defensively. "I have never seen this whole crowd relaxed. The riddle may unlock for me when I do."

On Wednesday morning at breakfast Paul Charbonneau was solicitous, concern in his friendly eyes. "The book, it does not go well now?" he asked.

"No. It doesn't go. There are days like that. How did you know?"

Charbonneau shrugged. There was a certain complacency in his smile. He liked the role of Sherlock Holmes, Monsieur Lecoq, or Arsène Lupin, showing off his powers of deduction.

"It is not difficult," he said. "Always when you write on the machine you whistle. It is most remarkable that you can do so. Yesterday the music of the whistling was sad, of a great melancholy."

Keller Barkley was only vaguely aware that he whistled when he tried to concentrate. There had been complaints in city rooms where he had worked, but he never heard his own whistling and was never conscious of carrying any tune in his mind. On Wednesday, after his exchange with Charbonneau, he tried consciously to suppress the whistling, and he could not work. He tried then to introduce gay or schmaltzy tunes for the benefit of his worried landlord. When he did that, he was merely whistling and not working.

"To hell with it!" he said at length. "Let it come out sad. What do I care?"

His writing flowed more easily when he did not think of it as writing, but the angels were not with him. He could make any given chapter read one way, or read another, depending upon where he placed the bias. He did not want bias, he wanted truth; and truth eluded him.

There could be no book without Valérie, without the understanding of Valérie, and that was an irony that had the laughter of devils in it. In order to write his book for Sally, he had to think of Valérie. When he thought of Valérie, the book, as he had planned it, fell apart. He had told her the truth, sitting on the bench and looking at the fountain. She was the key arch. If the girl who repudiated her claim to a vision was the same type of girl who refused to repudiate, then his difficulty was very great. Valérie in the role of Bernadette, of Mélanie, of Jeanne d'Arc was the Bernadette, the Mélanie, the Jeanne d'Arc of pious and popular belief. If they were each individual and different, having nothing in common with Valérie, then his thesis collapsed and he was back at the beginning of all his work, with nothing to write about and nothing to say.

And so passed Wednesday.

The Thursday breakfast table at Charbonneau's was bright with company. A Simard son and his wife had come from the mainland to take old Nicolas, the ex-Mayor, and his wife to a big Simard festival at Beaupré. Keller Barkley had met and talked with Nicolas and his wife, and now he met many more Simards from the island and the couple from the mainland. Nicolas, short, wiry, alert, and bubbling with vitality, insisted upon explaining the great occasion to him.

"Attend, monsieur!" he said. "It is an event of which you could write. In 1657, my first ancestor in Quebec, Pierre Simard and his son, Noel, landed at Beaupré from Pymoyen, which is near Angoulême in Old France. Three hundred years, monsieur! On the ninth, September, we celebrate that landing. There will be thousands of us, from *Les Etats-Unis*, from all Canada. From one man, those thousands!"

"It is remarkable!" Barkley said politely.

Some wry jester within him commented silently that there was a woman at the beginning of these Simards, too. And why was everyone so certain, always, that he could, and should, write about these prodigious feats of begetting?

"In 1725, monsieur, my ancestor on this island, the great-grandson of Pierre farmed land," Nicolas said. There was sudden emotion in his voice, a choked reverence. "The sweat of many Simards has wet this soil since, and many after us."

"In the phone book of the City of Quebec, there are 414 Simards," one of the mainlanders said, "and those, you comprehend, are merely the heads of families, and only those in the city, and possessed of telephones."

"You have something to celebrate," Barkley said.

One could not take it lightly. It was an impressive fact; not that so many people bore the same name, but that they all claimed a common ancestor. Barkley's mind went back to that plaque beside a roadside shrine, one of the few memories that he had of his grim trip to Ile-aux-Erables:

JOSEPH MASSE GRAVEL
1641
*Ses Fils Reconnaissants*
1941

The sons of Pierre Simard also remembered and were grateful.

Later, however, when the Charbonneaus were alone with him, Jeanne grumbled, scornful but without malice: "Simards!" she said. "And Gagnons! You would think that Adam was one of them and Eve the other. My family, Bouchard, is as old as either, but we make no such commotion about it."

"A Charbonneau was Archbishop of Montreal," her husband said, "and that is worth many names in a phone book." He gestured with his pipe and his eyes twinkled. "Not that we are without representation in this phone book of Quebec. But no! We are in it, and in two places, because I have ancestors who were poor spellers. Some of us are now Carbonneau."

The typewriter was repellent when Keller Barkley returned to it. He stared at it and it seemed to stare glumly back at him. They had both been wasting their time. He had nothing to say to it. The four walls pressed in on him, with their confounded windmills, the legion of children and dogs, the exposed hearts that faced each other. He swore softly, turned his back on all of it and walked out.

He told himself that he had failed to check one point of Céleste Drolet's story. She had mentioned her own ancestors and a bronze inscription that he should see. He did not try very hard to convince himself that it was important to anything that he was doing or would ever do; he merely went out to see it.

It was a long walk to mid-island. On stretches of the road where the trees were thin, it was murderously hot. The clouds had blown away after one day of futile threat and the weather was still August although the calendar read September. He had expected, in his ignorance, autumn coloring earlier than this in Quebec Province, but there was not a trace of it.

The plaque, when he reached it, was on a cement post beside a *calvaire*, a roadside shrine. Two men in rough work clothing, with clay heavy on their boots, were kneeling before the shrine, their backs to the road, rosaries in their hands. He felt embarrassed and self-conscious about stopping to read the inscription while they were at prayer. It was the season of heavy work and they were obviously workers. He wondered why they were praying, and for what. As he walked an unnecessary, hot, half mile up the road, he became annoyed with them.

"It is probably just a coffee break," he said. "An excuse to stop working."

He turned and walked back. The two men had finished their rosary and were sitting on the stone ledge with their backs to the shrine. They were smoking their pipes and talking earnestly, but they took time to lift their heads and say *"Bon jour."* Barkley said *"Bon jour"* in reply and stopped to read the inscription that he had walked so far to see:

ROBERT GAGNON
1657
MARC-ANTOINE GAGNON
L'Ile-aux-Erables
1726

That would be the first ancestor in the New World followed by the first Gagnon on the island. Below the names was an inscription in French which read:

> *This family is blessed in the sons and daughters that*
> *it has given to the service of God; from this island, 43*
> *priests, 7 Christian brothers, 94 nuns.*

The smokers had paused in their conversation to watch Barkley as he read the plaque. "There have been more since that was put up," one of them said.

"I don't doubt that."

Keller Barkley read the inscription once more and started on his return journey. The human statistics of this island were staggering. One might be amused by Nicolas Simard's hushed and reverent statement about all the Simard sweat in the soil, but when one had laughed, the soil was still a reality and there was no doubting the sweat, either. He was wasting quite a little of his own sweat, spilling it along this non-productive road. On either side of him were the fields where nothing was wasted. Men of the same continuing families worked them year after year, generation after generation.

"Do you know, monsieur," Paul Charbonneau said one day, "from where all these children come?"

"It seems to me that I've heard, but I've forgotten."

Charbonneau maintained a bland, poker face. "It is the pea soup, monsieur; the food of virility. In the olden days, there was always a big pot of pea soup simmering on the stove. Our people ate little else. In the days of my grandfather, a family of seventeen children was not remarkable. It was so even in the days of my father. Today, of course, there is still the pea soup in every kitchen, but there is much other food, even the food of factories."

"So the families have dwindled away to a dozen or so?" Barkley said.

"*Mais, oui! C'est comme cela.* Jeanne and me, we had only ten."

One did not have to take Paul Charbonneau seriously. He did not demand it. The island was another matter. It thrust itself and its living arguments upon one's attention. There were three small children walking on the road. At Barkley's approach, they stiffened to attention and said, "*Bon jour, monsieur,*" in polite chorus. He saluted them gravely and returned the greeting. It always happened when one met children here and he was still not accustomed to it.

He could see three houses from this point on the road, but he could not see the end of any one of the long, narrow farms. From these solid houses with their gaily colored roofs, shutters, doorways and window trims came the children. They went into the fields eventually, or married men of the fields, or went off into the forests to make new land, to the cities with a profession or trade, to the building of dams, to the new work of industrial towns, to anywhere and everywhere. However and wherever they went, they produced still more children and fed them into this vast incubator that was Quebec; all except those who, incomprehensibly, raised in this atmosphere of hungry life-begetting life, espoused celibacy.

"From this island, 43 priests, 7 Christian brothers, 94 nuns."

One could not understand the individuals, but one could see the results. Those workers in loneliness sublimated within the Church those powerful instincts that had produced them, making that Church itself as passionately strong as the society that it guided. One met that Church wherever one turned.

"They can have it," Barkley said.

He had been a celibate himself for a long time. It was not the way of life that he had chosen.

The thought of Valérie, suppressed for days, would no longer remain suppressed. She seemed to float out of the sun haze that hung above the road. He could see her, in imagination, walking along the road ahead of him, with her dancer's grace, her vibrant health, moving swiftly, eagerly. He saw her turn and smile, her pretty teeth visible for a moment in the parting of her lips, her dark eyes lighted.

He closed his eyes and she was lying in his arms on the toboggan, her cheek, her mouth, against his chest. He was holding her in the darkness before her own doorstep, the fullness and the softness of her body pressed against his own.

She couldn't love a man, Valérie said, who did not have work to do. On Ile-aux-Erables, Keller Barkley would not be worth a dollar a week. He would not know what to do when the work was heavy and if he did know, he couldn't do it. She would not be a beggar, she said, if a man supported her. She would cook and sew and care for him in a big house, with a big kitchen, with many rooms for many children. In the cities, which provided him with work that he could do, where would Keller Barkley find something like that?

What would he do in such a house? With a vegetable garden to put food on his table! What would he do with all of those children that Valérie wanted if he had them? He didn't know anything about children. He didn't understand them.

He walked steadily, stubbornly on. It made no difference. He had been running away from himself all week or slugging away at a typewriter in an insane attempt to slug himself into submission to an idea. He wanted the children of Valérie Rivard to be his children. There was no sense in pretending to anything else.

In a dim, uncomprehending way, he accepted the fact that Valérie's unborn children were a part of her and that no man could have her without accepting them. It was a staggering thought, an overwhelming thought, but one had to accept it because Valérie could not be divided into many women; the unity of her being was invincible.

So be it! If he had to build an habitant house of Quebec in Washington, in Maryland or Virginia, he would build one for her. He would import snow for her if she wanted it.

"Hell!" he said. "I'm worrying myself right down into the ground. I've got to see her."

He had reached the edge of the village and his pace quickened. It was a short walk to the Rivard house. He hesitated for a moment with his hand on the gate, then shrugged and strode up the path. Madame Lafleche, who opened the door for him, was anticlimax in person. Valérie wasn't home.

Madame Lafleche did not know where Valérie had gone nor when she would return. Neither did Valérie's father, who was, as usual, glad to see him. The old woman brought beer, and Louis-Charles, who seldom touched it, drank a glass with him. The cold beer was good after the hot road. Louis-Charles, however, was not at his best. There was no spark in him. To entertain him, Barkley told him about the two men whom he suspected of loafing when they knelt before the shrine. He told him of his bewildering encounters with Catholicism wherever he turned; the pictures of the exposed hearts in his room, Paul Charbonneau's solemn carving of a cross in the air above his food with his table knife.

Louis-Charles Rivard stirred restlessly. "I know," he said. "I could tell you of some really silly affairs. There is more damned nonsense in the Catholic Church than anywhere else on earth, including Soviet Russia." He made a weary gesture. "But there is more of everything else, too."

He was obviously a tired man and Barkley left after he finished his beer. Valérie had not returned, and now that he had lost that fierce, irrational momentum that had carried him along the road, Barkley was glad that she had not. He did not know what he would say to her if he met her. He had an impulse to visit André Drolet. He had never seen André at work. The impulse flickered briefly and died. Valérie might be there. He did not want to see her in the presence of André. He did not even want to think of her in connection with André.

His feet, without any conscious direction from his brain, had carried him to the edge of the graveled clearing. He stopped and looked at the Church of Saint-Thomas-Apôtre. Its spire dominated every view of the village and its influence dominated every aspect of life and of living in the place, but Barkley had never seen its interior. It was an integral part of the setting for the baffling key chapter of his book, but he had ignored it. Another scene with the Charbonneaus came to life in his mind. It had occurred on Sunday when Madame Charbonneau was urging him to attend the Mass. She stressed the beauty of the church.

"It is more beautiful than any place on the island," she said.

"It should be. It reaches into all of the pockets on the island, doesn't it?"

Barkley had not meant to be belligerent, but the words spoke themselves, and once they were said, he stood behind them. Madame Charbonneau was shocked, and showed it, then she was angry.

"For shame, monsieur!" she said. "We give but little, a very little for the good God who gives us everything."

Her husband moved into the situation, carrying compromise in heavy hands. "You must understand, monsieur, that a man would be ashamed if he put more beauty into his own house than into the house of God."

Barkley was in no mood to understand anything of the kind. "A man should put beauty into his own house if he can afford it," he said. "He lives there. And his wife does. And his children."

"Ah, yes. I agree. But, of course! I am a man of the world even if I live in a small place. I perceive your meaning. It is different elsewhere. I have traveled."

Paul Charbonneau gestured with his pipe to the framed mementos on the wall, pictures and souvenirs of his trip to France as a soldier in the First World War. Keller Barkley had seen those mementos and heard about them, all about them.

"In the cities you have wonderful museums, and I have seen them," Paul Charbonneau said patiently. "Your children may go to them and that is good. They learn to appreciate lovely things. Here we do not have beautiful museums or art galleries. We will never have them. Our children go to the church and it is very beautiful. That is the practical view, *n'est-ce pas?*"

It was the practical view and it was oddly touching. It silenced Keller Barkley, but he did not attend Mass.

He stood before the church now, remembering; regretting a little, as he often regretted, his impatience; the unnecessary vehemence that he put into arguments over matters of small importance.

It was afternoon and there was no Mass to complicate issues, no one around him to argue or to debate or to care whether he was interested in the church or not. He had no quarrel with beauty. Keller Barkley shrugged indifferently and mounted the steps.

267

The interior of the church disappointed him. He had been led to expect too much. It was much larger than he had anticipated, and it was easy to believe that, as the Charbonneaus assured him, it held the entire population of the island on special occasions such as the Midnight Mass of Christmas. The light was dim and there was a Cathedral hush, a chill, a distinctive odor that was probably a blend of time; of incense and candle wax preserved in the wood that remembered it. He had no impression of beauty.

The high altar, viewed from the nave, was baroque, elaborately carved, elaborately decorated, with too many candles, too much of everything. There were crown-topped niches to the rear of the altar on either side of the tabernacle, an ornate gold crucifix above the tabernacle itself. Fluted pillars stood high above the altar and behind it, flanking a huge dark painting. There were two angels, carved from wood but gilded and painted, standing on projections from the wall. The pulpit was inside the altar rail on the left side of the people in the pews, of heavy dark wood that was decorated with scrolls and images. The sanctuary lamp, suspended from the ceiling, was a huge affair of wrought silver, the flame in its glass of cherry red proclaiming the central fact of Catholic belief, that Jesus Christ Himself was present, whole and entire, within the tabernacle. The two side altars were simple in themselves but surmounted by Romanesque domes that overwhelmed them.

Keller Barkley lacked a precise architectural vocabulary and he could not phrase his critical reaction even to himself, but his net impression was that this church was a hodgepodge of ideas with no central theme, no compelling beauty. It left him unmoved.

There was only a single worshiper, an old man kneeling before the Saint Joseph altar on Barkley's right. Barkley moved down the center aisle for a closer look at the painting behind the main altar. It was sunlighted through windows high in the clerestory and it was obviously very old, the work of no ordinary artist. The figures portrayed against a somber interior were convincingly alive, the flesh tints still full and firm. It was a painting of Christ inviting Thomas, the skeptical apostle, to thrust his fingers into the wound made by the lance. The man who would not believe anything unless he could see it, feel it, test it with his senses, was on one knee, afraid at the point of proof to put his skepticism to a test. Keller Barkley studied the painting for a long time.

It was worth, in itself, the visit to the church. When he turned away from it, the church seemed more friendly.

He lingered, too, before the image of the Blessed Virgin. It was what André would have called conventional, in the same pose as André's image, carved from wood but painted in blue and white as his was not. The face was not quite that of a child, nor yet that of a woman. The Mediatrix looked down upon the beholder and there was an indefinable sadness in her expression.

Midway on the side aisle, Barkley paused briefly before a very commerical-looking plaster image of a nun in a brown habit carrying a bouquet of roses. He did not know the saint and the image itself was not worth a glance. Just beyond it, on the wall, was another painting dark with age. A plate beneath it stated that it had been brought from France in 1750 by the Jesuits who built the first church on the island, "destroyed by the enemy in 1759." There was something amusing about that.

"So nice of them not to mention the English," Barkley said.

The painting itself was of an angel in coat of mail who stood like a soldier, but without a soldier's weapons. His eyes looked confidently out of the canvas, friendly eyes in a strong face. A small card carried a quotation from Tobias 12:15—"For I am the angel Raphael, one of the seven, who stand before the Lord."

One of seven! There was power in that simple statement. Barkley was moved in spite of himself. He liked brave words when they were uttered without bravado.

He was beginning to understand this church. It was like a home in which many generations of a family have lived. The moderns of each generation had brought something new to it. The young had added their own ideas while the oldsters clung to the old. If one had the time to study it, this church would reveal much of the island's history, its changing tastes and its unchanging faith. Charbonneau had been right. The church, with its many roles in the life of the people, was also their museum.

He had reached another image. He recognized this immediately as André's work. It was boldly carved, stained but not painted. It was the image of an old man who carried a staff, a friendly patriarch who, if he wore habitant clothing instead of biblical robes, would pass well as one of *les anciens Canadiens*. He had a short beard, a mouth with gentle creases in the corners, eyes that seemed to recognize the man who faced him. The eyes alone were painted and they created a remarkable illusion of life. At the base of the image, the name of the saint was carved in block letters: Saint Joachim.

Barkley's memory stirred, then moved through fog. On his trip to the island there had been a church. His driver had wanted him to visit it. It was the Church of Saint Joachim. He had never heard of the saint but the driver said that he was the father of the Blessed Virgin.

"You like him, *hé?*"

He turned to the voice. "Very much indeed."

The old man who had been praying was standing behind him. He had been a big man once, no doubt, but he was frail and wasted now, his clothes hanging on him in folds and creases. His eyes were younger than he was and his skin was soft and clear, touched with pink. If it had been lined and leathery once, as so many of the farmer skins were, this man had been long years retired from the fields.

"I gave him to this church," he said proudly. "It cost me many dollars, an extravagant price, monsieur, but I wanted Saint Joachim in the church of my parish."

"Why?"

"He is my friend." The old man was gazing fondly on the statue of another man who was old. "Would you like to hear how I got acquainted with him, *hé?*"

Barkley looked at him warily. "How?"

"It is when the first baby comes. This one I want should be a boy. Not anything else. I never think of it. On one snowy night, a wicked night, I tell you, that baby comes. It is a girl. I do not know what to do about this."

The narrator paused, considering again his own predicament, permitting Barkley to consider it. "Then, monsieur, I think of Saint Joachim. I know about him, but not much. I do not pay much attention to him. Now I pray to him. Serious. Very devout. I say to him that he knows about the girl baby. Nobody ever had one girl baby better than him. Damn, no! So, I ask him to help me know about this baby and to be a good father, not always disappointed about it like I am."

There was a solemnity about the narrative now. The old man kept his eyes on the face of the image. "Saint Joachim helps me. You feel a thing like that, when a saint is helping you. Always you can feel it.

But he has to have his little joke, too. It is the pleasant thing about Saint Joachim. He likes a little joke."

Barkley's wariness increased. "What do you mean, 'joke'?" he said.

"The next two babies are girls, also." The old man made a despairing gesture. "I am slow to comprehend this. When I have three girls, and no son, praying to everyone else in Heaven to help me, I go to Saint Joachim again. I say to him that now I have learned about girl babies. I do not need to learn any more. He can stop helping me on this. The next one, she is a boy. After that, no more girls. Five sons I have and all of them live."

The old man smiled happily. "We have been friends many years, him and me. I wanted him in my parish church. Best friend I have in Heaven, Saint Joachim!"

Keller Barkley's emotions were touched in an indefinable way. He had an instant liking for the man beside him, a liking that extended, at least for the moment, to his invisible friend. It was all so simple, so naïve, so impressive in its warm sincerity, this tale told in the back of a church. There was no idolatry in it, no exalting of an image. The friendship existed before the image was carved. This man had placed a statue in his parish church as he would hang the portrait of an ancestor in his parlor, and for much the same motives. He had had a long life and the Heaven to which, no doubt, he aspired was no dull affair of harps and angels; it was a place in which he had friends, pleasant saints who offered neighborly help and who had a sense of humor, a place where he could enjoy conversation and an occasional joke.

"I am glad that you told me that story," Keller Barkley said. "I will remember it, and your friend, Saint Joachim, too."

"Thank you, monsieur."

They had walked together out of the church. The man blinked in the bright sunlight. "I cannot be hospitable," he said unexpectedly. "I would invite you to my home, since you are a stranger to it, but my wife is very sick."

"I am sorry." Barkley hesitated. "Perhaps you will visit my home. I am living at the hotel. We could have a glass of wine. Or beer, perhaps?"

The old man looked regretful. "It would be pleasant, but I cannot do it. I go no farther from my home than the church, and only when my wife sleeps." He looked suddenly into Barkley's face. "You will, instead, say a prayer with me, m'sieu, for my wife? I would have her live until I can go with her, if God permits. She is a very timid woman."

It was an invitation and a plea. Barkley had a swift mental picture of the two men praying at the roadside shrine, then sitting there and talking, smoking their pipes. Was it possible that you could ask a man to say a prayer with you as you would ask a man to have a drink? It was possible. It had just happened. He had accepted, out of politeness, or amiability, many invitations to drinks that he did not want, with people who meant nothing to him, in places that he disliked. But this?

"We have had many years together, my wife and me," the old man said.

That did it. Keller Barkley had not had many years with Sally, but he had accosted strangers in Lourdes, seeking a miracle for her. He had dispatched three separate strangers on a search for a doctor that rainy morning, like a general commanding troops. He could not refuse what he himself had sought. Another memorable line, slow to register on him, registered now. "She is a very timid woman." This man did not want her, his timid wife, to face a strange and frightening experience alone. He wanted to be there with her.

"Certainly I will say a prayer with you," he said.

"Thank you, m'sieu. Thank you."

The old man turned, almost trotting in his eagerness to return to the church. Only then did Barkley realize the fantastic irony of the situation in which he found himself. He was pledged to ask with his lips, with his mind, with his soul perhaps, for what his mind proclaimed impossible, the assistance of the invisible.

"I'll do it," he thought grimly. "I won't let this fine old codger down."

The old man genuflected before a pew halfway down the center aisle, then, on the point of entering the pew, he remembered suddenly that he was the host. He had extended the invitation. He stepped back to let Barkley enter the pew first. That simple action was like a challenge to Keller Barkley's thought. This man and he were strangers. It had obviously never occurred to his host, who never ventured far away from a sick wife, that he had asked prayers from someone who was not a Catholic. The idea would probably horrify him.

Keller Barkley squared his shoulders. He genuflected.

He made the sign of the cross, too, when the other man made his.

He fixed his eyes on the tabernacle. "I think that I have been trapped," he said silently.

That wasn't the thing to say. He had not come here to complain. He had come with a petition. He had made a bad start. From the corners of his eyes he saw the man beside him, eyes fixed upon the altar, his lips moving. How many hours had he prayed like this? It must have been pretty desperate for him all alone. He had sought so eagerly for company in his prayer, the elbow touch, the sense of someone beside him. Barkley fixed his eyes upon the altar, upon the tabernacle, then the crucifix above the altar.

How did one do it? How did one send messages to the unseen? The very thought of it made him self-conscious. He had not learned to do it even in the desperation of Lourdes. He had done there only what he had done on those occasional trips to Protestant Churches with his father. He had read meaningless printed prayers out of books, followed formulas, tried to do what others around him were doing. He had not talked silently to silent space. His promise today pledged him to do exactly that. He did not know how to begin, how to address the great Invisibility, within this Church or beyond it. One did not just say "God" as though it were a surname. The French word "Seigneur" made it easy for him. He could say that where he would have found the English equivalent "Lord" awkward. He said it and then the halting words formed in his mind.

"I haven't any right to ask favors," he prayed. "If You ever asked me for any, I didn't hear You, or I didn't pay attention. But I promised this old man that I would ask You to leave his wife with him for a little while. It would be a kindness if they could go together and what difference would it make to You?"

He stopped. That sounded argumentative. He could not even say a simple prayer without making an argument out of it. The silence pressed down upon him and it seemed a stern and disapproving silence. He turned his eyes to the side altar, to the image of the Virgin. Here was a gentler, more comprehensible spirit than the grim, enduring Figure on the Cross. She was not God. If he, Barkley, was a created being, she had not created him. She was not in authority over him. She was linked to awe and majesty but she was of earth. She was a woman who had lived in a small country village, not too essentially different from this one.

He did not know how to address her either, and he felt supremely foolish in attempting to address her at all. Neither the "Hail, Mary," of English nor the "*Je vous salue, Marie,*" of French came naturally to him. He drew a deep breath.

"You know my difficulty," he said desperately, "and you know his. I don't know how to pray, but help this old man and his wife, please."

He knelt there beside a man whom he did not know and the quiet enfolded him. He thought of Sally and there was no bitterness in him. He hoped that the old man would be more fortunate than he had been and that his wife would live. He hoped, incredibly, that there was another life out there in the invisible and that Sally had found relief from suffering and desperation in it, that someone had been kind to her as she had been kind, and that she understood, if she knew anything about him where she was, that he was groping his way through a very confusing fog and that he could not help the stupid mistakes he made.

Later, in his bed at Charbonneau's, he lay with his hands behind his head and stared at the ceiling. It had been an incredible day. He had lusted and he had prayed, as futile in the one as in the other, probably. At the end of it, he had found a strange peace. Someone had asked his help. Someone had asked him for something that he did not have and had never had. He had done his best and, in some unreasonable fashion, he had managed to pour water out of an empty jug. When it was over, the old man had stood on the steps of the church, shaking his hand and weeping.

Maybe they were both deceived. He had, perhaps, given nothing. The old man had, perhaps, received nothing. However, the gift which had passed between two people—a gift which could not be seen, touched, or tasted—had inspired gratitude in one and had brought the joy of giving to the other. Let the philosophers worry about that; Keller Barkley was no philosopher. He had received much on Ile-aux-Erables, but not until today had he been able to give anybody anything. For the moment, he was content.

# XIII

On Saturday night, the seventh of September 1957, Rosaire and Marguerite Gagnon gave a *veillée* in honor of Antoine Masson, who was returning to the seminary after his summer of working on the Gagnon farms.

Louis-Charles Rivard sat in his chaise longue with the pillows at his back, brooding glumly, after his daughter and André left. He had maintained a surface cheerfulness that was convincing while Valérie was present to observe him. He maintained no pretense with the beady-eyed Madame Lafleche, who had mixed his prescribed medicinal dose and who remained in the room, sitting opposite to him, waiting to see that he took it.

"It is unthinkable that anyone should marry Céleste Drolet," he said heavily.

"A man did."

"And paid too much for his folly."

"Marrying her was not his only folly."

"*Peut-être que non.* Beside it, all other stupidities are molehills."

"She did not become as she is alone. A spoiled woman is a man's work."

"No matter. She is as she is. I would not have my daughter marry her."

Madame Lafleche took a sniff of snuff, wrinkling up her nose. "Her son, Robert, is Céleste. Her son, André, is not."

"He has that to prove. I have almost loved him, but when he and his mother are one, I cannot tolerate it."

"He is kind. He has been hurt and he does not like to hurt others."

"Bah! He is strong and afraid to use his strength. What of tonight? He must take his mother to this *veillée*, this André, because she demands it. He does not make the house smoke with honest anger and compel her to go with her precious Robert. But no! A man with only one leg must walk the breadth of the island with his reptile of a mother, then return for the girl he has chosen and walk it again. *Pourquoi?* So the silly vanity of Céleste is flattered at my daughter's expense. He is no man for Valérie, this André, when he consents to such an outrage."

Madame Lafleche sat motionless for perhaps ten seconds, her lids drooping over her eyes. She tapped her fingernail on the lid of her snuffbox.

"And what manner of woman is the mother of the American?" she said.

"I neither know, nor care, if he has a mother."

"The American knows and he will not be indifferent to her. A Céleste Drolet speaking English is not to be preferred to one speaking French."

"There could not be two such women."

"There are many, and I have known them."

"You have probably known Moses and the prophets and Jacques Cartier!"

"I have lived a long time. Monsieur l'Américain is of the cities and a Protestant. His ways are not our ways."

Louis-Charles Rivard finished his medicine and lighted a cigarette. This clipper of umbilical cords, he reflected, was a shrewd old witch. She went to the heart of things. She perceived his liking for the American and, because she opposed that liking if it touched Valérie and André, she was aware of the weakness in the situation. She had not worried about the future of Valérie as he had, nor in the same way, because she could not. He had to talk to her. He had no one else.

"Valérie does not belong here," he said. "It was my folly that brought her to this small island. Her heart is in far places where her imagination takes her. She knows by instinct what some women never learn. She would grace any man's table, in a city home, or in a palace. She will never be less Catholic than she is. A man would be more Catholic, if he were a Moslem, knowing her."

276

Madame Lafleche snorted. She snapped the lid of her snuffbox as a gesture of impatience with words. "Valérie is a woman," she said. "A woman is happiest when she feels her roots holding her to the earth."

"Roots! Living on nothing? Bearing the grandchildren of Céleste Drolet?"

"Bearing her own children. I have delivered many women. I have never delivered one of a grandchild."

"Valérie is not such a fool as to marry a man who would submit her to the whims and vanities of that old imbecile."

Madame Lafleche rose and picked up the empty medicine glass. "A woman who is not a fool for a man if she loves him," she said, "is wise to her own disadvantage."

She walked stiffly away with the glass, and the eyes of Louis-Charles Rivard followed her. It was the same with all of them, always the last word! She was very sure of herself with him now, this Madame Lafleche. It was droll, when one thought of it, how any woman close to a man, any woman on whom he becomes dependent, moves all too readily into one, at least, of the many roles of a wife. Let her find herself even the least of those roles and she develops the assurance of a wife. After that, it becomes almost impossible to dislodge her.

He recalled the many arguments with Laure, his sister, when she was alive. He missed Laure. She had a good heart. This one was a better opponent because there was less nonsense in her. Madame Lafleche had lived close to birth and death through all of her years and she had her feet firmly set on the bridge between them. Admirable in a way! Realistic, certainly! Still, a life that had no time for absurdities was a dull life.

He stared at the blank face of the television set that Valérie had bought for him when he became trapped in one small spot of a big house in a bigger world. There was an excess of absurdities in this device, certainly, and some features that were useful. People, being essentially foolish when provided the opportunity, would, he had no doubt, accept the absurdities as useful also when the machine became part of their habit. It was a deplorable prospect, this surrender of a man's mind to a machine that was controlled by other men for profit. This TV must, of necessity, bring nothing but discontent to those it

277

enslaved; because contented people, happy with what they possessed, would not buy the ridiculous merchandise which must be sold to support this purveyor of pictures. The TV must, in all that it did, strive to make men and women discontented with what they had and forever restless to replace old possessions with new. The unhappiness of people, then, was its dedicated goal, and not their happiness. Even a fool should be able to see that inevitable fact, but fools would not see it, nor would many who considered themselves wise.

He had turned off the television after the news program, which was useful. He had been depressed at the big news of the day. Louis Stephen St. Laurent, Prime Minister of Canada from 1948 till June 1957, was bowing out of politics, resigning his leadership of the Liberal Party. Louis-Charles had followed the career of Monsieur Laurent for many years, agreeing with him and disagreeing with him, applauding him and criticizing him. Louis St. Laurent was older than he, but Louis-Charles had the feeling that he was losing a contemporary.

"*Je n' ai plus la force et la vigueur necessaires,*" the old leader said.

Louis-Charles could understand that statement and sympathize with it. He no longer had force or vigor himself. There was much else that he lacked. Life did not hold many comforts for one in his own predicament. There was little peace, and less dignity, left to a man when he could not even get rid of his own urine without the aid of a catheter, and often, which was worse, the aid of a barbarous old woman.

"If I could see the future of Valérie, I would be gladly finished with all of this sad comedy," he said fretfully.

He could not hope to see a grandchild, but it would be enough if the well-being of his daughter was in the hands of a man he could trust. André? He had been pleased at that prospect once. The boy had a quality that was rare in men. Valérie's mind and her soul could meet on common ground with his. The happy mating of minds and souls was as essential to a good marriage as the happy mating of bodies. They could have all three, Valérie and André, if he would be the man that he could be. As his mother's creature, he was nothing.

Tonight, and the fantastic escorting of Céleste to the *veillée* had determined that. André Drolet and his mother! Job and his boils!

The American? Louis-Charles thought about him, as he had

thought of him often. Keller Barkley was a man whom he liked, a man of decent instincts and fine impulses, of a good mind. His education, like his experience, lacked balance—a little of this and a little of that, with no strong connecting thread—so he was less mature in some particulars than he should be. That, in a young man, was not a fatal malady, provided that he was willing to grow. He would be a good husband, indulgent perhaps, but not weak. With him, Valérie would have a more pleasant and interesting life, with fewer hardships than an island marriage would bring to her.

There was a difficulty. This Madame Lafleche had seen it with her beady eyes and placed her bony finger squarely on it. One did not know the man's background or his family. There was no religion in him, no feeling for supernatural reality. It was not so much opposition to belief on his part as it was the utter lack of faith, which was a graver thing. This American's soul could not mate with Valérie's; he was spiritually impotent.

As though the passing thought of her had been enough to conjure her out of nowhere, Madame Lafleche was back in the room. She had brought the objects and devices upon which Louis-Charles was dependent. She brought his highball and placed it on the table beside him, checking to be certain that his pipe was within reach, and his cigarettes, his pad and three sharpened pencils, the bell with which he could summon her. Her mechanical thoroughness, emphasizing his dependence, irritated him unreasonably.

"Shall I turn on the television?" she said.

Louis-Charles looked at his watch. "I will have to endure something impossible before the ball game begins," he said, "but turn it on. Your beauty will suffer, no doubt, if you are deprived of rest."

The old woman turned on the set. She had learned to adjust it skillfully and she waited until she could judge the quality of the picture before she moved away.

"If beauty gained a woman nothing better than an ugly, evil-tempered old whale like you," she said acidly, "she would be a fool to cultivate it."

Louis-Charles chuckled as she flounced away from him. This had developed into a bright incident. He succeeded seldom in baiting her into such a retort. He made a mental note to dwell more often on the subject of her beauty. *Vanitas Vanitatum. Omnia vanitas!*

He fastened his pad to a clip board and started to rule up a box score. He liked to watch baseball. It rested a man's mind and stimulated his emotions. The season was nearly over in the International League. Tonight's game was next to the last of the season and the pennant was not yet decided. He frowned at the pad. Tonight, of all nights, baseball, which had relaxed him so often, was presenting him with yet another problem, one that threatened to spoil his fun.

Montreal, which had held his loyalty through a disappointing season, was playing Buffalo. It should be very simple. He should root, as always, for Montreal to win this game, even though a pennant or any advancement was impossible. Buffalo meant nothing to him, but if Buffalo defeated Montreal tonight and tomorrow, Buffalo would win the pennant. If Montreal defeated Buffalo and Toronto defeated Rochester, Toronto would win the pennant.

The prejudice of Louis-Charles Rivard was deep-rooted and uncompromising. He did not will pennants, or any other triumphs, to Toronto. He sighed as his pencil marked the pad. It was going to be very difficult for him to watch this game, wishing the victory for Buffalo over his beloved Montreal.

He closed his mind to the program on the TV screen preceding the game. His mind moved to the home of Rosaire Gagnon. Valérie was there, and André, and the American. He had noted in Valérie of late a seeming discontent with André, a feeling akin to his own. The American was, in many ways, an obvious and ingenuous young man. His eyes were filled with Valérie and he did not know how to blink them.

Tonight, Louis-Charles felt, would bring a climax in the life of his daughter. He could not help her. He had never been able to help her greatly in any affair of importance. He was a helpless bystander, as he was at a ball game, emotionally involved but powerless to change the result.

"It is the human dilemma," he said. "Who can live the life of another? Who would want to do so? *Il faut cultiver notre jardin.*"

Despite his attempts to reassure himself, he continued to be uneasy about Valérie. He was tired, very tired. He took a sip of his highball. He would feel better once the game began. He decided that he would enlist his emotions on the side of a Montreal victory, as he always had. He was too old a leopard to indulge in spot changing. Rochester, if all went well, might defeat Toronto, and a Montreal victory would do no damage.

It was pleasant to have that problem, at least, decently settled. He shifted his heavy body and committed himself to patience.

# XIV

A *veillée*, Keller Barkley discovered, was like a party in anyone's home anywhere, if one made allowances for the fact that Canadiens were not quite like anyone else anywhere.

The door of the Rosaire Gagnon house opened on the kitchen-living room. It was as large as three rooms of the model home at the Quebec exposition. Seeing it, Barkley could understand Valérie's dismay at the kitchen dimensions of La Maison Familiale. A large enameled stove faced the door and dominated the room. The floor was covered with patterned linoleum and normally there would be a large table where there was now a cleared space. He could estimate the size of the table from the indents on the linoleum where the feet had left their marks. The wood-paneled walls were hung with religious pictures, a commercial calendar, a black crucifix. Approximately twenty chairs were placed around the room, their backs to the wall, and the space left in the middle seemed as large as the dance floor of an average night club.

Marguerite Gagnon took charge of him as soon as he entered. She was not shy in her own home as she had been in Quebec. He was an old friend of hers after that experience. She was very pretty tonight, even prettier than she had been on the day of the exposition. It seemed incredible that she had eight children.

"Monsieur Barkley," she said, "you must meet everybody. They are demanding it."

He met a bewildering number of young people congregated in the kitchen. The men were husky, bronzed or sunburned; short and tall, dark-haired and light-haired, diverse rather than typed. Most of the girls were remarkably attractive, with two, at least, who were entitled to have "beautiful" written on their diplomas. He did not see Valérie nor André. He did remember Valérie's statement that he had not seen many girls lately. Certainly he had not seen these girls. A Hollywood scout might pass over Valérie for almost any one of them. He was not a Hollywood scout.

There was an atmosphere of excitement in the kitchen. Barkley felt it in the introductions and in the light and meaningless conversations around him. It was the excitement of anticipation, emotion that was temporarily caged. These young people had been working hard with little time for play. They were physically fit, wearing their best clothes, in the company of the opposite sex, and in the mood for a good time. He shared their anticipation for reasons of his own. Valérie would be here and from Valérie, one way or another, his life would take a new direction. He felt electricity in the air.

Marguerite was proud of her role as his guide. She considered him a personage and showed that she did. It was amusing and slightly embarrassing. She led him into the formal parlor, where the older people, and the married of whatever age, congregated. It was a cluttered, possession-crowded room, larger than Céleste Drolet's parlor, with ancestor portraits and religious prints occupying practically every inch of wall space. He met Monsieur le Curé again, who regarded him quizzically.

"Whether you accepted my advice or your own, Monsieur Barkley," he said, "I am pleased that you have stayed with us and that you are still a member of the parish."

He laughed and Keller Barkley laughed with him. It was, he thought, a remark that the old man in the church, and his friend, Saint Joachim, would consider a little joke, but French jokes very often had meaning behind them. He had an uneasy impression that the priest might be more serious than he seemed.

Céleste Drolet was sitting at the right of Monsieur le Curé and she was visiting royalty tonight, condescending to be here. It was impossible to converse with her because her attention was focused on the other room while she maintained the pose that nothing in these surroundings interested her, that she was accustomed to better things. Antoine Masson's intervention was a relief. He was bubbling with boyish friendliness.

"I have told my parents much about you, Monsieur Barkley," he said. "You are my most distinguished friend. I would have you meet them."

Barkley remembered Antoine's mother, the tall, heavy woman with the expressionless eyes who had opened the door for him at the presbytery, but he had never met Benoit Masson, who was *"le bedeau"* and had figured in several anecdotes of Paul Charbonneau's. Antoine's father was a stoop-shouldered, thin man whose pride in his son triumphed over an habitual humility.

"It is a wonderful occasion, this friendly assembly to compliment Antoine," he said. "We are honored that a writer of the United States attends it."

He was obviously not accustomed to making long speeches. He spoke slowly, selecting his words with care, and there was a dew of perspiration on his forehead. Keller Barkley liked him as he liked all public speakers with stage fright, and all people who found themselves improperly attired at a party, and all outnumbered, outgunned, outprovisioned people anywhere.

"The honor is mine," he said. "I am impressed and appalled by this wilderness of Antoine's. It will take a strong man to live in it."

"Yes." Benoit Masson forgot to be self-conscious. "It is a wonderful vocation, is it not, monsieur?"

These people all seemed to have that knack of looking at tasks and responsibilities that were incredibly, barbarously difficult and proclaiming them "wonderful"—an axe and a stand of trees in the wilderness out of which to carve a farm; a long strip of land to tend that would tire an ordinary man to walk; a family of eight or ten children to be brought into life and raised. Antoine's hand rested for a moment on Barkley's shoulder.

"I have thought many times of our conversation in the car," he said. "You gave me much to remember. Some day in my parish I will read some of your books, I hope, and remember again that I have known you."

"Books? My books are babies unborn, Antoine."

Antoine smiled. "May you have a large family, then. They will be good children, I am certain."

At the doorway of the formal parlor, as he was about to return to the big room, Keller Barkley met Rosaire Gagnon. Marguerite introduced them. Rosaire, at thirty-seven was short, blocky, powerfully built. He was round-faced, leather-skinned. His dark eyes were direct, searching.

"Monsieur Barkley," he said. "I have wanted to meet you. This is an affair of gaiety, but I would talk with you a minute or two if you will permit me."

"But, certainly. There will be ample time for gaiety."

"*Je le crois bien.* The night has not begun."

Rosaire Gagnon led the way to another door, which opened on a dark porch. Before he followed him, Barkley searched the big room with his eyes. Valérie had not yet arrived and her absence added force to Rosaire's statement that the night had not yet started. The man turned to Barkley when he had closed the door behind them.

"It was said by Robert Drolet to one of my nephews that you are writing a book about the vision of Valérie Rivard, and that you do not believe that it occurred."

"Robert does not know as much as he thinks he knows. What I believe does not matter. I have been trying to discover what people on the island believe."

Rosaire Gagnon nodded. "It is the reasonable attitude. So, I would talk to you." He drew a deep breath, bracing his shoulders back. "My land ends at the top of the bluff above the beach of Anse-Saint-Jean, east of the road. It is not straight, that bluff. It is an arc, curving in from the beach. It is the shape of the new moon and from any point of it, one may see the rock on which Our Blessed Lady appeared."

Barkley looked at him curiously. Here was no "if" or "maybe." Rosaire Gagnon was a forthright man, without compromise. He was looking into the darkness which obliterated the familiar landmarks of his farm, and he was evidently finding speech difficult, as had Benoit Masson, choosing his words carefully, one by one. "On the night of the vision, we prayed, Marguerite and me. You know what occurred."

"Yes. And I have met your daughter, Valérie-Marie. She is a lovely girl."

"That is true, but I thank you for saying so. You will hear many statements which are merely the words of people, monsieur, but evidence outweighs words, is it not so?"

"Usually. It depends on the evidence."

"Yes. I offer it to you." Rosaire Gagnon turned and his eyes were

285

stormily eloquent. He did not have to choose words now. He was releasing something that was pent-up within him.

"I have eight children. No child of mine has died. No child of mine has been seriously ill. No one else on the island may say as much."

"You have been fortunate."

"No!" The dark eyes were intent. "I have been blessed. The Mother of God stood upon this earth within sight of my land."

The silence seemed to vibrate with the force of that declaration for seconds after Rosaire stopped speaking. He looked out at his farm again, looking to the south, the direction of Anse-Saint-Jean, then he turned to the door. He had said all that he had planned to say and he did not know how to waste time.

"You will consider that, monsieur, when you write your book."

"Yes. I will consider it."

Keller Barkley followed the man into his house. He did not want to appear curt, but words came as hard to him now as they had to Rosaire Gagnon in the beginning. Such faith was impressive but it was not evidence. Rosaire, though his land abutted on Anse-Saint-Jean, knew no more about what had happened when Valérie was left alone there than did Keller Barkley. In terms of his own vocabulary, he had been "blessed," and in terms of Barkley's vocabulary, he had been "fortunate"; the difference lay between two men and their beliefs, fact was not involved in it.

"I tried to leave the book in my room," Keller Barkley thought, "but it seems to have come to the party."

Inside the house, excitement was no longer caged. Voices had risen, many people were talking at once, and there was much laughter. Keller saw Valérie immediately. She was standing beside André, engaged in animated conversation with two young men and a blonde girl. She was wearing the dress that she had worn to Quebec, but not the hat. She was lighted from within, too, as she had been in Quebec, delighted with life as she found it, and where she found it.

"Veillée is probably a magic word for her, as Carnaval was," Barkley thought.

He made his way across the room toward her and, as he did, André spoke to her and moved away in the opposite direction. It was odd, Barkley thought, that André should try to avoid him, if he had; but it did not matter. He stood beside Valérie again and her brown eyes came up to meet his.

"I did not know if you would speak to me or not," she said.

"You should have known."

"But no! All this week you have stayed away from me. You did not even say 'Bon jour.'"

"I came to see you once and you weren't home."

"You came to visit my father. He liked that very much. You did not wait until I returned."

Keller Barkley was not aware of anyone else in the room. The want of her was moving in him, drawing his muscles taut. "Did that make any difference to you, Valérie?" he said.

Her eyes dropped. "If you were angry with me, I would feel badly."

"Why should I be angry at you?"

She lifted her eyes, hiding whatever she thought or felt behind laughter. "Only *you* can answer that. Me, I know only why *I* am angry, when I am so."

There was an outburst of loud laughter from the other side of the room and Valérie whirled around, startled. Barkley, too, looked toward the source of the commotion. Robert Drolet had arrived with three other young men and they were in the center of the group that laughed. Something had been said, or something had been done, which did not concern Valérie or Keller Barkley, but it was enough to destroy the mood of the moment that they had together. There was a general movement of people in the room, a seeking of chairs. André had reappeared with a guitar. He seated himself in the middle of the room, tuning his instrument.

"He was merely going into another room to get his guitar, and I concluded that he was avoiding me," Barkley thought. "So much for eye-witness testimony!"

He and Valérie sat in chairs on the side of the room with the stove, facing the door. Robert's roving eyes discovered them and he ceased to be amused by the joke that he and his companions shared. He glowered across the room, then turned his back. If Valérie saw him, she ignored his existence.

"We will sing for a little while," she said. "The older people like it and it is part of a *veillée*. Later we will dance."

André played a few experimental chords, looked up with a lopsided grin and hit the strings. Inevitably, it was "*Alouette*," French Canada's greatest crowd warmer, probably the noisiest lark in all ornithology. Barkley sang with the others for a few bars, then they lost him. It was too fast and he was uncertain of the word sequence. Valérie had a sweet voice, deeper than he would have imagined, and she sang enthusiastically, with obvious delight in the familiar nonsense of the song. Once he had the crowd started, André took his smile away from them and gave it to her. He did not sing, but he played while Valérie sang; the singing of anyone else was merely incidental to him. Barkley, who sat close enough to touch Valérie, had the unwelcome thought that he was incidental, too; that she sang for André as he played for her.

The crowd sang "*En roulant ma boule*," and Barkley joined in. He remembered it vaguely from childhood French classes, and when he did not remember, he faked. Valérie turned and smiled at him when she heard him singing. It was a dazzling smile and he had a childish impulse to sing louder on the next number. André thwarted him. He swung into "*Vive la Canadienne*" and this was a tribute to the French Canadien girl. He made it a tribute to Valérie, his eyes smiling warmly at her. It was a tongue twister and Barkley could not keep up with it.

"Damn this guy!" he thought. "He is making public love to her."

He had an opportunity to observe the other singers since he was not singing himself. Many of them were paired off and to them the music was *pas de deux*. The girls who were not teamed with any particular youth sat together on one side of the room and sang challengingly at the young men who were seated on the other side. Robert sat with the stags and he was *un gaillard* when there were girls to smile at him. He sang lustily and he had a good voice. His eyes, however, flicked occasionally to Valérie.

The pattern of the *veillée* was suddenly clear to Keller Barkley. This was the first of many that would be staged, no doubt, in various homes as the fall weather brought a relaxing of the heavy work. Some of these couples would marry and then, at *veillées*, they would sit in the formal parlors. Some of the unattached males would cross the room to sit with girls of their choice. Girls who did not lure a youth across the room at the first few parties would try harder, become more alluring. Some of them would miss. And Valérie?

She was sitting with him, and she had chosen to sit with him. If he were an islander, that would have significance; it might have much, or none, with a visitor. He did not know. Some of the island girls married off-islanders. All of the Charbonneau daughters did. A visitor at one of these *veillées*, then, might be considered within the rules of the game, if he understood the rules. Still, there was André, who could not sit with anyone since he was playing. Valérie certainly held him within her orbit.

"I have been unfair."

He could not forget her saying that. It might mean that she regretted the feelings that she stirred in him because her own emotions were already involved elsewhere, or it could have the simpler, more direct meaning that he attributed to her at the time. A man could not know. He had to grope.

They all sang "*Au Canada*" and André let the guitar hang on the strap around his shoulder. He strolled over to Barkley and Valérie. His eyes were friendly when he looked at Barkley. He tapped the instrument with his fingers.

"Can you play Rock and Roll?" he said.

"Lord, no! I can't play anything."

"It is too bad. It would be a sensation."

Other young people crowded around, most of them with comments on the playing or suggestions for future selections. There was an exodus from the formal parlor. Monsieur le Curè, having approved the party with his presence, was taking his leave. Several of the older group left when he did. In the general milling around, Barkley lost Valérie. He did not know quite how it happened but when he located her, she was sitting with André at the other end of the room. Céleste Drolet was sitting, tight-lipped, not far away, watching them. The other Drolet had vanished. Robert and the three youths who had come with him, seemed to have left the party.

Barkley found himself teamed temporarily with a tall, blonde girl. He did not know how that happened, either. She was one of the two whom he had classified as probably beautiful. He had noticed her again in the group of unattached girls, wondering why she did not have at least two men, one on either side of her. He looked up suddenly and there she was. She had deep, soft, blue eyes and beautiful skin, deep peach in shade. He had been introduced to her but he did not remember her name.

"Here comes the fiddler," she said. "Now we can dance."

A magnificent old man was unwrapping a violin which was swathed in what looked like an old blanket. He was over six feet tall, with powerful shoulders and no apparent waistline bulge. He had a full and fluffy white beard that extended downward to his chest. It seemed almost sacrilege to call him "a fiddler."

"He looks like the Michelangelo Moses," Barkley said.

"Who?"

"Someone I used to know."

"He isn't. He couldn't be. Nobody knows him. He is Augustin Lepage. He is a hermit. He lives alone on the north shore. He never married."

"But he plays for *veillées?*"

"It is the only thing that he likes to do. He hardly ever speaks to anyone."

Barkley looked at Augustin with renewed interest. Here, evidently, was a novelty; a Lepage who was neither successful nor industrious. The man was tuning his violin, paying no attention to anyone. He wore a plaid lumberjack shirt and dark trousers that looked freshly pressed. His skin had a clean, fresh look and his eyes beneath bushy eyebrows were very blue. He was probably the black sheep of his family, but he was the most impressive-looking human being in the room, not excluding this luscious blonde. André crossed the room and spoke to him.

"André is the caller when we dance," the girl said.

André, of course, would not dance. Barkley hated the thought that came to him. It wasn't good sportsmanship to see advantage in another man's handicap, but he had to seek any advantage that he could find. He looked past the tall girl's shoulder, seeking Valérie. She was looking at him and for a moment their eyes met, then she turned away and joined a group of two men and four girls. Barkley regretted the blonde girl. He had not asked for such a gift.

"I have never spoken to an American before," she said.

"I am not an interesting example."

"I think so. I have never seen anyone who writes books." The soft blue eyes looked into his face for a moment as though they were trying to memorize him. "I have never read a book," the girl said.

Robert Drolet and his companions made another entrance, noisier than the first. Barkley understood the laughter and the good humor now. They had a bottle hidden somewhere outside and they kept slipping out for *un p'tit coup.* The other young men at the party, with a few exceptions, seemed to resent it, and Robert, semi-belligerent, was loudly derisive of the fact that he was disapproved. There was a situation building, but no one wanted to jeopardize the mood of the evening by taking too much notice of it.

André took the center of the floor to announce that the dancing would begin with a "reel carré."

The bow leaped across the fiddle strings and they were off on a variation of the American square dance. Barkley looked once into the soft, blue eyes of the blonde girl and then he lost her. André was a good caller, fast and unfaltering. Under his direction, the couples whirled, spun, bowed, curtsied, parted and came together again, changed partners and moved swiftly from one end of the room to the other. It was a long time, or seemed so, before Barkley met Valérie in this kaleidoscope of movement. Her eyes smiled at him, she floated into his arms and out again.

It was not as he had imagined dancing with her, but he took the moment that he had and looked forward to the next. Once, in an exchange of partners, Robert bumped him. It was deliberate, a form of body-blocking, and he swore when he did it. Barkley's jaw tightened. He wanted no trouble with Robert. There were too many Drolets in his life.

The music swirled into silence and the dancers spun into chairs, the girls fanning their faces with their handkerchiefs and the men mopping their foreheads. Keller Barkley took four fast gliding steps without music and slid into a chair beside Valérie.

"You did that well," she said, "but Philomène will be disappointed."

"Philomène? Is that her name?"

"As though you did not know! You were very interested in her."

"You do not believe that. You know that only one girl here interests me."

"That is very foolish."

"Why? Are you in love with André Drolet?"

It was blunt, but he had to know. Her eyes flashed up to his and there was hot resentment in them. "You have no right to ask that. If I were pledged to any man, I would not be sitting here talking to you."

The fiddler was playing again and the married couples from the formal parlor were having their turn at dancing. André did not have to call the cotillion that they danced. He dropped into the fortuitously unoccupied chair on the other side of Valérie. He did it easily, naturally, with the assurance of one who belonged there.

"Kel-lair," he said. "If you are equal to this dance, will you please invite my mother to dance it with you. She is being most unhappy."

Barkley hesitated only a moment. "Certainly," he said.

He bowed to Valérie and made his way, unwillingly, to the parlor. He could imagine no prospect less inviting than the prospect of leading Madame Drolet into the dance. He would not be stuck with her, of course, once they were in; they would be merely two more chips in the whirlwind of music. Still, there was Robert, her son, who should take care of her if none of these people who knew her were inclined to bother. André might have played a sharp trick on him, at the same time reserving Valérie for himself; on the other hand, one made outrageous requests only of those whom one regarded as friends.

"You do not want to dance with an old woman," Céleste Drolet said. Almost immediately she added, "There was a time when I did not have to wait for attention at a *veillée*, monsieur."

She was slender, swift-footed, and she danced well, but she seemed to be dancing from memory rather than with the music or through any feeling for the dance. Her eyes kept darting from side to side, either watching other people or alert to notice if they were watching her.

Keller Barkley started back to where he had left Valérie and André after he escorted Madame Drolet to the formal parlor. He was stopped momentarily at the edge of a group surrounding Robert. Robert was feeling his drinks and he was talkative, boastful of his exploits in Montreal, where he instructed many wealthy Americans in sports; many beautiful girls and many young men who were, by his account, pitifully inadequate until instructed by Robert. There was skepticism in the faces of the Canadien young men who comprised his audience, hostility in some.

"Tell us, Robert," one stocky youth said, "do you enjoy taking tips from the English and the Americans?"

There was blank consternation in the face of Robert for a second, then blazing anger. "I did not speak of tips," he said. "Who tells you this about tips?"

His eyes found Keller Barkley on the fringe of the crowd and his anger hardened into hatred. "It is a lie," he said belligerently. "Who takes the word of a foreigner against mine?"

Barkley was the only "foreigner" and the issue was suddenly his if he wanted to make it so. He wanted nothing of the kind. He did not argue, or quarrel, publicly with drunks in Quebec, Washington, or anywhere else, and he was not involved in the remark of the stocky youth. André was out on the floor calling another dance and he took advantage of the sudden shifting of the crowd to return to Valérie.

"It was good of you," she said, "to be kind to Madame Drolet."

"Only the thought was kind, and the thought was André's."

Her eyes clouded. "I wonder if you know," she said, "that you are much like him."

The music was urgent and it carried them from the side lines onto the vibrating floor. It was rolling in a swift tide now, with André playing his guitar under the frenzied fiddle, mixing up reels, quadrilles, and cotillions at a fast pace, letting those who would drop out. The joyful abandon of it took Barkley away from his introspective self. Valérie was his *idée fixe*, and when some other partner shared a few moments with him in the swift current of the dance, she was merely the shadow self of Valérie, filling in for her and making her return more thrilling, the brief intervals of her actual presence more intensely personal and exciting.

He realized, too, from the faces and the eyes of girls, as he moved in this shifting pattern of partners, that he was the substitute time and again for other men. There was more in all of this than dancing.

A girl might permit a young man to sit beside her if he sought her and was not objectionable to her, but the ultimate choice was hers. This ingenious method of dancing permitted her brief interludes with each of the other eligible males and she could encourage whom she cared to encourage, responding only to the music and not to the man when a temporary partner did not interest her. The man, of course, had the same right of choice. He could pursue when encouraged, or not pursue, or merely dance.

Valérie was elusive. Keller Barkley felt that she encouraged him to pursue, but only to a point. The man with whom he had to contend was not dancing, so he could not be certain about Valérie. The dance was a form of courtship, and in order to enter into it and be part of it,

a girl had to be courted. Well, he had courted her! His blood was hot
with the thrill of pursuit.

> *Mademoiselle, je peut plus danser*
> *La Bastringue, la Bastringue,*
> *Mademoiselle, je peut plus danser*
> *Parce ce que j' ai des cors aux pieds!*

The last whirl dissolved into laughter, with most of the dancers
singing the comic line about the man with corns on his feet. The
music floated into silence and the tension eased. The girls, obviously
following custom, found chairs together on one side of the room and
the men on the other. Only a very few couples sat together at this
stage and they were quite evidently pledged, out of circulation and
independent of game laws.

Keller Barkley was acutely aware of the fact that, at thirty, he was the
oldest of these young people with whom he was grouped. He was older
than many of the married couples who were relegated to the formal
parlor with the old people. He turned to the youth of twenty or twenty-
one on his right.

"The girls seem to have abandoned us," he said.

The young man flushed, embarrassed at being addressed by the
celebrity of the party. "They had enough of us while we danced," he
said. "They want us now to look at them."

It was as simple as that. Dance to wild, tantalizing music with a
swirling group of girls, the girl of your choice forever eluding you;
then sit, recovering your composure, and look at the girl, remote from
you, serene in the knowledge of being admired, under no necessity
for parrying your words or your advances!

"The damnedest sex trap in the world," Barkley thought. "No wonder they have a surge of marriages in the fall."

He tried to imagine surviving a series of *veillées*, with Valérie
eluding him. He couldn't do it. He was ready to burn all of his boats
now and say: "Here I stay!"

André remained in his chair, although the fiddler had vanished.
He plucked a few tentative notes and Antoine walked out onto the
floor. This was his party and he had not danced. He had visited with
the groups in the parlor and with friends around the room, now

suddenly he was in the spotlight, easily the most handsome man in the room, assured and smiling. André gave him his introduction and he sang:

> *Près de la fontaine*
> *Un oiseau chantait.*

From the two sides of the room, the voices of young men and young women answered him, joining their voices to his in the chorus:

> *Un oiseau, à la volette, un oiseau,*
> *à la volette, un oiseau chantait.*

Antoine continued to lead, repeating lines and picking up new ones, the regular pattern of the Canadien cumulative song, the side-line voices coming in strong on the "à la volette." As a song, there was no sense to it; as a battle of the sexes ranged in opposing forces across a room, it was wonderful. At the end of it, Antoine waited while André set a new mood. Everyone knew what was coming, even Keller Barkley. If French Canada could have only one song, this would be it:

"A la claire fontaine, m' en allant promener."

Antoine, when he let it out in a song like this, had a clear, strong tenor voice, and he knew how to project feeling. He reached the haunting refrain line, drawing the other voices in, and looked at Valérie.

> "*Il y a longtemps que je t'aime,*
> *Jamais je ne t'oublierai.*"
> (*A long time have I loved you*
> *Never will I forget you.*)

Keller Barkley held his breath, forgetting to sing. There was sadness in the song, a deep emotional quality, and Antoine captured every shade of meaning that was in it. He sang it well because he was a fine tenor and the feeling was there to be expressed, but he sang it to Valérie. No doubt of it. Antoine, in this moment, was expressing a forgotten composer less than he was expressing himself.

Valérie, too, forgot to sing. Her dark eyes seemed enormous, fixed upon Antoine's face, and there was a shadow on her face, tragedy or pain or regret or compassion, something beyond the reading, something that passed between the singer and herself, comprehensible to each of them but to no one else.

It was a matter of two seconds, perhaps, like the swiftest, most elusive encounter of a dance; then Antoine was on another verse, and when he reached the refrain again, he was not looking at Valérie. Keller Barkley was shaken.

"Antoine, too," he thought incredulously. "He's in love with her. This unhatched priest!"

A small boy moved across the line of chairs and whispered to him, a frightened little boy who had difficulty in making his voice obey him.

"M'sieu," he said. "You are wanted outside. It is of great importance."

He scurried away as soon as he delivered his message. Barkley hesitated. "*Il y a longtemps*," sang the voices. He wanted to share this to the end and he could not imagine who would want him. Charbonneau was his first thought. Something might have happened. His father knew where to reach him. Then he thought of Louis-Charles Rivard and he rose swiftly. If anything had happened to Louis-Charles, Madame Lafleche might want to break it gently to Valérie. She might send for him.

He tried to attract as little attention to himself as possible. They were all singing and "*A la claire fontaine*" exerted a spell. The boy had vanished in the direction of the door through which Barkley had gone to his discussion with Rosaire. Barkley stepped out of that door into the darkness, and when he had taken a half dozen steps, he knew that he had made a mistake.

The night was not as dark as it had first appeared to be. There was a high bright moon that lighted the cleared space between the house and the barn. Four or five figures moved in around him and Robert Drolet stood facing him. Robert was balancing on his toes and there was menace in him.

"Monsieur l'Américain," he said. "I resent this talk of tips in connection with my employment in Montreal."

The other youths were silent, spread out in a ring around the two protagonists. Keller Barkley felt fear like a cold wind on his body. He felt outrage, too, that he had been lured to this trap and outrage that he was falsely accused. He could not deny the accusation without giving way to Robert. He would not do that. There was no speech in him.

"I will have an apology," Robert said.

Keller Barkley drew a deep breath. He had never been better than an indifferent athlete at any time in his life. Robert was younger, stronger, a professional in sports if he was professional in anything. There was no mistaking Robert's intent.

"You can go to hell," Barkley said.

Robert moved with a cat's speed. His left hand flashed out before Barkley could raise his own hands in any kind of a defense. The blow landed high on his cheek, and the left hand, recoiling, pumped forward again to land against the corner of his mouth. Barkley brought his own right up as a clumsy guard for his jaw and missed awkwardly with his left. Robert hit him twice in the body, once on the protecting arm, then circled away, measuring him.

That measuring was again the tactic of a cat. Robert was very sure of himself and he could take his time. He circled Barkley, feinting with one hand and then the other, sneering at the clumsy, instinctive shifting of his opponent's guard, enjoying this moment of mastery and giving Barkley time to realize that he had no defense. Barkley's vision cleared after the first hazy moment under fire and he could see the hard, cold cruelty in the eyes of Robert.

"He does not want to knock me out," he thought. "He wants to make me last."

Keller Barkley was no longer afraid. Fear had gone with the first hurting blow. There was hot, desperate anger in him and he wanted to charge in and beat his enemy down. His fists moved back and forth. He had to keep turning like the hub of a wheel with Robert on the rim. Robert wanted him to charge, too. Finally he did.

He threw his left hand, grazing Robert's temple with it as the younger man crouched low. He did not succeed in unleashing his right. Robert hit him a half dozen times, to his head and body, sending him reeling back across the clearing. His legs felt rubbery and his eyes hazed again. Robert was crouched, weaving in front of him, giving him time to recover before launching another attack.

The other young men were silent, watching, their sympathies with one of their own against a foreigner. Barkley felt blood flowing down his right cheek. He brushed it off with his guarding right hand. The right hand was good for nothing else. His eyes were clearing again. He had been turned around in the circling. He was facing the door of the house. He could see it past Robert's crouching body. He saw it open as Robert did not. Robert danced in and hit him twice with left jabs, then danced back. Robert glided in again and a hurricane seemed to strike the clearing.

Barkley saw the tall, powerful figure of André behind the advancing Robert. He saw André balance, brace, and lunge. André's hand gripped Robert's shoulder, spinning him out of his charge, halfway across the clearing. His voice was sharp, savage.

"What is the meaning of this?"

Robert bounced like a tennis ball. His body turned and he came back to the attack on a new opponent with even greater savagery. He hit André twice and André would have gone down if one of the young men in the circle had not caught him. André had only a split second to regain his balance and he gripped the man who caught him, holding to him with his right hand while he hooked with his muscular left. Robert took the blow on his jaw, and as he staggered Antoine's arms went around him. Antoine held him with his arms pinned while he struggled futilely.

"In the name of God, stop this!" Antoine said.

The other young men moved in now, sobered by this unexpected climax to the baiting of a foreigner. They surrounded Robert, talking to him, and Antoine released him. The door opened again and Valérie ran into the clearing. She did not see anyone but André. He was standing, grimly intent, watching Robert, holding a handkerchief against the corner of his mouth where his brother's fist had cut him.

"André," Valérie said. "What happened? Are you all right?"

He did not look at her. "I am all right," he said. "Go with Antoine."

"No." Valérie looked around the clearing. There were other people coming out of the house now. Her eyes returned to André. "You are hurt."

"Antoine," André said. "Take her away."

Antoine took her arm and, after a moment's hesitation, she went with him. André crossed the clearing to Barkley.

"How are you?" he said curtly.

"Fine."

"We'll walk then. We'll walk to my place and I will fix you up. There's nothing better than walking when you're wounded, if you can do it."

His voice was gruff and he did not wait for Barkley to agree with him. He set his course for the road and Barkley followed him.

The *veillée*, as far as they were concerned, was over.

# XV

It was a silent walk from the home of Rosaire Gagnon to the atelier
of André Drolet. André made no overtures and Keller Barkley did not
feel like talking. There was nothing to say.

He had read of men who were beaten up, but it had always been
remote from him. Now it had happened, and the physical aspect of it
was relatively unimportant. He had been humiliated. He had stood
before another man, helpless and inept, unable to defend himself or to
retaliate when he was hurt. His imagination, which anticipated many
actual experiences, had not prepared him for the reality of this. In the
daydream world which he, like most men, visited occasionally, he had
never been helpless or defeated; always his imagination had assured
him that he would be able to do "something," even when opposed
to greater skill or tougher fiber. His "something" had been less than
futile, a clumsy fending that did not fend.

He had been rescued by a man who had only one leg, a man deprived
of normal balance, leg leverage, and agility. It was a question in his
mind, walking this dark road, whether Drolet, the rescuer, had not
humiliated him more than Drolet, the attacker. Between them, they
had left him no shred of glory, no tattered rag of pride.

There was, to crown the experience, Valérie.

She had not glanced at him. She had seen only André, worried over
André, spoken only to André. No one in that clearing had existed
for her. When André had sent her away with a curt command, she
had gone.

They turned off the road into the narrow path that led to André's workshop. André opened the door and snapped on the single-bulb droplight. He turned to Barkley and whistled softly.

"You'll need a bit of work," he said. "Sit in that chair. I'll be right back."

"I'm okay."

"Never think it."

André vanished into the other room and Barkley discovered that sitting in the chair was a reasonable idea. He felt all gone, used up, weary. André returned almost immediately with a first-aid kit. It seemed astonishing that he should have it until one considered the work that he did, the sharp tools that he handled. He had a can filled with cold water and a sponge. He sponged Barkley's face and the water stung.

"I am sorry about this," he said. "Sorry that it was my brother."

He put the can on the table, wadded some gauze, and clipped off a strip of adhesive tape. He worked swiftly, deftly, with a surgeon's skill. As he worked, he talked.

"I saw Jonicot, Rosaire's boy, speak to you," he said. "He looked frightened. That impressed itself upon me. There seemed no reason why he should bring you a message. Antoine observed him also, and he was curious as I was. When we finished 'Claire Fontaine,' and you had not returned, we went to look for you."

"And a good thing for me."

"Yes."

André stepped back. He had applied iodine to three or four places on Barkley's face and he had affixed the one pad. He went into the other room again and returned with a cold can of beer.

"Hold that against your eye," he said. "It may keep it from swelling too much."

Barkley tried it. It was difficult to hold, uncomfortable against his skin and a destroyer of the little dignity that he had left. He set it on the table beside the water can.

"Let it swell," he said.

André grinned. "It will be a black eye but nobody dies of that."

Barkley was aware when he looked at André that he was not seeing well out of that right eye. He was suddenly aware, too, of the ugly swelling of André's lip.

"You need a little first aid yourself," he said.

"I, too, must let it swell. It is inside my lip, a cut against my teeth. It will heal."

Their eyes met and there was a thought of Robert in the room with them. The fists of one man had done all of this damage and he had received little damage in return.

"It must not embarrass you, Kel-lair," André said, "that I was able to be of slight service. I was in your debt for taking care of my mother when I requested it. I am happy that I had the opportunity of paying that debt promptly."

He held out his package of cigarettes and Barkley accepted one. With one light stroke, André Drolet had wiped out the obligation, which Barkley was feeling, unexpressed. There was understanding in him. His use of "Kel-lair" was almost a pledge of friendship in which there could be no obligations incurred. Keller Barkley lighted the cigarette and flipped the match away.

"No, André," he said. "There was no debt. I told Valérie that there was only a kind thought and the thought was yours. I do not know if you are a better man than I am, weighing everything that we are. I am afraid that you may be."

He drew the smoke into his lungs, letting it trickle out, holding the words that he was about to say as long as he could hold them.

"Why haven't you married Valérie?" he said.

André stiffened. There was resentment of a personal question in his dark eyes, then there was nothing. He gestured with hands and shoulders, a fatalistic gesture, inimitably French.

"I have little to offer her."

"What does she ask?"

"It is her nature to give," André said slowly, "but it is not equitable to offer little to one who gives much."

This was very difficult. Keller Barkley looked at the small carving in its niche, the carving of a little girl with wonder in her face. The man who carved that image had given more than a little. He must have carved it long ago. It was lovingly done, every line of it.

"Your main difficulty is the vision, isn't it?" he said softly. "You are in awe of her because of what you believe she saw."

"Yes! And you would be if you were of our Faith." André lifted his head. "I look into her eyes and I remember that she saw the Blessed Virgin. You cannot know, Kel-lair, how that would be. For such a wonder there must be a purpose. I could not fulfill that purpose. She is more than a woman, Valérie."

"Yes. She is. But she is a woman, too."

Keller Barkley paused. He had never done anything more difficult than this. He had endured pain when he had no choice. Never before had he put himself deliberately on the rack.

"She did not see the Blessed Virgin, André," he said.

He spoke slowly, deliberately, with conviction in his voice. He did not know until the words were said that he had reached this point of positive conviction, with all of the evidence in and weighed and put away. André stared at him, his face slack, all of his defenses down.

"What do you mean?"

"I mean that she sees today what is not in the thing at which she looks. The miracle is inside of her, not outside. She sees marvels where there are no marvels. She looked at a cheap carnival with me and did not see it; she saw '*Carnaval*,' something of beauty that was in her mind."

André buried his face in his two hands like a man who prays. He was silent for a moment, then his hands dropped away, the fingers curving into fists.

"It is true," he said huskily. "She has always seen what no one else could see. But that? The vision on Anse-Saint-Jean? It was another matter. It was not in her mind that she saw the Blessed Virgin. She could only describe what she did see, putting no name on it."

"Did you ever see Saint Joachim?"

"But no. Of course not."

"I saw your carving in the church. Where did he come from? Did you use a model?"

"No. I never use a model. Only once." André flung out his hand. "My Jean-Baptiste, he is Antoine, because I felt him thus. For the others, no."

"Yet you saw them in your mind! So clearly that you could carve them. Is Valérie's mind like yours?"

"Yes. Yes. It is imagination. But the other?"

André rose and paced around the studio, his stride jerky and unrhythmical in this confined space. He spoke aloud, more to himself than to Barkley. "It is true what you say. You know the truth of such matters. You, too, have imagination. The being, or the creature of one's imagination has a short life unless one captures it in wood or stone or the pages of a book. We forget what we have imagined last year . . . last month. It could be as you say."

He stopped, facing Barkley. "This is a big thing in you, Kel-lair," he said. "To tell me this and to be patient while I understand it. I do not understand this gift from your mind nor why you have made it. I have seen your eyes when you looked at Valérie. *Mon Dieu!* That is not something of which two men can speak, but your gift is very great."

"No. I gave you nothing."

"Only the sweat and agony of speaking," Barkley thought. That was all he had given. He had not given Valérie to André because André already had her, all of her. It had been apparent through the long evening at the *veillée*, and crystal clear when she ran out of the house and called his name.

"I have been pouring water out of an empty jug again," Barkley thought, "giving to him something that I never had and never could have. Somehow, the water poured. He received something from me, an invisible something. Can you give somebody something that doesn't exist? I seem to have done it. And I came here looking for miracles."

André was pacing again. He stopped and lighted a cigarette. His face was tight, almost grim. "Tonight has changed many things. What, *mon ami*, can I give to you?"

"You have already given it."

The door opened suddenly, violently. Valérie came in breathless, closing it behind her, leaning against it for a moment.

"André," she said, "there has been a very unpleasant scene. I have to tell you before your mother reaches here. Rosaire was in a great temper when he discovered that Robert brought liquor to a house of the black cross."

Keller Barkley knew about the black cross from Paul Charbonneau. It was the symbol of the Temperance Society and all of the family, in a house that displayed it, was pledged never to drink alcoholic beverages of any kind. He could imagine Rosaire Gagnon, direct, humorless, sternly upright, when he learned about the fight and the drinking that preceded it. He had not known earlier because the older people bent backward to avoid interfering with the younger group, isolating themselves in the parlor.

"Your mother defended Robert and Robert claimed to her that he was attacked. She and Rosaire said some very harsh things to each other."

André stood straight, his back to the bench, his eyes on Valérie's face. "And now my mother is coming here?"

"Yes."

"We will await her."

There was hard strength in him, a grim intensity. Valérie, on the point of saying more, stopped. She turned to Barkley as though seeing him for the first time. Her eyes widened.

"Kel," she said, "you have been horribly hurt."

He smiled at her, knowing from the stiffness of his lips that his smile must be a gargoyle grimace. "A few fender dents, Valérie." He gestured toward the table. "André has been trying to roll them out with a beer can."

The door opened again and Céleste Drolet marched into the room, literally marched. Her body was ramrod stiff and there was a frightening rigidity in her features. Her lips were drawn tight and her eyes were cold, without light. She halted, facing André.

"You have disgraced yourself this night," she said. "I am ashamed that you are my son."

André's face was carved like one of his images, but with less expression. He gestured to Barkley without looking at him. "You will be so kind as to leave us, Kel-lair," he said.

Barkley was moving toward the door before André spoke. This was a personal affair, painful enough without the presence of an outsider. Valérie was staring at André, her hands clasped before her breasts.

"I will stop and visit your father on my way," Barkley whispered.

She did not turn her head. "Thank you, Kel," she said, "but please do not alarm him."

Valérie Rivard lived the longest minute of her life after the door closed behind Keller Barkley. André stood silent, looking at his mother, and there was nothing in his face that she, who knew him so well, could read.

"I never thought that I would live to see the day when a son of mine would seek the compliments of foreigners by turning against his own flesh and blood," Céleste said. "You have struck your brother, like Cain, and God will punish you for it."

305

"You do not speak for God," André said.

"Who speaks for God if I, your own mother, do not? Your fine Protestant friend?" Céleste half turned, pointing a stiff forefinger at Valérie. "Or that liar, with her tales of seeing the Blessed Virgin? To whom are you listening if not to me?"

"Sit down! I have listened to you enough. Now you will listen."

André straightened his body, pushing away from the bench. There was authority in his voice and Céleste recoiled slightly.

"Sit down!" he repeated.

There was sudden fright in the face of Céleste. Valérie felt it, herself, through Céleste and through her own nerves. She had never heard this voice of André's although she had heard him when he was angry. Céleste groped for the chair.

"I must accept this," she said, "since I am alone." She seated herself and her face was contorted as she looked up at André. "I have deserved better from you than this bullying, this tone of voice that one would use to a dog! I bore you. I gave you life."

André made a weary gesture. "As soon as I was old enough to hear you, I heard long complaints about your pregnancies. You bore no child happily. You gave no child life willingly. When you complained, I listened, but I knew that I was the result of a pregnancy that you resented. You blamed the life I have on my father. You cannot now take credit for it."

"This to me?" Céleste said incredulously. "I must hear this from my son?"

"The son of whom you have just said that you are ashamed," André said. "Now, what brought you here besides abuse? What do you want of me?"

"I want nothing of you," Céleste said. She was gripping the arms of the chair and her knuckles showed white. "You have driven your brother from his home. After tonight, he will return to Montreal."

André stood silent, looking at her. Valérie felt a dryness in her throat. This had to come. He was too big, too fine, to live in the shackles of his mother's petty tyrannies, but she wished that it could happen in some other way, without such cruel hurting. This scene could be and not hurt Céleste greatly because Céleste launched savage attacks habitually, and upon anyone who crossed her, inviting and seeming even to welcome the retaliation that she brought upon herself. André was not like that. He avoided quarrels or scenes even to the point of apparent weakness and indecision. The hurts that he suffered would be deep inside, where no one could see them. Céleste cried "Pity!" to the world.

"You have made your choice, I see!" Céleste was peering up at her son, her chin out-thrust, baffled perhaps at his silence. "Your own family means nothing to you. You have found those who mean more to you outside of your home."

She sat back in the chair, releasing her tense grip on the arms. "*C'est bien!* You will be rid of both of us. I will go to Montreal with Robert."

André nodded his head. "Yes," he said. "I think that will be best."

Valérie caught her breath. The face of Céleste Drolet seemed to collapse before her eyes, the rigid lines dissolving in an instant, the sharp, firm jaw going slack. It was impossible to know what Céleste expected from her ultimatum, incredible to believe that she expected to bring André to his knees by the threat of leaving him, after all that she had done to him and said to him. That she had expected some sort of victory from this trump card was certain. She stared at André, her face working, then she screamed.

"I can go! It will be best! You would drive me out of the home that I made for you, the home in which I raised you! I am old now. Someone else, you think, will care for you better. So there is no room for me in my own home. I can go among strangers."

She laughed hysterically and the laughing turned to wild weeping. She pounded the arms of the chair with her fists. André looked bewildered. He grimaced and threw out one arm in a jerky motion of protest.

"It was your choice," he said. "You wanted Robert. You have always wanted Robert."

Céleste rocked her body back and forth. "I have nobody but Robert. Robert would not do this to me. Robert would not order his mother out of her own home. He is only a boy, but he will take care of me. God will take care of me."

Valérie crossed the room. She went down on one knee, her arm across the older woman's shoulders. "Come, Madame Drolet," she said. "I will take you home. You are upset. It is not as it seems to you. Nobody——"

Céleste Drolet rose, shaking off her arm. "I know how it is," she said. "I know well enough. But I will go home. I will go to the home I have loved for the little time that I am permitted to have it."

She made her way to the door, her tottering walk in contrast to the march with which she had entered. Valérie walked beside her, not touching her. André took three long steps.

"Maman!" he said.

Céleste turned slowly, looking up at him. There was pity in his eyes, but no relenting in the grim lines of his face. The swelling of his lips robbed his mouth of firmness, making it grotesque.

"This talk of your home is nonsense," he said. "It is yours. No one would deprive you of it."

"But you would banish your brother?"

"I have not spoken to him."

"No. Your big fist spoke for you." Her lips curled and there was hatred in her eyes. "It was the way of your father and you are like him."

"I am. I have been like him even in his foolishness. He tried to make you happy by giving you what you wanted. So did I. There was no happiness in it, for you or for anybody."

Céleste stood looking at him, her head on one side. "So, now I must take orders from you, eh? I must do what I am told?" She shook a long thin finger in his face. "Well, remember this, when you're so proud of that father of yours! There's a lot of me in you, too."

She turned and opened the door, walking blindly into the night. Valérie glanced swiftly at André, nodded her head to reassure him and hurried after Céleste. Céleste was no longer faltering in her walk, she was walking with angry determination. Valérie touched her arm.

"I am sorry that this happened, Madame Drolet," she said.

"I can believe that as I believed everything else you told me."

"Yes. I never lied to you. In your heart, you know it."

Céleste slowed her pace, turning her head. Valérie touched her arm again. "Did you tell *me* the truth when you said that you wanted me to be your daughter?"

"That was long ago."

Céleste walked a half dozen steps. The light from a window in her own house was in her eyes. She whirled suddenly, her voice sharp.

"You do not deceive me," she said. "You have turned my son against me. You will marry him, I suppose. I will not be consulted. Well, marry him! But you will never be a daughter of mine."

She drew her thin body straight and anger left her. Her voice was cold. "You'll have no happiness, either," she said. "Don't deceive yourself that you will."

Valérie stepped back. "You are mistaken," she said softly. "You cannot rob me of my happiness, Madame Drolet. You never have."

She walked back, then, and her heart was hammering. She wanted beauty. She did not want this. "I am not a saint," she thought. "I will probably hate her at times, but not all the time. She is pitiful. I will try to love her. She is part of my life."

The cry of Céleste to André rang in her mind: "There's a lot of me in you, too." It was true. It had to be true; but whatever there was of Céleste in André, it was the better part of her. There was a better part. There were qualities that people had loved. It was her tragedy that she hid those qualities away.

"She will need me," Valérie said, "and she will not always hate me."

She opened the door of the atelier. André was pacing back and forth. He stopped when she entered. His face was drawn, lined with fatigue.

"I am sorry for this ugliness, Valérie," he said. "I could do nothing else. I had to draw a line. The demand that I escort her to the *veillée* was an absurdity when the Hamels would have driven her there. This affair of Robert's was more than too much. I could not tolerate it."

"You were very patient," Valérie said.

"I tried to be. She is my mother." André ran his hand through his hair. "She gave me no choice. I had to be firm with her. She knows now that I will not submit to these scenes, these dominations. I have taken a stand, once and for all!"

Valérie looked at him and compassion moved in her. She loved him more in this moment that she had ever loved him. He had suffered much and he could accept pain more easily than he could inflict it. She could not take from him the least part of what he believed that he had accomplished.

"Yes, André," she said gently. "You were explicit. You left no doubt. It was very difficult for you."

She extracted a cigarette from his package on the table and walked across the room with it. "Smoke for a few minutes and talk to me," she said.

He needed time and words and the solace of tobacco. His need was greater than her own and her need could wait. She watched him as he lighted the cigarette. His mouth was badly swollen and smoking was a problem upon which he was forced to concentrate. Her memory was suddenly crystal clear, looking at him, at his bruised lips. Robert had done that and she had not seen it. She had seen it happen on another day.

She was standing in the road and André had just told his mother that she had seen the Blessed Virgin. Céleste was kneeling beside her, asking questions. She could hear the questions and her own replies. It had never been so clear before in her mind. She saw Céleste leap to her feet and smash André in the mouth with the back of her hand. The awful shock and fright of that moment gripped her again. That was when fear had entered into her, fear that had made everything else hazy.

The memory film was unwinding and she could see details that she had never seen before. Madame Charbonneau and Mademoiselle Lepage were coming toward them on the road and Céleste was calling to them. The picture was sharper with every passing second. She closed her eyes, clasping her hands tightly together.

"Please, no," she prayed. "It is too late. I do not want to know. I never want to know."

She heard André's voice and she knew that he had been speaking when she had not heard him. "So Kel-lair and I came here and we talked," he said. "He is a man of rare honor. I am pleased that I know him."

Valérie's eyes cleared. The memory was gone. She could see André's face. She tried not to look at his mouth. There was intensity in his dark eyes and he leaned slightly toward her. Her need now was greater than his.

"André," she said.

He was standing and she rose to meet him, feeling his arms enfold her, wrapping her close to him. All of the want and the longing in him spoke in the one word, "Valérie." His cheek rested against her hair above her temples and when she raised her eyes to his face, he kissed her, pressing his broken mouth against hers until she drew away.

"No," she said, "I will not hurt you."

"You could not hurt me."

He held her with his left arm and brushed her hair back from her forehead with his right hand, gently, possessively.

"I have loved you a long time," he said. "You were a small girl holding my hand in the road when I first loved you."

His finger made lines on her cheek below her eyes. "You had tear-stains on your face."

"And dirt," she said.

"And dirt," he agreed solemnly, "and I loved you and I have never loved anyone else. Not even for a minute have I loved anybody else."

"You did not tell me."

"I could not reach so high. I cannot reach you now. You came down to me."

His arms tightened again and she caressed his cheek with her hand. She could not speak, but to the hushed quiet within herself, she whispered, "André, my André."

Keller Barkley pushed thought aside as he walked away from the atelier of André Drolet. He did not want to think about that cold-eyed woman, nor André, nor Valérie. He had lived physically tonight, and, improbable though it seemed, spiritually. He had projected himself into another dimension. He had grown. These people, who had so often made him feel younger than he was, could do so no longer. He had been older than André tonight, in fact as well as in years.

He saw the light in the window of Valérie's house and he stood for a moment looking at it. He had promised that he would visit her father. It was a stupid, impulsive promise, born perhaps of the anxiety that he had felt for Louis-Charles when the boy had brought him the message at the *veillée*.

"Please do not alarm him," Valérie had said.

He doubted that Louis-Charles would be alarmed by any tale of strife or violence that did not directly involve Valérie, but he might be disturbed and that would not be good for him. Barkley touched the dressing that André had taped on his cheek.

He would have to think of a light and humorous way of explaining that. It could not be a grim tale. It would have to be a narrative that carried the flavor of comedy. There was comedy in it, of course. There was always comedy in these swift, violent human explosions. Human pride always solved its problems by creating new and greater problems. Pride was a preposterous quality, the cap-and-bells of clowns.

"I can do something with that idea," he said. "The first step is to subtract my own pride from the equation."

He walked at random in the darkness, putting himself in perspective. When he could laugh, he strode to the door beside the lighted window and knocked. There was no answer. He considered ringing the bell, but that might mean awakening Madame Lafleche and he did not want that. He shrugged. No one ever locked a door on Ile-aux-Erables. The matter did not deserve debate. He opened the door and walked in.

He found Louis-Charles Rivard.

Nothing would ever alarm Monsieur le Notaire again, nor disturb, nor trouble him. His TV was still turned on, with no picture on the screen. His highball glass was shattered on the floor, the fragments surrounded by a small lake of liquid. On the other side of the chaise longue, his clip board lay, the attached pad neatly lettered with the figures of a ball score.

Louis-Charles had fallen forward, his body doubled up, his head against the table. His blank eyes stared at the far wall and there was surprise in his rigid expression rather than fear or horror. The fingers of his right hand gripped a rosary which they had sought in the small drawer of the table. The rosary had caught in the drawer and Death had not permitted him time to free it, but his heavy hand was closed around the crucifix, the string of five beads and the first decade.

Keller Barkley stood looking at him until the first shock passed, then he went to waken Madame Lafleche.

It was a long time later, when it was all over—the informing of Valérie, the tears and the excitement, the coming of the doctor and the neighbors—that Keller Barkley lay in his bed at Charbonneau's and looked again at the picture which was sharply engraved upon his memory. He could see every detail, even the small details that he did not recall noticing at the time. He could see the precise letters written on that pad affixed to the clip board:

7 Septembre, 1957

| | | | | | | |
|---|---|---|---|---|---|---|
| Buffalo | 1 | 0 | 0 | 2 | 0 | 0 |
| Montreal | 1 | 0 | 3 | 0 | 1 | 0 |

Louis-Charles Rivard had died after the sixth inning or during the first of the seventh, with Montreal leading, 5 to 3.

"He never knew how his ball game came out," Keller Barkley said.

That, somehow, seemed sad out of all proportion to matters of greater importance.

# XVI

Louis-Charles Rivard was buried on Monday in the cemetery on the
hill after a Requiem Mass in the Church of Saint-Thomas-Apôtre.
On Tuesday André left with his images for the new church on the
lower Saint Lawrence which had commissioned them. In the afternoon, Keller Barkley walked with Valérie to the beach of Anse-Saint-
Jean.

She was wearing a simple white dress with a small red ribbon at the
throat line. "My father disliked mourning most intensely," she said,
"and I promised him that I would never wear black for him."

She was grave, quiet, touchingly solemn. Barkley's intuition told him
that it was not alone her father's death that had changed her. She
had a new status, a new relationship to the world at large, to all men
save one.

"I told André that you asked me to walk with you," she said.

"And he didn't object?"

"No. He likes you."

Her eyes smiled. She was proud of this new sense of belonging, of
seeking a man's approval of her actions. It was something that Keller
Barkley could accept but he did not want to dwell on it.

"I have always wanted to walk at least once with you on the beach
of Anse-Saint-Jean," he said.

"Because of the book?"

"Only partly so. That beach is part of your story. I have never seen
you there."

They were passing Rosaire Gagnon's farm. Three children, small
distant figures, waved at them. Valérie ignored the personal allusion.

"Many people will miss you when you are gone," she said.

"I will miss many people."

"You have been very good for us, Kel. Everybody has remarked it. You are American and a Protestant, but you did not regard us as amusing, or with contempt. You did not hate us."

"You did not hate me, did you?"

"No."

They had reached the screen of birches. Valérie hesitated for a moment where the path curved down, then stepped forward. She did not follow it. She turned aside and seated herself on the rock that was shaped like a sleeping seal. Keller Barkley knew that rock. It had been the scene of a battle that he had fought with himself one night. He seated himself beside Valérie. Many things had changed since then.

He had learned to know the tides. Low tide today was 3:18. The beach was wide and lonely. The rocks were sharply defined, the big one to the west and the little one with the hollow doorway on the east. It was cloudy and the south shore was blurred. The breeze was blowing from the river with a touch of chill in it. Summer was packing up to leave as he was. At high tide tonight, when the ferry pulled away about eight o'clock, he would say good-by to Ile-aux-Erables. Valérie draped the sweater that she carried across her shoulders.

"Do you care to tell me now," he said, "what you believe yourself about the day of the vision?"

She had her chin resting on the palm of her hand, her elbow on her knee. She was looking toward the church steeple on the south shore, a thin bright shaft in a dark haze.

"Many people who write books," she said, "have wondered why no one has ever returned from death to tell us what it is like. No one has ever returned from childhood to tell us what that is like. I have thought about this, Kel, because I had to think about it."

"I know."

"A child does not have the words, or the understanding, in which to wrap an experience and keep it safe," she said. "We do not remember childhood. It is changed in our memory by everything that happens later, by new words we learn, new understanding. Does that sound absurd to you?"

"No. You are doing fine."

"I do not remember the part that is important. I do not trust my memory of the rest. So much of it may be what I heard later."

"What do you believe?"

"That is difficult. I know that I was not a liar. I would not willfully tell a lie to anyone. I told many people of seeing a figure on the rock. I do not remember telling them, but I told them. Since I did, I am certain that I must have seen a figure on the rock."

She straightened her body, turning to meet his eyes. Her eyes were marvelous: deep, brown, candid. Another word fitted them, too: innocent. Keller Barkley laid his own beliefs and disbeliefs aside, trying to enter into hers.

"Do you believe today that the figure was the Blessed Virgin?" he said.

She hesitated. "If it was, the vision was not meant for me. It was meant for Antoine."

Barkley gestured his protest with one impatient hand. "You can't believe that since you believe in supernatural beings! Could your Blessed Virgin make a mistake and appear to the wrong person?"

"No," she said gravely, "but *we* make mistakes. We do not see what we should see—often."

Keller Barkley picked up a handful of pebbles and started throwing them down the slope. He had settled this question a dozen times in his mind and it always returned, haunting him. There was a missing piece in the puzzle, a piece that he could not find.

"The life of Antoine was changed, completely changed, after that day," Valérie said. "He became a different boy."

"Events changed him, or circumstances. His life wasn't the same after he became involved in that affair, so he wasn't the same. That is very simple. Your own life changed because of it, too, and you did."

"No. Not in the same way. My life changed more than I did." Valérie was looking toward the south shore again and there was a brooding quiet in her. "I learned only one thing from it, while Antoine was guided into very sure paths." She paused. "I learned why God told us to love our enemies."

"Why?"

"Because they make us strong."

She rose abruptly and returned to the path. He had to hurry to catch up with her, but she slowed her pace when she reached the sand of the beach.

"You know, of course, that Antoine is in love with you," he said.

She broke step, lifting her eyes to his face. "Why did you say that?"

"I watched him when he sang to you."

She looked away, walking slowly toward the receding river. "We loved each other deeply when we were children," she said softly. "He was very brave and it was more difficult for him to be brave than it was for other boys."

"And now?"

"We will always love each other a little."

There was shock in that quiet statement. Keller Barkley thought of the wilderness parish to which Antoine aspired, of the lonely nights of a solitary man surrounded by those who live in warm companionship. The single touch needed to make the picture horrible was to imagine that one man loving a woman far away who was married to someone else.

"Is it possible," he said, "to feel like that and still be a priest?"

"But of course. We all have the same feelings. A man would not be a good priest if he could not feel deeply. Antoine would have found someone that he loved as a man loves if he did not follow his vocation. What he feels for me is not that."

Valérie stopped walking. Her clear eyes met his. "Every priest knows what it means to love someone. He has to know. He knows, but he puts it aside. He rejects it for himself." She drew a deep breath. "Unless one knows what one is giving to God, and knows that it is precious, there is no gift."

"You make it sound very simple, but it is not simple."

She walked another two or three yards, raised her eyes to the little rock, then dug a hole in the sand with her toe. "I was standing here," she said.

They were back to the day of the vision. Keller Barkley stood beside Valérie and looked at the doorway in the rock. It was definitely a doorway. The rock itself was black, with no lightening of gray tones on this cloudy day. There was a slight projecting ledge above the inlet, the rippling waters of the Saint Lawrence. Barkley had seen it before, and when he tried to see it through the eyes of a small girl, it was the same.

"You can understand Antoine better if you try," Valérie said. "I will always love you a little, too, because I love a memory that I have of you and because you did not spoil it. There is nothing wrong in that."

Keller Barkley forgot the doorway in the rock. He took one startled half step backward as he turned. Valérie was trying to make him understand a situation that was very clear in her mind. There was an earnest, almost anxious, expression in her eyes. She stood braiding her fingers together nervously and the breeze whipped her wide white skirt around her legs. The want of her surged up in him again. It was closer to the surface than he realized.

"I love you, too," he said huskily, "and the memory. More than a little, Valérie."

He did not mean to say it but it was said. They were two people alone in the wide emptiness of the beach and they could be two people alone in an empty world. There wasn't a sound or a living thing in motion. Valérie raised her hand in a small, brushing gesture of protest.

"No. You must not say that. It is not what I meant. I made a mistake that day in Quebec. A girl wants to be liked if she is enjoying herself and if she likes a man. A woman tries to attract even when she does not think about doing it."

She stopped, spreading her hands helplessly. "I did not try to make you care for me in a special way. I wanted you to believe in me a little. You were very kind, very fine, not for me; but I wanted you to respect my life."

Barkley's throat felt dry. She was explaining her remark—"I have been unfair"—but explaining nothing else. If all circumstances were different, he and Valérie could be madly in love with each other and remain in love with each other, seeking wonder in a world that provided little wonder for those who did not provide their own. She knew it as he did. She must know it. The want that was an ache within him was not a solitary thing. He remembered that moment when she was in his arms. She must feel it, too, to use her phrase, "a little."

"How could I not respect you, your life, everything about you?"

"Your book does not respect me," she said.

Her eyes, meeting his, were candid and unafraid, fearing nothing in him nor in herself. He always made the same mistake about her, building his molehills high. She meant what she said, literally, truthfully, without any subtle undertones. He was "not for her." She was

André's. She was merely trying to explain something to him. He clenched his fists and was startled when the tiny pebbles bruised his palm. He had not been aware that he was carrying them. He threw them away and, with them, more than he had consciously planned to throw away.

"There is no book, Valérie," he said. "I believed that there was, but it was a delusion. It doesn't exist."

"I don't understand, Kel."

"Neither do I. Maybe some day, because I have known you, because I have known the people of this island, there will be a book worthy of the memory of someone who wanted a book from me."

He did not look at Valérie then. He looked beyond her at the black rock, the tall, empty doorway. Valérie's voice seemed to come from far away. There was puzzled protest in it, reluctant protest.

"You cannot afford to waste your work," she said. "No man can."

Something was glowing in the back area of the doorway, the solid rock that made the opening shallow. It was like sunlight reflecting on a small mirror, only there was no sunlight. He stared at it, puzzled, and the light moved upward in an instant, a line of light like a crack in a door that seals a lighted room. He blinked, holding his breath, and then the door was open. There was a room behind it filled with dazzling light. He stretched one hand toward Valérie, groping for her, missing her.

"Valérie, look!" he said. "The doorway."

"Don't, Kel," she said. "That isn't funny. It's cruel. It's——"

He scarcely heard her. There was a woman standing in the forefront of all that silver and gold light. He could not see her hands or her feet and her face was veiled in reflection so that he saw no detail of it. She was standing motionless, looking at him. There was no expression that he could read.

"Please, Valérie, look!" he said.

He heard her footsteps behind him, walking away. There was desperation in the realization that he had not reached her, that she was walking away without sharing this. The figure in the doorway seemed to be clothed in white, a long white robe. She did not move or beckon. She seemed to be waiting to see what he would do.

"Valérie!"

He called and then he turned. She was only four or five steps away, a second away, or two. It had seemed longer. He took three long strides and gripped her shoulder, turning her.

"You're wrong," he said. "Mistaken. Look!"

He stood beside her, raising his eyes to the rock. The light was gone, the illusion of someone standing in the doorway, everything. The doorway was as black as the rock that framed it.

"I did not believe that you would do that, Kel," Valérie said. "I tried to help, to tell you everything that I could. It was cruel and unfair to make fun of me."

"I didn't."

"Not here. Not that way. Even if it was an experiment! You shouldn't have done it."

She was almost running and it was difficult to keep pace with her. "I tell you that I didn't," he said. "I saw——"

"No. If you had the understanding that I believed, you could not have done that." She had reached the path to the birches and she turned, facing him. "I have suffered all of my life, Kel, because I once asked someone to look at that rock. You shouldn't have mocked me. I didn't cheat or lie and I tried to be fair to you."

He never reached her again. She would not hear him and he left her at the door of the house where there was no Louis-Charles to hear him or to act as arbiter between them.

"I hope that you will be very happy, Kel," she said.

So, in the end, he hurt her and he wiped out the image that she had of him, the memory that she would "love a little."

"I must have been crazy," he said.

He could no longer believe in the light that blazed from the rock. It was irrational and impossible. He could not even summon up a clear memory of the illusion that, for a space of seconds, had held him paralyzed. There had appeared to be a woman, but what woman? He had no impression of detail, nothing that he could call back or examine on the screen of his mind.

"A mood," he said, "a concentration of thought upon a single subject, a long conditioning while I wrestled with that manuscript."

He walked the village road, in a direction opposite from Charbonneau's and did not notice. His mind swung back to Valérie. If she had only looked when he called to her! He would know definitely, then, if it was completely an illusion, something that appeared only on the retina of his own eye.

"I did not mock her or make fun of her," he said. "I really believed that I saw something."

He felt a sense of outrage that she should believe that he would do that to her, but his own inner cry of protest was an echo of her "I did not lie!" Eventually he realized that.

"It is time to go," he said. "I've stayed too long on this island."

The want of Valérie was dead in him, killed in the same blast that swept away her memory of him. They would go their way to their separate destinies, but he had not wanted it to end like this. There should have been a kinder curtain.

His stride broke as a startling thought struck him. He was wrong, perhaps. Maybe it was meant to end this way, kinder to both of them that it did. He shook his head. "I don't know," he said.

He passed the three buildings of the Turcottes which would expand and grow and become other buildings. He stood for a moment beside the Coopérative and looked toward the wide sweep of the river to the east. André was on his way to one of the package towns with the images for their new church. André, who loved his own people and the old ways, would have to depend upon the foreign capital which build package towns in Quebec Province for the money that he must have to live. This island would change and Quebec would change, because people had needs; Turcotte's need for employment of his sons, André's need for new, well-financed churches for his images, the need of people for things that their fathers did not even know. Some of these Canadiens would find English villains to blame, as men everywhere found villains, but while they cried out in protest, they would, each in his own way, be changing the world they knew.

Keller Barkley walked back to Charbonneau's and it was twilight now. He did not have very long. The Charbonneaus had been walking with muffled tread all day. They were genuinely sorry to have him leave. Well, he wasn't finding it any too easy himself. He stood for a moment looking back at the village. He had not said good-by to Monsieur le Curé. He should have done so. And Rosaire and Marguerite Gagnon, and little Valérie-Marie! It was just as well. There was no sense in making a production out of it!

He mounted the stairs to his room. He would probably, like a damned sentimentalist, miss all of these windmills and children and dogs and running streams. He glanced thoughtfully at the two exposed hearts. He no longer had any feeling about them. They did not belong anywhere else that he had ever lived his life, but they belonged here. He looked at the crucifix.

The staggering memory of the light in the rock came back to him and his mind could not support it. "It didn't happen," he said. "It couldn't have happened. There could be no reason for it."

His eyes dropped to the pile of manuscript beside his typewriter and Valérie returned for a moment, poignantly. He had never known her body and he would never see her children, but—of all the ways that he would never have anticipated knowing a woman—he had known her spiritually. He had known her intimately as a soul; he, who never spent a thought on souls, nor wondered seriously if he had one.

He lifted the manuscript and weighed it in his hands. It was heavy and more than the weight of hours was in it. He turned to the wide fireplace. He had experienced only the part of one season on Ile-aux-Erables. He would never experience the winter, nor the big snows, nor see huge logs alight. He could, however, anticipate the season since time was running out.

He laid a half dozen manuscript pages in the chimney box and struck a match. They flamed swiftly and he fed more pages to the blaze, playing them out slowly. He did not hear Paul Charbonneau approach nor know that he was standing in the doorway until he heard his voice.

"Monsieur Barkley, in the name of the good God, what is this?"

He turned, then, and read the stunned horror in the broad face of Monsieur Charbonneau, who was watching him feed to the flames the book of which he was so proud, the book that had been written in his house.

"Paul, my friend," Keller Barkley said softly. "I am burning incense."

A19